Nazarene Dream

A True Legend

Michael Vadok

authorHOUSE®

AuthorHouse™
1663 Liberty Drive
Bloomington, IN 47403
www.authorhouse.com
Phone: 1 (800) 839-8640

Published by AuthorHouse   06/27/2018

ISBN: 978-1-5246-8462-4 (sc)
ISBN: 978-1-5246-8460-0 (hc)
ISBN: 978-1-5246-8461-7 (e)

Library of Congress Control Number: 2017904476

Print information available on the last page.

*Any people depicted in stock imagery provided by Thinkstock are models,
and such images are being used for illustrative purposes only.
Certain stock imagery © Thinkstock.*

This book is printed on acid-free paper.

*Scripture quotations marked NIV are taken from the Holy Bible, New International
Version®. NIV®. Copyright © 1973, 1978, 1984 by International Bible
Society. Used by permission of Zondervan. All rights reserved. [Biblica]*

For Rosemary,
with eternal love
and gratitude

1

"Your Christ is a Goddamn fraud!"

Ariel answered his friend Saul's accusation with a slap to the face. Saul, hand on cheek, glared at Ariel, who regretted his attack the instant he delivered it.

"Forgive me, Saul. Let me—"

"I forgive the strike. But I don't forgive myself for stupidly joining your cult and thinking your horseshit messiah was coming to save us."

"He is! Where's your faith? Scripture says—"

"Scripture! I'm sick of all your scripture reading and prophecies. I wish I could read so I could check myself if you've been teaching us the scriptures honestly, or just inventing things to deceive us."

Ariel's shoulders slumped.

"You can't mean that, Saul. Go to any synagogue and talk to any rabbi. You'll hear the same words from the same holy books. I'd be chased out of town if I tried to pass lies off as scripture."

Saul moved a few steps back and glanced at the door behind him.

"Well . . . you've misread something or made some mistake in your calculations. It's been almost forty years since your crucified Christ Joshua supposedly won his heavenly throne. Where is this Christ of yours, Ari? All this time, things have just gotten worse and worse and we do nothing about it. Look at the situation with the pagans. The Romans have invaded, and they're having no trouble laying waste to city after city. Soon they'll conquer Jerusalem too and then, with the Greeks' help, destroy all of us."

"You don't understand," Ariel said, clenching his fists. "These disasters are signs that our Lord is about to return to us. Didn't he tell us to be ready for tribulation and the judgment? Don't lose faith now. God's on the verge of reversing our sorry state."

"You're blind! God's already judged us, and He's abandoned us to the Romans. It's because we hated our law and let the pagans take everything. If your Joshua ever returns, you and the rest of his sheep will be slaughtered by then. All we can do now is fight the Romans, hopelessly, and at least die honorably for our God. So I'm joining the rebellion: the Zealots."

Ariel clutched his own forehead with one hand and shook his head in disbelief.

"They may be rustics and bandits, as you say," Saul continued, "but they're the only ones defending the honor of our nation. So go ahead and wait around for your sleeping shepherd to awaken. I'm picking up the sword!"

"Saul, abandon this wicked plan of yours. You can't fight and murder your way into the kingdom. God, not man, will judge, and only your righteousness can save you. God wields the sword. God!"

"Man wields the sword; God guides it. That's what the Zealots say anyway."

Saul shoved open the door and bolted out to the street as if making a desperate escape from a den of poisonous snakes. Ariel was alone now in his little house of stone and mortar at the southeastern edge of Antioch, Syria.

Ariel prostrated himself on the cold brick floor with his head pointed south toward Jerusalem. He prayed.

"Where are you, Lord? How much longer? How many more people have to die before you set things right? Haven't we been faithful? Haven't we done what you asked? What more do we have to do? What more do *I* have to do?"

Ariel's head started to ache. He groaned and sighed for a moment before returning to his prayers.

"Oh Lord, I've given my life to you. Haven't I been a good rabbi? Haven't I followed your way correctly? Your servant Paul taught it to me. But he taught me the Greek scholars too; he encouraged me to study their philosophers and historians so I could look wise and learned in their eyes. Am I too friendly with these Gentiles? Or have I remained too attached to my own people?"

Ariel coughed. His throat felt tight.

"I know I should expect trials in the last days of this age, but we've lost so much. I've lost so much. So many of my friends, members of my church—and members of the other churches— are dead because of the fighting with the Greeks, and now the Romans. Of course, I don't despair for them. I know they'll live again when you bring the resurrection. I grieve for all those who've lost faith, for those who deny you and say you'll never return. Those who dare say that you were wrong and cannot, or will not, come to vindicate the righteous of this sorry world.

"No! I know they're wrong! But so many are leaving— abandoning you—so many from my church and the churches everywhere. Please, Lord, don't let the whole world go astray. What can I do to bring the people back to you? Help me, Lord. Come back to us, Lord. Save us, Lord. Save us—"

Ariel went limp and fell asleep on the floor. Soon he began to dream.

* * *

Ariel felt himself floating, rising. He could see much of Roman Syria below him. He floated over the Sea of Galilee. It was filled with blood, and the dead bodies of Jewish and Roman soldiers bobbed to the surface. A current of blood and bodies flowed southward from the sea down the Jordan River. He followed the river, floating above it all the way to Jericho, and then turned west to hover over Jerusalem.

The lower city was in ruins—nothing but rubble and ash. Where the Temple once stood was a ramshackle heap of broken stone slabs and splintered beams of cedar wood held together by blood, ash, and naked dead bodies in various states of decay and mutilation. The upper city was intact but unpopulated, save for a few hundred Roman archers who sat on the roofs of the houses and shot their arrows at vultures circling above.

Just outside the city to the west, Ariel saw a group of about a hundred people that he recognized: his church congregation. They were huddled together in a defensive stance while a pack of ravenous wolves encircled them and approached.

In a flash, half the wolves turned into a cavalry of Roman horsemen who snatched away half the congregants and carried them off to the hills to the north. There the horsemen erected crosses and nailed up the congregants.

Meanwhile the other wolves transformed into spear-wielding Jewish Zealot warriors who impaled the remaining congregants and took them to the Temple ruins. One by one, the warriors slit the throats of their captives and tossed their bodies onto the Temple heap. After the last body was loaded onto the pile, the warriors set the bloody mass alight. Thick black smoke swirled skyward.

The earth began to quake and crack. Lesions opened up in the ground and released more blood and black smoke until it flooded and choked all the land in and around the city. A sudden, fierce blast of what sounded like an enormous shofar shook Ariel to his bones. The firmament above cracked open, allowing blinding-white light to radiate through. A host of winged angels emerged from the light. Ahead of them a fiery chariot led the way, piloted by Joshua the Christ.

Joshua was clothed in robes that were as resplendent as the heavenly beams on which he rode. Seven archangels flew behind him: Michael the Protector, Gabriel the Messenger, Rafael the Healer, Uriel the Redeemer, Raguel the Avenger, Remiel the Deliverer, and Saraquiel the Reckoner. Behind the archangels flew an endless multitude of warrior angels armed with flaming swords.

Ariel's skull vibrated to the sound of a voice that sounded like a chorus of voices shouting in unison.

"Shepherd! Where are your sheep?" the voice said, blasting with the force of thunder.

One of the Roman archers aimed his arrow at the chariot and released his bow. The arrow shot straight into Joshua's chest, causing him to collapse. The chariot dipped and then careened all the way into the hills where the crucified captives hung. The downed chariot set the hills and crosses on fire, and the archers exulted.

Ariel felt himself falling, accelerating toward the aqueduct running through the middle of Jerusalem. He crashed into the wet stone and woke with a violent shiver. He was crumpled on the floor of his house and wrapped in a thin film of cold sweat. His head pounded.

2

Twelve-year-old Joshua stood on top of the stone plinth encircling a cistern in the courtyard of his father Joseph's house. He held a makeshift wooden play sword above his head and taunted his ten-year-old brother Jacob below him.

"Egyptian pig! Taste the wrath of the true God!"

Joshua jumped down and mock stabbed Jacob, who dropped the long stick that served as a play spear and fell, staggering and swooning, onto his back. Jacob gurgled and groaned as he pretended to die.

"Avenge me, Anubis!" Jacob cried.

Joshua raised his sword again and pointed the tip directly at Jacob's face.

"Vengeance belongs to God alone!"

With exaggerated flourishes, Joshua mock stabbed Jacob several more times before pretending to sheathe his sword in his belt.

"Can I be Moses now?" Jacob asked.

"Sure. Be like Moses and climb Sinai—by yourself. I have to study."

"That's boring," Jacob said. "You study too much. How far along are you anyway?"

"I'm almost finished reading Father's scroll of the minor prophets."

"I haven't even finished the Torah. You've gone through that and the prophets too."

"Yes, but I honestly don't understand a lot of it. I'll have to read it again and discuss it more with Father."

"You're really going to be a rabbi like Father, aren't you?"

"Maybe. If that's what God chooses for me."

"So Rabbi Joshua, tell me: who is the greatest prophet? Not counting Moses, of course. Is it Ezekiel because he saw the chariot of God?"

"Ezekiel! This is Ezekiel." Joshua raised his hands and started to act the part of a prophet. "Jerusalem you whore! Like your sister Samaria before you, you've prostituted yourself with every nation! You throw your children into the fires of Molech and commit adultery with the Assyrians and their idols! How eagerly you painted yourself like a harlot to fornicate with the donkey-dicked Egyptians!"

Jacob laughed. "It doesn't say that!"

"Yes, it does. I swear. And worse too. You'll see. You won't believe it."

"No! You're such a liar." Jacob gave Joshua a weak slap on the arm. "Just tell me who the greatest prophet is."

"Hmm, greatest prophet."

Joshua paced, thinking and scratching his head. Jacob sat down on the plinth and stared at Joshua.

"Well?" Jacob asked.

"You know, Jacob, I can hardly tell one prophet from another. They all complain about the sins of Israel and warn that God will punish the Hebrews. There's a lot about the Babylonians: how God will send them to attack Jerusalem and enslave everybody. And the prophets were right! The Babylonians did come and take the Hebrews to be slaves in Babylonia. Jeremiah predicted that the Hebrews would be there for seventy years before coming back to Jerusalem, and that's exactly what happened. I would definitely say that Jeremiah was a great prophet. He stayed faithful to God when most of the Hebrews turned to foreign idols. He spoke God's truth to the kings and priests, even when it got him thrown in prison."

Joshua sat down next to Jacob and continued to muse out loud.

"But Isaiah did too, two hundred years earlier. Isaiah saw far into the future, to the final judgment and resurrection, so he must have been a very holy man. Then there's Daniel, who survived the lion's den and knew the meaning of every dream and vision. He predicted Nebuchadnezzar's future and saw how the Persians and the Greeks would conquer our lands. And of course there's Elijah and Elisha with all their miracles. God Himself came to take Elijah up to heaven in his fiery chariot."

Jacob stared at Joshua. Joshua could tell from the look on his face that Jacob was getting impatient.

"Sorry, Jacob. You didn't want to hear all that. To answer your question, the greatest prophet is . . . is . . . I don't know. Let's go ask Father."

When Joshua and Jacob arrived at the door of their father's study, Joseph was preparing the couch for a mid-afternoon nap. The room was windowless and dark, the only light coming through the door to the adjoining courtyard. Joshua did the talking.

"Excuse us, Father. We have a question to ask you, if you can spare a moment."

"Come in boys." Joseph motioned for the boys to enter and sit on the couch. "What do you need to know?"

"Of all the prophets, not counting Moses, which one is the greatest?"

Joseph lit an oil lamp and placed it in a nook in the wall. The flame coated the room in an eerie orange glow. Joseph did not answer right away, so to make sure his father heard him, Joshua again raised the question.

"Besides Moses, which of the prophets is the greatest? Jeremiah, Ezekiel, Elijah?"

"I heard your question, Joshua. And what a question!"

Joseph stroked his beard and pondered.

"Well—of course, it goes without saying that Moses was more than a prophet, and I assume you mean the prophets after Moses, those of the books of the prophets that follow the Torah in scripture. But I imagine that the greatest prophet is one who came before Moses. Yes, I'm inclined to think that the greatest prophet is Enoch."

"Enoch? Is he one of the minor prophets, like Zechariah or Amos?"

"No. Enoch is a major prophet. Remember in Genesis, the early descendants of Adam? Enoch was from the seventh generation after Adam. He was so righteous that God took him while he was still alive up to heaven. He never truly died. But before God took him, He granted Enoch visions of all that would happen in the future. God also taught Enoch the history of the angels and what would happen to them at the end of time. Enoch passed this knowledge on to his son Methusela, who in turn gave it to his son Lamech, who passed it to his son Noah, the same Noah of the Great Flood."

Joseph paused to clear his throat. Joshua and Jacob sat in silent, rapt attention. Joseph continued:

"Enoch's prophecies are special, divine revelations that were secretly shared among only the most righteous men of God throughout the ages. But it's not a secret anymore. Men have written Enoch's prophecies down and translated them into different languages at various times in history, and some copies have gotten out to the world outside the holiest circles. There was a copy of it, in Aramaic, at my yeshiva in Jerusalem. I read it. It was very difficult. Even translated into Aramaic, its ideas are clearly very ancient, and much of its knowledge is hidden in mysterious and obscure symbolism. It even explains the movements of the sun and the other heavenly bodies. I have to admit that I could only partially understand it. But those who are more learned than I am say that Enoch's prophecies, which are the most ancient of all, reveal the entire history of our people, all the way to the end of time. And so far all its predictions have come true. Surely this is the greatest prophecy. And if it comes from Enoch, than Enoch must be the greatest prophet."

Joshua stared at Joseph, mesmerized. As he watched his father describe these wonders, with Joseph's face fiery and spectral from the flickering orange glow, Joshua felt like he was getting a tiny taste of what Moses experienced when he gazed upon the burning bush on Sinai.

"Holy heaven on high, Father," Joshua said, gasping. "I have to read that book."

* * *

In a matter of months Joseph managed to get himself a copy of the Book of Enoch. He bought it for forty-five drachma from another Sepphoris rabbi who collected literary works of all kinds and considered the Book of Enoch to be fake, pseudepigraphic scripture. Joseph gave it to Joshua as a bar mitzvah gift on his thirteenth birthday.

Joshua was thrilled to have it. It was a set of five scrolls comprising all one hundred and eight chapters of Enoch, written in Aramaic on parchment that was wrapped around plain oakwood rods. Each scroll was a sub-book of the whole, and they were named, in order: the Book of the Watchers, the Book of the Giants, the Book of the Heavenly Luminaries, the Animal Apocalypse, and the Epistle of Enoch. Whenever he got the chance, Joshua studied the scrolls. He read them, reread them, compared them to other works of scripture, puzzled over the meaning of difficult passages, and memorized his favorite chapters.

Each scroll had its own thematic focus. The Book of the Watchers was all about God's angels, and how hundreds of them watched the doings of mankind on earth and became frenzied with lust for human women. In Enoch's era these "watchers" descended from heaven to earth at Mt. Hermon and went out to have sex with all the beautiful women they could catch. The offspring of the fallen angels and their human consorts grew to become enormous and wicked giants who wrought havoc. The giants attacked and oppressed man and beast, and they warred against each other. Meanwhile the fallen watchers corrupted humanity by teaching men the ways of war and women the ways of witchcraft and seduction. Upon witnessing all the evil unleashed by the watchers, God sent his archangels to destroy the giants and imprison the watchers underground, where they were to wait for their final damnation at the End of Days. The souls of the slain giants became the invisible evil spirits that would torment humanity throughout history.

The Book of the Giants detailed the crimes of the most notorious giants and explained how the famous monsters and demigods of pagan religion were, in actuality, those same giants.

The Book of the Heavenly Luminaries explained the movements of the sun, the moon, and the stars, and the heavenly origins of rain, wind, and other weather-related phenomena.

The Animal Apocalypse was a history of the Jewish people from creation to the end times. It used animals to symbolically represent the main personalities of Hebrew scripture. Abraham, for example, was a white bull, while Moses was a sheep and Daniel was a ram. Entire ethnic groups were symbolized this way. The Jews, for example, were sheep; the Egyptians, wolves; the Philistines, dogs, and so forth.

The last book, the Epistle of Enoch, was a prophecy of the main events to occur throughout history until the end of time, with teachings to show mankind the ways of righteousness that would save them from the final judgment of the wicked.

The Animal Apocalypse in particular inspired many discussions and debates between Joshua and Joseph, and later between Joshua and Jacob, about who a particular bull was, or what nation the lions were supposed to represent, or who the white ram with the big black horns was supposed to be, or what the answer was to similar mysteries.

"Look, Jacob," Joshua would say. "In chapter eighty-nine it says, 'that white bull which was born among them fathered a wild ass and a white bull calf with it.' The white bull is Abraham, the wild ass is Ishmael, and the white bull calf is Isaac. I know this because the next passage says, 'but that bull calf fathered a black wild boar and a white sheep; and the former fathered many boars, but the sheep gave birth to twelve sheep.' The white sheep that fathers twelve sheep has to be Jacob, who had twelve sons, so the black wild boar is Jacob's brother, Esau. Their father, Isaac, must therefore be the white bull calf, and the wild ass is Ishmael, his brother.

"And listen to the next passage. 'When those twelve sheep had grown, they gave up one of them to the asses, and the asses again gave up that sheep to the wolves, and that sheep grew up among the wolves.' See? That's Jacob's sons giving Joseph to the Arabs, who then sell him to the Egyptians."

In this way Joshua taught Jacob—when Jacob would listen—the meaning of the Animal Apocalypse, and he did so with all the precocious authority of the rabbi he aspired to be.

3

Ariel gazed at the city from his roof as the sun sank in the distance and left purple and scarlet ripples in the darkening sky. Behind him, to the east, stood Mt. Silpios, a thousand feet high. Before him lay the Jewish Quarter of Antioch. Further west he could see the Greek part of town, itself bordered on the west by the Orontes River.

A man on a slow-walking donkey moved up the path to Ariel's neighborhood. Ariel noticed that the man swayed like he was half-awake and might fall off the donkey at any moment. As the rider got closer, Ariel saw that the man was dirty with grime and dried blood. He looked familiar.

"Could that be?" Ariel asked himself. "Yes, it is! Benjamin!"

Ariel climbed down the ladder and ran outside to meet his friend. When he reached him, Benjamin was lying face down on the donkey's back, his arms around its neck. He smelled like he hadn't washed for days. Ariel nudged him.

"Benjamin! Are you well? Speak! It's me, Ariel."

Benjamin looked up at Ariel. With half-opened eyes and an exhausted-sounding voice, Benjamin groaned.

"Ariel? Ariel! Thank God, I made it. You were right, Ariel. I made a mistake. Oh … Gamala … the war … falling …" His voice drifted off.

"Come, Benji, you're tired. Let's put you to bed. When you've recovered you can tell me all about your adventure."

Ariel helped Benjamin off of the donkey and then held him steady by the shoulders as he led him into the house. As soon as Ariel had lowered him onto the bed mat, Benjamin started to snore.

Benjamin slept well. He woke the next afternoon and washed himself with a sponge and a jar of water from Ariel's cistern. Ariel gave him a new tunic to wear.

The two old friends sat at Ariel's dining table, where Ariel laid out a breakfast of bread, olives, cheese, and figs. Benji was so hungry that he tore into his food like a wolf into a chicken. Sated after swallowing every last crumb, Benji relaxed, thanked Ariel for "restoring him to life," and began to tell his tale.

"Oh, Ari, for a moment I let the devil lead me almost to my ruin. At the time I thought I was doing the right thing, but now I realize it was wrong, so wrong. Christ forgive me, but I was seduced into supporting the rebels."

"No! Benji, how? Weren't you listening when I—"

"I know, I know. You were right. The rebels will do nothing but destroy us. They claim to want to liberate us, but they just want to martyr themselves. That's heroism to them. And they'll take the rest of us down with them. Believe me, I've learned my lesson. What the rebels are doing is even worse than you realize."

Benji sat back and took a deep breath.

"On my way back from Jerusalem after Yom Kippur, I stopped in Gamala to stay briefly with my sister. If you don't know, Jerusalem has war fever now. They're building walls, digging up trenches, doing everything to prepare for a Roman invasion. I did my atonement and left immediately, afraid of what might happen when the Feast of Tabernacles crowds showed up. I went through Perea and the Decapolis; that seemed safer than Judea or Samaria, where I assumed the Romans would be marching.

"In Gamala my sister Ruth put me up in the house she shared with her husband Zephani and her children. Zephi was excited and kept telling me all about how the rebels were going to defeat the Romans, how Gamala was safe from any attack, and how we could have freedom if we only fought for it. I told him to live righteously and trust God, and to be vigilant because Christ Joshua was coming soon to establish the new kingdom. I told him how unwise it was to get caught up in a pointless war. But Zephi wouldn't accept it. We argued back and forth, but eventually he started to persuade me. I began to entertain the idea that if all the turmoil was a sign of the end, and the judgment was at the door, then maybe Joshua would condemn me if I didn't stand against the pagans. Zephi quoted the famous words of Judas the Galilean: 'God will help us only if we actively seek to liberate ourselves and don't lose heart.' Forgive me, but for a moment I became convinced that if I supported the rebellion I would be doing God's will!"

Ariel shook his head. Benjamin continued.

"It was not like we were fighting men. We had no weapons in the house, and I'm not young. We hid in that house and prayed for the success of the rebels. But even we would get caught up in the madness, as you'll see.

"The city was teeming with Jews who had fled the fighting in nearby towns like Tiberias and Gadara. Many of them were rebels — young, confident warriors. We Jews were great in number, and Gamala seemed to be a refuge because . . . well . . . it *was* the safest place to hold out against the Romans."

"Safe? Really?" Ariel asked, raising an eyebrow. "Is any place safe where the Romans invade?"

"Well . . . no. Obviously, any place would have been dangerous, but this town was safe compared to anywhere else we might have been. Just let me tell you what happened and everything will be clear."

"All right," Ariel said, raising his hands as if to surrender. "I'll shut up and let you speak."

"Thank you, Ari. So . . . Gamala. We were on top of a high hill in the shape of a giant camel's hump, with a citadel fortress on the highest point, and towers all along the hill. On both sides of our camel's hump the people's houses were stacked along the steep slopes, level on top of level like the steps of a stairway. The Romans would have to climb the steep hillside just to reach us.

We also had a wall protecting the foot of the hill, and where the wall stopped we had unclimbable rocks and cliffs. Naturally we felt secure. With the refugees added to the native population, we had many armed young men who could fight, and even the unarmed were willing to hurl stones.

"But more people meant more stress on our supplies, and there just wasn't enough food or water for everyone. I was sick with worry that we wouldn't be able to hold out long under siege. And when the Romans came, how many of them there were! Soldiers, horses, stone-throwing catapults, machines that fired swarms of arrows and javelins—it was terrifying. They filled in trenches and built ramps near the walls so they could begin their assault. But our warriors were brave in spite of it all, and they prepared to meet any enemies who managed to get through or over those walls.

"I was high up the hill in my sister's house, with her, her husband, and her children. I went out onto the roof to watch the army below. In no time the Romans with their battering rams broke through the wall. They stampeded into the city, shouting, blaring trumpets, trampling, and killing. But our men were all over them. The Romans had to climb up the hill, through narrow and unfamiliar streets, while our men had the advantage of the higher ground. As the legion poured in, our soldiers jumped on them from all sides, squeezing them into the uphill streets and forcing them to flee to the upper city. I have to admit that I almost shit myself. When I saw the Romans coming up, even though they were struggling with the climb and the rough condition of the pavement, I dashed back into the house to hide.

"Then I heard a screaming multitude run down from the very top of the city. I peeked out a window and saw crowds of our soldiers pouring out of the citadel and the towers, running to meet the advancing Romans. They cut the Romans off in the middle of a street and attacked them viciously, while more Romans below them continued up in such numbers that there was nowhere to flee. They were trapped! While our warriors sliced up the Romans with swords and shot them down with arrows, the older men, myself included, as well as the young boys, joined the fight. We got onto our rooftops and flung rocks on them. Some boys even managed to get close enough to the Romans to strike their legs with wooden clubs and knock them off their feet. As they fell, we stole their weapons and used them to finish them off. We made their weapons our weapons!

"But then the trapped Romans found a brief escape. They started to push into—and climb on top of—the nearby houses. At once I ran to my sister's family and took them up to the citadel. What a spectacle I saw from there! All those houses packed with heavily armored Romans and their victims, and as many on the rooftops as well. The roofs couldn't support their weight, and they started to collapse. Remember that those houses are arranged like steps up a steep hill. When a house collapses, that house then rolls down on the roof of the house below it, collapsing its roof, and so on all the way down. It was an avalanche! Most of the residents could see what was happening and escaped down the alleys and streets as soon as they could. But many Romans, and some Jews, went tumbling with the rocks and debris down the hill. If they didn't die from the fall or from being buried under the load, they staggered blindly in the suffocating dust until the blade or club or stone of one of our soldiers finished them off.

"To see so many Romans die this way felt like a blessing from God! The people drove as many Romans onto the roofs as they could—and gladly. What a great victory for us that day, or so it seemed. Every Roman that could move abandoned the battle and fled back to their camp.

"But our elation didn't last long. We realized that we were now doomed. The Romans weren't going away, and they would be at us again, angrier and wiser. Our soldiers positioned themselves behind the wall breaches again, and the other men, armed now with Roman gear, hid themselves strategically throughout the city. But many of the houses were destroyed, and supplies were so low that hunger turned the people against each other. The fighting men started hoarding the food and water, depriving the already-famished women and children. Then the Romans returned with their war machines, and General Vespasian's son Titus arrived with reinforcements.

"I admit that I was one of the many who, seeing the hopelessness of the fight, and knowing the unguarded canyons and caverns of the terrain, secretly fled to the wilderness outside the city. Zephi did the same thing but took his family another way. From a cave at the opposite end of the valley I could see the huge, sheer cliff that ran up the south side of Gamala's hill, hiding the rest of the city behind it except for the citadel and the towers at the very top.

"Apparently some Romans were able to slip unnoticed into the city and set traps, because the following morning I saw the towers come crashing down. Immediately afterward I could hear the clamor of the Roman legions invading the city, and then the screaming masses getting slaughtered. I'm sure you can imagine how this turned out.

"I eventually learned from another witness that the Romans murdered everyone mercilessly and indiscriminately. It didn't matter whether you were a soldier or a civilian, a man or a woman, or young or old. The Romans even killed those who surrendered. Any Jews who survived the early assault fled to the top of the upper city and tried to fight from there.

"Now, God Himself turned against us that day and blew a fierce wind against the city—a wind that aided the Romans' arrows but turned our arrows back against ourselves. I myself didn't see it, given the position I was in, but I did feel the strong winds. All I know is that I saw the most horrendous thing. At the top of the cliff behind the city, I saw crowds of Jews gathering. And then falling. Some jumped to their deaths, others fell or seemed to be pushed. Then I saw men throwing their own wives and children down the cliff side. Then those men jumped. How desperate they must have been! I swear I saw thousands die this way."

"Judas Maccabeus!" Ari shouted. "That's an amazing and horrifying tale."

"Yes, and you can see the results of the spirit of evil that grips so much of our nation now. Gamala murdered itself. Now it's a ruined wasteland—a desolate graveyard. Because of the criminal Zealots. Yes, I blame them even more than I do the Romans. The ways of the Romans are well understood everywhere—they leave the cooperative in peace and destroy all who provoke them. But the Zealots—with their false piety—they say they'll liberate us and return our nation to God, but they're just thirsty for blood and martyrdom. The righteous way of our Christ? They have none of it. Exactly the opposite in fact. Those rebels trample the true way of God and bring nothing but ruin. That's what happens when people give themselves over to arrogance and wickedness, as the rebels have. In Gamala, more Jews killed themselves or died from famine than were killed by the Romans."

Benji took a few deep breaths. A wave of calm came over him.

"I believe Joshua will return. He's almost at the door probably. I'm ashamed of what he'll find, and I'm afraid of the severe and terrible judgment that's in store for our people."

Ariel placed a friendly hand on Benjamin's shoulder.

"Benji, you have nothing to fear, my friend. You're true to the way. As for those who walk in darkness and sin, they've brought judgment on themselves. But I understand what you're saying. Joshua is coming—coming to gather the righteous into his kingdom. The master comes to gather his harvest from the field, the field that he's sown with the word through us, the faithful. What kind of harvest will it be? I fear right now that the harvest will be meager. Let it not be so, but I see a meager harvest!"

4

While she sat at a table in the kitchen, Joseph's wife, Mary, broke a pomegranate apart and gave a piece to her nine-year-old son Judah.

"When will I be old enough to go with Father to the villages?" Judah asked.

"When your father decides you're ready. Probably when you're thirteen or so."

"And what do Joshua and Jacob do out there with Father?"

"They help him. They help him carry his things. They help him light a fire or prepare a meal. They help him manage the animals or assemble a tent—anything they can do that he wants them to do."

"I guess it's pretty boring then."

Judah picked some kernels from his pomegranate and nibbled.

"Well," Mary said. "It's not a tourist's pleasure trip. Your father is just going to the villages around Sepphoris to trade and let the people know about his synagogue. Produce and animals are cheaper in the villages, and while your father does business with the villagers he gets to know them and befriend them. Today he's visiting a friend with a vineyard. He's going to show him the proper way to make sukkot tents for the Feast of Tabernacles. Your father teaches the country people the Torah, and he answers their questions. And when they come to the city to attend synagogue, they go to him."

"Why don't they just have a rabbi live with them in the village?"

"They would if they could, but men like your father are special. Aside from rabbis, scribes, and the wealthy people, almost everybody can't read or write. So most people have to learn about the law and the prophets from one of the few men, like your father, who can read and understand scripture. It's a way for him to help the poor, which the Torah commands us to do. So study well when your father teaches you, because it's a privilege to be able to study Torah."

* * *

Joseph, Joshua, Jacob, and Piram, their donkey, walked southward from Sepphoris. Joseph led from the rear while fifteen-year-old Joshua led Piram, and thirteen-year-old Jacob walked alongside her. Piram carried a load of saddle bags containing the group's supplies. One big sack held some tent cloth and another had the tent poles and rope. There was a bag of bread, a sack of lentil beans, several water skins, two wine skins, a skin of olive oil, a bag of pomegranates, and a sack of barley grains for the donkey.

"Father," Joshua asked as Joseph moved closer to the donkey. "Why don't we ever go to Jerusalem? Aren't we supposed to?"

"Ah, Joshua," Joseph said. "Jerusalem. We should go to Jerusalem, and we will someday. But right now we have to go see Ephraim. I promised him I would teach his family how to make sukkot and properly celebrate the Feast of Tabernacles. They're going to Jerusalem for it this year. But we'll have to stay in Sepphoris then. We can't abandon all our neighbors who are too old, poor, or infirm to walk all the way to Jerusalem. I'm still their rabbi and they count on me."

"Which village did you say was Ephraim's, Father?" Jacob asked.

"Nazareth. We've been there before. That's the village where I stayed briefly when I moved to Galilee from Jerusalem. That was right before I married your mother in Sepphoris."

"Why did you leave Jerusalem?" Joshua asked.

Joseph paused and winced.

"Actually," Joseph said, "it's more honest to say that I *fled* Jerusalem. Jerusalem became a crazy place after King Herod died. Herod's son Archelaus took the throne in Judea and right away showed himself to be every bit the tyrant that his father was."

Joseph looked around as if he were about to share a dark secret. "Listen to this. At Passover some of our people protested at the Temple, demanding justice for those men who helped Herod murder some of our most righteous scholars. So Archelaus sent troops to bully them. Those troops attacked them in the middle of their Passover sacrifices and killed thousands without any justification. All the people fled the Temple and hid themselves in their homes. That's why the Passover festival ended early that year."

Joshua and Jacob moved closer to their father to better hear him. They listened with wide-eyed disbelief as Joseph continued his tale.

"Archelaus then sailed off to Rome to receive instructions from Caesar, leaving Roman soldiers in Jerusalem to harass the Jews in his absence. Things got bloody again. Jerusalem's men, with every justification of course, attacked the royal palace and the Roman soldiers there. By Pentecost the city was engulfed in war, with Romans and Jews killing each other everywhere. The Romans plundered the Temple, the Jews plundered the palace, and the fighting spread throughout Judea. I got myself out of there. I would've been killed if I hadn't. And I haven't been back since."

"And Jerusalem is still unsafe?" Joshua asked.

"It isn't at war anymore, but I'm not eager to go back. It still has problems. After Archelaus came back, armed with Caesar's permission to oppress our people, he tyrannized all of Judea. And now the Romans control Judea directly, without even a Herodian stooge in the middle—a stooge pretending to be a Jewish king while carrying out Caesar's orders. No, I'll stay away for now. Jerusalem is too dangerous, especially at festival time."

"But what about the commandments to observe the festivals?" Joshua asked.

Joseph halted the donkey and fixed a solemn gaze on his sons.

"Listen, my sons. The law is sacred. It exists to guide us and to give us life. But if observing the law means our destruction, then life comes before observing the law. That's why we're exempt from the laws of Temple worship and the Sabbath if they put us in danger. God gave us the law so that we would live, not so that we should die."

* * *

Nazareth was a tiny village of forty-nine simple clay and brick family homes perched on hills overlooking several small wheat fields and vineyards. Most of the male inhabitants worked in those fields or vineyards during the day while the women washed, cooked, and cared for their young children in the village proper. The hilltop position of the village offered an excellent view of the surrounding land, so early settlers called the place "Natzar Eretz," which more or less meant "watch place" or "site from which to watch the land." Over the years the name shortened to Nazareth.

Joseph and sons stayed two days and nights in Nazareth, bunking with Ephraim's family in a home consisting of one large, windowless room with a flat wooden roof and a basement chamber for housing livestock. On the first day, Joseph, Joshua, and Jacob showed Ephraim's family and some of their neighbors how to build sukkot with the materials and dimensions required by Jewish law. The villagers already had a basic understanding of how to celebrate the Feast of Tabernacles, but they wanted Joseph to authorize every detail as legitimate to assure them that they would not embarrass themselves in Jerusalem.

Joshua taught the children some of the history behind the festival.

"You sleep in a tent to remember that our ancestors slept in tents when they wandered the desert after escaping Egypt."

"We feast to celebrate all the blessings God has granted us in the Promised Land."

"Show respect to the ancestors, for they may appear to you in your tent. Each night be prepared for a visit from Moses or one of the prophets."

On the second day, Joseph and Joshua gathered with the men who would be making the pilgrimage and recited the most important festival prayers: the Shema (Deuteronomy 6:4–9, 11:12–21, Numbers 15:37–41) and the Hallel (Psalms 113–118). They repeated the prayers until each man could recite them from memory. Afterward Ephraim took Joseph aside to speak with him in private.

"Joseph, I'm giving you three sheep to thank you for healing my son of his fever. You can pick any three from my little flock."

"I'm grateful for anything you give me, friend, but I insist that you choose whatever it is. And I didn't heal your Isaac. God did. I only prayed and made the request on your behalf. If God willed it so, then count yourself blessed."

"You're too humble. God pays heed to the righteous, and you, my friend, are a righteous man. I insult you with my sheep. Here I am burdening you with animals you have no use for, except to sell in the markets of Sepphoris. An inconvenience for you. You deserve better. You've prepared us well for our festival trip, and we can afford it thanks to you. That vintner friend of yours, Samuel—the one you brought to me in Sepphoris—he's been a profitable client. He buys more of my grapes than anyone. I'll give you ten percent of what I've made from him this year. Here you are—forty Tyrian silver shekels! Buy yourself a horse, or two donkeys."

Joseph gasped. "Ephraim! I don't deserve this generosity. But I suppose I must accept it, reluctantly. You've never let a friend refuse a gift. You're a blessing: a man who pays his debts and then some. If Nazareth prospers, it's surely because you, more than anyone else here, are righteous in the eyes of the Lord."

Ephraim and Joseph embraced, and then walked back to the house. Ephraim was happy to provide such a handsome reward to his friend, because he knew that Joseph had brought similar good fortune to others in the village, and many of them nevertheless did not repay their debts to him.

* * *

Early the next morning, Joseph, Joshua, and Jacob loaded up their donkey to head north back to Sepphoris. Joseph had sold the tents and some of the food, so there were fewer saddle bags, and one of them was small but heavy with the coins gained from the profitable visit. After starting their walk, they noticed the loud jostling of the coins as Piram shuffled along. Embarrassed, Joseph added some barley grain to the coin sack to muffle the ostentatious jangling.

The morning was temperate and quiet, and the travelers' minds wandered. Jacob burned to talk with his father about all the possible ways to spend their new money, but he knew that Joseph would lecture him about the sinfulness of greed and pride. It wasn't long, however, before Joseph pierced the silence by reciting psalms and inviting his sons to join him, each taking a turn with a verse.

Joseph: "Shout for joy to honor God our strength, shout to acclaim the God of Jacob!"

Joshua: "Start the music, sound the drum, the melodious lyre and the harp; sound the new moon trumpet, at the full moon, on our feast day!"

Jacob: "This is a statute binding on Israel, an ordinance of the God of Jacob, this decree he imposed on Joseph, when he went to war against Egypt."

Joseph: "I can hear a voice I no longer recognize: 'It was I who relieved your shoulder of the burden, so your hands could drop the laborer's basket; you called in your trouble, so I rescued you.'" (Psalm 81)

Reciting psalms this way the three whiled away the time as they walked along the road.

When they reached the approximate halfway point between Nazareth and Sepphoris, they noticed two horsemen ahead of them approaching from the north. As the riders got closer, Joseph could see that they were tall, long-bearded men wearing tight turbans over their hair and swords at their belts.

"Don't even look at them," Joseph said to his sons. "Just keep going and mind your own business."

Joshua and Jacob fixed their gaze on the path right in front of them, not allowing their eyes to wander beyond the donkey walking a few steps ahead of them.

When the horsemen came within speaking distance, one of them, slightly shorter and somewhat older in appearance than the other, rode ahead past them and turned around to face them from behind. Joseph, his sons, and Piram were now caught between the two horsemen, with the taller one in front gazing down on them. Joshua and Jacob could no longer help but look at these frightening strangers.

The tall one spoke and betrayed a Samaritan accent.

"Give up your money and your bags," he said as he pulled out his sword and brandished it at Joseph. "No one will be harmed if you cooperate."

Joseph, trembling, walked toward the donkey. As he went through the motions of untying the saddle bags, he kept his eyes on the tall Samaritan. He took his time untying, and before finishing he spoke to the robber.

"God watches you." Joseph said.

"Yes, God watches all," the tall horseman said. "But I assure you that there are far more spectacular crimes occupying His attention at the moment."

When the saddle bags were untied and in hand, Joseph relinquished them with visible anguish, as if he were surrendering his own hand to the chopping block.

"I beg you to not do this," Joseph said. "Please, spare us and spare yourself the punishment for this sin."

The shorter robber leapt off his horse, drew a dagger, and began frisking Jacob, then Joshua, and finally Joseph. He found nothing valuable and climbed back onto his horse.

Joshua fumed with indignation. He began to recite from the thirty-forth and thirty-fifth Psalms of David.

"Evil will bring death to the wicked, those who hate the virtuous will have to pay; the Lord—" (Psalm 34:21)

Joseph shot Joshua a look of rage.

"Silence!" Joseph shouted. "What are you doing? Stop it. Obey at once!"

Joseph pleaded with the robbers: "I'm sorry. Forgive my son. He's having a fit of mad stupidity. Please ignore him."

Joshua continued undaunted: "Yahweh Himself ransoms the souls of His servants, and those who take shelter in Him have nothing to pay. Shame and dishonor on those who are out to kill me! Back with them! Cover with confusion those who plot my downfall! May they be like chaff before the wind, with the angel of Yahweh to chase them! May their way be dark and slippery, with the angel of Yahweh to hound them!" (Psalms 34:23, 35:4–6)

Joseph grabbed Joshua and tried to muzzle him with his hand, but Joshua slipped out of his grasp and leapt onto a nearby embankment. Joseph lunged at him again but Joshua dodged him, letting Joseph fall forward on his hands and knees.

"How dare you!" Joseph yelled.

Joshua pointed at the tall robber and continued his tirade of verse: "Unprovoked they spread their net for me, they dug a pit for me; but Ruin creeps on them unawares, the net they've spread will catch them instead, and into their own pit they'll fall!" (Psalm 35:7–8)

Joseph picked himself up to make another attempt at restraining Joshua, but the tall robber, without even having to dismount, kicked Joseph back down and signaled to his partner to face down Joshua.

Meanwhile Jacob was on his knees, frantic and praying. He recited from Psalm fifty-nine: "Rescue me from my enemies, my God, protect me from those attacking me, rescue me from these evil men, save me from these murderers!" (Psalm 59:2–3)

The tall robber laughed and then shouted, "Everybody just calm the fuck down!"

Joshua and Jacob quieted and allowed the robber to speak.

"Your wild floundering and sermonizing are very amusing, but our business here is done. Just be thankful to escape with your lives. And don't judge us so harshly because we're robbers. By robbing we show that we fear neither God nor men. Unlike those truly impious thieves—the burglars. They skulk and steal while hidden away from men's eyes—but in the full view of God—showing that they fear men more than they fear God. Reserve your condemnation for them!"

The robbers positioned themselves to ride and commanded their horses to begin trotting away southward. The robbers had just begun to get away when Joseph, Joshua, and Jacob took a moment to embrace. They were sad and traumatized, but relieved to be safe. Then Joshua, still incensed at the robbers, raised his hands in the air and yelled in the direction of the departing horsemen, quoting from the ninety-fourth and ninety-seventh chapters of Enoch.

"Woe to you who acquire silver and gold in unrighteousness and say: 'We've become rich and have possessions; and have acquired everything we desired.' Yea, like water your lies shall flow away; for your riches won't abide, they'll quickly depart from you, for you have acquired it all in unrighteousness, and you'll suffer a great curse. Woe to those who build their houses with sin; for they shall fall under the sword!" (Enoch 97:8-10, 94:7)

Joseph was about to admonish Joshua for his unnecessary provocation of the robbers when Jacob did something much more reckless. He grabbed a fist-sized rock and threw it at the shorter robber, hitting him in the back of the head. Unhurt, but enraged, the horseman turned around and started to gallop toward Jacob, guessing from Joseph and Joshua's shocked reaction that Jacob was the thrower.

As the horse approached, Joshua tried in vain to grab the robber's leg and pull him off. But Joseph was able to get to Jacob in time to push him away and off the road. In the process, however, Joseph was himself trampled by the horse, and he took blows from three of the horse's hooves: one in the head, one in the chest, and one in the leg.

The horseman steadied himself and, satisfied by the damage inflicted, galloped back to his companion to continue the journey south.

Joshua and Jacob rushed to help their father lying bloodied on the ground. To their horror they could see that Joseph's skull was crushed. Without question he was dead.

Joshua and Jacob tore their tunics and wept, overwhelmed by shock and grief. They remained so until enough time had passed for them to compose themselves and realize that Piram was missing. The donkey had wandered a short way off, spooked by the final charge of the horse, and in a matter of minutes Joshua and Jacob found her nearby. They draped their father's corpse over her, laid their hands on it, and prayed over it as they made their sorrowful journey home.

* * *

Months later, in Sepphoris, Mary pondered how she and her children would live without Joseph. Her marriage contract stipulated that she and the children would be supported by Joseph's family, but they were unknown to her, possibly dead, and in any event far away in Jerusalem. After years of hearing Joseph's horror stories about that city, she was not about to drag her children there to pursue uncertain prospects.

But staying in Sepphoris would also be difficult. Joseph still owed money on the building he used as his synagogue, and without Joseph's income they would have to sell their house to cover the debt. Joshua and Jacob could work as laborers for various builders in the city, but the pay would be meager and the family would have to move to a poorer part of town. In Mary's mind the poverty was acceptable, but the embarrassment of having to face the phony sympathy of her friends and acquaintances, who she knew would gloat at her misfortune, would be intolerable.

Mary decided that the best option was to move to one of the nearby villages where she could raise her family in a state of poverty with dignity. Nazareth was the natural choice because not only was her family known and admired there, but it was the village containing the most residents who were in debt to Joseph.

So Mary and her children moved to Nazareth, and the villagers were happy to welcome them. Ephraim's family helped Joshua and Jacob construct a new house near theirs. It had walls of stone and clay, a flat wooden roof, and room enough for Mary and her children.

Isaac, another friend of Joseph's, secured Joshua a job at Isaac's brother Asher's stone-working shop in Reina, a village two miles northeast of Nazareth. There Joshua earned money breaking limestone from a nearby quarry and transporting it to the workshop, where he cut, drilled, carved, and sanded the stone into jars, bowls, dishes, and cups. He also helped deliver finished wares to customers and marketplaces.

On the Sabbaths, Joshua set up a tent of meeting on a plateau at the southern end of Nazareth, where he invited the villagers to pray, sing hymns, and hear him recite scripture. Over time Joshua developed the confidence to deliver his own sermons at these meetings, where he expounded on scripture and told stories that illustrated whatever lesson he wanted to impart. The Nazarenes were impressed by his knowledge and authoritative demeanor, and they accepted his precocious preaching with warmth, but to them he was still only the son of a rabbi, a child imitating their beloved Joseph. When they spoke of him, they called him Joshua the craftsman—the young maker of stoneware.

5

After spending a week with some fellow church elders in the city of Iconium, Ariel returned to Antioch. He entered the north gate of the city and walked the main colonnaded road to a boulevard stretching east, which traversed the Greek neighborhood south of the amphitheater. This boulevard would take Ariel to the Jewish Quarter, where his home waited at the foot of a hill at the easternmost part of the city.

When he walked through the Greek neighborhood, he noticed a house with a man standing on the roof and a few people on the street outside watching him. These were a woman aged in her thirties, a teenaged boy, a young boy, and a young girl, all Greek by appearance. A middle-aged man with the beard and cloak of a Jewish scholar stood on the opposite side of the street and watched as well.

"Shalom, lord," Ariel said to the Jewish man. "My name's Ariel. Do you know what these people are doing?"

"Shalom," the man answered, shaking Ariel's hand. "I'm Naftali. The people here are welcoming the return of the master of the house. He'd gone missing for a few days. You're lucky you weren't here before; the city guards were rounding up Jews, myself included, and interrogating us about this missing man. They were worried that Jews had taken the man to sell or sacrifice. The woman there, the wife, was ranting about Christians taking her husband to eat his body and drink his blood. Can you believe such paranoid slander? Luckily the man showed up today and the guards let us go. I'm still here only because this family fascinates me."

Naftali pointed at the man on the roof and laughed.

"Why's he on the roof?" Ariel asked.

Naftali took Ariel aside and lowered his voice.

"These goyim, the Greeks, are crazy. It turns out the man was missing because he'd been carousing, and he drunkenly lost himself somewhere. When he got home his wife wouldn't allow him to come in through the front gate. She accused him of being under the influence of devils, so he'd have to enter the house 'the devils' way,' which is through the roof! Apparently this will force the evil spirit to exit the man through the hole in the roof after he lowers himself in. I just had to see such a thing!"

Ariel looked back at the house. Behind the front gate was a small courtyard flanked on the right and left by one-story rooms with sloping tiled roofs. Behind the courtyard the house had two stories and a tiled roof, upon which the man was now kneeling as he removed some of the tiles with the help of some tools.

When the man had made enough of a hole to drop himself through, he signaled his family with an upturned thumb and sat on the edge of the hole, dangling his legs inside. With his hands grabbing opposite edges of the hole, he slid down until he was hanging inside the house with only his gripping fingers visible, and in an instant he released his grip and fell in. His family clapped and whistled and went inside through the front gate.

"Remarkable!" Naftali said.

"I suppose the clapping and whistling scared away the demon," Ariel said.

Naftali shrugged his shoulders.

Ariel began to feel an uncomfortable sense that his lingering was voyeuristic and unseemly.

"Well," Ariel said. "It's been a pleasure, Naftali, but I must be going now. Shalom."

"Shalom." Naftali said.

As Ariel walked on, thinking about what he had just witnessed, he couldn't help remembering the story Benjamin told him about the Roman siege of Gamala, when the soldiers crashed through the roofs of the Gamalans. But there was something else, some story from the scriptures that he could only halfway recall, that the roof spectacle had awakened in his memory.

What was it? Oh yes, now I remember. It's in the books of the Kings, when King Ahaziah fell through the lattice of his roof terrace and was left immobilized on his bed. Ahaziah appealed to Baal-Zebub to heal him, but Elijah cursed him for his idolatry.

Ariel recalled Elijah's curse on Ahaziah.

You will not leave the bed you're lying on. You will certainly die!

Ariel pondered these cases of accursed men who fell through roofs for the remainder of his walk home, and upon arriving he opened up his scroll of the second book of Kings. There it was in the first chapter: Elijah cursing the idolatrous Ahaziah, Ahaziah sending a hundred soldiers after Elijah, Elijah bringing down fire from heaven to kill the soldiers, and Ahaziah dying on his bed as predicted.

Ariel put away the scroll and let his mind wander in a daydream. He felt inspired to see in the images of the falling men a metaphor for the dire straits of his war-ravaged people. He imagined feverish scenes: men chasing each other into fiery pits, desperate soldiers jumping off a cliff, wicked angels falling to earth through cracks in the firmament, and all of Israel begging a remote God to send down forgiveness and healing through the fissures of the shattered sky. He sifted through the mental detritus, and in an instant he saw it all coalesce into a coherent vision. He picked up a quill and a page of parchment and began to write.

6

Twenty-five-year old Joshua had grown into a tall, strong, and handsome man. Six days a week he walked two miles to and from the stoneware workshop where his lifting, carving, drilling, and sanding heavy limestone made his hands strong and his arms muscular. As he worked he often recited his favorite verses from scripture. It was a way for him to further solidify his recollection of them and to stave off boredom. His workmates would listen and sometimes request a particular story or ask him to explain the meaning of a puzzling passage. Joshua also entertained his coworkers with stories he made up himself, stories that were often based on scripture but altered to make them more appealing to his companions.

On Sabbaths Joshua continued to preach at his tent of meeting, and he drew dozens of Nazarenes to hear him teach the law and the prophets. He spoke with a confidence and authority that pleased his listeners, who loved to be reminded that they were the descendants of the great heroes of scripture. Joshua became a figure of fascination, especially to the young women who came to hear him speak. Mary was pulled into countless intrigues with other villagers trying to arrange their daughters into marriage with him. Nevertheless Joshua rejected all such proposed unions, insisting to his scandalized mother that it was not for him to get married and start a family. Mary harangued Joshua for his baffling reluctance to take on the proper responsibilities of manhood, especially when he was so spoiled for choice, but one Sabbath morning she visited the tent and saw Joshua give a surprising sermon that completely changed her thinking about her son and his marriage prospects.

This particular Sabbath was cloudy and windy, with a moisture in the air that suggested rain could come at any moment. Periodic wind gusts punched the tent cloth and caused it to bulge with a loud roar. A good crowd of about fifty Nazarenes sat on the grassy ground, huddled together in the warmth of body heat. Joshua led the congregation in the Shema prayer and some benedictions, and then began to preach.

"Enoch, seventh from Adam, who was so dear to the Lord that He took him while still alive up into heaven, received from God the most complete vision of the future ever given to any prophet, a vision that he shared with his descendants, and which passed from generation to generation through the most learned and righteous holy men of the ages. I'm fortunate enough to be familiar with this book. This morning I'll recite from some of it, and I'll add some of my own commentary to clarify its meaning for you."

Joshua began to recite from chapters ninety-one and ninety-two of Enoch.

"To future generations who shall observe righteousness and peace. Let not your spirit be troubled on account of the times; for the Holy and Great One has appointed days for all things. (Enoch 92:1–2)

"The word calls me, and the spirit is poured out on me, that I may show you everything that shall befall you forever. (Enoch 91:1)

"Hear, you sons of Enoch, all the words of your father, and hearken, as you should, to the voice of my mouth; for I exhort you and say to you, beloved: Love righteousness and walk in it, and draw near to righteousness without a double heart, and don't associate with those of a double heart, but walk in righteousness, my sons. And it shall guide you on good paths and be your companion. For I know that violence must increase on the earth, and a great punishment is unavoidable; the earth will be uprooted and destroyed." (Enoch 91:3-5)

As Joshua recited, he paced the ground and wore a serious expression that broadcast a gravitas that belied his youth. He looked into the eyes of the faces in the audience with an intensity that suggested it would be a grave sin to fail to pay attention. The occasional wind gusts that buffeted the tent raged like angry spirts trying to wrestle it to the ground, and they punctuated Joshua's speech with a subtle, disquieting menace.

"Unrighteousness shall again be complete on the earth, and all the deeds of unrighteousness and of violence and sin shall prevail a second time. And when sin and blasphemy and violence of every kind increases, heaven shall deliver a great chastisement, and the Holy Lord will unleash his wrath and judgment. (Enoch 91:6-7)

"In those days heaven will destroy all who love violence, wickedness, and deceit. The Lord will burn all the idols of the heathen and remove them from the whole earth; and He will cast the heathens into the grievous punishment of fire, to burn forever. (Enoch 91:8-9)

"And the righteous shall rise from their sleep, and wisdom will be theirs. But the Lord shall cut down all those who plan violence and commit blasphemy." (Enoch 91:10-11)

Joshua stopped reciting and began his commentary.

"Enoch begins here by referring to two punishing divine judgements upon the earth. To Enoch, who, if you remember, was the great-grandfather of Noah, these are visions of future events. The first is the Great Flood of Noah's time, a punishment of water. The second is a great punishment of fire. When is this fire coming? Listen carefully to what Enoch says."

Joshua resumed his recitation: "I, Enoch, was born the seventh in the first week, able judgement and righteousness still endured." (Enoch 93:3)

Joshua commented: "Enoch is talking about the first 'week' of history, the period from Adam until Methuselah."

Reciting again, Joshua said, "After me great wickedness and deceit shall arise in the second week; and in that week there shall be the first end. And in it a man shall be saved." (Enoch 93:4)

Joshua commented: "The first end is the Great Flood. The man saved is Noah. That's easy enough to see.

"The next verse reads: 'And after that in the third week, at its close, the Holy Lord shall elect a man as the plant of righteous judgment, and his posterity shall become the plant of righteousness for ever more.' (Enoch 93:5)

"This man, 'elected as the plant of righteous judgement,' could be none other than Abraham. Notice the word 'posterity.' Remember how God promised Abraham that he would be the patriarch of the great nation of the Hebrews. The third era of history ends with Abraham founding our people.

"Listen to the next verse: 'And after that in the fourth week, at its close, a righteous man will see visions of the holy, and the Lord will reveal a law for all generations, and He will command His children to build an enclosure for that law.' (Enoch 93:6)

"Obviously the 'law for all generations' is the law that God gave Moses on Mt. Sinai, and the 'enclosure made for it' is the tent of meeting where the first priests performed the sacrifices and protected the ark. So the fourth age of history is the time of Moses, including the bondage in Egypt, the Exodus, and the march to the Promised Land.

"Now listen to the next verse: 'And after that in the fifth week, at its close, the house of glory and dominion shall be built forever.' (Enoch 93:7)

"The fifth week is the age of Joshua, the Judges, King David and King Solomon, ending with Solomon building the Temple, the 'house of glory and dominion,' in Jerusalem.

"This is made even clearer in the next verse: 'And after that, in the sixth week, all who live in it shall be blinded, and the hearts of all of them shall godlessly forsake wisdom. And in it a man shall ascend; and at its close a great fire shall burn the house of dominion, and the whole race of the chosen root shall disperse to a new land.' (Enoch 93:8)

"The sixth week is the era that began with the kings after Solomon, continued through the schism between Israel and Judea, and ended with Nebuchadnezzar's destruction of the Temple and the Jews' exile to Babylon. The words are indisputable: 'a great fire shall burn the house of dominion.' It's a prophecy of the Temple's destruction. 'The whole race of the chosen root shall disperse to a new land.' This is clearly the Babylonian Exile. 'The man who shall ascend' could only be Elijah, who was taken up to heaven in the fiery chariot during the days of King Jehoram."

A few of Joshua's listeners began to nod off, but a sudden gust pounded the tent and startled them awake, as if the elements themselves demanded that Joshua's long-winded sermon be heard.

"Now listen carefully to the next verses: 'And after that in the seventh week shall an apostate generation arise, and many shall be its deeds, and all its deeds shall be apostate. And at its end the Lord will select the elect of the eternal plant of righteousness, and He will give them sevenfold instruction concerning all of His creation. And after this there will be another week, the eighth—that of righteousness—and the Lord will give it a sword so that the righteous may execute judgment on those who do wrong, and the Lord will hand the sinners over into the hands of the righteous. And, at its end, they will acquire Houses because of their righteousness, and the Great King shall be housed in glory forever.' (Enoch 91:12-13, 93:9-10)

"We know that the sixth 'week' ended with the Babylonian Exile, so the seventh starts with the return from exile: the return of the Jews to Jerusalem and Judea. In the seventh 'week' we have the rebuilding of the Temple, the rule of the Persians, the rule of the Greeks, the rule of the Hasmoneans, and the rule of the Herods and Rome. Yes, we are living in the seventh 'week' of history! Can there be any doubt? We certainly aren't in the eighth 'week,' the 'week of righteousness.' Clearly the sinners are not in the hands of the righteous; quite the opposite is the case. All power today belongs to sinners, apostates, and pagans. Even the holy city and Temple belong to the Romans now. Here in Galilee, we have a Roman sponsored king, Antipas, who answers only to Caesar. 'Apostate' is the perfect word to describe our times.

"But how far along are we in this seventh era of history? When can we expect it to end? Let's reckon from the prophecy. From Abraham to Moses was about five hundred years. From David to the Exile was five hundred years. A 'week' in the prophecy appears to be about five hundred years. And it's been about five hundred years since the return from the Exile. We're at the end of the seventh week! The new age of history, the righteous age, is almost here!"

Several audience members, eyebrows raised, looked at one another and shrugged.

"Let me finish reciting the prophecy: 'And after this, in the ninth week, the whole world will witness the righteous judgment. And all the deeds of the impious will vanish from the whole earth. And the Lord will write the world down for destruction, and all men will look to the path of uprightness. And after this, in the tenth week, in the seventh part, the watchers shall receive their eternal judgment, and the great eternal heaven will spring from the midst of the angels. And the first heaven will vanish and pass away and a new heaven will appear, and all the powers of heaven will shine forever, with light seven times as bright. And after this, there will be weeks without number, forever, in goodness and in righteousness. And from then on there will never again be any mention of sin.' (Enoch 91:14-17)

"Listen, people of Nazareth! The thousands of years of sin since Adam are coming to an end! Ahead of us is the age of judgment! First, the eighth week, when Israel will be restored to righteousness and all the godless apostates and sinners who pollute our Holy Land will be destroyed by God's own hand. For five hundred years Israel will be a new, sanctified kingdom and a beacon of light for the rest of the world. Then the ninth week, when the wicked of the whole world will burn, and the earth itself will be destroyed. And finally the tenth week, when heaven and earth are reborn, when Satan and his angels are cast into the fiery pit along with all the wicked, and the righteous will live on forever in God's eternal glory!"

Joshua looked up and gazed beyond his listeners as if he were transfixed by the heavens. Audience members murmured amongst themselves, pondered Joshua's mental state, and wondered how to respond. A few listeners stifled some quiet laughter, and a handful sneaked away and out the tent, but most just sat in awkward silence while Joshua stood in an apparent trance. Mary, burning with embarrassment, trembled with fear for her son.

Without warning Joshua projected an imperious tone of voice and resumed speaking.

"All you who are righteous, but poor and persecuted, robbed and ruined, brought low by the sinful powers of this world, your vindication is at hand!"

Joshua returned his gaze to the audience and paced. His former look of gravitas returned and his voice boomed like an angry prophet's. He recited from chapters ninety-four through ninety-six of Enoch.

"Woe to you, you rich, for you've trusted in your riches, and from your riches you'll depart, because you have not remembered the Most High in the days of your wealth. You've committed blasphemy and unrighteousness, and are marked for the day of slaughter, and the day of darkness, and the day of great judgment. Thus I speak and tell you: He who has created you will overthrow you! (Enoch 94:8–10)

"You, righteous! Fear not the sinners, for again the Lord will deliver them into your hands, that you may execute judgment on them according to your desires. Woe to you who repay your neighbor with evil, for you'll be repaid according to your works. Woe to you, lying witnesses, and to those who weigh out injustice, for you'll suddenly perish. Woe to you, sinners, woe to you who persecute the righteous, for your injustice will bring you persecution and a heavy yoke. (Enoch 95:3-7)

"Wherefore fear not, you that have suffered, for healing shall be your portion, and a bright light shall enlighten you, and you'll hear the voice of rest from heaven. Woe to you who devour the finest of the wheat, and drink wine in large bowls, and tread underfoot the lowly with your might. Woe to you who drink water from every fountain, for suddenly you'll be consumed and wither away, because you've forsaken the fountain of life. Woe to you, you mighty, who with your power oppress the righteous; the day of your destruction is coming. Many and good days shall come to the righteous in those days—in the day of your judgment!" (Enoch 96:3–8)

Mary was in tears. Her face burned and her head ached. She was dizzy with worry.

My poor son! All his studying and reciting has turned him into a crazed crackpot! He thinks he's found the key to God's unknowable mysteries. My Joshua! A doom sayer and a woe spouter! God prevent him from becoming some wandering recluse, preaching Jeremiads to the sheep and the goats! Who could ever marry him then?

* * *

After revealing the momentous prophecy of Enoch to the Nazarenes, and facing both the bemused indifference of his audience and the panicked objections of his mother, Joshua decided that he would be wise to revert to his more conventional style of preaching on the Sabbaths.

The day after the Enoch sermon, Joshua went to the stoneware workshop as usual. His friend and coworker Thaddeus had been at the tent service the day before, and as soon as Joshua arrived he asked him about it.

"Joshua! I heard your sermon yesterday. I was amazed. Can it all be true? You sound like a holy man—or a prophet."

Joshua scowled. "Are you making fun of me?"

"No, not at all. I was truly impressed."

"Then why didn't you come tell me in the tent? Why didn't you support me? You saw how everyone reacted."

"Yes, the people didn't receive your words well, if I'm honest. But that's just the thing. I was afraid to openly be your friend at that moment, the way everybody was talking about you and mocking you. I'm sorry; I was afraid. But they don't know you like I know you—how learned you are, I mean. You speak like a true prophet. You sound like John the Baptist."

"Who's John the Baptist?"

"He's a holy hermit who lives by the Jordan, where the Jordan meets the Jabbok. He used to be a priest in Jerusalem, but now he lives rough in the wilderness, preaching to his followers about the wickedness everywhere and how the great Day of Judgment is coming soon. Just like you were doing yesterday."

"You know him?"

"No, but I've heard about him, and he apparently agrees with you."

Joshua gazed into space. "I have to meet this John the Baptist. Where did you say he lived?"

7

Ariel stood at the podium on the dais four steps up from the floor of the synagogue. Behind him loomed the arch-topped alcove housing the tabernacle: the ornate wooden cabinet with an image of the tablets of the Ten Commandments engraved on its doors, behind which sat the ensconced Torah scroll. The congregation sat on wooden benches on both sides of a rug-covered aisle that stretched from the dais to the synagogue entrance.

It was the Sabbath and Ariel had finished the customary prayers, benedictions, and readings from scripture, including Second Kings chapter one, which he had chosen for that day's reading from the prophets. He was ready to begin the sermon that he had finished preparing the day before.

"Brothers and sisters in the Lord, I'm inspired today to offer you a puzzle, a riddle for you to ponder that's based on the story I want to tell you now. The story is about Joshua our Lord and his work of healing and forgiving sins. First, let me tell you the story and then I'll ask you the riddle."

The prospect of a riddle made many in the audience sit up to pay extra attention. With the audience fully engaged, Ariel told his story.

"We know that when Joshua was in Galilee, teaching the way of righteousness and declaring the coming kingdom of God, he healed many people. He cured lepers, paralytics, the deaf, the dumb, and demoniacs, among others. Once, when Joshua was in Capernaum and already becoming famous in the lake towns for his healing power and authoritative wisdom, he attracted a large crowd to Peter's house, where he was teaching the word. So many came to hear him that there wasn't room in the house for everyone, and a crowd formed outside.

"Four men came, carrying a paralyzed man on a portable sickbed. They wanted to meet Joshua and have him heal their incapacitated friend. But they couldn't reach Joshua because the crowds were so thick and impassable. So the four men climbed up onto the roof and made an opening by removing some of the planks. Then they worked together to lift the sick bed carrying their friend to the roof, and from there they lowered the bed with great care through the opening and down to Joshua.

"Joshua saw the faith of these men. They were not deterred, even when they could only get to Joshua by unusual—some might say improper or deviant—means. They dared to disdain all obstacles because they believed in Joshua. Joshua spoke to the paralyzed man: 'For such faith, let your sins be forgiven.'

"Now, some Pharisees were there, thinking to themselves, 'What blasphemy! Only God can forgive sins!' Joshua knew that the Pharisees were protesting in their hearts, so he confronted them, saying, 'Why are you such enemies of faith? Which is easier to say to this paralyzed man, "your sins are forgiven" or "get up, take your bed, and walk?" Since I want you to know that I can recognize the repentance that earns the forgiveness of God, I say to you, friend, get up, take your bed, and walk home!' The man got up, took his bed, and walked out in front of everyone. They were all amazed, having never witnessed such a thing before."

Ariel paused for a moment to let the story sink in. When some of the members of the congregation began to fidget and cough, Ariel spoke again.

"Now, I present this riddle to you: who is the paralyzed man in the story? If you think you have the answer, come see me. In any case I'll reveal the answer here next Sabbath. Go now in the peace of the Lord and Christ Joshua, brothers and sisters."

The congregation sang a closing hymn and filed out of the synagogue. Many of the faithful pondered the riddle as they made their way home, some deep in silent thought, others discussing it with their companions.

That night, two hours after the Sabbath had ended at sunset, Ariel received a visitor at his home. Zachariah, a fellow elder of the Christian sect in Antioch, had come to present his answer to the riddle. After exchanging the usual pleasantries with Ariel, Zachariah jumped right to his interpretation of Ariel's story.

"I think your paralyzed man is Israel. Your story is allegorical and the man represents the nation of Israel, paralyzed by its estrangement from God. Israel is hobbled by its erroneous ways as it's led by the four false philosophies, and each of the four men carrying the bed represents one of these philosophies. One represents the Pharisees, who abandon ethics for statutory ritual; one represents the Sadducees, who reject the prophets and rob the people; one represents the Essenes, who arrogantly set themselves above everyone else and consider themselves the only true Jews left in the world; and one represents the Zealots, who in their fervor to be independent of Rome at all costs bring ruin upon us all."

Zachariah smiled and nodded his head, smug with confidence that he had solved the riddle.

"Well, Zachariah," Ariel said. "You've certainly come up with an imaginative solution. You're right about the paralyzed man, but I only had four carriers because that's how many men you'd need to safely bring the paralytic up to the roof and then down through the opening. But I like your version much better. Well done! But what's Joshua's role in all this? I'm sure you've figured that out too?"

Zachariah blushed. "Well, now I feel foolish for how I went on about the 'four philosophies.' But as far as Joshua goes, I see Joshua as the Savior of Israel—the only one who can put Israel on the right path. I was going to tell you that the way of Joshua is the cure for all the 'crippling' ways of the Pharisees, Zealots, and all the others, but you've already put that to rest!"

Ariel smiled. "No. That's perfect, Zachariah. I did mean to say that Joshua is the cure for Israel's ills—the restorer of lost righteousness—but I probably had all your other ideas too, if only at the corners of my mind. Because you're right. All those groups *have* led Israel astray. Joshua had the answer all along, but he was rejected, and now Israel faces destruction. If only we'd all heed him, we'd be saved. You understood my basic message and then some!"

Ariel gave Zachariah a congratulatory slap on the back.

"Remember," Ariel said, holding up his index finger. "Joshua is the way to salvation, no matter what happens. Israel could fall into ruin, but soon the pagans will too, and Joshua will return to gather the righteous faithful into his kingdom. My message to our church is 'don't lose faith on account of the war.' Joshua is the Messiah and we must remain faithful because he *is* coming."

"Yes, absolutely, Ariel. I just hope our brothers in the church understand this. So many have abandoned the faith because of the Roman disaster."

"And that's exactly why I'm telling these allegorical stories in my sermons, to keep the church faithful."

"Stories? So you have more?"

"Yes. The Lord inspires me all the time—in dreams, visions, and perceptions that could only be from him. With the Lord's help I see so many ways that the war is the culmination of sins that are in direct opposition to the way of Joshua. Herod, the Pharisees, the Zealots, and everyone else who's taken us to war operate in a spirit of pure rejection of the Christ. And that's why things are turning out so badly for us. But if we follow the way we'll have the opposite outcome: salvation instead of destruction."

Zachariah furrowed his brow. "But aren't you worried that people won't accept your allegories? What if they say you're just making up stories about Joshua?"

"Look, I'm not trying to deceive anyone. The members of our church know the words of Joshua; they know the story of his ministry, his crucifixion in Jerusalem, and everything else. I'm not telling them that Joshua actually did exactly this or exactly that, at exactly this time in exactly that place, or anything like that. I'm being honest from the start. They know that I'm telling them symbolic stories designed to make them think, just like the Lord himself did with his parables. It's just a way to get them to see that the war isn't evidence that Joshua was wrong in his predictions or his teachings. The war doesn't weaken his message, it strengthens it!"

"As long as that's perfectly clear to everyone. We don't want to lead the people astray. I'll be sure to hear all your sermons from now on."

"Absolutely. But you know, it's interesting. As I've said before, I feel that the Lord is inspiring me to imagine these stories, that in some way he's sending them to me. What if Joshua is sending me memories of actual events in his life? Imagine that! The stories would then be literal truth straight from the Lord himself!"

Zachariah laughed.

"That would be incredible, Ariel, a miracle! Your mind really is on fire. Consider me amazed."

8

John the Baptist camped with a few disciples in wilderness caves west of the Jordan, near where the Jordan and Jabbok rivers met. He was tall and thin, with long, wavy black hair and a black beard about a foot long. He wore a camel skin tunic in imitation of Elijah, and he fed himself from whatever kosher foods he could scavenge in the desert. In practice this meant that he, and by extension his disciples, ate almost nothing but fire-roasted locusts, dates, and wild honey.

John and his disciples spent most of their time sitting in caves and starving, imagining their souls to shine cleaner and brighter with each new bout of hunger and deprivation. On more well fed days, when locusts and honey were plentiful, they found the energy to pray, discuss scripture, or tell each other parables designed to stimulate deep contemplation of the mystery of God.

On occasion people came to hear John deliver his famous and passionate exhortations to repent and be saved from God's imminent judgment. After the sermon John would invite his audience, no matter how large or small, to be baptized one person at a time by him or one of his disciples. The baptism was a symbolic cleansing of past sins and a formal declaration before God to commit oneself henceforth to a life of righteousness.

When Joshua came to listen to John, he approved of all he heard the Baptist say. When John baptized Joshua, he took him into the Jordan and prayed over him. Then he recited from Ben Sirach and Ezekiel.

"To the penitent God provides a way back, and encourages the lost. Turn back to the Lord and give up your sins, pray before Him and make your offenses few. Turn again to the Most High and away from iniquity, and hate what He loathes.

"Who in Sheol can glorify the Most High in place of the living who offer their praise? The dead can no more give praise than those who have never lived; they who are alive and well glorify the Lord. How great is the mercy of the Lord, and his forgiveness for those who return to Him!

"For not everything is within human reach, since human beings are not immortal in the flesh. Is anything brighter than the sun? Yet it can be eclipsed. How worthless then the thoughts of flesh and blood! God holds accountable the hosts of highest heaven, while all mortals are dust and ashes. (Ben Sirach 17:24–32)

"I will immerse you in clean water, and you will be clean; I will cleanse you from all your impurities and from all your idols. I will give you a new heart and put a new spirit in you; I will remove from you your heart of stone and give you a heart of flesh. And I will put my spirit in you and move you to follow my decrees and be careful to keep my laws." (Ezekiel 36:25–27)

John submerged Joshua and brought him up again. Joshua then spoke to John.

"If you will, let me become your disciple. I want to learn how to be pure and holy, so I can know God and do what pleases Him."

John smiled, but he felt pity for Joshua.

"It's not at all an easy thing you're asking me. Just living out here is an ordeal. Here we have no Roman comforts. Are you prepared to sleep in a cave, on the hard ground, and eat only the meager offerings of this harsh wasteland?"

"Yes." Joshua answered without hesitation.

"Hmm." John was skeptical. "Let me ask you a few questions."

John took Joshua into a cave and interrogated him like he interrogated all his potential new disciples. John tested Joshua's knowledge of scripture and demanded that he reveal his beliefs about it. John wanted to see if he and Joshua had compatible views of the world—if they shared a common understanding of how to live righteously and were in agreement that the current era of history would soon end in cataclysmic divine judgment. He also had Joshua tell him all about his past and how he lived his life. While listening and watching, John tried to discern any tell-tale signs that Joshua might be a spy or saboteur working for Herod Antipas, the Romans, or the high priests. He then tried to assess whether Joshua would be strong enough to endure the ascetic life, wise and worldly enough to interact well with the public, and ethical enough to be trusted as a new member of the Baptist community. At the end of the interrogation, John was satisfied that Joshua was not a threat and might make a good Baptist, so he brought Joshua into the fold, giving him the tentative status of a novice disciple.

Joshua soon developed a close bond of trust with John and the other disciples. Before long he became a fully accepted and respected Baptist.

* * *

Each disciple of John the Baptist had a particular day of the week on which he was given an hour in the evening to ask the master questions one on one. Joshua's first such session, on his designated evening of Sunday, occurred on the fortieth day after his baptism.

"Master, why did you leave the priesthood in Jerusalem?"

"The Temple, I'm sorry to say, has become an abomination. Defying and insulting God has become the priority, not worshipping and obeying Him. When I served in the Temple I saw such brazen pollution. Priests ingratiating themselves with the Herodians with gifts from the holy treasury, even using the Temple funds for personal use. They made sacrifices on behalf of idolaters, and the high priesthood itself now goes to the highest bidder, regardless of family or qualifications. I couldn't stop it and I couldn't stand it, so I left. This wilderness is my temple now.

Here I can live in a state of purity. I feel closer to God here than I ever did in that profaned Temple."

"Are the priests in Jerusalem aware that judgment is at hand?"

"No, they refuse to accept it. They have their own interpretation of scripture and arrogantly dismiss all others. They don't believe that this age is soon to end, or that there will be a resurrection, even though the prophets proclaimed these things. The priests claim that the prophecies of Isaiah and the other prophets were either fulfilled long ago, or were purely metaphorical and not relevant to the future. They completely reject Enoch—as if they were in any position to judge Enoch! Today's priests, so counterfeit and venal, don't belong to that secret circle of holy men that has passed Enoch down through the generations. They reject it not only because it isn't part of their chosen canon, but because it exposes them for what they are: hypocrites and apostates. It makes perfect sense that they'd reject it—they think they're the masters of righteousness, so of course they oppose something that tells them they're doomed to be judged for their sins. But they deny the truth, and they'll burn!"

John threw a piece of dry bark into the fire. Joshua watched the bark sear into ash, and then he returned to his questions.

"What must I do to prepare for the coming judgment?"

"You must walk the righteous path."

"How do I walk the righteous path?"

"You dedicate yourself to always doing God's will."

"What is God's will?"

"You already know what God wills; it's only a matter of doing it."

"Forgive me Master, but I don't mean what God commands everyone to do in general. I mean what is God's will for *me*?"

John scratched himself on the head. "Oh. That God will tell you Himself."

"When?"

"You must pray and fast. Find a place of solitude, like Moses did on Sinai. There you must pray and fast until God sees fit to commune with you. That's when God will tell you what to do."

9

Ever since the war between the Jews and the Romans began, Ariel hated going into the Greek parts of Antioch. Before the war, the Jews and Greeks were at peace in the city, tolerating and respecting each other's equal status as citizens while mostly keeping to themselves and their own ways. But now the Greeks, in part to prove to the Romans their loyalty, made the Jews the objects of vile slanders and unjustified persecutions. The Antiochene Greeks even accepted a popular rumor, spread by the very son of the governor of the Jewish Quarter, that the Jews were plotting to burn down the city. This governor's son had converted to Greek paganism and encouraged the Greeks to believe every outrageous claim made against his own people. Every fire that broke out, regardless of its actual cause, was determined to be the work of the Jews, and was followed by a fresh mob assault in which any Jews within reach were slain. On calmer days that lacked such pretexts for violence, harassment was still the order of the day for any Jew caught out among the Greeks. Whenever Ariel, who was unwilling to hide his tell-tale beard or fringed cloak, had to walk through the streets of the Greek neighborhoods, adults cursed him and children pelted him with stones.

But on days when chariot races were exhibited at the Antioch hippodrome, much of the Greek population gathered there and left the other public spaces almost empty. Ariel loved to take advantage of such times to stock up on supplies at the agora market just south of the amphitheater. With the usual crowds gone, Ariel could shop without fear of harassment, rough handling, or pickpockets.

On one particular chariot race day, Ariel went to the marketplace, which was always scaled down on such days due to the lighter crowds. The shoppers were mainly Jews, but there were also a few Greeks and Romans. At one point Ariel passed a light-arms seller who was showing some swords to a Roman soldier.

"I need something sharp, light, and fast," the soldier said. "Something effective for fighting multitudes. My heavy sword is great against armor, but now I'm dealing with hordes of Jews who are poor in armor but rich in madness. I was just in Perea, fighting renegade Judeans, and I'll probably be sent to Jerusalem as soon as Vespasian returns from Rome."

"You were all the way off in Perea and now you're in Antioch?" the merchant asked, trying to establish a rapport with his customer. "How did that happen?"

"Antioch is our base. I'm in Vespasian's Syrian division. After Perea we returned here, and Vespasian left us here while he goes off to Rome to accept the emperorship and set the government to order. So here I wait, with a little time and freedom to recuperate and re-equip myself."

Ariel wanted to hear everything he could of this conversation, so he sat down on a bench off to the side of the arms shop, out of the sight of the soldier but close enough to overhear.

The merchant tried to prolong the chatter by feigning interest in the Roman's tales.

"Tell me more about your adventures in Perea."

"We marched into Gadara, the chief city of Perea, and the authorities there surrendered the city to us. The Gadarenes welcomed us happily and pledged their allegiance to Rome. The problem was the Jewish rebels, who had been causing trouble and escaped right before we got there. Vespasian put half of our legion under the command of General Placidus and sent us after the rebels.

"We caught up to them in Bethennabris, and what a dirty throng of bandits they were! No armor, no horses—just leather and livestock. But they were on fire to fight us. We lured them out into the open field outside the village, and then encircled them. They attacked us wildly, but ha! They were doomed. Our armor protected us from their spears and swords, while we easily butchered them with ours. That's where I regretted having my heavy sword. I could crush them with big blows, but I could have killed many more, and quicker too, if I'd had a lighter, faster weapon. There were so many of them; they were like beasts to the slaughter."

The merchant handed the soldier a short sword.

"Is this more what you're looking for?" the merchant asked.

"Yes," the soldier said, "but with a sharper blade."

The soldier thrust the sword into the air in a mock attack and used it as a prop as he continued his story.

"Finally the surviving Jews tried to flee back to the village. We easily kept up with them and picked off quite a few during the chase. But when they reached the village wall, the villagers inside shut the gate on them. They were terrified of letting us in with them—which was smart of them, honestly. We fought those trapped maniacs at our leisure and then attacked the wall. When we broke through—oh how we destroyed that village! We slaughtered all who dared face us, took all the plunder we could carry, and burned the village to the ground. But many rebel Jews escaped during the fray, so we had to go after them.

The soldier pointed the short sword to the west and sliced the air a few times.

"The rebels went west. They were probably trying to get to Jericho. There must have been twenty thousand of them. We followed them to the Jordan, where the gods had laid a cruel trap for them. Thanks to recent rains, the Jordan was swollen and completely unpassable. They had to turn around and fight us, which they did with mad desperation. We speared them and stabbed them and trampled them with our horses. Most of them died at our hands, but some two thousand of them fell or jumped into the Jordan and drowned, and a sad remainder of about two thousand more finally gave up and surrendered to us. Those we took prisoner, along with their livestock."

"Wait a minute," the merchant said. "I've heard of this battle. The Purge of Perea. That's the battle you're describing."

"Yes, probably. Is that what the people are calling it? Well, that's a good name for it. All those corpses floating down the Jordan! And the carnage wasn't over. We attacked all the rebellious villages in that area and beat them into submission. Some tried to escape in boats on the Dead Sea, but we took our own boats out to them and destroyed them. We cut them down and sank them. Dead Sea indeed! And, of course, the Jordan carried many of those other drowned rebels into the Dead Sea as well. What a sight that was—thousands of dead bodies floating in the Jordan and the Dead Sea!"

Ariel shuddered. The soldier's tale seemed unbelievable. If such atrocities were happening in Perea, it would not be long before nearby Jerusalem and the rest of Judea would come under Roman attack. With a deep sense of dread, Ariel stood up, purchased a few essential items in the market, and headed home. That evening he met with some of the other church elders and told them what he'd heard about the Purge of Perea. They already knew about it.

10

After years of self-deprivation and study under John the Baptist, Joshua had at last begun his quest to reach a more intimate communion with God by enduring a solitary trial in the desert. He wandered northward along the west bank of the Jordan, traveling only during the night. During the day he would find a shady tree or rock formation under which to sleep or pray. He ate nothing and his only sustenance consisted of occasional drinks from the river. After a few days he found a cave where he could rest and pray, free from the oppressive sun. He decided to stop traveling and remain in the cave as his chosen place of solitude.

The first night in the cave, Joshua sat with his back against a large rock and gazed out at the desert. The moon provided only enough light to reveal a vague, empty landscape. The heavy silence was broken only by sporadic intrusions: the buzzing of flying insects, the cries of night birds, and the rustling of light winds. At Joshua's feet lay the cedar walking stick covered with hyssop leaves that John had given him to ward off evil spirits. Joshua closed his eyes and prayed to God for guidance, hoping for some voice, vision, or sign from the Holy One. Nothing happened. His hunger tore at his insides. As the night cooled he wrapped himself in his cloak and fell asleep.

When he awoke it was early in the morning and flies assaulted him. He swatted them away as his eyes adjusted to the light of day. He felt itchy from the thin film of sweat and grime that covered him, so he walked to the Jordan to bathe. Once clean, dry, and refreshed by a long drink from the river, he returned to the cave. He sat against the rock again, the walking stick at his feet. Reeling from hunger and desperate for distraction, he closed his eyes and recited from the first book of the Psalms of David. He knew all forty-one psalms by memory, but he had picked out ten of those for special focus during his ordeal. He started with the first Psalm.

"Blessed is the one who does not walk in step with the wicked or stand in the way that sinners take or sit in the company of mockers, but whose delight is in the law of the Lord, and who meditates on His law day and night. That person is like a tree planted by streams of water, which yields its fruit in season and whose leaf does not wither—whatever they do prospers.

"Not so the wicked! They're like chaff that the wind blows away. Therefore the wicked will not stand in the judgment, nor sinners in the assembly of the righteous. For the Lord watches over the way of the righteous, but the way of the wicked leads to destruction." (Psalm 1)

Joshua next recited the eighth Psalm.

"Lord, our Lord, how majestic is your name in all the earth! You have set your glory in the heavens. Through the praise of children and infants you have established a stronghold against your enemies, to silence the foe and the avenger." (Psalm 8:1–3)

He then went to the fifteenth and sixteenth Psalms.

"Lord, who may dwell in your sacred tent? Who may live on your holy mountain? The one whose walk is blameless, who does what's right, who speaks the truth from their heart; whose tongue utters no slander, who does no wrong to a neighbor, and casts no slur on others." (Psalm 15:1–3)

"Lord, you alone are my portion and my cup; you make my lot secure. I will praise the Lord, who counsels me; even at night my heart instructs me. I keep my eyes always on the Lord; with him at my right hand, I won't be shaken." (Psalm 16:5–8)

Joshua followed these with Psalms nineteen, twenty-three, twenty-four, twenty-six, twenty-nine, and thirty-two. After a brief break to rest his voice and take some deep breaths, he repeated the ten-psalm cycle. As he recited, he began to forget where he was and whether it was day or night. He felt a strange dizziness, and the ground seemed to vibrate. He felt as if he were simultaneously moving and sitting still.

"The Lord is my shepherd, I lack nothing. He lays me down in green pastures; he leads me beside quiet waters; he refreshes my soul. He guides me along the right paths for his name's sake. Even though I walk through the valley of the shadow of death, I will fear no evil, for you are with me; your rod and your staff, they comfort me." (Psalm 23:1–4)

After reciting the cycle for the third time, the thirteenth Psalm came to him, as if someone had requested that he recite it. So he did.

"How long, Lord? Will you forget me forever? How long will you hide your face from me? How long must I wrestle with my thoughts and day after day have sorrow in my heart? How long will my enemy triumph over me? Look on me and answer, Lord my God." (Psalm 13:1–3)

Without thinking he returned to his chosen ten-psalm cycle. The psalms seemed to merge together into a single prayer with no beginning or end. Other psalms and scripture passages began to seep into the periphery of his mind, and he lost awareness of himself as a being separate from the words. The words were all that was. He fell into a trance.

Joshua found himself in the middle of a vast desert at night. He was holding a shining, golden scroll. A herd of black goats with fiery-red eyes and long horns creeped toward him. In a flash the scroll transformed into a golden loaf. Joshua broke pieces off of the loaf and tossed them to the goats. When a goat ate the golden bread it transformed into a bright-white sheep. Joshua fed all the goats and they all became sheep.

Then four black horses appeared and circled the flock of sheep. Each horse carried a dark, nebulous shade possessing the generic form of a man. The shades drew swords and slew the sheep. Black eagles and ravens swooped down to peck at the sheep's bloody carcasses and then flew away. One of the shades tossed a flame onto the pile of dead sheep, and the fire engulfed the heap. In an instant the fire went out and everything disappeared.

Joshua was alone in the desert again. He held in his right hand the hyssop-coated cedar staff, but it was now golden and radiating gold light in all directions. In the distance he could see an army of dark shades rushing toward him. The shades were generic humanoids like before, but now they had flaming-white eyes and round, fleshy pits where mouths ought to be. The shades whistled and wailed like winds through a desert canyon, and their mouth holes spewed hot, foul-smelling vapor into the air. As the shades approached, Joshua swung the golden stick and the light dispersed any shades that it touched. Joshua swung the staff like a berserk, cornered warrior and sent golden light everywhere, repelling every shade that came near. Soon all the shadowy demons were gone and Joshua was alone again in the desert.

Now Joshua held a large, golden ram's horn. He blew the horn and sent a distressing, bone-shattering blast into the cold void. An unseen force propelled Joshua skyward, and he found himself standing on a mountain top and looking down at the city of Jerusalem. A tall stone wall enclosed the city in a square, and busy civilians teemed within. On top of the midpoints of each of the four sides of the wall stood a giant. A deep and solemn male voice said, "Begin the harvest!"

The giant at the middle of the west wall was a Roman Caesar sitting on an ivory throne. He wore a laurel crown and held a massive trident. He stabbed his trident into the city below and brought it up with several Jerusalemites impaled on it. He put the trident into his mouth like a fork and devoured the impaled victims like a ravenous glutton.

The giant on the north wall was a Greek warrior in bronze armor standing on a pedestal. With his hand the giant scooped up some Jerusalemites and threw them into a wine press. He turned the press and blood dribbled out of a spout at the bottom.

The giant put his mouth to the spout and sipped like a baby at the breast.

The giant on the south wall was an Egyptian pharaoh, costumed in the shining robes and jewels of royalty and sitting on a golden throne. Four giant beasts stood abreast in front of the pharaoh: a lion, a crocodile, a python, and a wolf. The pharaoh threw a net into the city. After a moment he lifted the net up and it was filled with Jerusalemites. The pharaoh placed a quarter of his catch before each animal and laughed when the beasts tore into their prey.

The giant on the east wall was a Jewish high priest, dressed for Temple service in the sacred vestments. To his left was a bronze basin and to his right a golden altar. With his left hand the priest grabbed a citizen, and with his right he decapitated the citizen with a long knife. He then drained the blood into the basin and threw the body onto the altar. He repeated this process until there were twelve bodies on the altar and then set the corpses alight. The smoke rose skyward from the altar to an enormous, brilliant cloud. As the cloud consumed the smoke it darkened and began to pulsate. Lightning flashed within the cloud and started to shoot out at the city and the giants. The solemn voice from before issued a command from the cloud: "Let this ruined harvest burn!"

The lightning now burst out with wonton ferocity in all directions, striking every part of the city and overwhelming the giants. Everything struck by the lighting went up in flames. Soon the city was a blazing inferno, and Joshua could feel the heat rise to him. The heat increased, and right at the moment when he felt the heat would make his own body catch fire, he was alone in the desert again.

This time Joshua was in the familiar, actual desert in front of his cave. The sun, which by its position indicated that it was about nine in the morning, seared his skin. Somehow he had ended up about fifty feet outside the cave, and his cedar staff was missing. He ran back into the cave to get out of the sun and recover his bearings. A merciless thirst consumed him. He crept along the shadiest path he could find to the Jordan, left his clothes on a rock, and jumped in. After cooling off and drinking his fill he got out, dried quickly in the sun, and dressed himself.

As he headed back to the cave he saw in the distance a man walking toward him along the side of the river. The man looked about thirty years old, bearded, and dressed in a peasant's tunic. He stumbled about in a serpentine fashion, walking toward the river and then away from it in a regular rhythm. In his right hand he carried Joshua's cedar protection staff, which he waved as if fending off imagined assailants.

That's where it went!

Joshua was equally afraid and fascinated.

With a sudden jerk the man threw the staff into the river, where it drifted southeast toward the opposite side. The man continued walking.

God has brought me a test!

Joshua was nervous but excited. He crept up to the man as one might approach a frightened, injured animal before attempting to render it aid.

The man was tormented inside by voices. One voice, which sounded like a stern old man, badgered him with ceaseless commands and said, "Go to the water! Drink the water!" Another voice, of an angry old woman, countered and said, "Get away from the water! Don't drink the water!" Deep down the man wanted to drink the water, but he continued to waver. He was sure the voices belonged to demons, and he was afraid to upset either one of them.

When Joshua was about fifteen feet away from the man, he caught the stench of the man's long-unwashed body. The man did not seem to notice Joshua at all. Joshua got five feet closer. The man was mumbling to himself, saying something like "What do you know about water?"

"Quiet! Stop torturing me!" the man cried, startling Joshua.

This man has a demon for sure!

Joshua looked into the man's eyes and yelled, "Come out of him, spirit!"

Joshua got the man's attention. The man heard Joshua's voice louder than the internal voices, and he saw Joshua standing in front of him, gazing at him. The man felt threatened.

"Persecutor!" the female voice shouted.

"Run away from him!" the male voice shouted.

"Attack him!" the female voice shouted.

The man threw a punch with his right fist at Joshua, who blocked the blow with his left hand. Joshua grabbed the man's shoulders and looked into his eyes again.

With confident authority he shouted, "Come out I say! God Himself put me in your way to banish you! Release this man and go away!"

Some of Joshua's words echoed inside the man's head.

God Himself . . . release this man . . . go away!

The male and female voices weakened.

"Run away!" the male voice said.

"Danger!" the female voice said.

The man looked away from Joshua's gaze and tried to push him away. Joshua held firm onto his shoulders and started to push the man toward the river. Joshua remembered the popular legend that demons hate water.

That must be why he was wavering. He wanted to drink but the demon tried to keep him away from the water.

Joshua pushed the man into the water and, still holding on to him, went in with him.

The cool water shocked the man's senses. The wetness, Joshua's grip, the struggle—these things felt real. The words continued to echo through his mind.

God Himself . . . release this man . . . go away!

The male and female voices receded.

"Water!" they both screamed as if from a distance.

Joshua lifted the man up by the shoulders and then gripped the sides of his head, forcing the man to look at him. Joshua looked into the man's eyes and tried to project a fearless, wrathful intensity that would demonstrate his unwillingness to be intimidated by any demon. As if trying to subdue an army with the mere power of his voice, Joshua shouted, "In the name of the Most High God, come out! God wash this man and cleanse him of his sins! The will of God overtake you, impure spirit!"

The man saw Joshua clearly in front of him. Joshua's words reverberated through his skull.

Most High God . . . cleanse him of his sins!

The male and female voices were gone. The man was calm.

The man spoke: "God . . . wash . . . sins."

"Yes!" Joshua shouted, releasing the man's head and grabbing his shoulders again. "God forgives your sins."

"God forgives your sins," the man repeated. He stared at Joshua with a blank expression.

Joshua smiled and embraced the man.

"God has released you!" Joshua said. "Consider yourself baptized. Do you repent of your sins?"

The man stared back and said nothing.

A moment later the man shouted, "Repent!"

"Amen!" Joshua answered. He pointed south.

"Go. Go to John the Baptist. Tell him what God has done for you. I'm Joshua, his disciple. John can teach you the way of righteousness and save you from the evils of this age. Tell me, what's your name?"

The man looked at Joshua and pointed at him. "Joshua?"

"Yes, I'm Joshua. Who are you?"

The man hesitated and searched his mind. Then he remembered.

"Isaiah. My name is Isaiah."

Joshua embraced him again and guided him out of the river.

"Go Isaiah. Go in peace, with the blessing and protection of the Lord."

Joshua pointed south again.

"Just follow the river that way, Isaiah. It will take you to John. If I had food I'd give it to you, but there are date palms along the way. You'll see. Shalom!"

Isaiah walked southward along the side of the Jordan. A new, lone voice now sounded in his head. It was Joshua's, repeating the same hopeful words over and over.

Repent! God forgives you!

He walked a straight path and wavered no more.

Joshua sighed and walked back to his cave. He leaned against his favorite rock and tried to collect his thoughts and process recent events.

God has called me!

He was so beside himself with excitement and fear that he forgot his hunger for the moment. But in an instant exhaustion overtook him and he fell asleep. When he woke up, it was dusk. He was so famished that he felt like his insides were consuming his own body.

"This fast is over," he said.

* * *

When Joshua returned to John the Baptist, it was early in the morning. John was sitting, looking out the entrance to his cave, and munching on a fire-roasted locust. When he saw Joshua, he stood up and embraced him.

"I've returned, Rabbi," Joshua said.

"Hallelu Jah! Welcome. You must tell me how your fast went. Do you want something to eat?"

"Sure. I found some dates and honey on the way back, but all the walking has me hungry again."

Joshua took a roasted locust, bit a piece off, and chewed. When he finished eating he began his report.

"Rabbi, after days of fasting and praying, God sent me visions, terrible visions. He showed me what He wants from me, and I'm afraid. It's a heavy burden. But I also have faith, and I'm honored to do His will. And I cast an evil spirit out of a man! Did Isaiah come and see you? He—"

"Slow down, Joshua! You're saying many things very quickly and it's early in the morning still. Have mercy on your master. Isaiah? Did the prophet visit you?"

"No. Isaiah is the man who had the demon. I drove it out and told Isaiah to come see you. Did he come?"

"No. No one named Isaiah came to me. And no one came to talk to me about any demon. Why did you send him to me?"

"So you could cleanse him yourself, and get him to commit to a righteous life and be saved from demons forever, and—sons of a whore, now that I'm saying it, it does seem ridiculous. At that moment I felt like such a savior that I presumed to know what's best for that man—a man I didn't even know! He probably had his own family to get back to, his own obligations, God bless him." Joshua laughed at himself.

"Yes, probably," John said. "But you cast a demon out of him? That's remarkable—amazing even. What happened exactly?"

"Have you never expelled a demon before, Master?"

"Well . . . in the cities there are exorcists. Whenever someone has a demon, or a loved one with a demon, they go to the exorcists. There are many in Jerusalem. I leave demons to them! I'm not surprised you found a demoniac wandering in the wilderness, but can you imagine someone possessed by an evil spirit finding their way to me? On their own? Or someone with the patience to lead a possessed person all the way out here to me? People go to the nearest exorcist, and they're in the cities. Did your father have this ability? Did he exorcise demons?"

"I don't know. He healed people occasionally. Perhaps some of them were afflicted by demons. I never saw him with anyone like Isaiah. But I've seen exorcisms performed in the public squares of Sepphoris. Those all seemed like theater to me. I always assumed that demons haunted only hostile, dangerous places and persecuted only the most God-forsaken people. But now I understand that demons are everywhere. They're restless because the seventh week is coming to an end. They want to kill faith and drive as many men as they can away from God before He begins the eighth week and the age of righteousness. They're taking advantage of the sinfulness of our times to ensnare everyone, so that God's coming kingdom will be empty—as empty as they can make it. I saw this in my visions."

"Yes. Your visions. Tell me what you saw."

Joshua paused and collected his thoughts.

"Frankly, Master, much of what I saw was unspeakable and horrifying. I won't burden you with it. But I'll tell you the message that God was sending me with those visions."

John nodded his approval, and gestured with his hand a silent invitation for Joshua to continue.

"My visions showed me the woeful condition of our people. Almost all of them poor, unable to read the scriptures, and unaware of what's coming. The priests and rabbis feed them just enough of the word to enable them to live as decent Jews: obedient, orderly, and unchallenging to the authorities. Herod and his wealthy friends, including the high priests, take advantage of the ignorance and complacence of the people, holding them in a web of sin and maintaining an order of injustice in which the Herodians take too much from the people, give little in return, and hoard money for themselves and their Roman patrons. As the power of the rich increases, the ordinary, impoverished Jews fight among themselves over the scraps left them and ignore God as they fret over worldly concerns. Meanwhile God's wrath grows as He is ever more forgotten and disobeyed."

"Amen, Joshua," John said. "That's the state of things. God truly must have reached you. He's no liar."

"Yes. And these conditions make the people easy prey for the evil spirits who, as I've mentioned, are agitated over the coming age. If I fight for righteousness, as God commands me, I'll have to contend with the multitude of demons that Satan will put in my way. That demon I met by the river, I believe, was my first test."

"You're probably right about that." John said.

"Master, I look at our people and I feel sorry for them. They're like sheep without a shepherd. They're assailed on all sides by enemies who steer them away from God. I want to teach them the truth: the prophecies, the coming judgment, how to return to God, how to be worthy of His kingdom. I want to bring as many people as I can to the kingdom before the destruction begins. God has called me to do this. I'm afraid. This is a heavy burden. But I'll obey my God."

"God have mercy on you, Joshua. You truly astonish me. Are you sure you're ready to take so much on? You're talking about going out *there*—to the world—to a pit of vipers. If you can go out there, amid all that evil, and get people to repent and turn to God, then you're a true man of the Lord. I myself would be unworthy to unfasten the straps of your sandals."

John embraced Joshua.

"Don't worry, Joshua. Stay and strengthen yourself. Anything you wish to learn from me, ask me without hesitation. Benefit from my knowledge and experience. Think hard about your next steps."

"I will, Master. Pray for me."

* * *

For the next few days John continued to baptize and preach as usual, but made a point of always having his meals with Joshua. One morning, as John and Joshua shared a breakfast of dates and honey, they discussed Joshua's plans for his mission.

"You know," John said. "If you go around preaching everywhere, people are going to ask you to heal them of their ailments. That's what they expect of a holy man. Many came to me for healing when I was in Jerusalem because I was a priest. People sometimes even now expect my baptisms to heal them of one thing or another. Will you be able, or even willing, to heal people?"

Joshua stopped eating and looked at John with a wide-eyed, worried expression on his face.

"Moses! I didn't even consider that, but you're probably right. If they see me as a man of God, they'll look to me for a share of His healing grace, especially if they see me cast out demons. But my mission is to heal souls—to preach God's truth and lead people to His kingdom. Hopefully I can persuade them to repent and walk the righteous path. Then God might free them from the afflictions brought by sin. But to heal just anyone who asks? That's probably beyond me."

"You said your father healed people. What did you learn from him?"

"My father taught me how to cover flesh wounds with saliva and clay, and how to relieve pain by laying hands. He taught me how to tell a common fever from a deadly one. He taught me how to read skin diseases—to tell whether they're leprous or not—from the book of Leviticus. Once, a man came to him who had woken up deaf one morning. With saliva my father dislodged some foul, waxy residue from the man's ears, and the man could hear again. The man said an evil spirit entered him during the night and left that residue in his ears."

"The ailments of many are just like those, so what your father taught you will be useful. Many people will love you just for telling them that they aren't as sick as they'd feared, as if you yourself had persuaded God to forgive their sins and heal them."

"But what if they really do have a serious illness, or I fail to heal them?"

"It's always good to try what you can. If it's God's will that someone suffer, what can you do? But it's better to try and heal some than to not try and heal none."

"Yes. That makes sense, Rabbi."

John and Joshua sat in silence for a moment before John reopened the conversation.

"I don't know if you've decided where you'll go first when you start your mission, but I recommend you go to the towns around Lake Gennesaret—the Sea of Galilee. There's a man who's famous in Capernaum, a man named Zebedee. He has two sons who used to be disciples of mine. Their names are Jacob and John. They left me, but amicably, and they're still believers. Go see them and tell them you're a friend of mine. They'll probably help you—tell you about the people there and how to relate to them and so forth. You're not going to be able to do all the things you want to do all by yourself, so find assistants."

* * *

One night Joshua joined John for the evening meal and made an announcement.

"I've decided what to call myself from now on."

"You're changing your name?"

"No. But I've been trying to decide whether to call myself Joshua bar Joseph, after my father, or Joshua from Sepphoris, after where I was born and spent my childhood, or Joshua from Nazareth, after where I spent my young adulthood."

"Those are all good choices. Which did you decide?"

"Well, I rejected Joshua bar Joseph because it's so common. If people called me that, how would I be distinguished from all the other Joshua bar Josephs in the world? I would be forever confused with countless others. And Sepphoris is Herod's town. Herod Antipas lived there the same time I did, and the whole city supports him. If I called myself Joshua from Sepphoris, people would get the wrong impression about me. They would instantly assume I was sympathetic with Herod and his allies. But Nazareth is a village of the people, and it's where I discovered the meaning of the word and became a man. It's also so small that no one would confuse me with another Joshua from Nazareth. So I've decided to call myself that. Of the three, it's the most appropriate and convenient."

"It sounds like you've made a wise choice. Henceforth I will call you Joshua from Nazareth."

John stood up, looked out the cave, and lifted his hands as if he were addressing a crowd.

"Listen, wicked world!" John cried with mock severity. "I present to you the great Joshua of Nazareth, disciple of the great and famous John the Baptist!"

Joshua laughed.

11

A few months after the end of the war between the Romans and the Jews, when Ariel and the entire Jewish nation were still processing the total defeat of Israel, Ariel sat on his roof and steeled himself to go into the Greek-dominated center of Antioch. As much as he hated it, he couldn't keep himself away from the main city on this particular morning. Like everyone else in Antioch, he had learned that today was the day when Titus, accompanied by two of his legions and a shackled multitude of prisoners from Jerusalem, would march in triumph along the colonnaded main road that ran from south to north through the entire city.

His curiosity inflamed, Ariel burned to get a look at the Roman devils who had managed to destroy God's own Temple and flatten the holiest city in the world. He speculated that the Romans were some kind of divine instrument by which God had laid down devastating judgment upon His people for all their impiety, in particular their rejection of their own Christ. Ariel was convinced that the catastrophes of the war were but a prelude to the real judgment that was coming, when Messiah Joshua would exalt his followers over the pagans and the unrighteous in a new world in which God Himself would be king.

Eager to gaze upon the great Anti-Christ Titus, Ariel looked down on the city to see if there were any signs yet of his imminent arrival. He saw the streets filled with people. Men, women, and children all moved in the same direction: toward the main central road. But they weren't lining themselves along the sides of that road, as if they were waiting for Titus to parade by; they were filling the road and traveling along it toward the south gate of the city. Ariel realized that the Antiochene crowds, impatient to salute their hero, were going out to meet Titus before he even entered the city. It seemed as if all the Greek citizens were joining this crowd, leaving their neighborhoods empty and desolate.

Hope rose inside him.

If I stay back from the crowd enough, I should be able to avoid encountering any Greeks.

Far to the south Ariel could discern an immense and impressive-looking body of horses and armed men.

That must be Titus. Time to get closer.

Ariel began his cautious walk into Antioch, keeping a safe distance from any crowds and looking out for Greeks. The city turned out to be the ghost town that he'd hoped for, quiet except for the vocalizations of animals and the stirrings of the wind. When he reached an empty, tree-lined plaza about two hundred yards from the central road, Ariel noticed that the crowd ahead had stopped moving forward. He figured that the front of the crowd had at last met Titus outside the city and was now following him into Antioch, causing the spectators in the city to plant themselves where they were and wait. Ariel found a climbable oak tree nearby and scaled it to get a better view.

After about half an hour the crowd exulted, cheering and crying out because Titus was near. Ariel saw the Roman road-paving and camp-building crews file by, followed by the royal chariot that carried Titus. Four black horses, standing abreast, pulled it while an imposing squad of bodyguards marched in front and along the sides. The guards wore shining helmets and breastplates, and they carried a variety of weapons, including fasces, axes, spears, and swords. At the center of the chariot stood Titus, armed, armored, and helmeted like a magnificent conqueror. Ariel tried to get a good look at his face, but the helmet, at that distance, was too much of an impediment. Behind the chariot walked a cavalry of a few hundred horsemen, armed and armored for war. Some six thousand infantrymen, some with spears, others with swords or bows, followed. Then a few hundred more horsemen, a few thousand more infantry, the corps of trumpeters and ensign carriers, and at the end about a thousand nearly naked male prisoners, shackled at the wrists and ankles and chained together in rows. The prisoners looked tired and emaciated, but otherwise healthy, except for a few that had dramatic battle scars or missing limbs. Trident-wielding guards walked alongside the prisoners and maintained an orderly march by poking any straggling captives back into line.

As Titus passed, the spectators gave the straight-armed Hail Caesar salute, which Titus answered by raising his sword in a proud gesture of triumph. When the spectators saw the prisoners, they shouted "Take ours too!" over and over again, which in short order transformed into "Take our Jews!" The gleeful proclamation of hate soon infected the entire multitude of spectators, who maintained the chant throughout the parade. Some even chanted it on the way home after it was all over.

Ariel did not hang around long enough to witness the whole parade. He began his return home soon after the crowd started its frenzied chanting. As he made a hasty retreat through the empty streets back to the Jewish Quarter, the plodding rhythm of "Take our Jews!" receded behind him.

When Ariel reached the proximity of his home, he saw a tall, slender man clad in a black cloak and hood standing at his door. Ariel hesitated and felt a cold wave of dread overtake him.

What demon ensnares me now?

The dark figure saw Ariel and removed his hood. The man looked emaciated, almost to a frightening, skeletal degree, but Ariel recognized him.

"Aaron!" he shouted.

The two men ran to each other and embraced.

"Hello, Brother," Aaron said. "It's good to see that we aren't both lost. Unbelievable what's happened, isn't it? Still believe in your Christ Joshua, do you?"

* * *

Ariel and Aaron sat opposite each other at the dining table. Ariel pushed a plate of bread and oil towards Aaron.

"Eat. You look like you could fall dead from hunger."

Aaron dipped a piece of bread and nibbled it.

"Thank you, Brother. But I've been slowly reacquainting my body to food. I'll eat a little. I don't want to overdo it too soon, hungry as I am; my insides might explode. Some of the other famished Jerusalemites that escaped the Romans gorged themselves as soon as they got their hands on food. They collapsed writhing and died. Horrifying!"

"As you wish, Aaron. No wonder you managed to survive. Christ! I feared you were dead. Is it really as bad as everyone says? Is the Temple really gone? Jerusalem burned to the ground?"

Aaron brought his fist to the table, then opened his hand and waved it as if discarding crumbs.

"Crushed utterly. Ashes to the wind. A few towers still standing, maybe, but otherwise it's ruined—a tomb for an entire people. A tomb, but plundered, with the bodies desecrated and left exposed—an abomination. Holy shit! Look at me. The scribe, the scribbler. I was working for priests at the Sanhedrin, recording first fruits and tithes, documenting trades and payments, serving men of wealth and rank. And then, before I knew it, I'd become Saraquiel, the Reckoner, counting dead bodies like so much grain! For whom? How pointless! Now our dead vastly outnumber our living, and the living are mostly prisoners."

Aaron noticed the bloodstone amulet hanging from Ariel's neck. A chalice was engraved on it, with a crown of thorns above it. Three Aramaic words circumscribed the images like a ring: Anointed, Crucified, Risen.

"Ah, there he is!" Aaron cried, as if catching a burglar in the act. "Joshua—the crucified Messiah. That pretty much sums it up, doesn't it? Jew, crucified. I saw thousands crucified, in all sorts of depraved ways. The Romans raised a forest of crosses outside the walls of Jerusalem. For a time they hung hundreds of unlucky Jews a day—to intimidate the Zealots and make them surrender."

Aaron laughed with contempt.

"As if that would have any effect on those madmen," Aaron said. "Crucified Jews. What does that mean to a pack of villains who were already crucifying the Jews, their own people, within those city walls? They had us all nailed to crosses, one way or another. Some onto the cross of treacherous murder, like anyone who dared to escape the city to get but a mouthful of food—those they slayed, accusing them of going to the Romans. Likewise anyone with money, or food, so they could take it for themselves. And, of course, anyone who was esteemed by the people or otherwise threatening to their tyranny in any way. They killed them all. But the rest of us—we who escaped their blood lust and greed—we were nailed to the bigger cross: the cross of famine."

Aaron closed his eyes and winced. He kept his eyes closed for a moment and then opened them with a start as if waking up.

"God, what a horror!" Aaron said, as if groaning from pain. "Man is a devil, I tell you. All it takes to turn a man into a devil is to deprive him of food. I saw people in such desperation that they clawed tooth and nail at their own mothers, wives, husbands, brothers, and children even, to take the tiniest crumbs from them. People murdering each other over a handful of grain. Men, women, and children reduced to chewing sandal leather and dried animal turds. The houses and streets choked with dead bodies, with no survivors to bury them except those too hungry and weak to bother. Imagine, if you can, the stench of a city of rotting corpses."

"Father of Christ!" Ariel shouted. "How did it all happen? Who's to blame?"

"Who's to blame? Weren't you listening? Didn't I say that man is a devil? Man is to blame."

Aaron pounded the table with his palm and shot a fierce stare at Ariel, who averted his eyes and fidgeted with his hands.

Aaron noticed Ariel's discomfort, so he softened his expression and demeanor to put Ariel at ease again.

"But I know what you mean," Aaron said. "You want to know who bears the *primary* guilt. I will go back—back to the beginning."

Aaron cleared his throat and sighed.

"You may remember, Ari, that Eleazar, the Temple governor, was the first to declare war against the Romans. He, with the support of many priests and Levites, stopped all Temple sacrifices by and on behalf of the Romans and all other non-Jews. Eleazar was fanatical about expelling the Romans and winning independence for our people. He and the like-minded priests persuaded some of the fighting men to join their cause, and they managed to kill the Romans who guarded the Temple.

"All of Jerusalem became divided. Two groups formed: one for war and one against. Simon, Ananias, all the priests that I worked for, sided against war. Then our side recruited our own fighters to attack the others. Eleazar's soldiers took the Temple as their base, and ours attacked them from the outside. God forgive us, but we polluted that holy ground with bloodshed. Throughout the city families divided—son against father, brother against brother— over whether or not to fight the Romans. Stupidly, we were killing each other before the Romans even came to the city. This was our sorry state when John came. You've heard of John? John of Gischala? And Simon bar Gioras?"

"Yes, of course. The leaders of the biggest Zealot armies. I hear the Romans are going to execute them."

"Yes. Well, Jerusalem's end began when John of Gischala came to the city with his degenerate followers. John led an army of marauders gathered from all parts of the countryside. These were low-life criminals who killed and robbed whomever they could. He brought thousands of them into the city, and thousands more from the pro-war faction in Jerusalem joined him. He came pretending to be a liberator. He convinced many that he and his men would protect the city from the Romans and restore Jewish rule in Judea. But he really came to conquer Jerusalem himself and plunder it.

"The first thing John did was falsely accuse various powerful and wealthy men of plotting to hand over Jerusalem to the Romans. He killed them and confiscated their wealth. Next he chose new high priests from the pro-war faction and forcibly imposed them over all other religious authorities. This of course was a grievous violation of the law; they dared to dishonor the ancient and sacred rules of priestly succession. They replaced legitimate priests from the correct families with unworthy sycophants who could now overrule any opposition to John's policies. It was a complete mockery of the very religious law that John was claiming to protect!

"The highest-ranking legitimate priest, Ananus, was outraged, and he enlisted everyone he could to the cause of overthrowing Eleazar and John. My employers, myself, and the rest of the anti-war faction joined Ananus and set out to retake the Temple from the robbers. Many of the citizens also were disgusted by what the Zealots were doing and joined us. Outside the Temple we met John's thugs and attacked. We gave them as good a thrashing as they gave us. Rocks and spears flew from both sides; swordsmen clashed everywhere! Eventually we forced them into the Temple, where they polluted the sacred ground with the blood of the dead and wounded."

"Christ Joshua!" Ariel cried, interrupting. "No wonder Jerusalem was destroyed. The holiest of hallowed ground, where anyone in the slightest state of impurity is forbidden to tread under penalty of death, trampled on by murderers soaked in blood. That kind of desecration could never avoid arousing God's wrath. Son of a—I can't believe it!"

Ariel calmed himself and Aaron continued his tale.

"We thought we'd gained the upper hand against John, but then the Idumeans came. Some agent of John must have gone to the Idumeans and told them vicious lies about what was happening in Jerusalem, because all the armed men of Idumea showed up—claiming to have come to rescue the city from Ananus. John managed to sneak the Idumeans into the city without Ananus knowing, and with their help he started to slaughter our men. We were no match for their doubled numbers, and thousands of us were slain, including Ananus himself. Ananus! So wise and virtuous, and so skilled at persuasion. No one could replace him, and his death utterly crushed our morale. We were defeated."

Aaron shook his head, sighed, and rubbed his eyes for a moment before speaking again.

"Next the Zealots and Idumeans attacked the ordinary citizens. Any men with money they slew in order to steal it, and those who were poor but fit for fighting they imprisoned, hoping to recruit them. Those that refused suffered death by torture. All the citizens began to lock themselves in their own houses, afraid even to make a noise—so terrified they were of the Zealots. But eventually the Idumeans caught on to what was really happening and saw the Zealots for the villains they were. When they learned of all the Zealots' crimes and injustices, all while Jerusalem still remained undisturbed by the Romans, they felt tricked and returned home, embarrassed to have gotten involved.

"With the Idumeans gone, John's thugs went on a rampage. Every wealthy man they could find they killed for his money; every popular man they killed to prevent him from arousing the people against their crimes. The Romans hadn't even arrived, and the people were trying to flee the city—to get away from the tyranny of the Zealots. And if the Zealots caught anyone trying to leave the city, they killed them for 'desertion.' The roads out of the city were littered with the dead bodies of those who tried to escape, and the Zealots wouldn't even bury them, or even allow them to be buried. Anyone who tried to bury one of these was killed for 'aiding deserters.'"

Aaron released a bitter half laugh from deep within him.

"It's like you said, Ari. How could we not be doomed then, in that place, imprisoned by madmen who piss on our law, who leave our dead desecrated like that? At that point our destruction was assured!

"And so it was, for that was when Simon bar Gioras came to Jerusalem like a curse directly from God. This Simon, a savage and a marauder, collected under him an army of criminals and freed slaves from all over—from Galilee to Idumea. Forty thousand armed men! He reportedly robbed and burned all the villages he could, all the while hiding his plunder in caves. He came to fight John over some dispute over money, or women, or maybe just out of criminal rivalry—I don't know.

"But John didn't want to fight Simon; he wanted to focus on raping the city. John's men went around murdering and stealing as they pleased, with total impunity. So we who were hiding in the city, under the authority of the high priests, made a rash and foolish decision, purely out of desperation to be rid of John. Matthias, who was the high priest now that Ananus was gone, convinced us to appeal to Simon—to ask him to save us from John. We embraced this doomed plan and sent Matthias to Simon with this proposal. Simon agreed and we let him into Jerusalem. The people welcomed him like a savior, but we soon realized how sadly mistaken we were about him. We now had Eleazar and John with their hordes in the Temple, coming out to abuse the people at whim, and Simon in the city with his robbers preparing to fight John.

"Now, it wasn't stupid enough that two factions of Jews were going to fight each other while the Romans were on their way, because Eleazar and John started to fight between themselves over which of them should rule the Zealots. So Eleazar and his men attacked John's from the priestly court, and John countered from the outer courts. Imagine the obscene spectacle. Eleazar's archers shooting down on John from the Temple's holiest court and John's war machines hurling boulders in retaliation, cracking the walls of the inner Temple as if it were the most profane den of pirates. Simon capitalized on this absurdity and attacked John from outside the Temple. So from without and within, three mad armies of brigands polluted the Temple with ceaseless destruction and murder, as if they were trying to destroy Jerusalem themselves and make the siege of the city that much easier for the Romans!"

"Well that's what they ended up doing, God damn it!" Ariel shouted, worked up in a frenzy.

"Absolutely, Brother. And this insane war among the divided Zealots quickly doomed everyone in the city thanks to the utter blindness and greed of Simon and John. Because, you see, Simon, with all the citizens in his thrall, could take whatever food and supplies he wanted from the city, while John relied on the loot he'd stolen from the people. And Eleazar, I imagine, raided the storerooms of consecrated food in the Temple. So in order to weaken Simon, John sent his troops to burn the storehouses of grain in the city, while Simon, in retaliation, had his troops burn whatever of John's supplies they could find. The brigands torched the whole neighborhood around the Temple, destroying grain meant to last years. The Zealots started the famine before the Romans had even arrived, although the Romans would eventually do their part to starve and murder us as well.

"When Titus arrived with his legions and started to set up camp outside Jerusalem, Eleazar, John, and Simon finally came to their senses and stopped fighting each other. The Romans, with their numbers, arms, and war machines, scared the Zealots enough to make them unite to defend Jerusalem as they'd originally promised. And the Zealots did have occasional success against the Romans—burning down their catapults and ambushing their troops and so forth—but ultimately the Romans broke through the city walls and gained easy access into Jerusalem.

"But before they actually invaded, they offered the Zealots a chance to surrender peacefully. That's when they raised the crosses, the thousand or so crucified Jewish prisoners of war I mentioned before, meant to intimidate the Zealots into giving up. When the Zealots refused peace, we fully expected the Romans to instantly raid the city and kill us all, but they chose a crueler trick. Titus ordered his legions to build a wall around Jerusalem to trap us inside and prevent any supplies from getting in from outside. The Romans took to building that wall like a hive of busy bees. They divided into groups of a hundred or so and spread out all around. They worked ceaselessly—with inhuman energy—and completed the wall in only three days. The wall was done before the Zealots had even recuperated from their previous fighting."

Ariel shook his head in disbelief. Aaron nodded and continued his recollections.

"Now the Romans just waited for the famine to do its work. As time dragged on, food got scarcer and scarcer and people more desperate. Even the Zealots, who had stolen so much from the people, began to run out of food and taste hunger. They started to raid private homes, robbing families of all their food and leaving them to starve. Bread became precious, like gold, with people hiding it and eating it in secret. This is when the horrors I mentioned before started, when people came to blows over scraps, and weren't ashamed to rob food from their own children. The Zealots were the worst of all, even murdering women and children to take their crumbs.

"I saw my own supply of food dwindle, and as I hid in my room with hardly a cup of flour and a jar of oil, I prayed over it. I beseeched God to multiply it like he did for Elijah and the widow of Zarephath. No such luck!

"I can't remember how many days I'd gone without food when I saw the Temple burning and the Romans slaughtering the Zealots. Out of desperation I decided to flee. I took a dagger from one of the many corpses lying in the streets and ran out toward the Roman camps. I pretended to be on the attack so no Zealots would think I was deserting. When I reached the Romans, I threw away my dagger and surrendered. I was saved! I was a prisoner—but saved.

"I was put into a company of other Jewish prisoners. The Romans gave us food, and I was tempted to devour it, but I knew to take it easy. That's when I saw others, not so disciplined, swallow down enough food into their hollow bodies to die from it. The Romans seemed perfectly content to let their prisoners die this way."

Aaron's voice was weak and hoarse. He drank some water.

"Don't say anymore," Ariel said. "Let yourself rest. Leave the rest of it for later."

"Yes. You're right. I *am* tired. But I've almost reached the end of my tale. Let me be done with it."

"All right. Finish if you must, but don't overexert yourself."

"We were held awhile in the camp, and then they told us the war was over and chained us together. They marched us north all the way to Caesarea Philippi with Titus and his legions. The Greeks there lent Titus their hippodrome to celebrate his triumph. Titus put on a big spectacle, showing off his army and captured spoils, including us. The Greeks hailed him as the 'Conqueror of the Jews.' Titus presented gladiator fights, and the gladiators were us, the prisoners! Some were forced to fight lions or bulls, but I was selected for the 'war games.' They gave me a spear and shield, and put me into a group of prisoners assigned to kill another armed group—as if at war. Can you believe the depravity of it?

"In the chaos of the battle I stumbled onto a way into the underground passageways of the hippodrome, and I slipped away unnoticed during all the killing. I ran out of there like a madman, brandishing my spear at the few Greeks who saw me to scare them away. With everything that was going on, I imagine I wasn't even worth pursuing anyway. I escaped! I ran into the wilderness and made my way here."

"Holy shit, Brother!" Ariel said, gasping with astonishment. "I just saw Titus parading by here in Antioch. The devil is still here. I saw the prisoners. They must have survived those horrible games. Incredible!"

"Yes. And now I'm free, thank the Lord. But for how long? I fear we Jews are all doomed now to become enslaved to the Romans one way or another. But that's a worry for later. For now I'll regain my strength, bulk up a bit, and become presentable again before I go to Sepphoris to see my children, God protect them."

"Stay and take all the time you need."

Aaron smiled.

"You really should have had children of your own, Ari. I can't believe you let that fanatic Paul persuade you to be celibate. How can you still believe in Joshua after all that's happened? He was supposed to save the Jews, wasn't he? And look what's happened."

Ariel frowned.

12

Capernaum was a fishing village of about two hundred family homes on the north coast of the Sea of Galilee. A synagogue stood in the center of town, and along the shore were several docks, constructed from wood, basalt, and sand, that served the busy traffic of fishing boats. The centermost dock was the largest and longest of all of them, and a custom house stood where the dock began on the shore.

Silas, a tax official for Herod Antipas's government, was the chief administrator of the customs house, where he sold fishing permits, collected the duties paid per unit weight of each catch, rented out boats, and arranged contracts by which fishermen could pay their boat-rental fee with a portion of future catches. Only after paying the requisite duties and fees could the fishermen, usually in teams of ten or so, divide their spoils among themselves to sell as each saw fit.

Upon arriving in Capernaum, Joshua went to the customs house and asked Silas how to find Zebedee. Silas took Joshua outside and pointed out a tall, completely bald man with a long, white beard. Zebedee was yelling and gesticulating at a team of men who were equipping a boat for a fishing expedition. After convincing Silas that he wasn't there to fish, and therefore exempt from any need to purchase a fishing license, Joshua went out to meet Zebedee.

"Shalom, lord. Are you Zebedee?"

"Yes, I am."

"I'm Joshua, a disciple of John the Baptist. John sent me to meet your sons Jacob and John."

"What do you want with them?"

"John told me they could help me. I'm travelling through Galilee to bring the baptism of John to all who will repent of their sins and commit themselves to the righteous way of the Most High."

Zebedee shook his head and turned toward his crew.

"Jacob! John! You have a visitor. Elijah himself has sent his servant Elisha to prophesize to you today. Pray the news is good!"

Two bearded fishermen, twenty-some years of age, walked up to Joshua and Zebedee. Zebedee pointed to Jacob, then John, and then Joshua, identifying each in succession: "Jacob. John. Joshua."

Zebedee then moved down to the boat, leaving the three alone to talk. Jacob was slightly older and taller than John, but somewhat younger and shorter than Joshua.

"So, Joshua," Jacob said. "You're a follower of the Baptist?"

"I am."

Jacob and John took turns shaking Joshua's hand.

"We are too," Jacob said. "We used to live with him by the Jordan, in the wilderness between Samaria and Perea, but we prefer to be here—in civilization."

"Where we can eat," John said with a laugh.

"John's still there," Joshua said. "He's still preaching the word and baptizing pilgrims. But I've come to bring John's baptism of repentance to the people—to save as many as I can from the coming wrath."

Jacob hung his head down for a moment and then looked back up to face Joshua.

"If you're seriously doing as you say," Jacob said, "then I'm ashamed to not also be doing it. We should have done the same as soon as we left John, but by some wickedness we've abandoned God to focus on filling our bellies. John must have sent you to us to save us from ourselves—"

Jacob was interrupted by the sudden reappearance of Zebedee.

"Prophets!" Zebedee yelled. "Time to embark! The barbelia and tilapia are itching to jump into our nets. Let's go Jacob and John, and bring your Elisha with you. Elisha, get in the boat. If you're a man at all, prove it! Show us you can handle a net. Are you strong enough to haul fish from the sea? Sons, don't listen to this man, don't follow him if he can't prove his worth on the waves."

"But I have no license," Joshua said.

"We'll cover it for you. Relax," Zebedee said.

Jacob and John escorted Joshua onto the boat. John took Joshua aside to reassure him.

"Don't worry about my father and his bluster. He's just having fun. We'll show you what to do. Come. It'll be all right."

Zebedee stayed on the dock.

"Aren't you coming, Father?" Jacob asked.

"Bah!" Zebedee said as he made a dismissive gesture with his hand. "I have to stay ashore and find a new boat—for when you donkeys wreck this one and drown."

John laughed.

"Good," John said. "We'll be spared the dead weight."

The boat was twenty-seven feet long and nine feet wide, with ten men aboard: Joshua, Jacob, John, and seven others, plus sacks and nets. Jacob introduced Joshua to the seven other fishermen and the crew launched the boat into the lake.

About a mile from shore they started to haul in some respectably large catches of fish. Joshua helped the crew pull the nets into the boat, and his strength was perfectly adequate to the task. When the size of the hauls started to diminish, the crew sailed further away from shore in search of better fortune. After about an hour of drifting and pulling in meager catches, they turned the boat to go southeast. A cool wind blew from the north, and clouds approached them from the northwest.

Mere moments later the winds blew strong and seemed to come at them from all sides. The water began to undulate and high waves started to crash against the boat. The men collided into each other as they struggled to hold onto the boat amid the frequent, violent eruptions of water. They were soon caught between a powerful vortex of wind and merciless, pounding waves. The fisherman panicked and yelled curses into the void.

Joshua steadied himself between two fish-filled nets and began to recite from Psalm ninety-three. His voice boomed.

"The seas have lifted up, Lord, the seas have lifted up their voice; the seas have lifted up their pounding waves!" (Psalm 93:3)

A wave crashed right over Joshua, soaking him, but he continued.

"Mightier than the thunder of the great waters, mightier than the breakers of the sea—the Lord on high is mighty!" (Psalm 93:4)

A sudden jolt of the rocking boat sent Joshua tumbling into one of the nets, but he got right up, steadied himself again, and with a fearlessness that impressed the fishermen he shouted some verses from the hundred and first chapter of Enoch.

"Don't you see the sailors of the ships, and how the waves toss their ships back and forth, and how the winds shake them, and how they and their ships are in great trouble?" (Enoch 101:4)

Joshua lifted his hands, as if in supplication to heaven, but another violent jerk of the boat forced him to grab hold of the nets and steady himself again. Undaunted, he lifted his hands again and resumed his recital.

"And therefore they're afraid because all their nice possessions go on the sea with them, and they have bad feelings in their heart that the sea will swallow them and that they'll perish therein." (Enoch 101:5)

The wind slowed and diminished a bit, and the undulations of the waves became less frequent. Jacob and John each held onto Joshua to prop him up while they gripped opposite sides of the boat to keep themselves secure and steady. Joshua continued his recitation.

"Are not the entire sea and all its waters, and all its movements, the work of the Most High, and has He not set limits to its actions, and confined it throughout by the sand?" (Enoch 101:6)

The wind continued to calm, little by little, and the waves that crashed against the boat were now reduced in size and power. Joshua continued from Enoch.

"And at His reproof it fears and dries up, all its fish die and all that's in it; but sinners on the earth fear Him not. Has He not made heaven and the earth, and all that's in it? Who has given understanding and wisdom to everything that moves on the earth and in the sea?" (Enoch 101:7–8)

Now the wind was calm, and the water undulated in its natural, gentle rhythm beneath the boat. Joshua looked around and saw the fishermen staring at him, dumbfounded. He smiled at the fishermen and finished reciting the chapter.

"Don't the sailors of the ships fear the sea? Yet sinners don't fear the Most High!" (Enoch 101:9)

Led by Jacob and John, the fishermen erupted in applause and celebratory shouting.

"Praise Joshua!" they cried again and again.

After the shouting wore itself out, Jacob leaned back against the side of the boat and began to recite from Psalm one hundred and seven.

"For He spoke and stirred up a tempest that lifted high the waves. They mounted up to the heavens and went down to the depths; in their peril their courage melted away. They reeled and staggered like drunkards; they were at their wits' end." (Psalm 107:25–27)

John joined Jacob's recital and together they continued.

"Then they cried out to the Lord in their trouble, and He brought them out of their distress. He stilled the storm to a whisper; the waves of the sea were hushed." (Psalm 107:28–29)

Joshua then joined Jacob and John in their recital.

"They were glad when it grew calm, and He guided them to their desired haven. Let them give thanks to the Lord for His unfailing love and His wonderful deeds for mankind." (Psalm 107:30–31)

The relieved crew, having endured enough excitement for one day, headed back to Capernaum. The return was pleasant and uneventful. On the way, Joshua, Jacob, and John tested each other's knowledge of scripture, which turned out to be strong for all three—Jacob and John had studied well under John the Baptist.

Some of the fishermen did not give Joshua much credit for the calming of the storm. They thought the storm would have abated anyway, even without Joshua's theatrics; such was the fleeting nature of the squalls on Lake Gennesaret. Nevertheless they appreciated the event as an amusing and wonderful coincidence. The others, however, including Jacob and John, thought that they had witnessed a true miracle.

"Who is this Joshua?" Jacob asked John, amazed. "Like Moses or Elijah he commands the waters and the wind!"

* * *

The next morning Jacob and John postponed their usual fishing activities to help Joshua launch his ministry. The three of them prepared a sermon, and they agreed on a message that the brothers would each deliver in different marketplaces of the village. Jacob would make a public announcement in the west marketplace of Capernaum, and John would do the same in the east market. Each knew the ideal places to speak to attract the most attention.

Jacob stood on a grassy slope at the north end of the west marketplace, where his voice would carry easily to the people gathered below. He took a shofar from his bag and blew a long note. When he saw a sufficient number of eyes looking his way, he began his speech.

"Good people of Capernaum and elsewhere, attention! Our town is blessed today by great fortune and honor! Joshua, the illustrious prophet sent by John the Baptist himself, will be at the Capernaum spring, just a mile northeast of the village, today at the third hour, a mere hour and a half from now. He will be baptizing all faithful and penitent Jews in the merciful forgiveness of God. Come. Wash away your sins! Renew yourself in the Lord! Joshua the Nazarene has come! Joshua, the rabbi specially blessed by God, from whom all evil flees! I myself witnessed him command a storm to still itself! He saved my boat and he'll save you from your sins! Come to the Capernaum spring today at the third hour!"

Jacob repeated this speech every fifteen minutes over the next hour, and then made his way to the spring to assist Joshua. John, who delivered the same speech at the east marketplace, did likewise. About forty men and women followed them to the spring.

Joshua, flanked by Jacob and John, stood on marshy ground in front of the spring, a natural pool of fresh water surrounded by green reeds and plane trees. It had a small waterfall on the far side. He addressed the assembled villagers.

"People of Capernaum, I bring you good news from the prophets. Good news if you honor God and live righteously, bad news if you serve only yourself and cheat your neighbor. Good news to the honest fishermen of Capernaum, bad news to Herod, who robs from the Galilean poor to give to the rich of Rome. These days of injustice are coming to an end. God has appointed this time, when sinners and pagans are taking everything away from us, to unleash His vengeance. Soon, the enemies of God, those who profit and enrich themselves while ignoring the commandments, will topple under the weight of judgment. And you who suffer and struggle, faithful to the Lord while sinners prosper at your expense—your vindication is at hand. God hasn't forgotten the righteous, and He'll uncover every sin and injustice!"

Joshua began to pace before his audience, looking them over like a military officer assessing the battle-readiness of his soldiers.

"Enoch and Isaiah predicted the Babylonian invasion, the destruction of Solomon's Temple, and the Exile. But they also predicted another disaster, a much bigger and final disaster that's reserved for our days! Enoch said that it would come some five hundred years after the Exile. The time is ripe! Listen to what Enoch wrote about our age:

"When sin and unrighteousness and blasphemy and violence in all kinds of deeds increase, and apostasy and transgression and uncleanness increase; heaven shall deliver a great chastisement, and the Holy Lord will unleash His wrath and judgment. In those days heaven will destroy all who love violence, wickedness, and deceit. The Lord will burn all the idols of the heathen and remove them from the whole earth; and He will cast the heathens into the grievous punishment of fire, to burn forever. (Enoch 91:7-9)

"This prophecy is confirmed by Isaiah."

Joshua pointed to Jacob.

"Jacob!" Joshua shouted. "What does Isaiah say about the coming judgment? What does he say in chapter twenty-four?"

Jacob stepped forward and recited from Isaiah.

"See, the Lord is going to lay waste the earth and devastate it; He'll ruin its face and scatter its inhabitants—it will be the same for priest as for people, for the master as for his servant, for the mistress as for her maid, for seller as for buyer, for borrower as for lender, for debtor as for creditor. The earth will be completely laid waste and totally plundered. The earth will dry up and wither, and the heavens will languish with the earth. The earth is defiled by its people; they've disobeyed the laws, violated the statutes, and broken the everlasting covenant. Therefore a curse consumes the earth; its people must bear their guilt. Therefore earth's inhabitants will burn, and very few will be left." (Isaiah 24:1–7)

A few listeners sneaked sway from the audience and took the road back to the village.

"Friends," Joshua said. "You can save yourselves from this judgment. The way to save yourselves is to renounce sin."

"Renounce sin!" Jacob and John shouted in unison.

"The coming judgment is reserved for sinners!" Joshua added. "Listen to these revelations of Enoch: 'I have sworn to you, you sinners, by the Holy Great One, that all your evil deeds are revealed in heaven, and that none of your wrong deeds are covered and hidden. And don't think in your spirit, nor say in your heart, that you don't know and don't see that every sin is recorded every day in heaven in the presence of the Most High. From now on, you know that all your wrong doing will be written down every day until the day of your judgment. Woe to you, you fools, for through your folly you'll perish; and you don't listen to the wise, so no good will come to you against the wise, and so know that you're prepared for the day of destruction. Therefore don't hope to live, you sinners, for you'll depart and die; for there will be no ransom for you; because you're prepared for the day of great judgment, for the day of tribulation and great shame!'" (Enoch 98:6–10)

Joshua pointed to John.

"John!" Joshua cried. "Does Isaiah agree with this? What does Isaiah say?"

John took a deep breath, stepped forward, and recited from Isaiah.

"The floodgates of the heavens are opened, the foundations of the earth shake. The earth is broken up, the earth is split asunder, the earth is violently shaken. The earth reels like a drunkard, it sways like a hut in the wind; so heavy upon it is the guilt of its rebellion that it falls—never to rise again. In that day the Lord will punish the armies in the heavens above and the kings on the earth below. They'll be herded together like prisoners bound in a dungeon; they'll be shut up in prison and be punished after many days. The moon will be dismayed, the sun ashamed; for the Lord Almighty will reign on Mount Zion and in Jerusalem, and before its elders—with great glory!" (Isaiah 24:18–23)

A few more hearers made a furtive exit from the assembly and walked back to Capernaum.

Joshua resumed pacing and preaching.

"Isaiah, like Enoch, tells us about the fallen angels, the 'armies in the heavens,' that will be judged. Those fallen angels fornicated with women, begetting the giants, whose evil spirits torment us today. The evil spirits are so active and restless now! Have you noticed? They know that their judgment is at hand. They're in a hurry to corrupt as many as they can while God still withholds His hand. Protect yourselves! Faithfully give yourselves over to the Most High God! Evil men, and evil spirits, are no match for God! Your righteousness will put you under His supreme protection. Isaiah affirms it.

"Isaiah wrote, 'Trust in the Lord forever, for the Lord, the Lord Himself, is the Rock eternal. He humbles those who dwell on high, he lays the lofty city low; he levels it to the ground and casts it down to the dust. Feet trample it down—the feet of the oppressed, the footsteps of the poor.' (Isaiah 26:4–6)

"Enoch says in chapter one hundred: 'In those days the angels shall descend into the secret places and gather together into one place all those who brought down sin, and the Most High will arise on that day of judgment to execute the judgment among sinners. And over all the righteous and holy He'll appoint guardians from among the holy angels to guard them as the apple of an eye, until He makes an end of all wickedness and all sin, and even if the righteous sleep a long sleep, they have nothing to fear.' (Enoch 100:4–5)

"Listen to the prophets! The righteous have nothing to fear!"

Jacob, remembering his cue, interrupted.

"Master, who are the righteous? How can I become righteous?"

"Who indeed!" Joshua said. "John! Tell us what Isaiah says about the righteous in chapter thirty-three."

John cleared his throat and recited.

"Those who walk righteously and speak what's right, who reject gain from extortion and keep their hands from accepting bribes, who stop their ears against plots of murder and shut their eyes against contemplating evil—they're the ones who will dwell on the heights, whose refuge will be the mountain fortress. Their bread will be supplied, and water won't fail them." (Isaiah 33:15–16)

"Amen!" Joshua shouted. "The righteous will be saved. When this age of sin ends, the new age of righteousness will begin. The righteous will finally have their reward! Enoch says in chapter one hundred and three: 'I swear to the righteous, by the glory of the Great and Honored and Mighty One who reigns, that all goodness and joy and glory are prepared for them, and written down for the spirits of those who've died in righteousness, and that much good shall be given to you in reward for your labors, and that your lot is abundant beyond the lot of the living. And the spirits of you who've died in righteousness shall live and rejoice, and your spirits shall not perish, nor shall your memory from before the face of the Great One to all the generations of the world.' (Enoch 103:3–4)

"And in chapter one hundred and four he says, 'Your names are written before the glory of the Great One. Be hopeful; for before you were put to shame through sickness and affliction; but now you'll shine as the lights of heaven, you'll shine and you'll be seen, and the doors of heaven will open for you!'" (Enoch 104:2-3)

Joshua looked around at his audience, his expression intense with gravitas. Only about twenty-five of the original forty remained, but they were mesmerized. Sweat poured down Joshua's face and glistened in the morning sun. He took some deep breaths and then resumed speaking.

"Your ears do not deceive you. God promises resurrection to the righteous—life in the heavenly kingdom after death in this world. So live and die in righteousness; be resurrected into the kingdom of God!

"But I know that there are some who deny the resurrection of the dead, some who have authority and call themselves priests or rabbis. They're mistaken! No matter who they are, or what position they hold, they're at odds with the prophets of scripture. Isaiah, in chapter twenty-six, says: 'But your dead will live, Lord; their bodies will rise—let those who dwell in the dust wake up and shout for joy—your dew is like the dew of the morning; the earth will give birth to her dead!' (Isaiah 26:19)

"All the prophets agree. So don't be fooled. We—Jacob, John, and myself—have spent our lives learning and meditating on the scriptures. We fasted with John the Baptist in the wilderness and communed with God. We know the truth. You stand now at a crossroads. One path leads to death and fire, the other leads to life and the kingdom of God.

"Today, right now, commit yourselves to the righteous way, set yourselves onto the road to the kingdom. Confess your sins. Receive the baptism of repentance. If you sincerely repent, God will forgive you your sins. And He may heal you of whatever afflicts you. But always walk the righteous path and shun sin; new sins might just lead to new afflictions! Take this seriously. If you hope for forgiveness or reward from God, you must be ready to keep your end of the bargain and embrace a life of honesty, peace, justice, mercy, goodness, love, and faithfulness to God's law. Don't trifle with the Most High!"

Joshua, Jacob, and John lined up the audience members and led them one by one into the spring to be baptized. Each baptism began with a few verses from the Wisdom of Ben Sirach, chapter seventeen.

"Return to the Lord and leave sin behind, plead before His face and lessen your offense. Come back to the Most High and turn away from iniquity, and hold in abhorrence all that is foul. How great is the mercy of the Lord, His pardon on all those who turn toward Him!" (Sirach 17:25–26, 29)

After this the initiate confessed his or her sins. When all was confessed, the baptizer recited from Psalm fifty-one and had the initiate repeat after each verse.

"Have mercy on me, O God, according to your unfailing love; according to your great compassion blot out my transgressions. Wash away all iniquity and cleanse me from my sins. For I know my transgressions, and my sin is always before me. Against you, you only, have I sinned and done what's evil in your sight; so you're right in your verdict and justified when you judge." (Psalm 51:3–6)

Next the baptizer recited from Ezekiel chapter thirty-six before immersing the initiate in the spring water.

"I'll pour clean water on you, and you'll be clean; I'll cleanse you from all your impurities and all your idols. I'll give you a new heart and put a new spirit in you; I'll remove from you your heart of stone and give you a heart of flesh. And I'll put my spirit in you and move you to follow my decrees and be careful to keep my laws." (Ezekiel 36:25–27)

After all were baptized, Joshua laid his hands on each of them and sent them on their way while Jacob sang from Psalm forty.

"I waited patiently for the Lord; He turned to me and heard my cry. He lifted me out of the slimy pit, out of the mud and the mire; He set my feet on a rock and gave me a firm place to stand.

He put a new song in my mouth, a hymn of praise to our God. Many will see and fear the Lord, and put their trust in Him." (Psalm 40:2–4)

Some of the initiates had come to the spring with headaches, toothaches, sore extremities, muscle cramps, guilt over past misdeeds, or just general distress about hard life circumstances. More than a few of these, after undergoing baptism, felt relief from their ills and forgiveness for their sins. Others continued to suffer but hoped healing from God would be forthcoming. Almost all those baptized that day by Joshua, Jacob, and John, however, believed that they had come at least a tiny bit further into the good graces of God, if only for a moment.

As they walked back to the village, several of the newly baptized conversed with each other.

One asked, "Have you ever heard such command of the scriptures?"

Another said, "Never have I heard a rabbi preach with such passion and authority!"

Still another said, "He's no ordinary rabbi. He's a prophet, a man of God. We should listen to him."

13

Lucius and Dionysius, two elders of the Antioch Cristian sect, invited Ariel and Zachariah to Lucius's house to discuss with them the crisis of their diminishing congregations. The four men sat at a table in a small dining room that abutted a kitchen on one side and a simple courtyard on another. It was evening and a pair of oil lamps threw their flickering light onto the bare, plastered-brick walls.

Ariel and Zachariah reported that they had lost a number of their believers, most of them Jewish converts to the way, due to the skepticism about the Christ which was flourishing in the wake of the disastrous war against the Romans. Lucius and Dionysius, whose followers were mainly Greek converts to the way, reported that the war had a less potent effect on the faith of their congregations.

"Their faith is strong," Lucius said, "and unshaken by the devastation that so troubles the Jews. It's probably because, as Gentiles, they more readily accept the destruction of Israel as God's punishment for their rejection of the Christ. They're less attached to the traditional messianic hopes of the Jewish nation, so they can see that the recent tragedies are merely the beginning of the promised wrath and judgment that will precede the return of our Lord."

"Alas," Zachariah said. "So many of our followers were hoping the war would lead to the worldly triumph of Israel over the pagans, and a new kingdom of freedom and prosperity for the Jews after so much degradation. They despair of any salvation from God now that things have turned out so contrary to what they'd hoped."

Dionysius tried to encourage his friends: "Yes. You have the extra burden of having to explain to some of your brothers that the scriptures don't mean what they've always believed them to mean. But you've managed to get many Jews to see the light, haven't you? You just have to keep up the fight and reach everyone you can. We'll pray for you."

"Thank you, brother," Zachariah said. "Ariel and I appreciate your support."

Ariel, half listening to the conversation, stared into space.

"Are you all right, Ariel?" Zachariah asked.

Ariel blinked and refocused on his friends.

"Sorry," Ariel said. "I was just thinking about the dream I had last night, a dream about our Lord Joshua."

"Oh shit," Zachariah mumbled to himself. "Here we go."

"Tell it to us," Lucius said. "Please. I insist."

"Do you all want to hear it, really?" Ariel asked.

"Yes," Dionysius said. "We love hearing your dreams."

The others nodded their agreement, so Ariel described his dream.

"Joshua and his disciples were in a boat on Lake Gennesaret. They landed on the eastern shore in the region of the Gadarenes. After they got out of the boat and walked for a while, a man with an evil spirit came towards them. This man lived among some tombs in the hills, and he would scream and cut himself as he wandered about. The Gadarenes tried to restrain him but they couldn't. He was so strong and wild that he would even break free from iron chains and shackles.

"The possessed man ran straight to Joshua and fell on his knees right in front of him. The evil spirit shouted at Joshua: 'What are you here to do to me, Joshua, Son of God? Don't hurt me!'

"Joshua asked the demon, 'What is your name?'

"The demon answered, 'My name is Legion, for we are many. We beg you, in God's name, don't send us away!'

"An enormous herd of pigs was on the hillside nearby. The evil spirits begged Joshua: 'Send us into the pigs!'

"Joshua did as they asked. He shouted, 'Go out of this man! Go into the pigs!' The evil spirits obeyed, exiting the man and entering the pigs. The herd of about two thousand pigs rushed wildly down the hills to the lake where, frenzied by the possession, they jumped in and drowned.

"The men tending the pigs ran into town terrified and told everyone what had happened. The people ran to the scene and saw the formerly possessed man now in his right mind. They saw Joshua, and because they were afraid of his power, they begged him to leave the region. Joshua and his disciples left the region and returned to their boat. The formerly possessed man wanted to go with them, but Joshua told him to stay with his own people and tell them all that the Lord in His mercy had done for him. The man went and told people throughout the region about how Joshua had healed him. The people listened with wonder and amazement."

"Ari, Ari, Ari," Zachariah said, groaning. "*You* should be tied to a pig and sent into the lake to drown! I know what you're doing. The demons in your story—they're the Romans, and the pigs are the Zealots that the Romans drowned in the Jordan in that battle in Perea. You're talking about the Purge of Perea. No wonder you set in in Gadara; that's where the battle began, only it was the Gadara in Perea near Jericho. You know, even if you set it in the Gadara near Lake Gennesaret, as in your story, those pigs would have to run five miles before reaching the lake. It would make more sense if you set your story in Gergesa, which is right on the eastern shore."

"Zachary," Ariel said. "I'm just describing the dream I had. You shouldn't be surprised if it doesn't make sense. I didn't make it up; it just came to me in my sleep. Maybe I was dreaming about the Purge of Perea for whatever reason. I'm just telling you that this particular dream affected me, and I myself wonder what it means."

"Any dream featuring the Lord Joshua," Dionysius said, "should be handled with care and not dismissed lightly. You should write it down so we can study it at length; it probably does mean something."

Lucius was excited and, almost breathless, said, "Of course it means something. Dreams like this are messages from heaven! Ariel, you've been sent a message from Christ! We must decipher it."

"Please," Ariel said. "I can't assume that I've been blessed with the honor you suggest. But I suppose it's possible that something can be learned from the dream. It does remind me of other visions that I've had, visions in which Joshua exhibits signs—signs that portend events of the end times—signs that leave me puzzling over their meaning."

"Yes," Lucius said. "Joshua's exorcisms may have been more than healings. They may have been signs as well. Perhaps when he drove out a demon he showed us the kind of demon that others—the detractors who defy the way—would send our way as the judgment approaches. Aren't the Zealots, with their impious criminality and blasphemy, perfect examples of the kind of sinfulness that Joshua opposed? Didn't they bring the cruel Romans into Galilee, Perea, and Judea? Your dream *is* a sign, Ariel. It shows that Joshua foresaw the evil that the Zealots would unleash in our times, and he warned us with signs that we were too blind to see or understand at the time. You need to share your visions, Ariel, so people understand that the horrors we're living through now are the very signs of the judgment that Joshua warned us about."

"Hold on," Dionysius said. "Before we start proclaiming Ariel's visions to the world, we need to examine them carefully, lest there are demonic forces involved. Ariel, share with us all your visions and dreams about Joshua. We have to figure out their meaning and verify if they're truly from the Lord. If we can do that, then we can share them with the churches as authentic revelation."

"All right, brother," Ariel said. "That makes sense to me. I'll go along with your suggestion. Do we all agree?"

Lucius agreed without hesitation. Zachariah, with some reluctance, also agreed.

Lucius went to the kitchen and came back with some bread, oil, and dates on a large plate. The elders sat and snacked while Ariel shared some of his visions with them.

14

Joshua, Jacob, and John sat in glum silence on a hill overlooking Capernaum from the north. They were resting after a fervent session of anxious prayer, for they had just learned that Herod Antipas had arrested and imprisoned John the Baptist. Some of John's other followers informed Joshua in Capernaum before moving on to Tiberias to appeal to Herod himself for John's release, or failing that, to at least persuade Herod to spare his life. According to their report, some of Herod's soldiers sneaked into John's camp in the middle of the night and kidnapped him. The rumor was that John was being held prisoner in Machaerus, Herod's fortress just east of the Dead Sea.

Joshua spoke.

"Joazar, the synagogue official, has invited us to speak at the next Sabbath service. Let's prepare a sermon that honors John and addresses the injustices of our times."

* * *

The Capernaum synagogue was more crowded than usual that Sabbath. Most of those baptized at the spring were there, as were non-regular synagogue goers who came out of curiosity about Joshua. After beginning the service with the recitation of the standard prayers and benedictions, Joazar unrolled a Torah scroll, written in Hebrew, and read one verse at a time while his assistant Ishmael followed each verse with an Aramaic translation. The reading was from Exodus chapters twenty-two and twenty-three. Several passages in particular resonated with the audience when Joazar read them.

"If you lend money to any of my people, to any poor man among you, you must not play the usurer with him: you must not demand interest from him." (Exodus 22:24)

"If you take another's cloak as a pledge, you must give it back to him before sunset. It's all the covering he has; it's the cloak he wraps his body in; what else would he sleep in? If he cries to me, I'll listen, for I am full of pity." (Exodus 22:25–26)

"You must not cheat any poor man of yours of his rights at law. Keep out of trumped up cases. See that the man who's innocent and just is not done to death, and don't acquit the guilty." (Exodus 23:6–7)

"You must never accept a bribe, for a bribe blinds clear sighted men and is the ruin of the just man's cause." (Exodus 23:8)

After the reading Joazar signaled to Joshua, who got up to speak before the congregation. His tone was solemn, and his voice choked up from evident grief.

"John the Baptist, my teacher and my friend, is the greatest and most righteous man I know. A man singularly committed to God—and to bringing others to God. Subsisting on nothing but the barest necessities at his camp in the wilderness, he freely gives the precious words and wisdom of God to all who come to him. That is, he did until Herod, with no justification whatsoever, took him from us and imprisoned him like a criminal. For what crime? Piety? Uprightness? Honesty?"

Joshua's tone of voice turned indignant.

"Yes. Herod must have hated that John told people the truth, the truth about God's coming wrath which will upend all those who are false, grasping, abusive of the people, and eager to subvert justice for bribes and power. How Herod must have raged at John's honesty, his exposure of the crimes of the rich, and his popularity. That a righteous man could be so beloved and popular must have terrified Herod to the core. How afraid he must have been that the people might turn against him and his criminal ways. Well, whether John is free or imprisoned, we should continue, unafraid, to proclaim God's justice and to oppose the injustice that rules over us today!

"Listen. I want to hear from you. Say 'amen' if you've felt the bite of Herod's taxes."

Most in the congregation said, "Amen."

"Say 'amen' if you feel unjustly burdened by those taxes."

Most in the congregation, with enthusiasm, said, "Amen."

"Say 'amen' if you've ever been robbed by bandits."

Some in the congregation said, "Amen."

"Say 'amen' if Herod's soldiers defended you from those bandits or helped you get restitution."

Silence. Then a smattering of laughter.

"Say 'amen' if you've suffered undue loss at the hands of creditors."

A majority of the audience members gave up a lively "Amen."

"Say 'amen' if Herod's courts were impartial and held justice in greater esteem than the bribery of your creditors."

Silence. Then laughter.

"Say 'amen' if Herod has taken plenty from you but given you nothing in return."

The crowd pronounced a forceful "Amen!"

"Say 'amen' if justice demands that John the Baptist be freed!"

"Amen!" the people cried. The congregation muttered and stirred. Excited conversations broke out.

Joshua waited for his listeners to quiet down. They did, somewhat, but lingering murmurs of laughter and energetic chatter prevented the synagogue from falling into complete silence.

While the tittering congregation was still settling down, a man stood up and shattered the mood with an abrupt outburst.

"What do you want with us, Joshua, disciple of John? Do you want to destroy us by bringing the wrath of Herod on our heads? What do you have to do with us? Leave us out of it!"

An awkward silence descended and everyone turned to look at the heckler—a bearded villager, no more than forty years old, with a face red from rage.

Joshua gave the heckler a stern look and shouted at him.

"What evil spirit possesses you to make you afraid of Herod? Haven't you heard? Herod's wrath will come to nothing when put against the much greater wrath of God! It's to such as you that the prophet . . . the prophet . . . Isaiah . . . yes! It's to such as *you* that Isaiah wrote, 'Who are you that you fear mere mortals, human beings who are but grass, that you forget your Maker, who stretches out the heavens and who lays the foundations of the earth, that you live in constant terror every day because of the wrath of the oppressor, the oppressor who's bent on destruction?'" (Isaiah 51:12–13)

Joshua looked around at all the faces in the crowd and continued to quote Isaiah.

"For where's the wrath of the oppressor? The cowering prisoners will soon be set free; they won't die in their dungeon, nor will they lack bread." (Isaiah 51:14)

Returning his gaze to the heckler, Joshua shouted, "Out with you! Be gone, evil spirit who fears Herod but not God!"

Jacob and John stood up and pointed at the heckler.

"Out!" They shouted together. "Out! Out! Out!"

The crowd joined in. Everyone pointed at the heckler and chanted with Jacob and John.

"Out! Out! Out!"

The heckler looked around with obvious fear in his eyes. He released a loud grunt of frustration and fled the synagogue. The congregation hooted and applauded.

Joshua paced and waited for the excitement to die down. The morning sun shined through the synagogue entrance and onto the floor beneath him. When the audience was silent and looking his way, he resumed speaking.

"Have no fear of Herod. It's to such as him that the prophet Micah wrote, 'Woe to those who plan iniquity, to those who plot evil on their beds! At morning's light they carry it out because it's in their power to do it. They covet fields and seize them; they covet houses and take them. They defraud people of their homes, they rob them of their inheritance. Therefore the Lord says: "I'm planning disaster against this people, from which you can't save yourselves. You'll no longer walk proudly, for it will be a time of calamity.'" (Micah 2:1–3)

"In all sincerity I urge you to have no fear of Herod, and have no fear of Herod's master, Caesar, either. For it's to such as Caesar that the prophet Habakkuk wrote, 'Woe to him who piles up stolen goods and makes himself wealthy by extortion! How long must this go on? Won't your creditors suddenly arise? Won't they wake up and make you tremble? Then you'll become their prey. Because you've plundered many nations, the peoples who are left will plunder you. For you've shed human blood; you've destroyed lands and cities and everyone in them. Woe to him who builds his house by unjust gain, setting his nest on high to escape the clutches of ruin! You've plotted the ruin of many peoples, shaming your own house and forfeiting your life. The stones of the wall will cry out, and the beams of the woodwork will echo it. Woe to him who builds a city with bloodshed and establishes a town by injustice!'" (Habakkuk 2:6–12)

The sunlight was now shining on Joshua's cloak, as high as the fringes. Joshua signaled to Jacob, who stood up to sing Psalm fifty-eight.

"Do you rulers indeed speak justly? Do you judge people with equity? No, in your heart you devise injustice, and your hands mete out violence on the earth. Break the teeth in their mouths, O God; Lord tear out the fangs of those lions! May they be like a slug that melts away as it moves along, like a stillborn child that never sees the sun. Before your pots can feel the heat of the thorns—whether they be green or dry—the wicked will be swept away. The righteous will be glad when they're avenged, when they dip their feet in the blood of the wicked. Then people will say: 'Surely the righteous will be rewarded; surely there's a God who judges the earth.'" (Psalm 58:2–3, 7–12)

Joshua resumed speaking.

"'Surely there's a God who judges the earth.' These are the words of David. We can't ignore them. The righteous will be avenged and the wicked will be 'swept away.' All our prophets say so. But right now the wicked prosper and the righteous languish."

Joshua signaled to John.

"John," Joshua said. "Tell us what scripture has to say about our times, about the trials we endure in this age of injustice."

John recited from Enoch chapter one hundred and three.

"The righteous and good who are alive, they say: 'In our troubled days we've worked hard and experienced every trouble, and met with much evil and been afflicted, and have become few and our spirit small. And we've been destroyed and haven't found any to help us even with a word. We've been tortured and destroyed, and don't expect to live from day to day.'" (Enoch 103:9–10)

The audience listened and nodded their heads in silent agreement with the complaints that sounded so similar to their own. John continued.

"We hoped to be the head and have become the tail. We've worked hard and had no satisfaction in our labor; and we've become the food of the sinners and the unrighteous, and they've laid their yoke heavily on us. They've ruled over us, hated us, and hit us, and to those who hated us we've bowed our necks but they pitied us not. We complained to the rulers in our tribulation, and cried out against those who devoured us, but they paid no attention to our cries and listened not to our voice." (Enoch 103:11–14)

A few congregants whispered, "Amen." John quoted Jeremiah chapter twelve.

"You're always righteous, Lord, when I bring a case before you. Yet I would speak with you about your justice. Why does the way of the wicked prosper? Why do all the faithless live at ease? You've planted them, and they've taken root; they grow and bear fruit. You're always on their lips but far from their hearts. Yet you know me, Lord; you see me and test my thoughts about you. Drag them off like sheep to be butchered! Set them apart for the day of slaughter!" (Jeremiah 12:1–3)

Joshua took the floor to speak.

"These worries and troubles, expressed by our prophets long ago, are the same that torment us today."

Many in the audience whispered, "Amen." Joshua continued his sermon.

"So what, according to the prophets, is God's answer to all this injustice? Isaiah, Amos, and Zephaniah have some pertinent words for us. Isaiah wrote, 'Woe to you who add house to house and join field to field till no space is left and you live alone in the land. Woe to those who make unjust laws, to those who issue oppressive decrees, to deprive the poor of their rights and withhold justice from the oppressed of my people, making widows their prey and robbing the fatherless. What will you do on the day of reckoning, when disaster comes from afar? To whom will you run for help? Where will you leave your riches? Nothing will remain but to cringe among the captives or fall among the slain.' (Isaiah 5:8, 10:1–4)

"Amos, in chapter five, wrote, 'You levy a straw tax on the poor and impose a tax on their grain. Therefore, though you've built stone mansions, you won't live in them; though you've planted lush vineyards, you won't drink their wine. For I know how many are your offenses and how great your sins. There will be wailing in all the streets and cries of anguish in every public square. The farmers will be summoned to weep and the mourners to wail.' (Amos 5:11–12, 16)

"Zephaniah wrote, 'That day will be a day of wrath—a day of distress and anguish, a day of trouble and ruin, a day of darkness and gloom, a day of clouds and blackness. The Lord will bring such distress on those who've sinned against Him that they'll grope about like the blind. Their blood will be poured out like dust, and their entrails like dung. Neither their silver nor their gold will save them on the day of the Lord's wrath.'" (Zephaniah 1:15–18)

The sunlight was now shining on Joshua's entire body. He looked beyond the audience, as if he were gazing into the future. His illuminated face looked stern and commanding, like a warrior

107

both triumphant and terrible. He recited from Enoch chapter one hundred and three like a judge pronouncing a severe sentence.

"Woe to you, you sinners, when you've died, if you die in the abundance of your sins, and woe to those who are like you and say regarding you: 'Blessed are the sinners, they've seen all their days, and they've died in prosperity and wealth, and haven't seen tribulation or murder in their life; and they've died in honor, and without facing judgement during their life.' You know that their souls will descend into hell, and they'll be wracked in tribulation, and their spirits shall enter into darkness and chains and a burning flame of harsh judgment. They'll have no peace. This judgment shall be for all the unrighteous in all the generations of the world!" (Enoch 103:5–8)

Joshua relaxed his expression and his tone of voice, and he returned his gaze to the audience. He looked into their eyes, surrendered a gentle smile, and recited from Enoch chapter one hundred and eight.

"But the good, who love God and who, since they were born, longed not after earthly food, but regarded everything as a passing breath, and lived accordingly, whom the Lord tried much, whose spirits were found pure so that they should bless His name; He has assigned them their reward, because they've been found to love heaven more than their life in the world, and though they were trod under foot by wicked men, and experienced abuse and reviling from them, they blessed the Lord. The Lord will summon the spirits of the good who belong to the generation of light, and He'll transform those who in the flesh weren't rewarded with honor as their faithfulness deserved. He'll bring out in shining light those who've loved His holy name, and He'll seat each on a throne of glory, and they'll shine for time without end! (Enoch 108:8–13)

"All the prophets foresaw the Day of the Lord. After careful study of their words, John the Baptist, and we his disciples, came to the momentous realization that the Lord's Day is at hand. Listen! Enoch divided the world's history into five-hundred-year periods and predicted that the five hundred years after the Babylonian Exile—our period—would be the last before the destruction of our wicked enemies and the establishment of God's kingdom—the kingdom reserved for the righteous.

"Daniel predicted that after the Babylonian Exile, four kingdoms would rule over us in the age before the coming of the Lord's wrath. The first kingdom was Persia: a kingdom of the east. The second kingdom was a kingdom of the south: the Ptolemies of Egypt. The third kingdom was a kingdom of the north: the Seleucids of Syria. The fourth kingdom, a kingdom of the west, rules us now—the Romans. So the Day of the Lord is imminent; it's written in scripture! Prepare! There's no time to lose. Abandon all wickedness, repent, and live as God commands. It's we, our generation, who will witness the Day of the Lord!"

Joshua signaled to Jacob and sat down. Jacob stood up to lead the congregation in singing Psalm thirty-seven.

"Don't fret because of those who are evil, or be envious of those who do wrong; for like the grass they'll soon wither, like green plants they'll soon die away. Trust in the Lord and do good; dwell in the land and enjoy safe pasture. Take delight in the Lord, and he'll give you the desires of your heart. Commit your way to the Lord; trust in him and he'll do this: he'll make your righteous reward shine like the dawn, your vindication like the noonday sun. Be still before the Lord and wait patiently for him; don't fret when people succeed in their ways, when they carry out their wicked schemes. Refrain from anger and turn from wrath; don't fret—it leads only to evil. For those who are evil will be destroyed, but those who hope in the Lord will inherit the land. A little while, and the wicked will be no more; though you look for them, they won't be found. But the meek will inherit the land and enjoy peace and prosperity." (Psalm 37:1–11)

When the song was over, Joshua stood outside the entrance of the synagogue. As the people filed out, he blessed them and laid his hands on some of them. Many of the congregants left the service thoroughly impressed by the authority and charisma of Rabbi Joshua. Among them was a young fisherman named Simon.

15

Ariel stood at the podium in the synagogue and addressed the assembled faithful.

"Oh Levi," Ariel said, looking up as if beseeching heaven. "What has become of you? Levi, son of Jacob and father of the tribe of Levi, the tribe that gave us Moses, our lawgiver, and his brother Aaron, the first high priest. The tribe that God chose to take charge of the holy things: the ark, the tent, the Temple, the sacrifices, the law. God gave the law to Moses on Sinai, entrusting it to the House of Levi. It was to Levi that the priestly duties fell—to preserve, propagate, and empower the law for the tribes of Israel.

"But what will Levi do now? The Temple is destroyed. The priests are dead or dispersed. The sacrifices have ceased. God didn't give land to the Levites like he did the other tribes—the privilege of priesthood was its portion. And now even this is gone. And what will the Pharisees do? So much of their tradition is tied up in their countless regulations concerning proper tithing or proper Temple offerings and sacrifices. What use is that tradition now? A good portion of the book of Leviticus is rendered void, now that the Temple and its priests are buried. How we mourn for you, Levi!"

Ariel looked around at the faces of his congregation. Some were nodding their heads in agreement, while others looked teary eyed and dazed. Ariel sighed and spoke again.

"Now, I've heard some say that Jerusalem was destroyed because the letter of the law became more important to us than the spirit of mercy. I agree, but there's more to it than that. Much of the blame falls on the Temple priests, who corrupted and perverted the law after the Herodian kings got their greedy hooks into them.

"The Herodians' power over the priests enabled them to reduce the law to a mere tool for collecting money. In the reign of the first Herod, the priests gave up serving God and dedicated themselves to Herod. And who did Herod serve, besides himself? Not God. Caesar! How Herod loved his Caesar—here building temples and bathhouses for false gods and the emperor, there giving lavish gifts to every Roman official who could increase his power and standing with the Romans. And the Temple priests—with what did they busy themselves? Justice? Mercy? Charity? If only! They single-mindedly devoted themselves to their own wealth and status, which increased in proportion to how obediently they served Herod.

"The priests became contemptuous of the people, misleading them and taking advantage of their humble piety. The priests stood before the people and said, 'Come, come. Cleanse yourself of your sins! Bring us your tithes and your first fruits. Let us sell you our birds, goats, and sheep. We'll sacrifice them for you and win you the forgiveness of God. Don't worry if your sins are many, as long as you have enough money to pay for the sin offerings. And don't forget the Temple tax!'

"But at least they filled the Temple treasury. They would, of course, use all that money we gave them to help the needy of Judea, to educate the children, and to keep the Temple in good shape so God would be honored properly."

Hearty laughter arose in the synagogue. Congregants shook their heads and wagged their fingers.

"What?" Ariel asked in mock surprise. "They didn't? Oh, right. I remember now. They gave the treasury over to Herod and the Romans. They did it so they could get a share of the spoils.

Levi went to work for Herod and Caesar! Is it so surprising, then, that God let the Romans destroy Jerusalem?"

Ariel opened the scroll on the podium.

"Now I would like to sing one of David's psalms, a hymn about the first destruction of Jerusalem and the Babylonian Exile, which David foresaw. It's a hymn we can all appreciate, now that we ourselves have witnessed another devastation of our holy city. Sing along with me if you know it."

Ariel found Psalm one hundred thirty-seven in the scroll and began to sing it. He sang at a slow pace and in a tone of lamentation. About half the congregation joined him.

"By the rivers of Babylon we sat and wept when we remembered Zion. There on the poplars we hung our harps, for there our captors asked us for songs, our tormentors demanded songs of joy; they said, 'Sing us one of the hymns of Zion!' How could we sing one of Yahweh's hymns in a pagan country? Jerusalem, if I forget you, may my right hand wither! May my tongue cling to the roof of my mouth if I fail to remember you, if I don't consider Jerusalem my highest joy." (Psalm 137:1–6)

Ariel kissed the scroll and rolled it up. After a solemn moment of silence he looked out into his attentive but fidgety audience and resumed his sermon.

"Recently, brothers and sisters, I was in the middle of a fast, mourning our nation's desolation and praying for God to have mercy on our people, when I went into a trance. I had visions—a series of visions about Christ Joshua."

Ariel's listeners fell silent.

"In my first vision, I saw him walking along the edge of the Sea of Galilee, teaching the people who had come to hear him. As he walked, he caught sight of Levi, son of Alphaeus, a man from a well-regarded family. This Levi was working at the tax-collection tent, serving in a position of less status and honor than we might expect, given his noble upbringing. Joshua approached him and said, 'Follow me.' Levi, without hesitation, got up and followed him.

"In my next vision, I saw Joshua and his disciples at Levi's house, sharing a meal. Many tax collectors and other sinful people were there also, eating with Levi and his guests. Some teachers of the law—Pharisees—saw this and asked Joshua's disciples, 'Why does he eat with tax collectors and sinners?'

"On hearing this, Joshua said to them, 'It's not the healthy who need a doctor, but the sick. I have not come to call the righteous, but sinners.'

"Then I saw some people approach Joshua and speak to him. They said, 'John the Baptist's disciples and the disciples of the Pharisees are fasting, but your disciples aren't. Why is that?'

"Joshua answered them: 'John's disciples are right to fast, because they're mourning his imprisonment, and the Pharisees' disciples have reason to fast because they've lost the true sense of the law, having buried it under the tangled thickets of their elaborate tradition. But how can the guests of the bridegroom fast while he's with them? They can't, so long as they have him with them. But the time will come when the bridegroom will be taken from them, and on that day they'll fast.'"

Ariel took a deep breath. The synagogue was as still as a tomb.

"In my third vision, I saw Joshua and his disciples walking through grain fields, and as they walked along, some of the disciples began to pick and eat from the heads of grain. Some Pharisees were watching and they said, 'Don't you know that today is the Sabbath? It's unlawful to pick grain on the Sabbath!'

"Joshua answered them: 'Have you never read what David did when he and his companions were hungry and in need? Ahimelech the high priest allowed David to enter the house of God and eat the consecrated bread, which is lawful only for priests to eat, and David gave some of it to his companions too. In their time of need, David and his companions had a right to sustenance that took priority over the Temple law. So the law of higher priority overrules the law of lower priority. Be assured that my disciples have done nothing unlawful by picking the grain. It's only your tradition that says you can't pick grain on the Sabbath.

The law says in Deuteronomy 23:25, "If you enter your neighbor's grain field, you may pick kernels with your hands, but you must not put a sickle to their standing grain." If we were to put a sickle to this grain, we would be violating the commandment against theft. If reaping your neighbor's field is theft, but picking grain with your hands is not, then on the Sabbath reaping is unlawful work and picking grain is not. Yes, to sow or to reap is work, and is unlawful on the Sabbath, but picking grain is never work. It's reward. Can you forbid eating on the Sabbath? You fail to understand that the Sabbath was made for man, not man for the Sabbath!'

"In my fourth vision, Joshua entered a synagogue, where there was a man with a withered hand. Some Pharisees were there looking for a reason to accuse Joshua, so they watched him closely to see if he would heal the man on the Sabbath. Joshua said to the man with the withered hand, 'Stand up in front of everyone.'

"Joshua asked the Pharisees, 'Which is lawful on the Sabbath: to do good or to do evil, to save life or to kill?' But they remained silent.

"He looked around at them in anger, deeply distressed by their stubborn hearts, and said to the man, 'Stretch out your hand.' He stretched it out and his hand was completely restored."

Ariel cleared his throat. His congregation gazed ahead, entranced.

"In my fifth and final vision, Joshua met with Levi on a mountainside. Joshua said to him: 'Levi, son of Alphaeus, you're now healed of your past sinful ways. You abandoned tax collecting and learned from me the correct understanding of the law. Now I must take the name Levi away from you, because soon that name will lose its meaning. The name of Levi will be nullified when the Temple and the priesthood are destroyed. So henceforth you will be called Jacob, son of Alphaeus. But I already have a disciple named Jacob, so you will be the new Jacob: Jacob the Younger. I do this because when Levi is gone, he'll be replaced by the new Jacob: the new Israel.'"

Ariel paused, walked down the steps from the dais, and sat down on a nearby bench. The members of his congregation stared at him and wondered what it all meant.

16

Joshua, Jacob, and John enjoyed considerable success in Capernaum. They brought more people to the synagogue than anyone ever had, and increasing numbers of people came to them to be baptized. Their message appeared to be well received. Joshua believed it was time to take his ministry to the other villages nearby. He had a particular interest in a village a few miles west of Capernaum named Seven Springs, which did in fact have seven springs near it.

One morning Joshua decided to walk over to Seven Springs by himself to investigate the place. He had just started make his way along the Capernaum shore when Simon, the young fisherman, noticed him. Simon ran to Joshua and kneeled before him.

"Shalom, Rabbi. I'm your servant." Simon said with head bowed and eyes averting Joshua's direct gaze.

"Shalom, brother." Joshua said. "What do you need?"

"I just want to say that it's an honor to meet you, Rabbi Joshua. I'm Simon. Count on me to be your servant. Is there anything I can do for you? Maybe I can help you. If you're on your way to another town on the lake, I can take you in my boat. Where are you going, if I may ask?"

"I'm going to Seven Springs. It's very close. Thank you, but I don't need your boat."

"Of course. But let me take you anyway. I won't charge you anything; it will be my privilege. Spare yourself the heat and the dust. Spare yourself the wear on your sandals and feet. Save some time, however brief. Brighten a poor fisherman's day!"

Joshua hesitated and took a good look at Simon. He seemed harmless enough.

"All right. Take me in your boat."

Simon's boat was small. It could carry no more than ten fishermen when fully loaded with nets and equipment. But Simon co-owned it outright with his brother Andreus, which Simon mentioned with great pride to Joshua. With just Joshua and Simon on board, Simon rowing and Joshua facing him, the boat seemed roomy to excess. Out on the lake Simon was a fountain of nervous chatter.

"I'm just a simple man, Rabbi. I can't read, and the only scripture I know is whatever others have taught me. And I don't remember it all exactly, not like you. You seem to know it all, by memory no less. How did you become so learned?"

"It's just a matter of reading, rereading, and reciting so much that it becomes engraved on the heart. I had the luxury of study because my father was a rabbi. Later I studied under John the Baptist."

"Yes, of course. I heard you speak about John the Baptist in the synagogue. Very moving—powerful. You electrify the audience when you speak! The village can't stop talking about you. Is it true that you heal people and drive out demons?"

"No, not me. I only invite people to repent of their sins. If their repentance is sincere and they trust the power of God, then God forgives them and heals them. I pray and intercede on behalf of the penitent, but God does the rest."

"Right. Of course. Has God healed many of those who've come to you with their burdens?"

"He often has, yes. But again, it all depends on the person's faith and their seriousness about following the way of the Lord."

"I see."

Simon looked around as if hoping to not be seen by onlookers and stopped rowing. He dropped the oars in the boat and began to tear up.

"I'm an accursed man, Rabbi! My parents and two of my brothers are dead; only I and my brother Andreus remain. My wife died only a few years ago. An evil spirit, a malaria, entered her—my child too. He was only two years old! My wife's mother lives with us because her husband died. The three of us live together, broken by grief. We're a sad house of sorrow. I'm stalked by the Angel of Death! And my pitiless neighbors slander me— they say I fornicate with my mother-in-law. They spread false rumors about me; they say my misfortune is punishment for my sins. What can I do, Rabbi? What can I do?"

Joshua gripped Simon's shoulders and looked straight into his tear-moistened eyes.

"Simon, for God's sake, calm down! You sound like David in his darkest lamentations, when his most blood-thirsty enemies were at his heels."

Joshua recited from Psalm one hundred and two, taking care to exaggerate his voice and gestures to feign melodramatic anguish and make himself comical.

"My days vanish like smoke; my bones burn like glowing embers. My heart is blighted and withered like grass; in my distress I groan aloud and am reduced to skin and bones. I eat ashes as my food and mingle my drink with tears. My days are like the evening shadow; I wither away like grass." (Psalm 102:3– 5, 9, 11)

Simon blushed and turned his face away in shame. Joshua laughed and gave Simon a friendly grip on the arm.

"I'm sorry, Simon. I don't mean to make light of your pain. I'm just trying to amuse you—in my own clumsy way. I want to help you. Maybe I can."

Simon looked at Joshua's face and discerned an expression of sincere compassion. Simon relaxed and returned a faint, hopeful smile.

"Tell me, Simon. Aren't you an upright man? Aren't you honest and trustworthy in your dealings with your neighbors?"

"Yes, Rabbi. I am."

"And aren't you faithful and obedient to your God?"

"Yes."

"And in spite of all your suffering and loss, do you have compassion for the destitute and those who are unjustly persecuted?"

"Yes. I do."

"Then you're not cursed. You're blessed! The problem is that we're living in the final evil age, when the wicked prosper and the righteous suffer. Do you think John the Baptist deserved to be imprisoned by Herod? Rejoice that you suffer for your righteousness. Soon God will judge the world and the righteous will be saved. Then it will be the wicked who suffer, while the upright prosper. Rejoice! It's for such as you that David wrote, 'How abundant are the good things that you've stored up for those who fear you, that you bestow in the face of all, on those who take refuge in you. In the shelter of your presence you hide them from all human intrigue; you keep them safe in your dwelling from accusing tongues.'" (Psalm 31:19–20)

"But Rabbi, I'm a sinful man!"

"You just said you were an upright man. Which is it?"

"It's . . . it's both!"

"Of course it is. Who hasn't sinned? But are you ready to abandon sin and commit yourself wholly to righteousness?"

"If that's what it takes to be saved, then yes."

"Very good then. I remember another psalm of David that you should know. Let's see . . . oh yes . . . I can recall it now: 'The righteous cry out, and the Lord hears them; he delivers them from their troubles. The Lord is close to the broken hearted and saves those who are crushed in spirit. The righteous person may have many troubles, but the Lord delivers him from them all; He protects all his bones, not one of them will be broken.'" (Psalm 34:17–20)

Simon felt great relief. Joshua made him feel like there was hope for him.

Joshua took Simon's hands in his and said, "Come. Pray with me. Repeat each verse after I say it."

Joshua recited from Psalms forty-six and one hundred eighteen: "God is our refuge and strength, an ever present help in trouble. Therefore we'll not fear, though the earth give way and the mountains fall into the heart of the sea, though its waters roar and foam and the mountains quake with their surging. The Lord Almighty is with us; the God of Jacob is our fortress. (Psalm 46:1–3, 7)

"I'll not die but live, and will proclaim what the Lord has done. The Lord has chastened me severely, but He's not given me over to death. Open for me the gates of the righteous; I'll enter and give thanks to the Lord. This is the gate of the Lord through which the righteous may enter. I'll give you thanks, for you answered me; you've become my salvation." (Psalm 118:17–21)

Joshua let go of Simon and said, "If you're serious about embracing the way, then you'll have to confess your sins and undergo the baptism of repentance."

"Here, in the lake?"

"No. If you're ready, we'll do it in one of the seven springs."

"However you wish. I'm your servant."

As the boat approached the shore of Seven Springs, Joshua reclined at his end of the boat. He raised his head and hands toward the sky and recited from Psalm thirty-two.

"When I kept silent, my bones wasted away through my groaning all day long. For day and night your hand was heavy on me; my strength was sapped as in the heat of summer. Then I acknowledged my sin to you and did not cover up my iniquity. I said, 'I'll confess my transgressions to the Lord.' And you forgave the guilt of my sin. Therefore let all the faithful pray to you while you may be found; surely the rising of the mighty waters will not reach them. You are my hiding place; you'll protect me from trouble and surround me with songs of deliverance." (Psalm 32:3–7)

When Joshua and Simon came ashore, they went straight to the nearest spring, where Joshua performed his usual rituals of confession and baptism. Afterward Joshua insisted that Simon row his boat back to Capernaum without him because he wanted to explore Seven Springs on his own.

Upon returning home Simon bragged to Andreus about his new friendship with the renowned Rabbi Joshua. Andreus was impressed.

* * *

While in Seven Springs Joshua learned that one of the springs was reserved for lepers. Lepers, and only lepers, were permitted to use only that particular spring for bathing. Joshua went to that spring and prayed. After a while three men with apparent skin disorders, which marked them as lepers in the eyes of the community, came to the spring. Joshua greeted them and offered to examine their skin without charge. The three men accepted and Joshua performed a diagnostic test on each of them. It was the first time Joshua provided this service, which would become a staple of his ministry.

Joshua would take aside any person who had a skin disorder suspected of being leprosy and examine the sores on their body. If the sores were white spots, without white hair protruding and without any flesh eaten away, he would next ask the person a routine litany of questions: How long has your skin been like this? Have the sores increased or decreased in size? Have the sores multiplied and spread or have they diminished?

If the person answered that the sores had been visible for two or more weeks, with no change in size over that period, and either diminishment or no spreading, then Joshua would pronounce them clean. He would also declare clean those who had seen their white, hairless sores break out all over their body, as this was a sign of the body shedding the disease and recovering.

To all he declared clean, Joshua said, "Go and show yourself to a priest, and make the offering for your healing prescribed by Moses. Then you will be free to reenter the community."

If the sores were new, he would tell the person to observe their skin over the next two weeks and watch for the signs of cure or disease, which he would describe to them with great patience and care.

If the sores indicated leprosy, he would advise the person to camp away from the community, repent of their sins, pray to God, and watch for any changes in their condition.

In all cases he would end the examination with a prayer for God to heal and protect the examinee.

The three men that Joshua met that particular day at the spring turned out to have non-leprous skin conditions and he pronounced them clean. In awe and gratitude the trio fell to their knees and thanked Joshua. Their voices cracked from irrepressible emotion.

One of the men said, "I'm sorry, lord physician, that we have no money to give you for your kindness. Please forgive us."

Overcome with humility and pity, Joshua answered: "I'm not a physician or healer. God alone heals. I'm His servant, Joshua from Nazareth. My work is to bring people to God, not to take money from the needy. I've helped you by merely following the skin examination instructions that Moses wrote for us in chapters thirteen and fourteen of Leviticus."

"We're illiterate and not very familiar with that particular scripture," the man answered. "But thank you, lord Joshua, for all you've done for us by the grace of God!"

When the three men returned to town, they assured everyone that they were cleansed of their leprosy. They insisted that their cure was due to the healing power of Joshua the Nazarene.

* * *

When Joshua returned to Capernaum, Simon went to him and introduced him to his brother Andreus, who was a slightly smaller and less hirsute version of Simon. The two brothers went to hear all of Joshua's sermons and public speeches. Andreus believed that Joshua's teachings were true, and he marveled at his prodigious and poignant interpretations of scripture. Joshua baptized Andreus at the Capernaum spring, along with several other people, some of whom claimed that Joshua had healed them of their ailments that day.

17

Ariel and Zachariah were sharing some wine in Ariel's study.

"It doesn't stop, Ari. Fewer and fewer people are showing up to our meetings and services. I fear we're right about the impact of the war."

"Yes, unfortunately. That and all the hostility from the Greeks. I'm sure some have left Antioch forever. I just hope that wherever they go, they keep the faith."

"Yes, well, I have to admit that I can understand people's skepticism and disappointment. With all that's happened, I'm not surprised that some would feel that God has abandoned us. Some of the Jews who reject our risen Lord have been talking about the war as punishment for the sins of our nation, and I think they're right, in a way. When we took up arms against the Romans, we by no means were faithful to the law. In fact, we trampled and defiled it like the worst villains and traitors of our history. After soaking even our most sacred institutions in the blood of the basest crimes and impieties, how can we expect salvation? Perhaps our redemption's been cancelled! What if the Lord, on his way to collect the righteous and start the new age, saw what the Zealots and Sadducees were doing in the Temple and decided to turn right around and leave us to the devil? What then?"

Ariel finished his cup and refilled it.

"I confess that I've worried and prayed to the Lord about this very question myself. I assure you that you can let go of your catastrophic imaginations. Remember the remnant: the righteous elect that remain after God's wrath—the blessed ones the prophets wrote about and Joshua taught us about. All who sincerely repent and embrace the way can be saved. Listen. This reminds me of something. I recently had a vision, another vision sent to me from the Lord. It's relevant to this issue. Would you like to hear it?"

"Absolutely."

"All right." Ariel put his cup down and sat closer to Dionysius. "This is what I saw: Joshua came with his disciples to the town of Gennesaret on the shore of the lake. Many of the townspeople came out and gathered around them. A synagogue leader named Jairus fell at Joshua's feet and begged him to heal his dying daughter, who was bedridden in Jairus's house. Joshua agreed to go with Jairus and help his daughter.

"As they went, the townspeople followed and crowded around Joshua, pressing against him tightly to be near him. A woman was among them, a woman who had been unclean from a bloody discharge for twelve years. She had exhausted all her money on doctors but nothing helped her. Nevertheless she thought that if she could only touch him, even his clothing, she would be healed. So she pushed her way through the crowd and managed to touch Joshua's cloak from behind him. At that instant her bleeding stopped and she was healed.

"Joshua noticed what had happened and turned around, asking, 'Who touched my clothes?'

"Peter answered, 'Who isn't touching your clothes, Rabbi? Look at how everyone's pressing against us!'

"Joshua ignored Peter and kept looking for the person who had touched him. The woman then fell at Joshua's feet and, trembling from fear, confessed what she'd done.

"Joshua said to her, 'Daughter, your faith has healed you. Go in peace and remain healed from your affliction.'

"At that moment some people came from Jairus's house and told Jairus that his daughter had died. Jairus tore his clothes in grief, but Joshua, overhearing, told him, 'Don't be afraid; have faith.'

"Joshua took Jairus, Peter, Jacob, and John and, leaving the rest of the crowd behind, rushed to Jairus's house, where people were crying and mourning the dead girl.

"'There's no need for wailing,' Joshua said. 'The girl's merely asleep.'

"The mourners all thought Joshua was crazy, but the girl's parents sent them all out and brought in Joshua with his three disciples. Joshua went to the girl and, holding her hand, said, 'Get up little girl.' At that instant the girl, who was twelve years old, stood up and began to walk. Her parents were amazed and overjoyed.

"And so ends the vision." Ariel said.

Zachariah pondered Ariel's story and then gave his assessment.

"This vision of yours is all well and good, as far as it goes. Joshua heals a woman and raises a dead girl back to life. A pretty standard miracle story. There are so many stories about Joshua healing people and raising the dead. I'm not sure this adds much to what we already know. Am I missing something?"

"Try harder Zachariah. Think! The woman had bled for twelve years. The synagogue leader's twelve-year-old daughter rose from the dead. What does that tell you?"

Zachariah thought for a moment and then said, "Joshua . . . healed a woman and raised a girl from the dead. I don't see what else there is to say."

"For the love of the Lord, Zachariah!" Ariel said, sighing with frustration. "Don't you understand anything? The woman who bled for twelve years is our nation, polluted by her sins. She's unclean for *twelve* years to indicate that she represents our nation of twelve tribes. Her bloody discharge is a symbol of Israel's sinful and unclean state. By going to Joshua and believing in his power, she's cleansed. This means that there's salvation for Israel in spite of her sins, as long as she seeks out Christ Joshua and places her trust in him.

"The girl, on the other hand, is the innocent and pious Jewish nation that seems to have died. She's *twelve* years old and the daughter of a pious family. She isn't entirely dead. She'll rise again to life through the grace of Joshua. Our nation can still be restored to righteousness, but it will require obedience to the Christ."

Zachariah groaned.

"You son of a whore, Ariel! You and your allegories again. I ought to send you into the desert tied to a camel . . . with a beehive hanging from your neck!"

The two friends laughed, poured some wine, and drank.

18

One morning, while Jacob and John were fishing, Joshua climbed to the top of a hill near Capernaum to pray, recollect scripture, and prepare his next sermon. When he finished, it was the fourth hour after the dawn and he began his descent to the village. Simon and Andreus met him along the way.

"Shalom, Rabbi," Simon said. "Forgive us for disturbing you. Can we speak with you for a moment?"

"Speak, brothers," Joshua said as he guided them to a shady tree nearby.

"Rabbi," Simon said. "Is it true that you and the sons of Zebedee are leaving us to preach to the other villages?"

"Yes. We will preach to the other villages, but we'll soon return to check on the flock here, to make sure it hasn't gone astray. We want to take the word to all Jews, but we also want those who've received it to remain strong in it and stay faithful to the way. We who are shepherds—we care for our sheep."

"But if the shepherds keep adding sheep to the flock," Andreus asked, "won't they need to hire more shepherds?"

"Yes, eventually." Joshua said.

"Hold on, Andreus," Simon said. "You're getting ahead of yourself. Let me speak."

Simon turned to Joshua.

"Rabbi, we believe that you teach the truth. And we want to be worthy of God's kingdom when judgment comes. If you would permit it, we also wish to be your disciples and your servants. We want to accompany you on your travels and learn from you the ways of God. Before you say anything, let me assure you that we can make it worth your while. We'll provide you with the best of our catch and gains from our sales. We'll carry your burdens and prepare your meals. Whatever you ask, we'll do. We're your servants."

Joshua was surprised and he blushed a little from embarrassment. He looked at the brothers, felt bad for them, and decided to discourage them.

"I appreciate your generosity and your faith in me, but I'm afraid you don't know what you're asking. Jacob and John studied under John the Baptist, like me. They know the scriptures and are experienced preachers. They're inured to hunger and hardship. Will you be able to endure such things and learn scripture as if it were engraved on your heart? Will you have the patience? Will you be able to proclaim the word to the people, even when they hate and reject you? Are you prepared to stand up for righteousness when confronted by the wicked? Are you willing to contend with evil spirits?"

"Let us prove what we can do and let us take on whatever responsibilities you judge fit for us. Perhaps we're unworthy, but test us before you judge, if you will, Rabbi."

"I'll think about it. I'll give you my decision after the Sabbath."

* * *

That evening Joshua discussed Simon and Andreus's proposal with Jacob and John.

"I don't think it's a good idea." John said. "They're neither scholars nor speakers. What can a pair of uneducated neophytes do for us, except cause us trouble and embarrassment?"

"They aren't asking to become scholars or preachers." Joshua said. "They want to be students. They'd pay for their instruction by catching and cooking fish for us, and by helping us with mundane chores. It might be a convenient arrangement."

"What if they turn out to be good students?" Jacob asked. "What if they learn so well that they become worthy to do all the things we do? They'll want to be partners and not servants. That could be good for us, but that could also cause problems."

"I think that's highly unlikely to happen." Joshua said. "If we take them on, we'll eventually learn what they're capable of, but they'll have to prove themselves little by little. We'd only give them responsibilities they're ready for. If by some miracle they excel, so much the better. Imagine five of us, all preaching the word and all sharing in the daily tasks."

"In that case they'd be valuable assets," Jacob said. "We could reach more people."

"That's wonderful to imagine," John said. "But what if they become a burden to us? Isn't that a more likely outcome?"

Joshua gazed into space as if he were trying to perceive something far away.

"In all honesty I only see opportunity here." Joshua said. "We can let them serve however they can, and for only as long as they're useful to us. But if we can get these men, these simple, ordinary men, to understand the truth and embrace it wholeheartedly, then think of what that means. We'd have proof that we can turn the hearts of the unlearned. That's a valuable test for us. However well we can teach Simon and Andreus—that's how well we should be able to reach all the others who are like them. While we teach those two the word and the way, they'll teach us how best to conquer the hearts of the humble. How can we afford to miss that lesson?"

"It sounds like you've made your decision." John said.

"Well, you've convinced me, Joshua." Jacob said. "If they're good men, as you say, then I see nothing wrong with us and them working together and learning from each other."

"Do you agree, John?" Joshua asked.

"I'll go along with it," John answered. "But I'll keep a careful eye on those two, and you should too."

"I have eyes to see and ears to hear." Joshua said.

* * *

The day after the Sabbath, Joshua met Simon and Andreus at the docks.

"I'm going to test you two." Joshua said. "Prove yourself worthy and I'll make you my companions and disciples."

"Hallelu Jah!" Simon shouted. "What's the test?"

"Hold on. I'll get to it. First, though, I want to know more about all the fish you said you'd catch for me. What is the biggest haul that you've ever caught in one day?"

"Five hundred and fifty pounds." Andreus answered.

"Five hundred and seventy-five pounds." Simon countered.

"I want you two to go out and net a catch of at least six hundred pounds. Every day show me your catch before you sell it. You pass the test the day you catch six hundred pounds or more."

"But that could take . . . we might never . . . how can we—" Andreus said, eyes wide with disbelief.

"Andreus!" Simon yelled. "Stop whining! Have some faith. We accept your test, Rabbi. Come on Andre, let's get going."

At once the brothers began to prepare their boat.

* * *

Simon and Andreus plunged into their fishing efforts with more alacrity and devotion than they ever had before. They fished at all hours and trawled vast expanses of the lake. Each day they brought massive hauls to the markets and made good money. On their tenth day of work they managed to capture six hundred and two pounds of fish. Andreus ran to Zebedee's house to fetch Joshua and brought him to the market, where Simon was waiting with their prize catch.

Joshua looked over the pile of fish, confirmed the weight with the merchant, and congratulated the brothers.

"Now I want you to add the money from these fish to all the rest of the money you made fishing since you began the test, whatever you haven't already spent. I'll come to your house tonight to see it."

* * *

When Joshua went to Simon and Andreus's house that night, Simon sat him at a table and Andreus brought him a plate with a large piece of roasted tilapia, some bread, and olive oil.

Simon whispered to Joshua: "Please excuse my mother-in-law, Lois. She's fuming in her room, enraged because she thinks we're abandoning her."

"Did you explain to her that if you join me, you'll only be making trips around the lake, and that you'll often return to Capernaum?" Joshua asked, keeping his voice soft and low.

"Yes, but she doesn't believe it. She's convinced that we're taking all our money and leaving her to starve."

"After your first return home she'll be reassured."

Andreus entered carrying a watermelon-sized cloth sack, which he left on the table in front of Joshua. Simon opened it and dumped out its contents. Bronze and silver coins of various sizes cascaded out of the bag, jostling and jangling before coming to rest in a pile.

"Haven't we been productive?" Simon asked with a smug grin.

"Yes, indeed." Joshua answered. "Now I'll give you your next test. I want you to take all this money and give it to the poor. Give some to the orphans and some to the widows. Help the indebted restore their solvency. Buy food for the hungry. Compensate the robbery victims for their losses. Do the same for the victims of extortion or unjust court rulings."

Simon and Andreus listened with mouths agape.

Simon, his voice straining with grief, protested: "Rabbi, we worked so hard for this. Don't we deserve to keep it?"

"Absolutely you do. But you have to decide whether you want to make money or work with me. Worldly gain or the kingdom of God? I accept your choice either way, but I won't accept divided disciples. You can serve money or God, but not both. Pick the one you love more and commit!"

Simon wavered, but Andreus spoke with confident resolve: "We choose God. Worldly wealth will last but a short time, but the kingdom is forever. Besides, the kingdom is coming to replace this world soon anyway, so what choice do we really have?"

After brief hesitation, Simon nodded and put his hand on Andreus's.

"Yes." Simon said. "We choose God. We'll do as you say with the money."

"Wonderful! It looks like you might yet become true disciples, able to capture the hearts of men as well as you capture fish in your nets."

Lois, a fit and attractive woman of forty-some years of age, bolted into the room like a furious wind.

"Kingdom of God!" she shouted. "You rubes have really lost it now! Is this the bogus prophet you're going to go away with? Give him all our money and leave me destitute? Are you really falling for all this end times and judgment horseshit?"

"Watch your tongue, sister!" Joshua snapped. "You're insulting the holy word of God more than you're insulting me!"

"Silence woman!" Simon shouted. "Don't dare talk to the rabbi that way!"

Simon raised his hand to suggest the hard strike that he would deliver Lois if she persisted in her rudeness.

Joshua tried to defuse the tension by addressing Lois in a low and calm tone of voice.

"Sister, I understand your concern, but I assure you that Simon and Andreus will come with me for just a little while and then we'll all return. And so it will be with all our travels. You won't be abandoned. Capernaum's our home, and we'll always find our way home. To prove to you my seriousness let me—"

Joshua sifted through the pile of coins and made a second pile consisting of about one-fourth the original.

"Here. This is for you, sister. This will feed you for months. We'll call it the widow's share. You are a widow, aren't you?"

Lois ran her fingers through the coins as if caressing the hair of a beloved child. She exhaled with relief and calmed herself.

"I suppose that's reasonable," she said before getting up to wait on the men.

19

Dionysius sat at his desk reading Ariel's Aramaic manuscripts of his visions. All the visions and dreams that Ariel had described to his friends were there, preserved in ink on parchment for convenient reference and study. There were four manuscripts. One was a version of the story about the paralytic who was lowered through the roof to be cured by Joshua. Another was the story of Joshua healing the hemorrhaging woman and raising Jairus's dead daughter to life. A third manuscript told the tale of how Joshua called Levi from the customs house, taught the Pharisees the correct interpretation of the law, and gave Levi the new name of Jacob. A fourth manuscript was an account of the demoniac-pig episode from Ariel's dream.

As Dionysius perused the manuscripts, he heard a knock on his door. It was Ariel. Dionysius welcomed him with a cheerful "shalom" and invited him to join him in his study.

"How do you like my written versions, Dion?"

"I love them, Ari. There are good lessons in these visions of yours, lessons that should be shared with all believers."

"Yes. I think so too. What do you, personally, perceive those lessons to be?"

Dionysius paused to think for a brief moment and then answered.

"Well, I think the main point is that Joshua showed us the way to become cleansed and healed of our sinfulness, so that we might win the kingdom of God. But those who neglect the way and continue in their errors face disaster. Joshua warned us with his words and signs that we'd be destroyed if we didn't correct ourselves, and look—it was all fulfilled. Look at what's happened to us, to Israel, thanks to the apostates and Zealots. They led the people down the erroneous path, the path Joshua warned us about, and desolation was the reward. The people need to learn—to understand that Christ Joshua was and is our salvation, our only salvation, in this time of judgment."

"Ah, well said, Dion. I won't disagree with any of that. You understand. Now, if only we can persuade more people. I was just in the synagogue today, listening to some Pharisee refugees from Judea—stubborn, hard-headed Pharisees—and they taught blatantly false doctrine. They were trying to mislead the people and turn them away from Christ. The outrageous things they said, I couldn't help myself, I argued with them. I couldn't let their falsehoods go unopposed."

"What exactly did they say?"

"They said that Joshua couldn't be the Messiah, and they defended their claim with pathetic reasoning. They said the Messiah can't be Galilean, but I told them to read Isaiah chapter nine: 'In the future He will honor Galilee of the nations . . . the people walking in darkness have seen a great light . . . for to us a child is born, to us a son is given . . . and he'll be called Wonderful Counselor, Mighty God, Everlasting Father, Prince of Peace' (Isaiah 9:1–2, 6)

"They said the Messiah is not supposed to suffer and be crucified, so I referred them to Isaiah chapter fifty-three: 'He was despised and rejected by mankind, a man of suffering, and familiar with pain. Like one from whom people hide their faces he was despised, and we held him in low esteem. Surely he took up our pain and bore our suffering, yet we considered him punished by God, stricken by Him and afflicted. But he was pierced for our transgressions . . . and by his wounds we're healed.' (Isaiah 53:3–5)

"They said the Messiah belongs only to the Jews and has nothing to do with Gentiles. Can you believe that? I told them to reread Isaiah chapter forty-nine: 'It's too small a thing for you to be my servant to restore the tribes of Jacob and bring back those of Israel I've kept. I'll also make you a light for the Gentiles, that my salvation may reach to the ends of the earth' (Isaiah 49:6) Then I referred them to chapter fifty-six: 'Foreigners who bind themselves to the Lord to minister to Him, to love the name of the Lord, and to be His servants, all who keep the Sabbath without desecrating it and who hold fast to my covenant—these I will bring to my holy mountain and give them joy in my house of prayer. Their burnt offerings and sacrifices will be accepted on my altar, for my house will be called a house of prayer for all nations.'" (Isaiah 56:6–7)

Dionysius laughed.

"That should have silenced those Pharisees," Dionysius said. "Showing them their error so clearly with proof from Isaiah. Well done my friend!"

"You'd think they would surrender to reason right then and there, but no! They only grew fiercer in their stubbornness. They insisted that Joshua wasn't resurrected—that Peter had only seen Joshua's ghost. And since many dead people have appeared in ghostly form, there's nothing special about Joshua and no reason to suppose he's the Messiah. What perverse reasoning!"

"Amen! That argument's founded on wind. How can they be so ignorant? Christ Joshua was raised from death in body, and in body he ascended to heaven. How dare they insult the Christ like that? How did you answer those dogs?"

"I told them the same thing you just said. Then I told them that it was misguided Jews like them who brought devastation onto Israel. I got right in their faces and repeated that lamentation which is so popular with those of us who regret the war: 'For every four thousand Jews killed in the war by the Romans, five thousand were killed by their fellow Jews.'"

"Then you ran away like a hare to avoid a beating!" Dionysius said before breaking into laughter.

"Of course I did," Ariel said, smiling. "I'm not an idiot. I'm a man of peace."

20

Joshua, Jacob, John, Simon, and Andreus went to Seven Springs in Simon and Andreus's boat. After performing a few baptisms and sermons they started to develop a decent following, and one supportive villager, named Phillip, offered his home to Joshua's group for lodging during their stay. It was a convenient arrangement for both parties. Phillip lived alone in a large, four-room, basalt-stone house, so there was room enough for everyone to sleep in comfort. Phillip was glad to have the company. Joshua and his friends were a welcome respite from his usual lonely isolation.

During their time in Seven Springs, Andreus devoted himself to fishing, cooking, trading, and providing for the material well-being of the rest of the household, while Simon spent all the time he could learning scripture from Joshua, Jacob, and John.

One evening Simon went to speak with Joshua.

"I don't know why my brother so plays the woman and lacks my enthusiasm for the word." Simon said. "Do you want me to talk to him?"

"If I were to have you speak to Andreus," Joshua said, "it would be to praise him. To me it seems he shuns instruction only because he has no need for it. He behaves as if the word has already taken root in his heart and grown to maturity. He puts himself last and the rest of us first. It's people like him who will be all the more exalted in the kingdom. He who wants to be first in the kingdom must be the servant of all."

Simon burned with embarrassment and failed to summon anything to say in response. He cast his eyes downward and crept away, humbled and silent.

The sun was setting and Joshua called his disciples together. He invited Phillip to join them. He took them to the top of a hill overlooking the lake and had the men sit around him.

"Andreus!" Joshua called. "Tell me. Who suffers?"

Andreus, bemused, hesitated a moment, and then asked, "Don't we all suffer, Rabbi?"

Joshua laughed.

"Yes, of course." Joshua said. "But I'm talking about people in the world who are especially notable for their misfortune, who arouse special sympathy in your heart. Tell me, Andreus, who suffers?"

Andreus took a moment to think.

"The poor." Andreus answered.

"Yes indeed, the poor." Joshua said. "That's the kind of answer I'm looking for. Think about the poor, my brothers. They certainly suffer, but I say to you in all seriousness that the poor are blessed. Yes, blessed are the poor. For to them belongs the kingdom of God."

Joshua looked around at his five listeners, whose eyes were wide with attention.

"David," Joshua said, "when he looked ahead to the days of our generation—these evil times before the salvation of Israel— wrote in his Psalms: 'You evildoers frustrate the plans of the poor, but the Lord is their refuge.' (Psalm 14:6) He also wrote, 'Who is like you, Lord? You rescue the poor from those too strong for them, the poor and needy from those who rob them.' (Psalm 35:10) So be assured, brothers. By the authority of the prophets the poor shall be vindicated in the end."

"Simon! Tell me. Who suffers?"

"The hungry, Rabbi. The hungry."

"Yes," Joshua said. "That's correct. But I say, blessed are those who hunger now, for the time is near when they'll be satisfied. When David foresaw the age of righteousness, he wrote, 'The poor will eat and be satisfied.' (Psalm 22:6) and 'The Lord upholds the cause of the oppressed and gives food to the hungry.' (Psalm 146:7)

"John! Tell me, who suffers?"

"The humble and downtrodden."

Joshua sifted through the scripture stored in his mind. After a moment of reflection, he alighted on the verse he was looking for.

"Yes," Joshua said. "The humble. Blessed are the humble, for theirs is the kingdom of God. Solomon wrote in Proverbs, 'Better to be lowly in spirit along with the oppressed than to share plunder with the proud.' (Proverbs 16:19)

"Jacob! Tell me, who suffers?"

"The . . . mmm . . . the . . . those who mourn."

"Yes," Joshua said. "That reminds me of a wonderful psalm: 'Those who sow with tears will reap with songs of joy. Those who go out weeping, carrying seed to sow, will return with songs of joy, carrying sheaves with them.' (Psalm 126:5–6) It's true. Blessed are those who mourn, for they will be comforted.

"Phillip? Would you like to join us? Do you have anything to say about the suffering in the world? Will you tell us who suffers?"

Phillip sat in silence. His mind at that moment was blank. He shrugged his shoulders, embarrassed.

Simon tried to encourage Phillip and said, "Don't be meek. We're all friends here."

Phillip smiled.

"The meek." Phillip said. "We, the meek, suffer."

The men laughed.

"True," Joshua said. "You've reminded me of one of my favorite psalms, the thirty-seventh: 'A little while, and the wicked will be no more; though you look for them, they won't be found. But the meek shall inherit the earth and enjoy peace and prosperity.' (Psalm 37:10–11) So take heart, you who are meek, because you also are blessed. Blessed are the meek, for they shall inherit the earth."

Joshua looked up at the evening sky and raised his hands as if in supplication.

"Blessed are those who hunger and thirst for righteousness," Joshua said. "For they shall be filled. David said, 'Even in darkness light dawns for the upright, for those who are gracious and compassionate and righteous. Good will come to those who are generous and lend freely, who conduct their affairs with justice. Surely the righteous will never be shaken; they'll be remembered forever. They'll have no fear of bad news; their hearts are steadfast, trusting in the Lord.'" (Psalm 112:4–7)

Joshua lowered his hands and looked on his disciples.

"Andreus! Tell me. Who prospers?"

"The rich!" Andreus answered without hesitation.

The other disciples nodded in agreement.

Joshua smiled.

"The rich, of course." Joshua said. "They prosper now, but I say to you, woe to the rich, for they've already received their comfort. Their wealth won't survive the judgment. Solomon in his wisdom said, 'Don't wear yourself out to get rich; don't trust your own cleverness. Cast but a glance at riches, and they're gone, for they'll surely sprout wings and fly off to the sky like an eagle.' (Proverbs 23:4–5)

"So prepare yourselves for God's coming kingdom, where your righteousness will earn you heavenly rewards, but your wealth will be lost and useless. A psalm that I often sing in prayer, especially when I'm horrified by this unjust world, beautifully explains the folly of envying the rich: 'Don't be overawed when others grow rich, when the splendor of their houses increases; for they'll take nothing with them when they die, their splendor won't descend with them. Though while they live they count themselves blessed—and people praise the prosperous—they'll join those who've gone before them, who'll never again see the light of life. Their forms will decay in the grave, far from princely mansions. But God will redeem the upright from the realm of the dead; He'll surely take them to Himself.' (Psalm 49:15–19)

"Simon! Tell me. Who prospers?"

"The well fed." Simon answered.

Joshua laughed.

"Have you been fasting, Simon?" Joshua asked. "Well, if so, then bless you. For I say sincerely, woe to those who are well fed now, for they'll go hungry. The prophets leave no doubt about it. Solomon in Proverbs wrote, 'Don't join those who drink too much wine or gorge themselves on meat, for drunkards and gluttons become poor, and drowsiness clothes them in rags.' (Proverbs 23:20–21)

"How often have I proclaimed it to the people? The ancient prophesy of God's beloved Enoch says, 'Woe to you who devour the finest of wheat, and drink wine in large bowls, and tread underfoot the lowly with your might. Woe to you who drink water from every fountain, for suddenly you'll be consumed and wither away, because you've forsaken the fountain of life.' (Enoch 96:5–6)

"Jacob! Who prospers?"

"Rabbi, I say those who laugh at the humble and righteous— the arrogant."

"Amen, Jacob." Joshua said. "I solemnly promise that they won't be laughing on the Day of the Lord. When Jeremiah warned Jerusalem that Babylon would destroy her for her sins, he spoke the word of God to the arrogant sinners. What was true then is even truer now—now that an even bigger judgment looms: 'The Lord will set out a feast for them and make them drunk, so that they shout with laughter—then sleep forever and not awaken.' (Jeremiah 51:39) So I say woe to those who laugh now, for they'll weep and mourn!

"John! Who prospers?"

John looked around and searched his mind for an answer.

"The liars!" John said with a touch of venom in his voice. "The wicked deceivers who pretend to be holy and good, but exploit the weak and try to advance themselves with their false piety.

Those like the Herodians and the priests who support them. They seem to be prospering quite nicely, and they're much admired."

"Amen." Joshua said. "Woe to such as those that you've described so well. Such false prophets and hypocrites thrive in every wicked generation. But I say woe to those whom the world speaks well of, because that's how the false prophets were treated in past evil ages."

Joshua closed his eyes. He fell into a brief spell of concentration, and then reopened his eyes with a start.

"The Lord," Joshua said, "spoke to Micah: 'As for the prophets who lead my people astray, they proclaim peace if they have something to eat, but prepare to wage war against anyone who refuses to feed them. Therefore night will come over them, without visions, and darkness, without divination. The sun will set for the prophets, and the day will go dark for them. The seers will be ashamed and the diviners disgraced. They'll cover their faces because there's no answer from God.' (Micah 3:5–7)

"Again I say woe to those, like the false prophets, who win the admiration and praise of the wicked. But likewise, blessed are those whom this wicked generation hates and persecutes for their righteousness. Blessed you are if you're rejected and insulted for your righteousness. Rejoice, because great will be your reward in the kingdom. Rejoice, because in this same way the wicked persecuted and rejected the true prophets before you. Do you think Jeremiah was greeted with praise when he warned Jerusalem about God's wrath? Do you think he was loved by the unrepentant sinners he tried to correct? These are his own words: 'I'm ridiculed all day long; everyone mocks me. So the word of the Lord has brought me insult and reproach all day long!' (Jeremiah 20:7–8) How do you think Isaiah was treated? Did Judea thank Isaiah for preaching God's words of warning—for trying to save her? Listen to Isaiah's own words: 'I offered my back to those who beat me, my cheeks to those who pulled out my beard; I didn't hide my face from mocking and spitting. Because the Sovereign Lord helps me, I won't be disgraced. Therefore I've set my face like flint, and I know I won't be put to shame.'" (Isaiah 50:6–7)

Joshua paused and looked at his disciples.

"Go now and take your rest." Joshua said. "Think about the things I told you here when you pray and when you lie down to sleep."

Joshua walked in the direction of the springs, where he would often pray alone. The disciples shuffled into Phillip's house. On the way in Simon draped his arm around Andreus.

"Tomorrow, Andreus, we'll fish and cook together. It's not right that you do all the chores. Together we'll serve our masters. And together we'll study. Forgive me for neglecting my share."

"Thank you, Brother," Andreus said, putting his own arm around Simon. "If that's how you'd have it, you're certainly welcome. No forgiveness is necessary."

Phillip remained outside and watched Joshua walk away.

21

Ariel stood at the podium in the synagogue. On both sides of the narrow aisle that stretched from the podium to the entryway, members of his congregation sat, filling the synagogue to about half capacity. Dionysius was among them, waiting with great anticipation because Ariel had promised to reveal another of his dreams during the sermon. Dionysius fidgeted and yawned during Ariel's opening prayers and readings, and he made a listless attempt to sing along to the following hymn, but he sat up straight and perked up as soon as Ariel rolled up his scroll to indicate that his sermon was about to begin.

"God feeds the faithful." Ariel said, projecting his voice to be heard by all inside. "We know this. When Elijah was in Zarephath, in the country of Phoenicia, he met a starving widow, a victim of the drought that afflicted that land at the time. She only had a pinch of flour and a spoonful of oil left, and was going to use it to make bread as a last meal for her and her famished son.

"Elijah himself was suffering from hunger, and God had sent him to the widow; He told Elijah that this woman would provide food to him. Elijah told her to bake a small loaf for him with her remaining flour and oil. But that was all the food she had in the world, so she protested that she couldn't give any to Elijah. But Elijah told her to have faith in God, and that God would provide. So she baked a loaf for Elijah, and there was still enough flour and oil left for her to make bread for herself and her son. Elijah stayed with the widow in Zarephath many weeks, and each day she would make bread for Elijah, herself, and her son, using only that last flour and oil that she had. God made sure that the flour and oil wouldn't run out for all that time—until the drought ended. God feeds the faithful.

"And remember Elijah's successor, Elisha, who, having only enough bread to feed twenty men, gave this bread to a hundred men. Those men ate until they were full, with some left over! God feeds the faithful.

"And now let me tell you about a similar event that you may or may not remember. One afternoon, Christ Joshua and his disciples were discussing among themselves the things they'd taught that day and all the things they'd done for the people. After their busy day they were hungry and tired, so Joshua told them to come with him in the boat and go to a quiet place in the Galilean countryside to rest. But soon after they landed, many people who had recognized and followed them started to gather and crowd around them. Joshua felt sorry for the crowd that had come to see him; they seemed like so many sheep without a shepherd. So he spent some time teaching them the word.

"But it was getting to be late in the day, so his disciples told him to dismiss the people so they could return to their villages and have something to eat. But Joshua said, 'Give them something to eat yourselves.'

"The disciples protested: 'How can we feed all these people? It would take four hundred silver shekels to buy enough bread for them!'

"'How many loaves do you have?' Joshua asked.

"The disciples checked and said, 'Five—and also two fish.'

"Joshua told his disciples to have everyone sit down on the grass in groups of fifty. He took the five loaves and two fish and, looking up to heaven, gave thanks to God before breaking the loaves and fishes and giving them to the disciples to distribute to the people. The whole crowd, numbering about five thousand, ate and was satisfied, and there was food left over as well. When the disciples collected the scraps of bread and fish, they had enough to fill twelve baskets!"

The synagogue congregation was attentive, but some listeners were looking around with evident dismay. No one in the audience had ever heard this story before. Ariel continued.

"After all this happened Joshua told his disciples to get into the boat and go ahead of him to Bethsaida, while he stayed behind to dismiss the crowd and then go into the hills to pray alone. It was late at night when Joshua finished praying, and when he looked out at the lake he could see the disciples struggling in their boat against the wind.

"Joshua went out to them by walking on the surface of the lake. As he approached them, the disciples saw him walking on the water and cried out in terror because they thought he was a ghost. Joshua said, 'Don't be afraid! It's me!' and got into the boat with them. The wind calmed down and the disciples were amazed by their master. They didn't understand what was happening, just like they didn't understand what had happened with the loaves. Joshua and his disciples landed at Bethsaida at the break of dawn."

Some members of Ariel's audience began to murmur among themselves.

"Where is he getting this?" they asked each other. "I've never heard this before."

Ariel paused to allow his listeners to return to full attention, and then continued.

"After spending some time preaching to the Jews around Bethsaida, Joshua was moved by the spirit to travel to Tyre in Phoenicia. He wanted to get some quiet time for contemplation, and he hoped that the Tyrians, being Greek pagans, wouldn't recognize him and would therefore leave him alone. But many people guessed his identity from the widely circulating stories about him, so he had to contend with unwanted attention from the curious and needy public. One particular woman—she was Greek, but she had been impressed by tales of the great rabbi's powers of exorcism—knelt before him and begged him to cast out the evil spirit that haunted her young daughter.

"'I was sent to redeem the lost sheep of Israel,' Joshua said to the woman. 'Let the children eat first; it wouldn't be right to give the children's bread to the dogs.'

"'But Lord,' the woman said. 'Even the dogs under the table eat the children's crumbs.'

"Joshua was impressed by the woman's words. He told her, 'For such a reply, your daughter is healed. Your faith has rescued her.'

"When the woman returned home she found her daughter completely free of the demon. Meanwhile Joshua went back to Galilee, rejoined his disciples, and took them east of the Jordan into the territory of the Greeks. He wanted to see if they, like the Tyrian woman, had ears for the word and faith enough to accept the way.

"While preaching to the Greeks, Joshua was joined by a large crowd that stayed in his company for three days. This crowd had run out of food, so Joshua told his disciples, 'I feel for these people; they've been with me three days and have nothing to eat. They're far from home and will surely collapse on the road if I send them away hungry.'

"His disciples asked him, 'Where in this remote place can we get enough bread to feed them?'

"'How many loaves do you have?' Joshua asked them.

"'Seven,' they answered, 'and a few small fish.'

"Joshua had the crowd sit down on the grass. He took the loaves and fishes, gave thanks to God, and broke them so the disciples could distribute them to the people. The crowd of about four thousand ate until satisfied; then the disciples collected the left over scraps. They gathered up enough to fill seven baskets.

"After the crowd went home, Joshua got into the boat with his disciples and traveled to Magdala. Upon landing, they were accosted by some Pharisees who recognized Joshua. They wanted to test him, so they asked him to give them a sign from heaven.

With an exasperated sigh he said, 'Why does this generation ask for a sign? I tell you truly, no sign will be given to it.'

"As he and his disciples walked on, Joshua said, 'Disciples, beware. The people's bread is tainted by the yeast of the Pharisees and of Herod!'"

Ariel ended his sermon right there, walked to a nearby bench, and sat down. Confused looks and whispers traveled in waves through the audience.

One listener asked, "What's he talking about? What does it all mean?"

Another said, "He must be fasting, the way he can't stop talking about bread."

Ariel overheard, and right away he stood up and started to pace down the aisle, glaring with frustration at his audience. He sighed and began to rebuke them.

"Do you really not see? Can you not hear? Are your hearts too hardened to understand? When Joshua broke the five loaves to feed the five thousand, how many basketfuls of scraps were left over?"

A man in the audience answered, "Twelve."

"And when Joshua broke the seven loaves to feed the four thousand, how many basketfuls of scraps were left over?"

A few audience members chimed together, "Seven."

Ariel was indignant. He asked them, "Do you still not understand?"

They didn't.

22

When Joshua finished praying he walked back toward Phillip's house. Along the way, in a remote area outside the village, Phillip met him.

"Lord," Phillip said. "I hate to further disturb you, but I must confess to you. My undisclosed sins burn me from within."

Joshua took Phillip to a nearby area littered with several smooth, tortoise-sized rocks and sat on one of them. With an open hand he motioned a silent invitation for Phillip to sit on a rock next to him.

"Tell me what's troubling you, brother." Joshua said.

"I'm beside myself with shame, Rabbi." Phillip said after sitting down. "My hospitality to you and your friends is founded on sin."

Phillip cleared his throat and looked back toward his house.

"My house . . . it wasn't always so empty." Phillip said. "I had a wife and two daughters. But my wife was unfaithful, and I had her stoned with her accomplice. I was so possessed by rage that I avenged myself on my wife's lover's family too. His widow . . . her marriage contract allowed her to inherit his farmland. When the tax collectors came, I provided false testimony, which helped them settle the debt by taking her land. She and her children . . . they were left destitute. And I've done similar things with other people, and I've profited from it. I became such a help to the tax collectors that they invited me into their ranks. It's true. I myself became one of them!"

Joshua looked at Phillip with wide eyes and reared back in horror.

"I know, you must be disgusted with me," Phillip said. "But I confess it. I'm a tax collector. I've enriched myself by burdening innocent people with unfair and excessive taxes. I've helped Herod rob Galilee, while grabbing a sizeable portion of the spoils for myself. That's how I live so well. I even married off my daughters with dowries paid for by the honest people that I ripped off. Everything is paid for with the wages of my sins. So I'm destined to be among the condemned when judgment comes! Is there anything I can do to be saved? Is there any hope for me at all?"

Phillip was in tears. Joshua stood up and gazed at Phillip for a moment, thinking about what to say. The awkward silence dragged on just long enough to cause Phillip to start to tremble when Joshua at last began to speak.

"The sins you've described to me are indeed serious. If you wish to be forgiven, you'll have to sell everything you own and use the money to make restitution to those you've wronged. You just confessed to me, but have you confessed to the Lord? Have you undergone baptism?"

"No. I was too afraid to admit the extent of my iniquity. But I'll do it—I'll atone. I'll do it. There's hope then, isn't there?"

Phillip paused and looked down at his own feet, which were sandaled in fine leather.

"Oh, Rabbi," Phillip said. "How can I repay everyone I've wronged? There are so many. Perhaps there really is no hope for me."

"The road ahead will be difficult for you, but you have to take it step by step. Start by making amends with one person, and see how that goes. Maybe you'll find that it's not as difficult as it seems, and perhaps your victim will forgive you. Carry on until you've completely repented and atoned, and then commit yourself to the righteous way. But don't delay. God's wrath is near."

"Yes, Rabbi. I'll do it! There's a farmer that I cheated—he lives nearby in the country; I'll go to him first, as soon as I sell everything. Pray that I can redeem myself, Rabbi. Pray for me!"

* * *

Joshua and his four disciples remained in Seven Springs for another two weeks, proclaiming the kingdom and turning people to the righteous way. They spent the following two weeks in Capernaum, returning to minister to their followers and to gain new ones. During this time Joshua also inspired some detractors. Some people rejected Joshua's apocalyptic claims and dismissed his healings as tricks. Herod's agents, wary of Joshua's growing popularity, began to spy on his sermons and baptismal gatherings to discover if he was saying anything about Herod. For the moment they were satisfied that Joshua was a zealous but harmless religious crackpot.

During this time Phillip sold his property and prepared himself to make restitution to those Galileans he had cheated as a tax collector. He was about to go off to make amends to Tholomeus, a farmer who lived near the town of Gennesaret (two miles south of Seven Springs), when Joshua and his disciples returned. Phillip asked Joshua to go with him to Tholomeus's farm, and Joshua obliged.

Tholomeus lived in a small, four-room house with his wife and two sons near an olive orchard just outside Gennesaret. Basalt-stone walls and a wood-plank roof enclosed two bedrooms, a kitchen, and a general-purpose room that contained a table, chairs, and most of the farming equipment. A ramp behind the house led down to a basement where Tholomeus kept an ox and a donkey.

Tholomeus's eldest son, Bartholomeus, was collecting olives in a basket when Joshua and Phillip arrived. When Bartholomeus saw Phillip, he dropped the basket and ran to confront him.

"What fresh extortion do you have planned now, tax man?" Bartholomeus asked. "Is it not enough that we're on the verge of losing our orchard to your greedy gang of thieves? Find another carcass to pick over, vulture!"

Joshua raised his hands in a gesture of peace and addressed Bartholomeus.

"Fear not, friend. I bring you good news. I'm Rabbi Joshua of Nazareth, and my friend Phillip here has abandoned his old way of wickedness. He's trying to please the Lord now. Believe it! He's here to restore to you your rightful property. Phillip?"

Phillip knelt down in front of Bartholomeus.

"It's true," Phillip said. "I'm trying to atone for my sins. I've brought the money that will allow your father to pay off what I over taxed him and keep his farm. And I've added more to compensate for the wrong I've done, as the law commands. I'm sorry for the injustice I've done. Forgive me if you can."

Bartholomeus looked at Joshua and Phillip and marveled as if he were looking at two talking donkeys rather than two men.

"I . . . I don't know what to make of this," Bartholomeus said, trembling. "Swear to me. Swear to me by God that this isn't some trick!"

"I swear to you that this is no trick." Phillip said. "May God burn me up right here in front of you if I'm not serious. I pledge to be your slave if I'm being dishonest with you."

Bartholomeus stared at Phillip as if waiting to see if he would burst into flames. Phillip looked up at him and flashed a sheepish grin.

"Show me the money you brought." Bartholomeus said.

Phillip removed the sack that was hanging from his shoulder and handed it to Bartholomeus. Bartholomeus looked inside and saw what looked like hundreds of silver coins. He stood wide eyed and motionless for a moment and then looked back at the house.

"Come," he said. "My father is the one you need to settle accounts with."

Bartholomeus, still carrying the bag, walked to the house with Joshua and Phillip following. When they reached the front entrance, Bartholomeus told them to wait outside while he went in to talk to his father. After some excited discussion in the house, Bartholomeus and his brother Dan came out carrying a wooden chair with their father sitting right on it. Apparently the old man had completely lost the use of his legs. Bartholomeus's mother also came out and stood in the doorway to watch the proceedings.

"My son tells me that you men have had some kind of miraculous conversion," the old man said. "Forgive me for not letting you in, but I'm worried about what might happen to my family and our home if you turn out to be demons disguised as tax collectors."

Tholomeus laughed. Joshua shrugged and Phillip knelt down in front of the old man.

"I've sinned against God and against you, neighbor." Phillip said. "Please forgive me. This man, Rabbi Joshua, has taught me about the way of righteousness and he's helping me to earn forgiveness for my sins. I've brought you the money to pay off the unjust debts I imposed on you, plus half more to provide proper restitution as commanded in the law. I gave the money to your son. Please accept it along with my sincere apologies."

"Yes. My son showed me the silver. I accept your act of repentance."

Tholomeus looked at Joshua.

"So you're the man who drove the devil out of this tax man?" he asked.

"I teach the word of God, and Phillip chose to accept it and repent of his sins." Joshua answered. "Devils are another matter."

The old man laughed.

"Well," he said. "May God allow you to convert all of Herod's tax men as you have this one!"

"Amen," Joshua said. "The harvest is great but the workers are few."

The old man looked at Joshua and felt an irresistible urge to embrace him. Forgetting for the moment about his legs, he stood up in an instant and wobbled to Joshua to take him in his arms. Everyone gasped with astonishment.

"Praise God!" Joshua said, exulting.

"Praise God!" they all shouted as Bartholomeus, his mother, his brother, and Phillip dropped to their knees around Joshua and Tholomeus, who remained in each other's arms.

The old man's healing seemed to be a miracle. In reality, his legs had healed years before. Originally he lost the use of his legs after getting kicked by a mule when Bartholomeus was still a child. After many failed struggles to walk again, he adjusted to an immobilized life and despaired of ever again standing upright on his own. He let his legs atrophy while his sons carried him from bed to chair and back again for years, managing the farm by directing his wife and sons to carry out all the physical labor. At some point during all that time his legs healed on their own from the original injury, but by then Tholomeus had abandoned all efforts to rouse his legs enough to reawaken them. He persisted in that state of learned helplessness until that emotional day when Joshua and Phillip came to visit.

* * *

Over the next few weeks Phillip went to all the Galileans he had cheated and made restitution, sometimes traveling with Joshua and at other times going with Jacob or John. When it was all done, Joshua performed a celebratory baptism of Phillip to proclaim his new life of commitment to God. Now free of worldly possessions, Phillip traveled with Joshua's group as a helpmate and student, hoping to one day become qualified to preach the word and the kingdom like Joshua, Jacob, and John.

Meanwhile Joshua continued to preach in Gennesaret, Seven Springs, Capernaum, and the countryside between and nearby, always assisted by at least two of his disciples. Bartholomeus found time to attend a few of Joshua's sermons, and he soon became convinced that Joshua was right about the imminent judgment of the world and the glorious kingdom that awaited the righteous. After one particular sermon in Gennesaret, Bartholomeus approached Joshua to speak to him in private.

"Rabbi, you've made me a believer. I want to follow you wherever you go and learn how to live righteously so I can gain the kingdom of God."

"Bartholomeus. Blessed Bartholomeus. It's a pleasure to see you again. But what are you saying? Don't you have a farm to manage and parents to take care of?"

"Yes, but much has happened. My father died, may he rest in peace, and I inherited the farm. I work as before, but now my brother fights with me out of jealousy that I own twice his share since I'm eldest. And now new tax collectors have come to harass us. It's endless trouble over property that doesn't even matter anyway—since judgment is upon us, as you say. I renounce it all and I repent! My father's death must be a sign that it's time for me to leave worldly concerns behind. Please help me, Rabbi."

"Bartholomeus, your father's death means you and your brother have to take care of your mother. Don't you know the commandments?"

"Of course, but things would be better if I left. My brother would love to have the whole farm to himself, so he could hire laborers and be the master. And my mother . . . well . . . she'd be happy to just have me visit occasionally; she's really had enough of me. It would be peace for them and peace for me."

Joshua looked at Bartholomeus and frowned.

"This cup you're asking to drink is bitter, more than you know," Joshua said. "We wander like dogs with no home. Are you ready for that? Are you willing to be a servant to the rest of us? You'll have to study with the utmost discipline—until you can recall the word at will. Can you face the wicked and denounce sin? Will you aid and comfort the sick? Can you stay true to the way even when accosted by Herod's agents and the demons who haunt the air?"

Bartholomeus paused to think for a moment.

"I believe I can do those things," Bartholomeus said. "But I'll do whatever you think I'm fit to do. Even if I can't become a rabbi or teacher of the law, at least let me serve some use to you. It's enough for me to learn how to please my God."

Joshua thought for a moment while he paced a small piece of ground. He stopped and faced Bartholomeus.

"I don't know what to do with you," Joshua said. "But I admit that I'd like to learn what kind of man you are—and you're a believer at least. Maybe you can prove yourself useful. The harvest *is* great and the workers *are* few. You may join us, but prepare to suffer."

Bartholomeus knelt down and grasped Joshua's ankles.

"Thank you, Rabbi, thank you! I'll serve you faithfully, you'll see. I'm your dog. Just let me say goodbye to my family first."

"Bartholomeus, you need to decide here and now whom to serve. If you can't leave your old life behind then by all means go back to it, but don't try to serve two masters. If you go back, stay and forget about me. I can't have disciples with divided hearts. If you want to follow me, then prove to me right now that you can give up everything and commit. This is your first test. Choose!"

23

Dionysius was as puzzled by Ariel's sermon as the other congregants were. As soon as the synagogue service was over, Dionysius looked for Ariel to talk to him and get an explanation.

Ariel was already walking back to his house when Dionysius caught up with him. The two talked while they walked.

"Ariel! That was quite a sermon. I suppose that whole tale about Joshua feeding the crowds and walking on the water and so forth came from another dream of yours."

"You suppose correctly, Dion. Did you discern any special signs or meaning from it, or did it leave you as perplexed as the others?"

"Honestly, I'm perplexed. I mean . . . it's glorious if Lord Joshua multiplied bread like Elijah and walked on water, but anyone would think so, and your dreams always seem to carry meaning beyond the obvious. I beg you to tell me what it all means."

"Believe me, I was as confused as you are at first, right after seeing it all unfold in my dream. But after reflection, I believe I understand it finally."

"So . . . tell me."

"Well, I noticed the similarity of Joshua's loaves miracle with the food miracles of Elijah in the book of Kings, so I opened the scriptures to see if they could help me. When I reread Kings, I saw that when Elijah multiplied the flour and oil of the widow of Zarephath, it was a time of famine due to a long drought.

Later, when Elisha multiplied the oil and the loaves, the people were suffering from famine because King Ben Hadad of Aram had besieged them. I couldn't help but be reminded of the recent famines of the war: the one in Gamala and the one in Jerusalem. I soon realized that Joshua's multiplication of the loaves and fishes was a sign—a sign heralding the devastating famine that would afflict Israel as judgment neared."

"Wait. Joshua miraculously feeds multitudes and that's a sign of future famine? How so? It doesn't make sense."

"But it does, Dion. Think about it. Look at Elijah. He was a rare remnant of righteousness during the wicked days of King Ahab. God punished Israel with drought but gave Elijah the miraculous power to multiply food. Joshua had the same power, but when *he* used it, he was warning us of the famine that God would send if we rejected the way and continued in our sins. Joshua, our righteous Messiah, fed the hungry. Israel, stubbornly sinful, rejected Joshua and suffered the punishment of famine. Can you see how righteousness and sin, and feeding and starvation, are set against each other? It's what the Greeks call 'antithesis'"

Dionysius thought hard for a moment and then smiled.

"Oh, I can see it now. It does make sense. Feeding and famine... good and evil. But why two feeding miracles? Wouldn't one be enough?"

"I wondered about that too. But I think each feeding miracle has its own meaning. Look at the first one. It happened in Galilee among the Jews. Joshua broke five loaves and two fishes. I thought the five loaves might have something to do with the five loaves of consecrated bread that David took from the Temple when Saul pursued him. But it didn't fit, and I didn't get anywhere with it. But look. Five loaves and two fish. When the Romans conquered Gamala in the war, wasn't that the fifth city of the countryside around Lake Gennesasret they'd taken? Think about it."

Dionysius paused to reflect.

"No, you're wrong," Dionysius said. "The Romans first took Sepphoris, then Gabara ... then Japhia ... then ... uh ... Jotapata, then Tiberias, then Magdala, and then Gamala. That's seven."

"Yes, but Tiberias and Magdala are right on the lake, while the others are in the countryside. The countryside—where grain is grown. Grain for making bread. Tiberias and Magdala are on the lake, where they get—"

"Fish! The two fish! I get it now. Tiberias and Magdala are the two fish. You're right, Ari. Gamala was the fifth city taken from the Jews, if you look at it that way. The fifth in the countryside."

"And Gamala is where the first big famine struck. And when the Romans rampaged through the city, how many Jews died at the hands of other Jews or by suicide?"

"Five thousand. Holy shit, Ari!"

"And how many died at the hands of the Romans?"

"Four thousand!"

"And ever since, what have people said about the war?"

"For every four thousand Jews killed by the Romans, five thousand were killed by Jews."

"Right! So look at the other feeding miracle. It took place in the Decapolis, where the Greek pagans live. Joshua fed four thousand there. Now, after the destruction of Gamala, the Romans took only two more cities in the countryside: Gischala in Galilee and Jerusalem in Judea. After taking Gischala, the Romans went south to Jerusalem. On the way they took three small towns along the Mediterranean coast: first Joppa, then Jamnia, and finally, Azotus."

"A few small fish!"

"Yes. With Gischala and Jerusalem, we now have seven loaves and the coastal towns give us the fish. And Jerusalem is where the Romans achieved their final triumph against us."

"And it's where we had our worst famine."

"Of course. Now look at the other details of the dream. When Joshua fed the five thousand, there were twelve basketfuls of scraps left over."

"Twelve tribes. The Jews."

"And when Joshua fed the four thousand, there were seven basketfuls of scraps left over. Seven."

"Seven . . . uh . . . seven days?"

"Think, Dion. What city is famous for its seven hills?"

"Rome!"

"Exactly. Joshua gave a sign that war and famine were coming to punish Israel for its sins, and the Romans wouldn't be the guiltiest party in it. If the Romans killed four thousand, the Jews would outdo them by killing five thousand. For all the blame the Romans have for destroying Israel, the Jews themselves have more. The Jewish fanaticism that inspired the Zealots to war—that's the yeast of the Pharisees. The collaboration with Rome that helped the Romans ultimately destroy Israel—that's the yeast of Herod. Those errors of the Pharisees and the Herodians corrupted the nation until the 'loaf' finally rose, and Israel was served up a feast of banditry, invasion, and famine."

Dionysius slapped Ariel on the shoulder.

"Seven sons of a whore! That dream of yours was a true vision from Christ Joshua himself. How else can you explain it? How blind I was! But now I see it. The crowds sat down in groups of fifty, like the groups of fifty soldiers sent by Ahab to kill Elijah, who then brought fire from heaven onto them."

"Or the prophets persecuted by Jezebel. They hid in the cave in groups of fifty."

"And the groups of a hundred, they remind me of Roman centuries, led by centurions to attack Jerusalem. There were groups of a hundred in the vision too, weren't there?"

"I believe so. Yes."

"And that crowd in the Decapolis. They were with Joshua for three days, right? Didn't the Romans take three days to build the wall around Jerusalem that doomed the city to starvation?"

Ariel's eyes grew wide.

"You're right! Wow, Dion. You perceive things that I wasn't aware of."

"Well, the Lord is thorough when he sends a sign. Ha! Those Pharisees who met Joshua and demanded a sign—and then Joshua told them, 'You'll have no sign.' Hilarious! Blind Pharisees! The irony is beautiful."

Ariel and Dionysius had made it to Ariel's house.

"Good night, Ari," Dionysius said. "I must get home. But I'm meeting with you again tomorrow, here at your house. We still have to discuss the faithful Phoenician woman and Joshua walking on the water."

"No. Forget that, Dion. Those signs are simple to explain and I'll do so right now, before you leave, and you won't have to bother me later."

"All right then. By all means, enlighten me."

"By walking on the water, Joshua showed that he had the same power over water that Moses and Elijah had. The disciples struggling against the wind in the middle of the lake is a sign of the turmoil they would suffer after their master's death. And their terrified reaction when mistaking Joshua for a ghost is a sign of the opposition they would face in those days, after the resurrection, when the hard-hearted non-believers would accuse them of merely seeing Joshua's ghost.

"Now, as far as the Phoenician woman is concerned, you surely understand, don't you? She shows that Gentiles, as well as Jews, can prove their worthiness for the kingdom if they have strong faith in the Lord.

"There. That's all I have to say. Go home now and get some rest."

24

Joshua decided that it was time he and his six companions went to Magdala to preach the word. He gathered his party together and revealed his plan.

"Brothers, we've done well in the villages, persuading people to follow the way, but it's time we took our ministry to Magdala—the big city. But I must warn you of a few things first. Magdala is heavily populated—some forty thousand souls—and prosperous. That means many temptations and traps await us. Be on your guard for tricksters, thieves, and prostitutes. They'll try to take advantage of your simplicity and good will; they only want to hurt you and rob you.

"Also, where there's money, Herod's agents follow, so there will be many more of them than you're accustomed to seeing. Here in the countryside the tax collectors hunt easy prey—the illiterate and the unlearned—the simple, honest, virtuous people of the land who readily give in to legal deception and exaggerated threats. We know this all too well from experience. But in the city many people are sophisticated, educated, and wealthy. To rob such people, Herod's men resort to more brutal tactics: torture, kidnapping, murder—nothing is too criminal or outrageous for them in their pursuit of unjust gain. These hard-hearted men will be everywhere, and they'll notice any gatherings where Herod is criticized. So tread carefully. Focus your efforts on bringing people to the Lord and be discreet when denouncing Herod.

"There will also be proud and arrogant people who'll look down on us for being poor and simple. They'll reject us and our message because they care too much for their pleasures and possessions. Don't despair over them; we'll just go on convincing everyone we can—those that have ears to hear. Not every seed sown grows to fruition. The word of God—it's like seed sown in a field. Yes. I have a parable for it. Let me share it with you."

Joshua stretched out his arms and projected his voice as if giving a sermon.

"What's it like to preach the word? It's like a farmer who goes out to sow his seed. He scatters the seeds, and some fall along the path, where birds come to eat it. That's what happens when the word you preach reaches those who walk the wayward, open road. They're unrepentant sinners who have no regard for God, so Satan comes and easily takes the word away from them before they even notice.

"Other seeds scatter onto the rocky and shallow soil, where they spring up quickly but just as quickly wither in the sun because their roots barely cling to the topsoil. Such are those who hear the word gladly at first, but as soon as they encounter the hardships of following the way, they give up and go back to their sins and comforts.

"Some seeds fall into the thorny brush, which tangles and strangles the seedlings so they fail to sprout grain. They're like those who hear the word and believe, but because they're too occupied with their wealth and their worries over how to best their neighbors, they don't allow the word to produce any fruit.

"Finally, some seeds fall into deep, rich soil, where they grow into a good crop that multiplies fifty or a hundred fold. Such are those who hear the word, believe it, and put it into practice. They produce a crop of goodness for themselves and the world that multiplies fifty or a hundred times what was sown."

Joshua stopped speaking and the disciples were silent. Mild breezes caressed the grass and swayed the tree branches as if to confirm to the disciples that nature herself approved of Joshua's words.

"Take these teachings of mine to heart." Joshua said. "Come. Let's prepare for the journey to Magdala."

* * *

Joshua's party took Simon and Andreus's boat to travel to Magdala. On the way Simon and Andreus did some fishing and caught enough to feed the whole group. About halfway from completing their journey, they all agreed to land ashore to cook and enjoy their meal.

Joshua and his companions sat down in a shady grove of laurel and oak trees. Simon and Andreus prepared the fire for cooking the day's catch, while Phillip and Bartholomeus laid out a basket of bread and a basket filled with pomegranates. When Phillip caught the scent of the roasting fish, his appetite awakened and he began to think about the pleasures of food. He turned to talk to Bartholomeus.

"It's strange to me that we have to be taught what to eat and what not to eat," Phillip said. "If God wants us to hold certain foods detestable, why didn't He just make them smell and taste awful? When I'm in Scythopolis or some other pagan town, and the people are cooking their pigs and rabbits and snakes, am I perverse for enjoying the smell? Why must the forbidden and unclean be so tempting? And what is it about those foods that's so dangerous? The pagans seem to eat them without harm to themselves."

"It's not that the forbidden foods are bad for you," Bartholomeus answered. "Bad for your body, that is. It's that they're bad for the people as a whole. If Moses and the tribes had raised pigs, being in the desert as they were, they would have all died from drought because pigs need tons of water to wallow in everyday; without it they can't survive. That's why the pagan pig farmers have to be near rich springs or large lakes. Without them, the pigs would use up all their water.

"And can you imagine if the people took up a taste for rabbits? Put a few rabbits on your farm and soon you'll have thousands of them eating up all the crops! And snakes? If snakes become acceptable at the table, people will seek them out and bring them home. But who really knows which snakes are poisonous or not?

"Pagans who do these things seem to do fine, but the more they do them, the quicker they die out as a people. That's why the pagan peoples never survive over the long run—that and their other sins—because they do things that eventually bring famine or sickness or something else to the whole tribe and everyone dies. It happened to the Jebusites, the Hittites, the Sodomites, and to every nation except ours, because God knows what's good for us. God gave us a law that allowed our people to live, as long as we followed it. But of course now that the end times are here, even many Jews, especially the rich and powerful, neglect the law and live like the pagans, just as the prophets predicted they would. Those apostates will share the fate of the pagans."

Before Phillip could respond, Joshua approached them.

"Bartolo," Joshua said. "I didn't realize you had so much to say about the dietary laws. You understand them well. Here, before we eat, is a perfect time for a lesson on such things. Brothers! Gather around!"

The disciples encircled Joshua, sat, and focused their attention on him.

"Brothers," Joshua said. "We're privileged to be Jews. Because of the unshakeable faithfulness of Abraham, the loyalty of his children, and the righteousness of Moses, God rewarded us with His law, a law that reveals secrets to us that are denied the pagans. Consider the dietary laws. God told us what to eat and what not to eat—not to deprive us, but to protect us. Thanks to God's merciful law, we shun the pig: a foul and gluttonous beast that devours everything, including carcasses and turds. Thus we're spared the dangers and sicknesses that the pagans, who love their pork, sooner or later succumb to. Likewise we avoid the shellfish, reptiles, and insects. We're blessed to know the difference between what's harmful for us and what's beneficial.

"Now, perhaps you think that we need not concern ourselves with these matters, now that the cataclysmic judgment is near. After all, what's a little sickness when God is about to spill the blood of nations? There's merit to this argument, but I say keep kosher. Do it, if for no other reason than to show respect to your Most High God. Why test the Lord and invite sickness and trouble if you can avoid it? If you start eating forbidden foods, you may get away unharmed, but you'll have to go all the way to the Temple in Jerusalem to make the appropriate sacrifices and atone for your transgression, and we don't have time for that! So if you want to follow me and participate in my mission, keep kosher.

"Nonetheless we must admit that there are far weightier matters at hand. The fire of judgment is coming for all the nations, Israel included. But violations of kashrut are the least of the reasons for it. You know the law; eating forbidden food is not a capital offense—we don't stone a man for it. But there are other, much more serious kinds of impurity that defile our nation. How can I explain this?"

Joshua paused a moment to think and then resumed his lesson.

"When I lived with my master John the Baptist, may the Lord save and protect him, I ate a diet strictly within the bounds of the Torah. In fact I was well inside the line of the law, having taken on John's diet of nothing but fruit, honey, and locusts. How holy my eating was! But imagine my surprise—my shit still stank like shit!"

The disciples laughed, except Simon, who only flashed an awkward grimace. When the laughter subsided, Joshua continued.

"Have any of you taken into your body anything as filthy and vile as some of the things that come out of your body? Never! Even the cleanest, most pure foods to be found in all the Lord's bounty become, when taken into the body, horrendously polluted and degraded into shit for the sewer. Ponder this. It's the nature of our worldly flesh to become unclean—to decay—to die. It can't be helped.

"But some try anyway. My master John told me about his days in Jerusalem, about the Pharisees there who study and interpret the law. Those men know the law well, but they add their own regulations to it to satisfy an obsession with external purity. 'Wash your hands before you eat,' they say. 'Plates are clean, cups are unclean,' they say. 'Food caught in the shade of an idol is unclean,' they say. They insist on following a hundred such rules, none of which are in the law. What do they gain for all their extra troubles? Well, they're clean—supremely clean—on the outside! They wash themselves so much they have the appearance of cleanliness, and appearance seems to be what matters most in our corrupt age. But I assure you that none of us will ever wash the stink off our shit!

"Listen. The uncleanness that comes out from within is much worse than any impurity that comes in from without. It's what comes out of a person that truly defiles them. It's the evil a man harbors within—his hate, lust, arrogance, greed, and his desire to steal, fornicate, and kill—these make a man unclean indeed, unclean from deep within where things aren't so easily or visibly washed away. So be clean on the inside."

Joshua took a quick drink from his water skin and then picked up a pomegranate from the basket.

"Which pomegranate would you rather eat?" Joshua asked. "The one with a dirty and bruised shell but fresh kernels inside, or the one with a clean shell but rotten kernels inside? Which cup would you rather drink, the one that's clean only on the inside, or the one that's clean only on the outside?

"God is coming to gather His harvest. He'll collect the good fruit and throw out the bad. The skin of even the good fruit will be discarded in the end, whether it's clean or not. The fruit within is what matters. Do you think God will accept rotten fruit just because it's properly washed?

"Yes, the Torah has been life for Israel. And now Judea forsakes the law and God prepares the Day of Wrath for her. The Pharisees teach a perversion of the law, a tradition of outer cleanliness to hide the rotten godlessness within. But I teach you: be faithful to the law—the true law. Obey the commandments, shun sin, trust God, love one another—and you'll be clean inside. And if you're clean on the inside, how great your cleanliness will be!"

25

Ariel and Dionysius sat on the couch in Ariel's study, both of them tipsy from wine.

"Joshua, Joshua, Joshua," Ariel chanted in his boredom. "Dion, do you ever worry that we're wrong about Joshua? That we've been misled, and Joshua isn't the Messiah after all?"

"What are you talking about? Has the wine put you in a hopeless mood? You know I'm faithful to the end. How can you doubt after all your visions?"

"I don't doubt. I'm asking if you ever do. But you've answered me. I'm just worried about all the brothers and sisters who *are* losing faith because of what's happened with the Romans. We're losing our flock, Dion. We need to do something.

"Listen to this—today I ran into some more Pharisees from Jerusalem. They taunted me. 'Where's your Joshua?' they asked me. 'Where's your king? The Temple's destroyed, Jerusalem's in ruins, and the people are enslaved or dead. Is this the kingdom your Christ promised?' I'm sick of arguing with those hypocrites. *They* brought all this ruin on us. They're the ones who supported the Zealots. They were the ones who turned the people against the way."

"Amen to that, brother," Dionysius said, lifting his cup in the air.

"Dion, listen. I've made a decision. I'm going to Jerusalem. If I'm going to make sense of all these catastrophes, I need to see the ruin with my own eyes. Maybe if I prostrate myself in the holiest place on earth, God will clarify everything for me, or at least send me more signs to help me understand things. So I'm going to ask Chief Elder Evodius to grant me leave. He should have no trouble adjusting to my brief absence, given all the recent desertions from the churches. Congregations throughout the city are half what they used to be."

"Jerusalem? That's a dangerous trip you're planning, Ari. I'll go with you. We'll be safer together than you'd be alone. I'm not afraid. My life is in God's hands. Yes. Until the bitter end!"

"Are you sure, Dion? We'll have to take a ship down south—at least to Joppa."

"Joppa! There's nothing but Romans there."

"Azotus, then. We'll have to go all the way to Azotus and then straight east to Jerusalem. We'll keep our heads down and draw absolutely no attention to ourselves. The Romans won't know we're there."

"Joshua save us! Ship travel? What about storms? Winter's barely over. Remember that huge storm that hit Joppa during the war? That night when all those rebels sailed out to sea to avoid Vespasian's ground troops? I heard that the storm tossed all those ships into each other—or into the rocks along the shore. Thousands of men drowned!"

"Calm down, Dion. You said you were in God's hands to the bitter end, remember? There won't be any storms like that, and even if there were, God will protect us. Don't you remember how Joshua used to command the storms to still themselves? God is greater than the sea. Besides, it will be safer on the sea than on land where bandits and Romans roam. If you really aren't as courageous as you claim, then stay in Antioch. But I'm going. With God's protection and Joshua's guidance I'm going!"

26

Magdala was known by the Greeks as Tarichea, which meant "dried fish," in honor of its largest and most famous industry. For the Jews, who made up the overwhelming majority of the city's population, "Magdala" was a shortened, Aramaic version of the Hebrew name Migdal Nunayah, which meant "citadel of fish." Along the lakeshore there were scores of docks of various sizes, serving hundreds of boats dedicated to catching fish from the Sea of Galilee or transporting dried fish to all the other towns around it. Just inland from the docks were the massive warehouses where fish were smoked, salted, and crated for transport. In addition to fish, Magdala exported enough other goods, especially dyed textiles and agricultural produce, to make it a major commercial port.

As they walked the Magdalene streets and learned the layout of the city, Joshua and his companions came across a neighborhood of grand complexes that housed some of the wealthier citizens. The disciples gazed upon the splendid homes of multiple floors, large courtyards, and tiled roofs as busy urbanites rushed by them.

Joshua halted when he heard a woman screaming from one of the nearby houses. He heard a sporadic sequence of anguished cries and angry yelling, clear and audible over the ordinary street noise. Joshua was amazed that the people around there seemed to take no notice of the screams. He approached a middle-aged man standing nearby.

"Shalom, lord," Joshua said. "Could you please tell me what all the raving is about, and why nobody's doing anything about it?"

"Shalom," the man answered with a smile. "Pay no mind to it, friend. That's just Mary, one of the rich girls, having one of her fits. She does it all the time. She's haunted. We're all used to it around here."

Joshua perked up and looked at his companions.

"Demons. I know it," he said.

Joshua's followers looked around and tried to hide the trepidation that came over them.

"Do you know, friend, this girl, her family?" Joshua asked the man.

"Yes."

"Then go! Tell them that Rabbi Joshua the Nazarene is here. Tell them I'm an exorcist. I and my companions can help this girl."

The man looked over Joshua and his party, and then shrugged as if incredulous. Without hurrying he walked to Mary's house and knocked on the door. A young man opened the door and the older man informed him of Joshua's offer. The young man demanded to be taken to Joshua, and the old man led him to the street.

"You're Rabbi Joshua of Nazareth?" the young man asked.

"Yes. I am him."

"I'm called Matheus son of Nathan. My sister Mary is possessed by an evil spirit. Come help her!"

Matheus led Joshua into his house, up the stairs to the second floor, and into the room where Mary was. The disciples followed but stayed in the entryway on the first floor.

Mary, a young woman modestly dressed in the colored linen of the wealthy merchant class, had both hands tied together with rope at a wooden bed post. She stretched herself lengthwise along a rug on the floor, pulling on the rope as if trying to break it. She twisted her body in a kind of rhythm, rotating her hips clockwise and counterclockwise while her legs, wrapped around each other, slapped and scraped the rug like the tail of an out-of-water fish suffering its last moments of life. She growled behind gritted teeth and a tense, angry face that betrayed an uncommon beauty in spite of the frightening contortions. At times she shouted loud, wordless vocalizations and kicked her feet in sudden, violent spasms. Mary's mother, Salome, kneeled close by, praying and attempting to comfort Mary with gentle caresses and reassuring words.

When Joshua entered the room, Mary recoiled and Salome stood up. Matheus introduced Joshua to his mother and she kneeled in supplication before him.

"By all that's holy, Rabbi, please heal my daughter." Salome said. "In the name of God, save her!"

"Have faith, sister," Joshua said. "Matheus, go get Jacob and John to help me, and bring me a jug of water."

Jacob and John ran to Joshua's side, with Matheus following with a jug full of cool drinking water. Meanwhile the other disciples crept up the stairs, crouched near the door, and leaned their heads in to observe the proceedings. Matheus gave the jug to Joshua, who tried to place it near himself on the floor until Mary kicked at it and almost knocked it out of Joshua's hands. Joshua ordered Jacob and John to hold down Mary's feet; each kneeled on a side of her and they wrestled her feet together and held them firm against the floor, Jacob holding the feet and John holding the ankles. Mary bucked her body in protest, arching her back and punctuating her angry screams with violent thrusts of her pelvis.

Joshua approached Mary and looked into her eyes with an intense, fearless gaze.

"Foul spirit!" he shouted. "You can't hide in this woman! God uncovers all! Come out of her!"

Mary growled and writhed, twisting and contorting herself against Jacob and John's efforts to restrain her.

"Recite with me," Joshua said to Jacob and John. He began to recite Psalm three, and Jacob and John joined him.

"Lord, how many are my foes! How many rise up against me! Many are saying of me, 'God won't come to the rescue.'" (Psalm 3:1–2)

At the third verse Matheus and Salome joined the recital.

"But you, Lord, are a shield around me, my glory, the One who lifts my head high. I call out to the Lord, and He answers me from his holy mountain. I lie down and sleep; I wake again, because the Lord sustains me. I won't fear though tens of thousands assail me on every side. Arise, Lord! Deliver me, my God! Strike all my enemies on the jaw; break the teeth of the wicked. From the Lord comes deliverance." (Psalm 3:3-8)

As they recited the psalm, Mary continued her tortuous undulations and repeated "rabbi, rabbi" over and over in a low groan while looking in every direction and chattering her teeth. When the psalm ended she began to growl and chant, "Baal Zebub, Baal Zebub, Baal Zebub . . ."

"Do you think I'm impressed by that name?" Joshua shouted. "I know that's not your name! No demon would surrender their true name so easily. I command you, in the name of God Most High, tell me your true name!"

Mary shook and squirmed. She groaned and grunted. Then she raised her voice and barked, "Baal . . . Baal Shechazaz . . . Baal Shechazen . . . Baal Azazeschechazen!"

"Liar!" Joshua shouted. "You're spouting gibberish! You won't confuse me! I will call you False Baal, because that's what you are—a false, lying spirit! In the name of God Most High, Lord of all that's in heaven, on the earth, and under the earth, release this woman! Leave her!"

On that command Joshua sprinkled some water on Mary's face. She let out a startled, high-pitched scream, which she sustained for several seconds. She felt the water drip down her face: at first itching, then, as it made its way to the sensitive tissue near her nostrils and lips, intense and agitating. She unleashed another scream, high pitched at first but falling low at the end, as she twisted herself and pulled at the rope. In a few moments the irritation from the water subsided and she calmed her exertions somewhat.

Noticing the minor change in Mary's demeanor, Joshua tried to bypass the demon and make a direct appeal to Mary herself.

"Mary, if you have ears to hear, listen! All who truly repent and put their complete trust in the Lord will have their sins forgiven and can't be dominated by any evil. God can't be conquered! Have faith and let God release you from this unclean spirit!"

Mary's writhing slowed, and she rocked her body back and forth with reduced violence. Her screaming stopped, replaced by steady seething and agitated exhalations that, although disturbing, were more tranquil than her earlier, more furious vocal assaults. Joshua came closer and looked into her eyes.

"Foul spirit! False Baal!" Joshua shouted. "You're no match for the Almighty Lord God! You have no right to oppress this woman by entering her! You have nowhere to go but out!"

Joshua grabbed the sides of her head and glared into her eyes with an intensity that was both tender and terrible. He could feel the muscles of her neck relax. Her countenance lost its raging fury and calmed to a bland expression of sweaty fatigue.

In a low and imperious tone Joshua commanded the demon: "Leave this woman! Leave this woman! Leave this woman!"

Jacob and John joined the chant: "Leave this woman! Leave this woman! Leave this woman!"

Matheus, Salome, and the four disciples watching at the door joined the chant: "Leave this woman! Leave this woman! Leave this woman!"

Mary's body went limp. Joshua signaled to Matheus to go to the rope binding Mary's hands and get ready to untie her. The others continued to chant until Joshua signaled them to stop.

"Matheus!" Joshua shouted. "On my command you will unbind your sister, and you, foul spirit, will also unbind her, and never enter her again! If you ever come near her again, all of God's curses will be upon you, and fiery chains will hold you in the abyss forever! In the name of the Most High God, Lord of all creation, unbind her!"

Matheus untied the rope, Jacob and John released their hold, and Mary collapsed on the rug. At first she didn't move at all, but in a moment she curled up and abandoned herself to convulsive sobbing. Matthew and Salome embraced her and rocked her as they might a young child.

"It's over, Mary," Matheus whispered into her ear. "You're free. Rest and be still now. You're free."

"Jacob, John," Joshua said. "Recite Psalm ninety-one, second half."

Jacob and John, their voices solemn, obeyed.

"If you say, 'The Lord is my refuge,' and you make the Most High your dwelling, no harm will overtake you, no disaster will come near your tent. For He'll command His angels concerning you to guard you in all your ways; they'll lift you up in their hands, so that you won't strike your foot against a stone. You'll tread on the lion and the cobra; you'll trample on the great lion and the serpent. 'Because they love me,' says the Lord, 'I'll rescue them; I'll protect them, for they acknowledge my name. They'll call on me, and I'll answer them; I'll be with them in trouble, I'll deliver them and honor them. With long life I'll satisfy them and show them my salvation.'" (Psalm 91:9–16)

Matheus, Salome, the disciples—all were amazed by what they had witnessed. Matheus and Salome walked Mary into another room and laid her onto a bed, where she fell asleep in an instant. Matheus and Salome returned to Joshua, showered him with profuse thanks, and offered him and his disciples lodging in their home for as long as they needed.

* * *

Mary's demonic fits had started a while after suffering sexual abuse at the hands of her stepfather, Lamech. The abuse traumatized her, and she felt powerless to do anything about it. If she dared accuse the perpetrator, she would either be disbelieved or judged a guilty accomplice to the "fornication," which would then require her to suffer the mandatory death by stoning. Her bottled-up rage and frustration developed into a psychosomatic distress that felt to her like the invasion of an unclean spirit, which in her darker moments drove her to unleash the furious and bizarre fits that so disturbed the household.

Mary's ferocious, infernal ravings frightened Lamech enough to keep him away from her, and they elicited a new kind of sympathetic attention from Salome and Matheus that they had never shown her before which, in the secret recesses of her subconscious mind, comforted her. Whenever a possession episode provided a satisfactory level of catharsis for her inner turmoil, Mary would revert to her normal behavior and Salome would thank God that the demon had left her alone for the time being.

Meeting Joshua, however, motivated Mary to cast her demons forever from her mind. In his performance of the exorcism, Joshua exhibited a commanding and compassionate charisma that held Mary spellbound. His words, his voice, and his confidence projected a power of suggestion that she could not resist. Surrendering to Joshua's will gave her a strange but welcome feeling of liberation. In Joshua Mary saw a man of high purpose, driven by the Lord to rescue the world from itself. The concerns of her previous life now seemed trivial, and she became determined to learn all she could from the great rabbi.

As Joshua got to know his new hosts, he learned that Matheus and Mary were well educated. Both could read Aramaic and were knowledgeable of scripture. Matheus could write in Aramaic and also read and write a little in Greek, all skills that eluded even Joshua. Mary and Matheus attended many of Joshua's sermons and baptismal events throughout Magdala, and they both were inspired to become his disciples. Joshua put them through his usual vetting and interrogations, and they had no trouble proving themselves qualified to take on discipleship.

* * *

The large population of Magdala was a great harvest of souls for Joshua and his followers to bless with the news of God's imminent wrath and the saving wisdom of the word and the way. Due to the enormity of the task, Joshua and his disciples remained in Magdala for several months. During this time the newer members of Joshua's party learned from their more experienced companions: those who had mastery of the scriptures taught the less learned whatever they lacked; veteran preachers trained the novices; the shrewd taught the innocent how to assess the trustworthiness of strangers; the best fishermen and cooks taught their skills to the others; and the three former disciples of John the Baptist shared their methods of baptism and healing.

The people of Magdala brought several schizophrenic and otherwise mentally disturbed people, who were all assumed to be possessed by evil spirits, to Joshua for healing. Joshua's attempts at exorcism were dramatic performances, delivered with a forceful, psychologically suggestive, and commanding authority that was irresistibly hypnotic, and which distracted the victim from his or her hallucinations. They were often successful, or at least appeared to be so to observers. The fact that he did not charge any money for his services, and seemed interested only in fighting the forces of evil, gave Joshua an aura of credibility that the professional exorcists could only dream of achieving.

One day, after impressing a Magdalene crowd by freeing a man from a demon, Joshua encountered hostile opposition from a well-known exorcist for hire named Avaran who resented Joshua's popularity.

"It's by Baal-Zebub, prince of the demons, that he drives out demons!" Avaran shouted. "He's a sorcerer!"

Joshua turned to Matheus, who along with Jacob was with him at that time, and asked, "Who's this who accuses me?"

"It's Avaran, a professional healer. He makes good money curing people of various ills and evils," Matheus answered.

Joshua confronted Avaran.

"Avaran! You're gravely mistaken. How is it possible that I cast out demons with the power of the king of demons? Then Satan casts out Satan, and Satan is at war with himself. How does that make any sense? Satan invades people and then sends me to undo his work? How wonderful! Satan thus divided against himself will surely destroy himself and put you out of business."

The crowd laughed, but Avaran countered.

"No! That's not what I'm saying. You conjure demons to enter people so you can send them out again and look like a healer. You're a sorcerer!"

"That's a clever idea," Joshua said. "How interesting that it comes from the man who has every reason to employ such a scheme: the man who heals for money! Why should I pretend to be a healer if I gain nothing from it? My only scheme is to bring people the word of God and the way of righteousness. That's a strange strategy for a devil. Jacob!"

"Yes, Rabbi?"

"Tell me what you think. Who's the more credible healer—the one who heals to show people the power and mercy of God, or the one who heals to show his own power and profit from it? Which does the work of God and which does the work of Satan?"

"Isn't it obvious, Rabbi? He who heals without seeking gain is God's agent. He who heals for gain is suspect."

Many in the crowd nodded in agreement. Joshua returned his attention to Avaran.

"Avaran! I tell you in all seriousness that your blasphemy is the most brazen I've ever witnessed. For one might be forgiven for blaspheming against the unseen and unknown Father who dwells in the heaven beyond the firmament and is unreachable by mortal flesh. But to witness with one's own eyes the healing mercy of God, the glory of the Most High made manifest in our world, and to still call it Satan—that's an eternal blasphemy, for then you reject God after He's revealed Himself to you. What kind of faith is that? If God's goodness and glory are Satan to you, then who's your god? Consider well whom you serve!"

The crowd was hushed as it hung on Joshua's words. When Joshua paused, Jacob broke the silence. He pointed at Avaran and shouted, "Out Satan!"

Others in the audience copied Jacob's gesture and joined him when he repeated, "Out Satan!" Soon the whole crowd was jeering at Avaran and chanting, "Out Satan!" Had Avaran not run away at that moment, some in the crowd would have grabbed him, taken him out of town, and stoned him to death.

27

Ariel and Dionysius managed to buy their way onto a large merchant ship that had Azotus as a stop. The trip was smooth: no storms and no trouble on board. When they disembarked at the port, they changed their clothes to make themselves look like wandering scavengers. They reasoned that they would appear too impoverished and insignificant to arouse the interest of bandits or soldiers. As a further precaution they would stay off main roads as much as possible, choosing instead to skulk through abandoned fields and orchards, or to sneak through desolate wilderness likely to be shunned by even the roughest of bandits. All the stealth and deviation from the easier roads meant a slower than normal journey, but they made the thirty-five mile trip to Jerusalem in five days, eating the fruits of fig, olive, and date palm trees along the way.

They were on a hill a half mile west of Jerusalem when they first caught sight of the city. Some of the western protective wall was still standing, and in front of it an entire legion of Roman soldiers was camped. They decided that the safest thing to do would be to sneak over to the hills south of city, travel behind them to stay out of view, and then climb up the eastern hills until they reached the Mount of Olives, where they would have an excellent view of the whole city.

The valleys behind the southern hills were littered with dirt mounds piled onto mass graves, trenches left over from the war, and the crumpled wreckage of catapults, ballistae, and other, less identifiable engines of battle. This detritus provided plenty of places for Ariel and Dionysius to hide whenever they spied any wayward Roman soldiers on patrol.

When they reached the Mount of Olives, they found some remnants of an abandoned Roman camp but no people, Roman or otherwise. Dionysius breathed a deep sigh and admired the spring-fresh, verdant slopes, which were colored with patches of wild flowers and crowded with a multitude of olive trees.

"This is it, Ari. The very site of our Lord's passion. Sacred ground!"

Ariel, searching among the trees for a hidden place that could provide a complete view of the city, failed to hear Dionysius. Dionysius rushed up behind him and tried to get his attention.

"Hey Ari! Ari!"

"What?"

"Do you think that when Christ Joshua was on his way to Jerusalem with his disciples . . . that . . . that he knew he would be killed—that he was going to be sacrificed for our sins?"

"Of course. He's the Messiah, isn't he?"

Ariel looked to the west and caught a view of the entire ruin of Jerusalem. He pointed to show Dionysius where to look, and they both gazed upon the once great city.

The Temple, located in the northeast and once the most prominent feature in the skyline, was an uneven shambles of broken stone and burnt cedar. The only wall around the Temple Mount still standing was the western one, an anomaly of intact rectitude amid the surrounding devastation, like an undisturbed tombstone that marks the violently ransacked grave of a despised monarch. Just northwest of the Temple Mount were the crumbled remains of the North Quarter, its buildings reduced to rubble and its Fortress Antonia a sad stump of spent charcoal. The New City, or "Bezetha," which lay beyond the destroyed north wall of the North Quarter, was a vast expanse of ashen wasteland. Southwest of the Temple Mount, the empty husks of burned and broken mansions of the rich and the royal marked the upper city, where only three of Herod's towers, and the city wall connected to them, remained intact, providing the backdrop to the camp of the Roman legion left to guard conquered Jerusalem. East of the hills of the upper city lay the valley of the lower city, once the neighborhood of Jerusalem's poor, and now a deserted basin of pulverized stone covering the forgotten dead bodies of thousands of victims of war and famine.

Ariel and Dionysius were both moved to tears at the sight. They prostrated themselves as if beseeching God's mercy, and Ariel, as if in mourning, recited Psalm seventy-nine.

"Oh God, the nations have invaded your inheritance; they've defiled your holy Temple, they've reduced Jerusalem to rubble. They've left the dead bodies of your servants as food for the birds of the sky, the flesh of your own people for the animals of the wild. They've poured out blood like water all around Jerusalem, and there's no one to bury the dead. We're objects of contempt to our neighbors, of scorn and derision to those around us. How long, Lord? Will you be angry forever? How long will your jealousy burn like fire? Pour out your wrath on the nations that don't acknowledge you, on the kingdoms that don't call on your name; for they've devoured Jacob and devastated his homeland. Don't hold against us the sins of past generations; may your mercy come quickly to meet us, for we're in desperate need. Help us, God our Savior, for the glory of your name; deliver us and forgive our sins for your name's sake. Why should the nations say, 'Where is their God?'" (Psalm 79:1–10)

Ariel and Dionysius were still face down in their pose of supplication when they felt the sharp pressure of leather shin guards in their backs. Two Roman soldiers had crept up to them during the prayer and were now on top of them. The soldiers grabbed the hands of their captives, pinned them behind their prone backs, and locked each pair of wrists into iron shackles. The soldiers then yanked their prisoners up onto their feet and held them in place as three more soldiers appeared. One of the three wore a helmet and armor that indicated his rank of decurion.

"Search them," the decurion ordered his two companions in Greek.

The two new arrivals obeyed, patting down Ariel and Dionysius while the original two soldiers held them by the shoulders.

"Nothing!" each soldier reported, spitting in disappointment after completing the search.

"Then take them to General Rufus," the decurion ordered. "You know the procedure."

"We ought to just kill these Jews here," one soldier said. "They don't have money and they're too weak to be useful as slaves."

"Be that as it may," the decurion said, "all such decisions have to get the general's approval first."

"He doesn't have to know," the soldier said. "Who cares about a couple of worthless Jews?"

"You'll follow your orders!" the decurion snapped. "All captured Jews go through Rufus. He decides their fate."

The soldier submitted and joined the others as they proceeded to shackle their captives' feet, chaining Dionysius's right foot to Ariel's left foot.

"March Jews!" one of the soldiers shouted.

Ariel and Dionysius, terrified, staggered forward as two soldiers walked behind each of them and goaded them with strikes from the flat sides of their swords any time they failed to keep pace. The soldiers marched them westwards, down into the Kedron valley, and then into the east end of Jerusalem south of the Temple Mount. As they marched through the ruined city, their eyes staring straight ahead, they witnessed up close the dire state of their beloved capital. Inside the city they could smell the stale stench of death and defeat, a dusty aroma of burnt and rotten flesh, charred wood, chalky limestone dust, and the excrement of scavenging animals. Out of the corners of their eyes they could detect piles of human bones of every type filling pits or ruined house foundations. Where there had once been homes and streets full of activity there was now just a crushed landscape of rocky debris, an immense, God-forsaken graveyard.

Halfway through their march through Jerusalem they began ascending the hills of the upper city, where the smells were the same, but stronger and more sickening. Ariel and Dionysius glanced around them at the broken stone shells that were once mansions—they were now the dilapidated tombs of citizens who died unable to escape the doomed metropolis. In some of the less decrepit domicile ruins they glimpsed charred human skeletons piled high like lumber. Soon they reached the still-standing trio of towers that Herod the Great had built to honor, respectively, his wife Mariamne, his brother Phasaelus, and his friend Hippicus. They marched past the towers, exited the western reaches of the city, and entered the Roman camp outside the west wall.

At the center of the camp stood a newly built wooden fort with palisade walls, outer cloisters topped by sloping roofs, and an iron-hinged wooden gate in the middle of the front façade. Ariel and Dionysius were marched to the gate, where a guard looked them over before opening the gate to allow the captives and captors through. Ariel and Dionysius got a quick look at some of the inside of the fort—stables, grain stores, busy iron workers, soldiers training for battle—when a tall, burly officer in impressive armor and fancy military regalia approached.

"Hail Caesar!" the soldiers said as they gave the straight-armed salute.

"Hail Caesar," the officer answered with raised hand.

"General Rufus, we caught these Jews sneaking around the Mount of Olives."

"Very well, soldier," Rufus said, looking over the captives. "Do you speak Greek?"

"Yes," Ariel answered.

"Who are you?" Rufus asked. "And what are you doing in Jerusalem?"

Although Dionysius knew Greek, Ariel did all the talking for the two of them.

"We're simple rabbis, lord, on our way to our homes in Antioch. I'm Ariel and my friend here is Dionysius. We're not here to make any trouble. We were only looking at Jerusalem from afar, to see if what everyone was saying was true and as bad as reported, when we were captured."

Rufus laughed and said, "I'm Terentius Rufus, the reason your holy city is 'as bad as reported.' Caesar appointed me to bury this city and reduce it to wilderness, as a lesson to all who contemplate defying Rome. I command this legion. We're the destroyers and the levelers. And we forbid Jews to trespass here in our wilderness. Forget this land. Don't try to recover or resurrect anything from it. Let its ruin be a monument to the invincibility of Rome."

"Please, lord, let us go home. We're harmless. We have nothing to do with the war. In fact, we always opposed the Zealots. They're heretics—apostates from true Judaism—offenders of God. We're dedicated to the way of righteousness and peace."

"The way?" Rufus asked, raising an eyebrow. "Are you followers of the Nazarene, Yesucristos?"

"Yes, we are," Ariel said. He pulled out his bloodstone amulet from under his tunic and showed it to Rufus.

"Well now. Perhaps I won't have to kill you after all. You may be of some use to us. Do you know who Tiberius Alexander is?"

"Do you mean the general from Alexandria, the commander of all the emperor's armies?"

"The one and the same. He's my superior officer. Only Titus and Vespasian are ranked higher. And he's a Jew! Or rather, he was. He renounced the Jewish superstition and adopted the true Roman religion to advance himself in our military. And how mightily the gods rewarded him for his loyalty! You Jews should take him as an example and a lesson. Join the rest of the world and accept the benevolent protection of Rome. You can see, in the results of your rebellion, how foolish it was to attack your protector. And after all we did for you! We gave you special privileges, allowing you to be citizens, and yet also to worship your hateful god and disrespect our gods. How many times did we protect you and indulge you when the rest of mankind wanted to destroy you?

"But I digress. I'm railing against those ingrates, the rebels, while you assure me that you're not of their kind. So, if you're opposed to the rebellion, you surely would like to see this war ended, correct?"

"Lord, forgive me, but isn't the war already over?"

Rufus laughed and said, "It's as good as over, yes. But some of your stubborn compatriots insist on carrying on the fight. If you can believe it, a horde of rebels is right now trying to fight off our army at Machaerus. And that's where you come in, my Jews. Since your former countryman Tiberius Alexander insists on employing Jews as spies and informers as much as is practical, and since your appearance gives every indication that you would worthless as slaves, I'm sending you to Machaerus. There you will assist the commander, Bassus—"

"We won't kill for you, lord, if that's what you plan for us," Ariel said, interrupting with a boldness that made Dionysius tremble. "It would be preferable to us, a blessing in fact, to be martyred right here rather than add to the destruction of our already devastated people."

"No, no, no," Rufus said. "Nothing of the sort. You'll be translators—information gatherers. You'll persuade the rebels to abandon their error, so that there can finally be peace. Peace makers—that's what you'll be! Yes. I won't kill you. I'll give you the chance to prove yourselves valuable as peace makers. But if you abuse this generosity of mine and betray us, Bassus will kill you. You can count on it."

Ariel opened his mouth to speak, but Rufus waved his hand to signal that speaking was now forbidden.

"I've made my decision. You're going to Machaerus."

Rufus called to a centurion: "Demetrius! Take these two Jews and prepare them to be transported. Have some of your men take them to Bassus at Machaerus. I'll write down all the instructions for you to take to him in a letter. Be ready to go as soon as I send it to you."

28

One Sabbath morning Joshua was in a valley right outside the western reaches of Magdala, teaching the word to his disciples and a small crowd of locals. The valley and the low, sloping hills surrounding it were lush and green, spotted by clusters of red and purple wildflowers that swayed with the mild breeze. After Joshua had finished his sermon and dismissed the crowd, individuals with special petitions lined up to approach Joshua one by one to receive a blessing, a healing touch, or brief counsel on a particular matter of concern. The last of these petitioners was a burly, hirsute man of forty-some years who was accompanied by his son, who looked like a younger, more slender version of the father.

"Rabbi," the father said. "You're clearly a learned man who knows the way of justice. I beg you to help me resolve a dispute with this one, my son."

"That will depend on the nature of the dispute," Joshua said. "But I'll listen to your concern, brother. Tell me, uh . . ."

"Jashen," the father said, patting himself on the chest. "My name's Jashen, and this is my son Thomas."

"All right, Jashen and Thomas," Joshua said. "Thomas—'twin'—that's an unusual name."

"Yes, well," Jashen said, "he was born a twin but his brother died in the womb. I named him Thomas so he'd always remember to live a worthy life, for the sake of his twin who was denied his."

Joshua smiled and nodded as if he approved of Jashen's explanation, and then waited for Jashen to make his point.

Jashen halfway opened his mouth to resume speaking when Thomas interrupted.

"Go ahead, Father. Tell him all about how you're unfair with me."

Jashen, offended, glared at Thomas and said, "Impudent boy! Go ahead then, if you're so wise. Go ahead and tell him your side of it."

"Rabbi," Thomas said. "My father is a prosperous but unfair man. All my life I've been a faithful son to him, obedient to every command. But I go unrewarded. All this while my lazy lout of a younger brother is indulged. My brother took his share of the family estate, sold it, and went off to squander it on easy living and whores. When the money ran out, he dared to come back to the ranch so he could mooch. And what does my father do? He welcomes him back like a returning hero! He slaughtered our finest cow and feasted to celebrate the return of his worthless son. And I, the ever faithful, never even had so much as a goat given to me. My father is stingy to the good and generous to the wicked."

Before Joshua could respond, Jashen jumped in to defend himself.

"Let me tell my side of it now. Good son—yes, you're a good son; you've been obedient to me without fault. That's true. But that's why you're so privileged in my home. You're the first born and heir, and I treat you like my partner in all things. Everything I have is yours. You're the co-master of the fields, the animals—everything. Don't you appreciate your special status?"

Thomas, arms crossed, rolled his eyes and frowned. Jashen grabbed Thomas by the shoulders and shook him as if to wake him up to reason.

"But your brother," Jashen said. "When he left, it broke my heart. I'd lost him and I was aggrieved. I was sick with worry that he might never return. So when I saw him returned to me, I was beside myself with joy. How could I not be? My dead son was returned to life!"

Thomas opened his mouth to respond but Joshua raised his hand to signal silence. Joshua ran his hand through his hair and paced the ground in thought. After this brief moment of reflection, Joshua returned his attention to the pair.

"I have something to say to you, Thomas, and another thing to say to you, Jashen. First, Thomas. Thomas, understand your father. When you're tending your sheep, or whatever animals you tend—let's just say they're sheep for the sake of argument—and one strays far from the herd, don't you go searching for that lost one? Don't you put the other sheep out of your mind for the moment so you can recover the stray, even if it's only one sheep out of a hundred? And don't you rejoice over recovering that lost one more than you do over the ninety-nine who never caused you any worry? So it is with your father. You never caused your father to worry, so he went about his business contentedly and you never saw him angry or distressed on your account, but you took his satisfaction for cold indifference and felt unappreciated. Your father rejoiced at your brother's return precisely because the grief he suffered at his loss was finally relieved. And so it is with your Father in heaven when one of His children who's lost in sin repents and returns to Him.

"Now I address you, Jashen. Jashen, understand your son. Too often in this wicked world we give all our attention to the bad things and the harm that others do us. Meanwhile we go on as if we're blind to the good and ignore it. We take the ones we most love for granted. Worse, we feel entitled to abuse them in ways we never would a stranger or even an enemy. If you love your son, Jashen, show him. Cherish him! You're losing one son just as you've recovered the other. Love one another. Love one another or lose one another! So promise me, Jashen. Promise me that you'll celebrate the loyal devotion of your son Thomas. Show him you appreciate him. Reward righteousness as it's deserved, as your heavenly Father does. Can you do this, Jashen?"

Jashen blinked as if waking from a spell. He looked at Thomas, felt a hesitant wave of tenderness rise within his breast, and embraced his son.

"Forgive me, Son. I've not appreciated you as you deserve. You're my beloved . . . my heir . . . my life!"

Thomas wiped a tear from his own cheek and Joshua turned to him.

"Thomas, promise me you'll love your father and your brother. Don't let your love grow cold. Appreciate all that they suffer and do for you. Can you do this, Thomas?"

Thomas looked at his father and said, with deep humility in his voice, "Forgive me, Father. I didn't understand your pain. I'm a child!"

Thomas and Jashen embraced again.

Joshua laid his hands on them, blessed them, looked up, and scanned the horizon. He appeared to be entranced for a moment. He shook himself as if waking and started to pace.

"Don't forget, though," Joshua said, "that there's a danger to riches. The more riches you pile up, the more you obstruct the path to God's kingdom. And God's judgment approaches."

Joshua signaled for his disciples to gather around him.

"Disciples! These two here are Jashen and his son Thomas. They're new friends of ours and they seek the way of God. I'm worried about you, though, Jashen and Thomas. I'm afraid that money has brought you troubles and may continue to be a stumbling block for you."

Jashen and Thomas looked at each other and shrugged.

"Friends, disciples, what good are worldly treasures, really? Especially now that God's judgment looms and stands ready to strike down all that is wicked and unworthy. How secure are your possessions? How long will you have them? Even if we have them all our lives—our short, fleeting lives—what do we ultimately gain? And can't our possessions be destroyed or stolen at any time? As David says in his thirty-ninth Psalm: 'In vain they rush about, heaping up wealth, without knowing whose it will finally be.' (Psalm 39:6) Amass for yourselves heavenly treasure that can't be destroyed or stolen.

"Another psalm . . . which is it? Oh yes. I remember. The forty-ninth: 'Why should I fear when evil days come, when wicked deceivers surround me—those who trust in their wealth and boast of their great riches? No one can redeem the life of another or give to God a ransom for them—the ransom for a life is costly, no payment is ever enough—so that they should live on forever and not see decay. For all can see that the wise die, that the foolish and senseless also perish, leaving their wealth to others. Their tombs will remain their houses forever, their dwellings for endless generations, though they had named lands after themselves. People, despite their wealth, don't endure; they're like the beasts that perish. Their forms will decay in the grave, far from princely mansions. But God will redeem me from the realm of the dead; He'll surely take me to Himself.' (Psalm 49:5–12, 15)

"In Psalm sixty-two, David says, 'Though your riches increase, don't set your heart on them.' (Psalm 62:10) So where is your heart? Is it set on earth or on heaven? No one can serve two masters. You'll hate one and love the other. You'll be devoted to one and despise the other. You can't serve both God and money.

"Therefore I tell you, don't worry about your body, what you'll wear, what you'll eat or drink. Life is more than food or clothes or possessions. Look at the birds of the air; they don't sow or reap or store away in barns, and yet your heavenly Father feeds them. Aren't you much more valuable than they are? Can any one of you by worrying add a single hour to your life?

"And why do you worry about clothing? See how the flowers of the field grow. They don't labor or spin. Yet I tell you that not even Solomon in all his splendor was dressed like one of these. If that's how God clothes the grass of the field, which is here today and tomorrow thrown into the fire, won't He much more clothe you? So don't worry, saying, 'What shall we eat?' or 'What shall we drink?' or 'What shall we wear?' For the pagans run after all these things, and your heavenly Father knows that you need them. But seek first His kingdom and His righteousness, and all these things will be given to you as well. So don't worry about tomorrow; tomorrow will worry about itself. Each day has trouble enough of its own. Worrying about tomorrow won't help tomorrow. It will only hurt today."

Joshua stopped speaking and sat down on a large rock to rest. The disciples all introduced themselves to Thomas and Jashen, and after the customary pleasantries Thomas and Jashen dismissed themselves.

As they walked home, Thomas and Jashen talked and shared their wonder about Rabbi Joshua.

"I think he might be the wisest man in the world," Jashen said. "Or the craziest."

"Yes," Thomas said. "He seems to be a bit of both."

"All that preaching about the danger of wealth—as if poverty weren't a worse danger!"

"And what was all that about birds not hoarding food in barns? They would if they could."

"You're right about that, Son. I've seen the birds struggle and fight each other for their food. Don't tell me they don't worry about what they are to eat."

"And someone has to make the clothes we wear. What are we to do, cover ourselves with the flowers of the field?"

They laughed together, and Jashen said, "God gives to those who take care of their own."

"True!" Thomas said.

After walking a while in silence, Thomas asked his father, "But all those things he said about us, about how we should get along—that was good, right?"

"Oh yes, Son. Absolutely. He really set us straight on that!"

29

Demetrius was already under orders to lead his hundred infantry men to Machaerus to provide reinforcements to Bassus, so he made room for his two prisoners in a supply cart designated for carrying the horses' hay. By Rufus's orders, Ariel and Dionysius were bound, blindfolded, and knocked out with a sedative mixture of wine, myrrh, and a tiny trace of hemlock. Demetrius laid the sleeping rabbis onto the hay bed like a pair of grain sacks and covered them with a top layer of hay that concealed their presence.

When Demetrius's troops departed Jerusalem, they took the public road to Jericho and arrived there in one day. The next day's march took them to Perean Gadara, and on the third day they reached Bassus's camp east of Machaerus.

When Ariel woke up, the blindfold was gone and he found himself on a leather cot inside a small tent. His wrists were shackled and a Roman, clad in leather armor, sat on a chair opposite him. The Roman threw Ariel a small loaf of barley bread and a water skin.

"Eat," the Roman ordered, in Greek. "When you're finished I'll give you your instructions."

Ariel devoured the bread and washed it down with one giant gulp that emptied the water skin.

"Listen carefully, Ariel. I'm going to send you out to the valley in front of the gate of the fortress. You'll have to climb up to that gate and join the Jews there. Your official story is that you've escaped our camp. I'm going to give you some false intelligence to share with them to confuse them. But before I do, let me explain what your main objectives are. You need to learn what kind of army they have behind those walls. How many men? How well supplied? What weapons? Are there secret tunnels? What are their plans? Are they expecting reinforcements to come help them? How do they operate? Do they have special weaknesses? Keep your eyes open."

"Whoa . . . whoa there. This is too much," Ariel said. "I can barely follow you. And this isn't what General Rufus told me I'd be doing. He said—"

"Ariel, shut up. Don't forget your friend, Dion. We're holding him hostage and he's at your mercy. If you're useful to us then he'll live, but if you don't cooperate he dies. For his sake, perform your duties with care. You need to take these orders seriously. Understand?"

Ariel inhaled to calm his nerves and groaned.

"I understand. I'll cooperate."

"Good."

The Roman took a saw from his belt and approached Ariel.

"Spread your hands and make the chain taut," the Roman ordered.

Ariel obeyed and the Roman began to saw through the chain. Halfway through the chain the Roman put away the saw and took out a hatchet. Laying the chain across a wood stump, he raised the axe. Ariel moved his head back and the Roman plunged the blade into the weakened link of the chain with frightening speed and precision. The chain broke at once.

"There," the Roman said. "Now you look like a real fugitive."

Ariel flexed his arms. The chains rattled as he reaccustomed himself to his normal range of motion.

"Listen carefully," the Roman said. "In exactly one week you need to return to me with everything you've learned. Find a way to sneak back to our camp in the middle of the night. Go to the stable at the south end, the third stall on the right. Give your report to the man waiting there. It will probably be me, but whoever it is, address him as 'Scipio' to confirm who you are. Do a good job for us and you and your friend will be spared. Got it?"

"Understood."

"Good. Now, here's what you'll report to the Jews, the 'secret plan' that you 'discovered during your imprisonment' . . ."

30

Late at night, while Joshua was alone on the roof of Mary's house praying, he recalled the encounter he had that day with Jashen and Thomas. He couldn't help thinking about his mother and siblings, and how long it had been since he last saw them.

David's sixty-ninth Psalm came to him.

You, God, know my folly; my guilt is not hidden from you. (Psalm 69:5)

Joshua felt a sickening, visceral wave of shame pulse through his body. He imagined his family back in Nazareth: abandoned, rejected, and convinced that Joshua hated them. He resolved to return to them, if only for a spell, to tell them about his mission and reassure them about all he was doing.

The next morning Joshua gathered his disciples around him and told them that he was going away for a week to Nazareth. He revealed his anguish over familial regrets and insisted that they continue to preach, baptize, and heal the sick while he was away.

"You can't go alone, Rabbi," John said. "Jacob and I will go with you. It'll be safer that way."

"I appreciate your concern," Joshua answered. "But I'll be all right. I know the villages and the countryside. It should only take two days to walk to Nazareth. I'll be in no danger. And even if I were to encounter bandits or the like on the road, how would you help me? Fight them off with scripture? Don't worry about me. Trust God."

The next morning Joshua packed a bag with some salted fish, bread, dates, and figs, and then put a few coins in a small purse which he put into the bag with the food. After hanging a water skin from his belt, he went to his disciples to give blessings and goodbyes and to thank Salome and Lamech for their generous hospitality. He left the house, said a quick prayer, walked west out of the city, and took the country road toward Nazareth.

* * *

When Joshua was near Nazareth he decided to visit the stoneware workshop in Reina where he had worked in his youth. To his great surprise and joy he found his friend Thaddeus still working there. He was much more amazed, however, to find his own brother Jacob working right alongside him. The three of them embraced, elated to be reunited.

"Thaddeus," Joshua said. "How did you rope Jacob into working with you in this desolate crag?"

"Someone had to replace you," Jacob said. "It might as well be me. It's better money than tending sheep or working for a vintner."

"Jacob is the next best thing to having you around to entertain me with stories and sermons," Thaddeus said. "He's almost as well versed in scripture as you are, and he's imaginative like you too. I've learned a lot from him, as much as a scholar."

"Well, it's good to see you've kept up with your studies, Jacob," Joshua said. "Hopefully you don't hate me after I've abandoned you for so long."

"All the hard feelings are gone now," Jacob said. "I forgave you long ago. I know now how important it is to you to save the world, or whatever it is you're doing. But our mother still grieves. She's turned all of Nazareth against you. I'd avoid going into town if I were you, after all the stories she's told about her 'mad, traitor son'—her 'disappointing, ingrate son.'"

"It's a shame she feels that way," Joshua said. "But I understand it. Whatever the case is, I'm going to face all the hate and blame, if that's what I have to do to explain myself to her. What about the two of you? Do you think I'm crazy?"

Jacob answered, "If you're still preaching the imminent judgment and urging repentance from sin—"

"I am." Joshua said, interrupting.

"Well," Jacob said, "then I think your beliefs aren't crazy. The scriptures back up what you teach. What may be crazy, though, is the hope you have of convincing all the ignorant, misled donkeys in our country. The people are beaten, Brother. Every day Herod impoverishes us a little bit more—in wealth and in spirit."

"That's exactly why I'm in such a hurry to spread the truth." Joshua said. "As hard as it is, I feel compelled by God to play the shepherd—rounding up a herd of wayward sheep."

"Well, good luck to you, Brother," Jacob said, shaking his head.

Joshua looked around the workshop and indulged in a brief spell of nostalgia. For a moment he imagined the sweet, simple life of the stone cutter: the concentrated devotion to the process of cutting, drilling, chiseling, and sanding a raw block of limestone into a beautiful vessel in which to store the purest water.

"You know," Joshua said as he came out of his reverie. "What you're doing here is not so different from what I do. I have a disciple—a rough, hard-headed fisherman from Capernaum. He's simple and unlearned, but malleable and completely committed in his faith. I've been chiseling away his baseness and reforming him into a real scholar of the word. I think when I'm done with him he'll be a shining vessel of righteousness. If I can do that with someone like him, there's hope for our people."

Joshua looked at Jacob and Thaddeus and smiled.

"Jacob, Thaddeus, I know you're both wise men—believers and masters of the law and the prophets. Come. Join me! I lead a group of eight disciples who wait for me in Magdala. We're bringing many people back to God. The harvest is rich, but the workers are few. You'd be welcome members of our group. Just as you chisel and reshape these rocks, you could refine and transform men. What do you say?"

Jacob and Thaddeus looked at each other and Jacob shrugged. "This is a big burden that you propose for us," Jacob said. "But we'll consider it, given the sadness of our times. Let us think about it and discuss it with each other."

"Think about it then!" Joshua shouted, indignant. "But while you do, think about what you'll say to the Most High Judge when He asks you to defend your worthiness for His kingdom!"

With that abrupt outburst Joshua left the workshop and continued on his way to Nazareth.

* * *

Joshua was walking by a fenced-off vineyard when he saw the hills of Nazareth. A few workers were examining some vines and Joshua waved a silent greeting, but the workers just looked askance at him and went right back to their inspection.

It was noon when he began to ascend the hills that cradled the villagers' houses. On his left, vineyards spanned the nearby landscape for acres, reaching the borders of grain fields and grassy valleys farther off. On his right, sheep and goats hid in hollows or huddled under shady laurel trees on the rolling foothills. Ahead, most of the villagers were resting and taking their midday meal indoors, sheltered from the searing sunlight. Occasionally Joshua caught sight of women or children outside their homes, but as soon as they saw him they whispered to each other and hurried back inside.

When he finally reached the old home of his youth, Mary's house, he caught a glimpse of the grassy plateau where he had once preached under a tent. It was now enclosed by a fence and reserved for the grazing of sheep. He shook off the memory and braced himself to face his mother. Fearing that he might be denied entry, Joshua walked right into the house without knocking.

Mary sat rapt in concentration as she worked at a loom when Joshua walked in. Startled, she jumped up and reeled back.

"Who are you?" Mary asked, panting with fear.

"I'm your son, Mother. Joshua."

Mary, shocked, inhaled as if girding herself for battle and approached. As soon as she saw him in the light she embraced him.

"Joshua! Joshua, you hateful, disloyal son!" Mary cried. "Tell me you've come to your senses at last. Tell me you're no longer a fanatic—that you've given up your dangerous wandering. Tell me you're finally ready to be a settled, responsible man—a real man."

Joshua freed himself from Mary's embrace.

"No, Mother. I can't stop what I'm doing. God has called me, and I won't refuse. God has called me to teach the word to all who lack it, and to bring sinners to repentance before the judgment. You have to accept it. Try to understand, Mother."

Mary grimaced with deep disappointment and slapped Joshua across his face. Joshua stood firm, ready to take more blows if necessary.

"Do whatever you have to do to extinguish your rage, Mother."

Mary glared at her son.

"If you haven't changed at all, then why are you here? Have you come just to torture me?"

"No! I came to explain to you what's happened to me. God—"

"Blasphemer! How dare you invoke God while you try to excuse your reckless behavior! Forgetting your family, disdaining your mother—why do you hate me, Son? How can God approve of you being so thoughtless and cruel? Don't you know that I suffer? You don't realize I worry to death over you—not knowing what trouble you're in or whether you're even alive? What is it, really, that has you so spellbound out there, that you feel entitled to abuse your mother this way? Tell me, wise rabbi!"

"Mother, listen. I'm captured by nothing less than the kingdom of God! Everything else pales before it. I'm sorry, Mother, but it's true. I'm like a man who finds a priceless treasure in a field. What does he do? He hides it again and then gladly sells everything he has to purchase that field. I have to give everything else up— family, a wife, money—to serve a far greater thing. All these worldly things that everyone runs after—they soon won't matter because the new age is dawning, just as the prophets said it would. Surely you recognize this too. Did Father not teach you the scriptures?"

Mary scoffed. "Now you mock me for being a woman? I dedicated my life to my family, something you apparently wouldn't understand. Ungrateful child! Grow up!"

"Mother, I don't judge you. I would never judge you. You're a blameless, righteous woman. I know that I've hurt you. But it had to be. It was God's will. The kingdom will be yours too. Just accept the will of God. Have faith!"

Mary's eyes welled up and sprouted a few tears.

"Joshua, I'm sorry, but I just don't believe you. You're saying that our world is going to end—that God is going to just wipe everything away and begin again, making everything right this time. That's crazy. It's the same thing the deranged hermits preach! It breaks my heart that you believe it. All I want is for you to be well again. Please, come to your senses."

Mary got on her knees, looked up, lifted her hands, and prayed.

"God! I pray to you to heal my son! Bring him back to me. Please make him abandon his insane dream. Convince him to settle down, marry, and be a responsible family man. Please, Lord. I beg you. Save my son!"

Joshua looked down at his mother and pitied her.

"Mother, the only thing you lack is faith. But I have faith for the both of us. When you see God's judgment come, then you'll know that I'm telling you the truth. It won't be long, Mother."

At that moment Joshua was interrupted by the sudden arrival of Jacob and Thaddeus. Jacob saw Mary in her agitated state and immediately went to her and embraced her.

"Mother," Jacob said. "I hate to do this to you, but I must go with Joshua. He knows the truth and he's doing what God commands him to do. Now I also must obey. I finally have the courage. Don't worry Mother. Don't be sad. God Himself supports and protects us. Soon you'll see that all this is happy news. God bless and protect you, Mother."

Mary pushed Jacob away and pointed an accusing finger at Joshua.

"Now you've bewitched Jacob too? Now I lose two sons?"

Mary rushed into Joshua and attacked him with furious punches and feeble kicks. Jacob grabbed her from behind and pulled her off of him.

"Thaddeus!" Jacob shouted. "Get me a cup of the formula!"

Thaddeus went into the kitchen and came back with a cup filled with wine mixed with myrrh. Jacob pushed Mary into a chair and forced her to drink the cup. He held her down until she was calm. In another moment she was out. Joshua kneeled in front of Mary and said a brief prayer for his mother to be delivered from her doubts and accept the will of God. When Joshua finished, Jacob told Joshua and Thaddeus to wait for him at the workshop.

"I'm going to stay here and take care of our mother until Simon and Judah return. They're her faithful sons—her good sons. She'll be all right with them. Then I'll meet you at the quarry."

"Are Simon and Judah going to be all right with you leaving?" Joshua asked.

"They're going to have to be. I'm never here much anyway. They'll accept my decision sooner or later. I'll leave before any fighting can start!"

Joshua and Thaddeus left and headed back to the workshop.

"You're doing the right thing, I assure you," Joshua said to Thaddeus as they descended the Nazarene hills.

Joshua reflected as he walked.

Someday, when the time is right, I'll return and set my family straight for once and for all!

31

Ariel left the Roman camp as dawn was breaking. Behind him long embankments surrounded the tents, stables, war engines, and guard towers of the Romans. Before him stood the village-fortress of Machaerus, which capped the top of a three-thousand-foot-high, steep-sloping hill. At the apex sat the citadel—a three-hundred-square-foot stone castle with ninety-foot-high walls and towers twice that height at the corners. Below the citadel a village of about five hundred residents clung to the slope like a smaller version of Gamala, its houses lined up like the steps of a wide stairway.

The village was enclosed by four thick stone walls that made a trapezoid with towers at the vertices. The lowest face of the citadel formed the top, two fifty-foot-high walls extending from the top towers made the sides, and a long, fifty-foot-high wall connecting the bottom towers formed the base. This base wall had a two-floor observation tower in the middle, with the bottom floor serving as the main gate and entryway into the village. The eastern corner of the village was connected to a massive aqueduct that fed immense cisterns below the village.

Ariel observed his immediate surroundings. He was in a valley in front of the base wall that protected the lowest part of the village. The main gate was ahead to his right about a hundred yards away. At regular intervals along the base wall, heaps of earth lay, waiting to become the foundations of Roman siege ramps. On top of the base wall he could see a few soldiers patrolling along the rampart walkway—young, bearded, and leather-clad swordsmen of the Zealot resistance.

Ariel ran straight ahead to get closer to the wall and attract the attention of a soldier. He waved his arms and showed off his wrist shackles to indicate that he'd escaped the Roman camp. A soldier saw him and called over some of his companions. They took a good look at Ariel and waved to signal that he should move over to the main gate. Ariel obeyed, and the first soldier ordered the others to go down to meet the fugitive there.

The soldiers frisked Ariel for weapons before bringing him into the lower floor of the gateway tower. Two of the soldiers took Ariel off to the side and into a guards' quarters to question him.

"What's your story?" the taller soldier asked, speaking Aramaic.

The soldier wore a plain iron helmet without a face mask. The shorter soldier lacked headgear and had long, wavy, black hair.

"My name is Ariel bar Hananiah. I was travelling through Judea, on my way home to Antioch, when the Romans captured us—me, I mean. They brought me here as a slave—"

"Wait," the helmeted soldier said, interrupting. "You said 'us.' Who else was with you?"

"My friend. He was captured with me."

"Where is he now?"

"I don't know. I think he's in the Roman camp. We were separated."

The helmeted one stroked his own beard and stared at Ariel with a doubtful look on his face.

The other soldier said, "You forgot to—"

"Oh shit, you're right," the helmeted one said.

"I hate to do this, Ariel," the helmeted soldier said. "But we're going to have to confirm that you're really a Jew."

The soldier motioned his hands to indicate that Ariel would have to lift his tunic for a penis inspection. Ariel understood and lifted his garment while the helmeted soldier performed a quick examination of his member. Satisfied, the soldier rose and allowed Ariel to re-cover himself.

"Circumcised!" the helmeted soldier declared as if it were a small victory. "And legitimate. Not a new scar like on some of the false Jews the Romans send to spy on us."

The other soldier nodded his approval.

Returning his attention to Ariel, the helmeted soldier said, "Call me Ethan. This one's Ezra. Tell me, Ariel, what good are you to us? Did you learn anything useful about the Romans during your servitude?"

Ariel took a deep breath and tried to remember his false, scripted report. His voice trembled with a faint, almost inaudible trace of nervousness when he spoke.

"Yes. They have horrible things planned for you. When they finish building their war engines, they're going to catapult more than just boulders into this fortress. They have jars full of poisonous snakes that they want to launch into your village. And the snakes will want to stay, thanks to the barrels of pestilent rats the Romans hope to send your way. They have wine skins filled with poison to throw into the cisterns, and other wine skins filled with menstrual blood. They want to insult and defile you as they destroy you. And—"

Ethan broke out in riotous laughter.

"What an outrageous fable! You're either crazy, Ariel, or you're spreading Roman lies. Either way, I don't like it. I should slay you right here, but now I have to see if the Romans are even half as depraved as you say they are—if they're planning anything even remotely similar to what you describe. I'm going to have to imprison you, Ariel, but as soon as the Romans' snakes hatch from their jars, I'll release you and make you my special advisor on Roman tactics."

Ethan called a soldier from outside into the room.

"Gilal! Help Ezra take this jackal to the detention tower."

Ezra pinned Ariel's wrists together behind his back and tied them with rope. Gilal, a taller version of Ezra, entered and grabbed one of Ariel's biceps. Ezra grabbed the other, and the two soldiers led Ariel, who went along with them like a pliant mule, into the village. Ariel was furious with himself.

Damn it! I knew they wouldn't fall for that Roman horseshit! Now I'm totally fucked. Fucked!

The soldiers marched Ariel eastward along a path between the base wall and the neighborhood right behind it. Brigades of Zealot soldiers, engaged in conversation and routine military chores, huddled in alleyways and against the wall, but aside from a few disinterested looks they ignored the marching trio as it made its way to the corner where the aqueduct met the base wall. They turned and climbed up the hill along the side wall to a two-story, square tower built into the wall. Ezra unlocked and opened the iron entry door, and Gilal led Ariel up the steps to the top floor. At the top of the stairs a bare stone hallway led about thirty feet to a dead-end wall. Along the hallway to the left, there were three wooden doors spaced at regular intervals, and the wall opposite was identical. Gilal opened the third door on the left, untied Ariel, shoved him into the cell, and locked him in.

"If you have to piss or shit," Gilal yelled through the door, "use the chute!"

Ariel, wide-eyed, looked around the cell. It was dark, with only one narrow archer's slit—a six-inch-wide and eighteen-inch-high opening in the wall directly ahead of him—to allow the morning light and dry desert air to penetrate the ten-foot cube of a cell. When his eyes adjusted, he saw a wooden bench against the wall to his left. The room was otherwise unfurnished—an empty brick box. Ariel turned to the wall at his right and spied the chute that Gilal mentioned. It was a six-inch-square opening in the floor at the corner where two walls intersected, and below it a steep, stone slide descended to an opening in the tower wall facing east. Anything passing through the chute would be ejected out to the deep and rocky valley behind Machaerus.

Ariel remembered that Machaerus was the place of John the Baptist's imprisonment and beheading. He wondered if he was in the same tower, perhaps even the very cell, that had held the great martyr. He shuddered with horror as he imagined the Lord's forerunner standing in an awkward squat over the chute, missing the mark on occasion, and kicking wayward turds down the slide to tumble beyond the steep cliff to the lifeless abyss below.

Ariel sat down on the bench, leaned his head back against the wall, and agonized over his situation. If he couldn't make it back to the Roman camp in time, Dion was going to die. Was there any way for either one of them to escape? Ariel contemplated confessing everything and hoping for mercy. But wouldn't the Zealots just kill him if they found out he was sent to spy for the Romans? It looked like he and Dion were doomed. He shook from dread and terror as despair gripped him. Desperate for mental distraction, he got up and poked his head into the archer's slit to focus his attention on the world outside.

The view directly ahead allowed him to see the lowest section of the village, the protective base wall below it, and the valley below the wall. The Roman army was amassing in the valley now: getting into formation behind earthen embankments, building up siege ramps, and scrambling to complete construction of the various war engines.

A sudden clamor arose and a brigade of about fifty Zealots surged out of the village gate. They were led by a wild-haired, young warrior who distinguished himself from the other soldiers by his bright, silvery cape which, when it flapped in the wind, reflected the sunlight in a way that resembled flames following in his wake. The insurgents attacked a surprised troop of ramp-building Romans and dispatched them like lions pouncing on a helpless herd of heifers. After the skirmish the Zealots fled back to the gate and into the village in as sudden a rush as they had left it. About thirty dead Roman infantry men lay scattered about the unfinished siege ramp. Ariel couldn't see a single dead Zealot. Behind the village wall the Zealot brigades exulted with celebratory shouts. A few of the soldiers lifted the silver-caped warrior onto their shoulders and paraded him through the village streets.

"Eleazar!" the soldiers shouted, lifting their swords into the air. They inspired the villagers to join them in chanting their hero's name.

"Eleazar! Eleazar! Eleazar!"

Several times throughout the day Eleazar led large and enthusiastic groups of Zealots out on similar lightning-fast raids against the frustrated Roman building corps. Each successful foray resulted in a new scene of village-wide celebration. Ariel was fascinated. For the moment, he even forgot his own grim troubles. But when night came, and the battling opponents ceased fighting to retreat to their respective camps, Ariel remembered the harrowing peril he was in. He laid himself prostrate on the brick floor and began to pray for deliverance. With his uncertain future looming black and heavy on his mind, he prayed until sleep overtook him.

32

Joshua had only been gone five days when he returned to Magdala accompanied by Jacob and Thaddeus. Before leaving Nazareth, Joshua had persuaded Jacob and Thaddeus to keep secret the fact that Jacob was Joshua's brother to avoid stirring up any jealousy or suspicion of favored treatment. Joshua called Thaddeus and Jacob "old friends from Nazareth" when he introduced them to the others. To avoid confusing the two Jacobs they adopted the convention of calling Jacob son of Zebedee "Jacob the Elder" or "Elder Jacob," and the new Jacob "Jacob the Younger" or "Young Jacob." In spite of their mastery of scripture, Young Jacob and Thaddeus joined the group as humble novices, sharing in all the chores and studying how the others performed their duties.

Over the months Joshua became a minor local celebrity in Magdala. He charmed the curious, aroused adulation in believers, inflamed hostility in doubters, and won only indifference from those too worldly to concern themselves with vociferous religious provocateurs. To the disciples' alarm, Joshua also attracted ever-increasing attention from the Herodian security and tax agents. Joshua and his disciples made scrupulous efforts to avoid aiming direct accusations at Herod, but their message of divine wrath against those who abuse the poor was subversive enough to draw a rising number of Herodian soldiers to their gatherings. Joshua took it as a sign that it was time to move on to another part of

Galilee. So one morning while the disciples were together having breakfast, Joshua announced that they would soon be moving on to Tiberias, the other great city on the western shore of Lake Gennesaret, just five miles south of Magdala.

"Tiberias?" Bartholomeus asked. "That's the capital of Galilee—Herod's home. We'll be in constant danger!"

"Maybe so," Joshua said. "But now's the time. We need to spread the word to the people of Tiberias while Herod and his men are still uncertain about us—before we get into any trouble that could impede our progress. Besides, I don't want any disciples with me who abandon their work because they fear danger."

Bartholomeus fell silent, chastised and embarrassed.

"We'll take a few days to prepare for the move," Joshua said. "John and Elder Jacob, you should go first to assess the state of things. Find out what the people know about us and what Herod's men are up to. Find a good place for us to stay, whether it's with sympathetic people in town or at an appropriate uninhabited site. The rest of us will wait here for your return."

Mary approached Joshua.

"Rabbi, you want to move to a new city, but as we've been ministering to the people here in Magdala I've been troubled by something. How do we know if we're really changing people's hearts and bringing them to the Lord? For me at least, it's hard to tell if we're convincing them. This city still seems as sinful as ever."

"Mary," Joshua said, smiling. "You and Matheus weren't with us yet when I addressed this very issue, but let me just tell you, and all of you here who have or haven't heard it before, that it's not for you to worry about whether or not someone takes the word to heart. We're like farmers sowing seed. When the farmer scatters seed on the ground, he doesn't know which seeds will find rich soil or which will fall between the rocks; which will sprout only to get choked by weeds or which will get eaten by the birds. He lets the seeds grow on their own, not knowing how the plants will be until they grow from the ground. But once the plants have grown to maturity, the grain ripe and the weeds poking themselves out of the dirt, then the farmer knows the harvest has come, and only then does the farmer know the quality of his crop. Like the farmer, we won't know the results of our efforts until judgment comes. Then God will take his fruitful crop with Him into His kingdom and burn the weeds. Do you understand what I'm telling you, brothers and sisters?"

A random round of yeses and amens wafted in the air, followed by silence.

Simon broke the silence: "How can we let Mary, a *woman*, travel with us? It would be a scandal. We'd be the butt of the vilest gossip! All's well here, where Mary lives honorably in her family home, but out on the road? It can't be done!"

Joshua was indignant.

"You're yelping like a frightened dog, Simon. Mary has her brother Matheus with us. He can be her guardian and protector. Isn't that right, Matheus?"

"I *am* her guardian and protector," Matheus answered with equal indignation. "But I too am worried about you travelling with us, Mary. Righteous as you all aspire to be, brothers, I'll have no mercy on anyone who tries to defile my sister in any way. Come near her, and I'll make you regret it. I'll pound any one of you brutes!"

Mary rolled her eyes at Matheus's threats.

"I've seen how some of you gaze at her," Matheus said, looking in John's direction. "I'll seriously cripple any of you!"

John shrugged in silent, disbelieving protest while Joshua raised his hands to indicate his disgust at the new direction of the discussion.

"Calm yourself, Matheus," Joshua said. "There's no reason for you to get worked up like this. Have you learned nothing in your time with us? Isn't it clear to you what we're all about? I think I can safely speak for all of us and say that Mary's honor is safe with us. If I'm wrong about that with respect to any of you, then whoever has this trouble must leave us right now. You're all here because you chose to commit yourselves to the way. If you can't accept this burden then by all means go! And if your lust is causing you to struggle in spite of your faithfulness to me, do whatever you must to squelch it. I won't have my mission collapse because one of you can't stay true to the right path! Do you really dare to greet the final hours of the age and face your Most High God while waylaid under a base fever for fornication? If your eye is your trouble, rip it out. It's better for you to enter the kingdom with one eye than to be cast out with two! If your hand is causing you to stumble, cut it off. It's better for you to enter the kingdom with one hand than to be cast out into the fire of judgment with two!"

Joshua began to pace and the others stood in silence. He shot a quick glance at Matheus and then returned his attention to the whole group.

"If you have any kind of problem or disagreement with your fellow disciple, go and discuss it between just the two of you. If you reconcile, then peace be with you. But if you don't, let one or two others hear the case and help decide it, in accordance with the law that states, 'a matter must be established by the testimony of two or three witnesses.' (Deuteronomy 19:15) If you still can't resolve the problem, bring it to me and I will decide. If you won't listen to me, then you and your problem can go to the devil!"

Joshua let out a light-hearted laugh. Mary then stood out in front of everyone and addressed Joshua.

"Rabbi, I've always been honored that you would have me as your disciple, and I'm humbled that you would include me in your further journeys. But I have my own concerns, besides those of Simon and Matheus. You see, as I've worked with you all here in Magdala, preaching the word and guiding the lost, I've learned that many men don't take me seriously as a teacher. For them my sex is a stumbling block that prevents them from accepting the word when it comes from me. And as believers and students of the word, we women often have trouble with rabbis who wish to limit our learning—because to them our sex makes us unworthy to study the law and the prophets.

"So I propose to you that I start my own ministry here in Magdala—a ministry for women. I can teach the women all the things you've taught me, but without all the difficulties that arise when women are taught by men. I think it would help bring many women to the kingdom who otherwise might be excluded due to their sex. I believe God calls me to this special mission. Let me try this, Rabbi, here where I have some wealth and respect, and see how it goes. I forever remain your disciple. What do you say, Rabbi?"

Joshua stared at Mary with his mouth agape for a moment and then smiled.

"Well, this settles things nicely, doesn't it?" Joshua said. "I think your idea is excellent. If you're determined to walk this path then I say do it! I suppose you also want to stay, Matheus—to help her and be her guardian?"

"Yes and no, Rabbi," Matheus answered. "I'm forever your protector, Mary, but as a man I don't see how I can help you if you want to work exclusively with women. In that case why have a guardian? Besides, you don't need my help. You're a better student of the way than I am. But I do need *your* help, Rabbi Joshua. I need your guidance and your wisdom. I'm not ready to leave you. Whatever Mary decides, I must insist on following you wherever you go, if you'll allow it. And if you also can accept that, Mary."

Mary embraced her brother and said, "Yes, Matheus. Go with Joshua. I'll be all right. I promise."

Joshua embraced both of them and addressed the group.

"Disciples! We have lessons to teach, penitents to baptize, sick to heal, evil to vanquish. Let's conquer the day! Come John and Elder Jacob, tell me your plans for your reconnaissance mission to Tiberias."

* * *

A few days later, when John and Elder Jacob were off reconnoitering Tiberias, Joshua prayed alone in the hills west of Magdala. He prayed in a state of firm devotion, knees on the ground but body rigid and straight, hands lifted heavenward, face to the sky, and eyes closed in deep concentration. When he finished, he let his body relax and sat down on his heels, which made him feel like he was falling back to earth. He opened his eyes halfway to ease his return to the harsh daylight.

Joshua flinched and reared back in frightened surprise. A young man was kneeling prostrate before him.

"What's this about?" Joshua said while looking all around to see if anyone else had snuck up on him.

The man looked up and smiled.

"Rabbi! It's me, Thomas. Don't you remember?"

Joshua recognized the man who, a few months before, he had helped reconcile with his father, Jashen.

"Oh, right. Thomas. I remember," Joshua said as his startled nerves calmed. "How are things going now with you and your father?"

"Oh Rabbi," Thomas said, sighing. "I have no father."

"What? What happened? Did he die?"

"No. Nothing like that. We've separated, my father and I, all over . . . well . . . over you really."

"What are you talking about? Didn't you two understand what I taught you? Explain yourself."

Thomas got up and sat next to Joshua.

"All right, Rabbi. Here's what happened. After we left you and returned home, my father and I got along wonderfully. Every day he told me how much he loved me and how proud he was that I was his eldest—how deserving I was to be his partner and heir. He held me up as an example for my brother; we both worked hard for my father, but he awarded me the more important tasks—the greater responsibilities."

Joshua nodded his head as he listened but stayed silent while Thomas told his story.

"But all this time I couldn't stop thinking about all those things you said about wealth and the judgment and the kingdom of God. I started to see our lives on the estate in a different light. Here we were, expanding our land holdings, increasing our livestock, getting richer from our crops, and any day now God is going to unleash His wrath on the wealthy and rescue the poor. It felt like with all our mounting prosperity we were just digging our own graves. I confronted my father about this; I told him we should be living more modestly and doing more for the poor. But he just laughed. He thought I was joking.

"Every night I prayed to the Lord to forgive us for being so selfish and arrogant towards our less fortunate neighbors. I became obsessed with the wickedness of the world and the punishments to come for all who don't repent. One incident in particular put me into a fit of worry. A neighbor of ours, Obed, became so indebted to the tax agents that he was going to have to give them his farm—the house, the land, the animals, everything. My father, shrewd man that he is, knew that the value of Obed's property was more than his tax debt and more than what the tax agents were going to sell it for. So he gave me a good sum of money and the responsibility to buy all of Obed's property from the tax collectors—not to rescue the poor man from the tax men, but to take advantage of his misfortune. Obed's family was going to be left destitute so my father could add more to his already enviable estate. I couldn't bear the injustice of it!

"So I just gave the money to Obed so he could pay his debts and keep his farm. Obed was so happy. He wanted to come thank my father, but I told him that my father wasn't at home. When I returned, I told my father what I'd done and he was enraged. I told him that his money may not have bought him more worldly property, but it *had* gone to purchase us a little estate in heaven. He demanded that I go back and undo it, but it was too late and I wouldn't. He tore his clothes and sent me away. Now I'm dead to him."

Joshua stared at Thomas, incredulous.

"What are you going to do, Thomas, now that you've robbed your father, although for a righteous purpose?"

"I'm going to live a life of poverty and prayer—devote myself to God. I'll renounce this world and earn a place in the kingdom of heaven!"

Thomas got back down on his knees.

"Please, Rabbi. Teach me," Thomas said. "Show me the way to the kingdom."

"The law and the prophets, properly understood, show the way. Do you know them?"

"Not as well as I want to."

Joshua ran his hand through his hair and sighed.

"You want to be my disciple? Maybe that would be the right thing for you, I don't know. But you've proven yourself willing to forsake family and fortune to pursue justice and mercy. I must give you credit for that. But our life is not easy. All who follow me must drink a deep cup of sorrow and hardship."

"I'm ready."

"Well, listen. Come and stay with us a little while. Learn and serve and do as we do. If our ways suit you, and you us, then you'll be a disciple."

"As you wish, Rabbi. I'm yours!"

Joshua brought Thomas to the other disciples and reintroduced him.

"Disciples, this is Thomas. Do you remember when he came to us with his father, Jashen? He'll be living with us for a while. Treat him like a brother, because his heart is set on the kingdom. He tried to steer his father, a rich man, to the way of righteousness, but his father refused and sent Thomas away. Now Thomas has found us, God be praised.

"By joining us, Thomas has chosen the better part of the law. What do I mean by this? Sometimes the law is in conflict with itself, and you must choose to break one commandment in order to avoid breaking another, higher commandment. The sixth commandment, for instance, says, 'You shall not kill.' But when wicked foes threaten the survival of the righteous in times of war, or when sinners violate the most serious strictures of the law, God says, 'Put the transgressors to death.' Because it's better for the righteous to kill a few of the wicked than for a few of the wicked to destroy or pollute the righteous.

"Likewise, consider the fifth commandment, which says, 'You shall honor your father and your mother.' Thomas has disobeyed and abandoned his father. This is usually a grave sin. But to stay loyal to his father, Thomas would have to join his father in his sins and his rejection of God—for Jashen forsakes righteousness and exploits the poor; he's deaf to the word and devoted only to his own greed. Jashen forced Thomas to choose between his father and his heavenly Father. If you must choose, always choose your heavenly Father! If your father or mother is wicked and hates you for your righteousness, love and obey your heavenly Father over them. Continue to pray for your parents' repentance, but don't let their obstinacy prevent you from following the right way. Your heavenly Father is greater than your worldly father. Whoever loves their father or mother more than their heavenly Father is unworthy to be my disciple! Likewise, whoever loves their son or daughter more than their heavenly Father is unworthy of me!"

* * *

After a few days Elder Jacob and John returned from their survey of Tiberias. They reported that some of the people there had indeed heard stories about the Galilean prophet named Joshua who healed the penitent and pronounced fiery judgment upon the wicked. They also said that the Herodian authorities of Tiberias seemed to be tolerant of preachers who kept silent about politics, but they cracked down on anyone who made overt criticisms of the status quo. More than anything, the Herodians were busy extracting as much tax revenue as they could from the Tiberian populace. Elder Jacob and John warned that the tax agents were squeezing fishermen in particular with special zeal, and were enjoying a subsequent bonanza from unjust confiscations of fishing vessels. The disciples therefore decided to leave their own fishing boat in Magdala and under the care of Mary for the time being. They would journey to Tiberias on foot.

33

On Ariel's second day of imprisonment, a soldier brought him a loaf of barley bread and a large jug of water, both meant to last him several days. Eleazar went back to his usual exploits, and Ariel was happy to watch. The battle developed into a real siege, with other Zealot brigades besides Eleazar's attacking different sections of the Roman lines, and the Romans entering the fray with sporadic success. Dead bodies from both sides of the conflict now littered the valley. Before long the ramps, ballistae, and catapults would be ready to escalate the violence and allow the Romans to invade the village, but not on this particular day. When the day's fighting ended, Ariel returned his attention to stark reality. He prayed and fretted over his desperate circumstances.

What do I do, Lord? Am I to die before you return? Help me, Lord!

Ariel despaired of either he or Dionysius escaping with their lives. He couldn't live with the guilt if he let Dion die to save himself. He accepted that he'd have to admit everything to the Zealots and plead for permission to rescue his friend, however doubtful it was that he'd be granted that liberty. It was the only chance that he and Dion had, so he resolved to do it the next day—even if it killed him. It was the right thing to do. It's what Joshua would have done.

The next morning Ariel slept late and woke to the sounds of battle. He got up to watch the action. Zealots snuck up on busy ramp builders, sometimes surprising and slaughtering them with great success, other times falling into a rout when ready Romans waiting in ambush caught them off their guard. Amid all this back and forth, Eleazar had a banner day conducting his lightning attacks. He and his troops went on a destructive rampage, utilizing stealthy maneuvers to knock down ramps, burn up siege engines, and kill Romans before they even knew they'd been attacked. Whenever he returned to the village after an expedition, the adoring populace, as always, saluted and chanted the name of their irrepressible champion.

In the late afternoon there was a lull in the fighting as both armies returned to their camps to rest and recuperate. It had been an especially taxing session of violent exertion, and both sides of the conflict suffered their share of torn flesh, shed blood, broken bones, hacked limbs, and crushed skulls. Eleazar, however, deviated from his usual habit of retreating to the village and instead stayed outside the gate to boast and joke with his compatriots, who watched him from the ramparts. He sent the soldiers into fits of giddy laughter as he gesticulated to mock the enemy in comical reenactments of the day's best victories, all in open and reckless contempt of the Roman camp below. Proud, arrogant, and assuming the Romans were done for the day, Eleazar entertained the troops on the wall with careless disregard for the fact that he was alone and unprotected on the battlefield.

Without warning a Roman fighter who had been hiding behind a collapsed siege ramp leaped out and charged at Eleazar from behind. The Roman rammed into Eleazar with such speed and force that he knocked the wind out of him and stunned him into a confused stupor. In shock, and too immobilized to so much as unsheathe his sword, Eleazar hung like a corpse over the Roman's shoulder while the soldier carried him off in a frantic run to the Roman camp. By the time the astonished Zealots gasped at this incredible reversal of fortune, it was too late for them to do anything. Eleazar was already in the hands of the enemy.

The distressed Zealots of Machaerus had begun to wail for their stolen hero when General Bassus, tall and dressed in full battle armor, emerged from a tent in the center of the Roman camp. Some of the general's guards followed him and dragged a bound and subdued Eleazar with them. Bassus approached a tall embankment that was in full view of both the citadel and the village and ordered his guards to take Eleazar to the top of it. There they began to strip Eleazar of his clothing. First they took his shiny cape, held it in the air, and offered it as a trophy to the general. Next they removed the iron plate that protected his torso and threw it to the ground, followed by all of Eleazar's leather armor from his torso, legs, and feet. A guard ripped off Eleazar's belt, and another cut off his linen tunic and loincloth, leaving him standing completely naked. Two of the guards each picked up a flagellum and positioned themselves to begin whipping Eleazar's flesh.

The Zealot warriors all groaned from grief and outrage at this spectacle, and the entire village complex erupted in a loud and disorderly chorus of protest. All Machaerus seemed to plead for Bassus to show mercy to Eleazar. Bassus was amazed by what he heard—by how much the Zealots adored this one man. He raised his hand to signal the guards to cancel the whipping. The clamor from the village calmed somewhat, as if hopes were raised that Eleazar would be spared. Bassus felt that he now had, through Eleazar, the power to manipulate the will and morale of the Zealots however he might wish. Delighted, he conceived a wicked plan.

Bassus issued a command to his guards that sent them running off to a nearby area of the camp. They came back carrying two wooden beams. The guards climbed to the top of the earthen mound, dug a deep hole into it, and set one of the beams to stand straight up from inside the hole. They attached the second beam, which was cut to allow it to fit at right angles with the first, to the top of the vertical beam to make a T-shaped cross. Projecting his voice for all to hear, Bassus announced that Eleazar would be crucified.

The outcry from Machaerus reignited even fiercer than before. Gasps and wails accompanied hysterical shouts that demanded that Eleazar be spared. Zealot warriors wept and beat their chests with the flat sides of their swords. Villagers dropped to their knees to pray and to plead for God to intervene. Soldiers watching from the citadel banged their heads against the nearest hard object they could find.

Ariel was astonished by what he saw.

Holy shit! They're going to crucify him!

Ariel had never witnessed an actual crucifixion, but as a devoted follower of Joshua the crucified Christ he couldn't help thinking that Eleazar's imminent execution would be imbued with some kind of sacred significance.

Is this a sign? Is God sending a sign?

Eleazar fell to his knees, dropped his face and bound hands to the ground, and pleaded for mercy. Bassus just smiled. Eleazar then turned toward the village and posed in supplication to his compatriots.

"Whatever you do, don't let this happen!" Eleazar shouted. "Save your son!"

Ariel was unimpressed.

Pathetic. That's not how Joshua faced the cross!

Many soldiers and villagers of Machaerus answered Eleazar's pleas with affectionate gestures that demonstrated their love and loyalty. The frenzied crowd fired up its vehement outrage and roared desperate demands for Eleazar's salvation.

Ariel worried.

This fanaticism for Eleazar is going to be the death of us all. The crucifixion will throw the Zealots into a suicidal fury, and no one will survive that chaos. I'm going to die with the Zealots here on this rock. This is it, Dion, wherever you are. There'll be no mercy for either of us today!

At that moment Ariel noticed a party of six men marching with great solemnity down the village steps that led to the gate. Two looked like high-ranking military officials, two appeared to be scribes, and two were dressed in the magnificent attire of well-heeled nobility. They went through the gate, proceeded across the valley, and headed straight for Bassus and Eleazar.

"Holy son of the bitch of all bitches!" Ariel yelled to himself in disbelief. "A negotiating party? Is the whole town going to surrender just to save that one stupid Zealot? Is this how it ends?"

When the party reached Bassus, various men of apparent authority from both sides exchanged formalities and began to deliberate. After a brief negotiation, the men recorded statements, signed papers, stamped seals, and shook hands. Bassus ordered his guards to unbind Eleazar and put clothes on him. They dressed him in a new linen tunic, returned his leather wear, and put a Roman officer's cloak around him. Bassus kept Eleazar's breastplate, weapon, and cape for himself. The Jewish scribes and military officials stayed with Bassus and Eleazar in the camp while the two men of noble dress returned to the Machaerus fortress. The Zealots and villagers understood that Eleazar had been freed and they exulted with deafening cheers of celebration and relief.

Ariel's heart pounded with wild, overflowing joy at the prospect of getting out of his crisis alive.

"Hallelu Yah!" he cried. "You've answered my prayers, Lord!"

In spite of his elation at the turn of events, Ariel couldn't help feeling indignant toward Eleazar. It amazed him that Eleazar could be so impious that he would allow all the citizens of Machaerus to give up their town just so he could save his own life.

The two apparent noblemen went through the village and citadel, announcing the surrender and urging everyone to prepare to evacuate within twenty-four hours. They also reported that upon leaving Machaerus, the Jews would be reunited with Eleazar.

After an hour passed, Gilal came to Ariel's cell.

"Everyone's evacuating, Ariel," Gilal said. "The fight's over. Leave before the Romans change their minds and kill us all!"

Ariel picked up the water jug and finished its remaining contents with one gulp. Then he grabbed the half-eaten loaf, left the cell, and headed down the stairs.

I have to find Dion! There's no reason for them to keep him now. If I can get to 'Scipio,' I should be able to get him to release Dion to me. Why not?

Ariel headed towards the south stable of the Roman camp.

With all the commotion of Jewish crowds moving out of Machaerus, and Romans preparing for their new mission of destroying a soon-to-be-empty village fortress, Ariel found it easy to sneak unnoticed into the southern stable. He went straight to the third stall on the right and found Dionysius there waiting.

"Dion!" Ariel shouted, surprised and elated to be reunited with his friend. "How did I not know I'd find you here?"

The two friends embraced and shed tears of relief.

"Thank the Lord you're alive, Ari! After the Zealots gave up, my captors let me go and said you'd come here eventually. It's a miracle! What's happened to you?"

"I have the most unbelievable story to tell you, Dion. I'll tell you everything on the way home. Let me just say right now that God has answered all my prayers! He even sent me the sign I was looking for. Now I know that Joshua's returning soon for sure! I have great news for everyone. Come, Dion. Let's go!"

34

Joshua and his ten disciples were about halfway to Tiberias when they began to hear unusual noises coming from the wooded area to their right. Joshua hushed his companions and turned his head to listen.

"It sounds like men," Joshua said in a low, quiet voice. "Arguing . . . now struggling . . . now striking . . . grunts . . . shouts of pain. Something ugly is happening in the woods."

The disciples heard it too.

"Elder Jacob, John, listen," Joshua said. "Sneak up, well out of sight, and find out what's going on. Then report back immediately. We'll wait here. Whatever you do, don't get discovered. But if you find trouble, whistle once to tell us you're coming our way, twice to tell us to come your way."

"I think I know what it is," Phillip said, whispering just loud enough to be heard by his companions. "It's probably tax agents roughing somebody up. I'll go with Jacob and John. I can help keep them out of trouble."

"Careful," Joshua whispered. "Keep yourself and the rest of us out of trouble too."

Elder Jacob, John, and Phillip skulked into the woods, every few steps hiding behind oak or terebinth trees to stay as invisible as possible. They followed the noises and soon found an elephant-sized rock half-embedded in the ground. Phillip signaled with his hand for Jacob and John to lay low while he poked his head out from behind the rock to take a peek.

Phillip saw a narrow path of dirt and grass ahead that cut through the woods and led to a clearing about a hundred feet away. The clearing was spacious with a few trees spread far apart from each other in the middle of it. Two tall, thick-trunked oaks each served as a hitching post for a pair of saddled horses. A pair of short terebinth trees with trunks branching out like double-pronged forks each held a man dressed in common peasant garb. Each man's neck was caught at the throat inside a trunk fork as if the tree were choking him. Above the back of each man's neck a wooden board was nailed to the forking branches to hold the man trapped in place. Four men of average build, dressed in the leather armor of Herodian law enforcers, were busy tormenting the two captives. Each captive had two tormentors, one striking his victim's body with some kind of rod or flagellum, the other spitting verbal abuse at his victim's face and punctuating the message with frequent slaps and punches.

Phillip signaled to Jacob and John that the three of them should make their way back to the other disciples. They exited the woods in the same stealthy way they had entered them and reunited with their companions.

"Just as I suspected," Phillip said under his breath. "Herodian tax collectors. Four of them, ganging up on a couple of rural folk. The hog-humping thugs have those two stuck in trees by the neck; they're flogging them without mercy. But we can take them, if we work together. I say we do it. If we don't, they'll kill those poor saps. We have to save them. Isn't that what we're all about—justice, mercy, salvation? How can we face our Lord's judgment if we permit this crime?"

"He's right, brothers," Joshua said. "This could be a test from the Lord. What's your plan, Phillip?"

"Well, there are eleven of us and four of them. We can put two of us on each thug, with three of us left over to assist. I'll start things by riling up the horses. This will distract the robbers; then four of us can knock them out and take their weapons. With the right-sized rocks, we can easily take them down. I've worked with these types; they're not well-trained fighters. Once we have them out or subdued, we cut or untie the horses free and send them running. This is important. We can't have any of the tax men galloping off to tell their friends or bosses about us. Next we'll tie up the robbers and free the peasants. If we each do our part, it'll be easy."

"This is crazy," John said, struggling to keep his voice down.

Simon nodded in agreement and said, "Yes. This isn't our fight. We're not fighters. What are we doing?"

The others, however, voted them down and wanted to try Phillip's plan. Matheus and Thomas in particular were eager to fight, and they relished the chance to inflict some well-deserved punishment on the Herodian persecutors.

"Brothers," Joshua whispered. "We're on the side of righteousness here. God will protect us. If you're a true disciple of mine, you'll trust God and do His will."

Simon and John fell in line with the others. Phillip picked up a rock the size of a brick.

"Each of you find a rock like this one," Phillip said.

They all grabbed the nearest such rock they could find from the plentiful supply along the side of the road.

"Phillip, lead us!" Joshua said. "I think the two Jacobs, Andreus, and myself should be the first to strike and take their weapons, unless circumstances favor others. Do you accept that, brothers?"

All nodded their assent.

"What else should we know, Phillip?" Joshua asked.

"When I raise my hand like this, with my finger pointed at me, that means I'm about to do something on my own and you should hang back. If I raise my hand like this, finger pointing to the sky, that means rush and attack. Grip your stone well and strike hard against the back or side of the head. Like this."

Phillip demonstrated the move with a harmless mock strike of his rock against Bartholomeus's head.

"Remember," Phillip said. "Absolute stealth. Stay silent and invisible."

Phillip, Elder Jacob, and John crouched and sneaked into the woods as they had before, using the trees as cover and keeping their eyes and ears wide-open for danger. Joshua and the rest followed their example and took meticulous care to be quiet and well hidden.

As they crept through the woods, many of the disciples filled the mental vacuum left by their silence with anxious misgivings about the impending ambush. What a moment ago appeared to be an urgent call to heroism was now, with each nervous step, looking more and more like a foolhardy leap into an unfathomable abyss. As their dread and self-doubt grew heavier, their senses became heightened and distorted, and soon their rising terror made them vulnerable to tricks of the mind. Breezes became the whispers of evil spirits. Twigs snapping underfoot evoked the clicking teeth of hungry beasts. Buzzing insects suggested the trembling warnings of disapproving guardian angels. Birds whistled mocking accusations of hubris in the face of inevitable failure.

Bewitched by these illusory perceptions, they failed to notice that the noises from the clearing had diminished. Only the occasional groan or kick against the dirt now emerged from their feared destination, but their panicked imaginations magnified those sounds and made some of the disciples think they could hear demons clawing at the earth from the underworld.

As they approached the elephantine rock, a sudden rumbling of thunderous cacophony from an indiscernible location rattled their nerves and shocked their senses. In reality, four horsemen rushed northward along the nearby road that the disciples had just left behind. Joshua, Phillip, Matheus, and Thomas, less terrified than the others, pressed themselves against thick trees to hide while they clutched their stones and anticipated an attack. The others immediately dropped their rocks and dove into bushes or flattened themselves on the ground, convinced that indomitable enemies had come to murder them. Soon the horsemen were long gone. Phillip looked past the boulder and made a brief scan of the area.

"Damn it!" Phillip shouted. "We're too late! Shit! All you cowardly cunts lying in the grass, get up! That was them! The four taxmen—that was them who just went by! Come on, everyone! Follow me and pray those two hapless rustics aren't dead!"

When they reached the clearing they found the two men with their necks still stuck in the trunk forks. They appeared to be unconscious, with their tunics torn and their bodies marked up with bloody cuts and welts. Elder Jacob and John pulled hard on one of the nailed boards until it popped off. Matheus and Thomas did the same to the other board. Joshua pulled one victim up from his tree, laid him on his back, and splashed water from his water skin onto the victim's face. Simon did the same to the other man. When they felt the water hit them, both men opened their eyes wide and reared back in fear, as if they expected a new round of torture to begin.

"Hallelu Yah!" Joshua shouted with relief. "You're alive!"

One of the bloodied men rubbed his eyes and looked around.

"You're Jews," he said.

"Yes," Joshua said. "But not from Herod. You're safe now."

The man looked over at his beat-up companion.

"Judas! Are you all right?"

"Yes, I think so. Just the usual tax-jackal injuries. What about you? How do you feel, Simon?"

"The same, God be praised."

The new Simon looked up at Joshua and asked, "Did you see those pricks get away? There were four of them."

"We might have," Joshua answered. "I did see four guilty-looking Herodian horsemen gallop past us. I suppose they must be the same who are responsible for this bloody crime. I'm just glad we found you still breathing. Please, take your time recovering. Let us clean you up and make sure you're not badly hurt. Simon, is it? And Judas?"

"Yes. I'm Simon and this is my younger brother Judas. Thank you for freeing us from those damn fork collars. Those pigs left us to die!"

"I'm happy to help anyone suffering abuse at Herodian hands, friend." Joshua said. "I'm Joshua. These are my companions."

Joshua introduced all of his disciples—he continued to call them "companions"—to Simon and Judas. Afterward Andreus, Andreus's brother Simon, Elder Jacob, and John started to clean up the injured brothers by applying oil to their wounds.

"So, Simon," Joshua said. "If it's all right with you, tell us how you got into such trouble with those tax collectors."

The new Simon took a deep breath and said, "I'm not ashamed to admit that Judas and I saw a pair of taxmen out here on the road and decided to ambush them. We thought there were only two, but then the other two came later. There was a fight, and they managed to subdue us and collar us in the trees. That's when they started to beat and berate us."

"What devilry were you up to . . . ambushing those men, as you say?" Joshua asked, disapproval evident in his voice.

"It wasn't common robbery," the new Simon said. "I swear to you, we didn't take the money for ourselves. That money belongs to the people. The tax collectors are the robbers! We put all the money we recover from tax collectors into the treasury of the synagogue. The elders then distribute it to the needy. We're just returning Jewish property to Jews."

"I suppose this time they got away with all the money," Joshua said. "Did you ever get your hands on it? Is that why they tortured you, because they thought you had money hidden somewhere?"

"No, not at all," Judas said, entering the conversation. "We never had the money. They wanted more than money. They were torturing us for information. They wanted us to betray our friends."

"Your friends?" Joshua asked.

"Yes," Judas answered. "There are many of us. We're all over Galilee—Judea too. We spy on the Herodian traitors to learn their plans and habits. And whenever we get the opportunity to strike, we take it."

"All right, that's enough out of you for now," the new Simon said to his brother. Turning back to Joshua, new Simon said,

"Before we say any more about ourselves, please tell us about you, friends and rescuers. What luck is responsible for bringing us together like this?"

"Well, have either of you heard of Rabbi Joshua of Nazareth?" Joshua asked.

"No," new Simon answered. "Neither the rabbi nor the town."

Joshua laughed.

"I'm Rabbi Joshua of Nazareth. My companions here are my disciples. We travel around to inform people that the time predicted by the prophets has arrived. It's true. God's judgment is near and we all must repent of our sins and make ourselves worthy to be admitted to His kingdom. We teach God's law to those who've forgotten it—to give them a chance to reconcile with their heavenly Lord. We baptize the penitent—following the example of the great Baptist, John. Sometimes we heal the faithful of their ills, if God wills it. We've returned many stray sheep to the Lord—in Capernaum, Seven Springs, Gennesaret, Magdala— and now we're on our way to Tiberias."

"Tiberias is where we live," Judas said. "We can help you get settled there, if you wish; it's the least we could do to repay your kindness, Rabbi. It sounds like you men are doing good work— teaching people the truth."

"Yes," new Simon added. "The prophets say that these are the last days of the pagans. Our people's deliverance is due to occur soon. We're always watching—watching for the moment when Herod stumbles, when our people can rise up and return our land to God. Soon the Romans will learn that we won't accept—we'll never accept—any authority other than God. We'll make it too costly for Caesar to oppress us. We'll make the Romans regret ever trying to plunder us and turn us against our God!"

Joshua laid a friendly hand on new Simon's shoulder.

"Your zeal is impressive, Simon," Joshua said. "But I assure you in all seriousness that you don't need to worry about fighting and rising up and revolting against Caesar. God will take care of all that. When judgment comes, it will be a divine cataclysm, like the Great Flood. God will ride down from heaven on His chariot, leading an army of angels. They'll upend the world. They'll cast the wicked who now rule us down from their towers—and throw them like weeds into the fire. And He'll gather the righteous faithful into His heavenly kingdom as a farmer gathers a fruitful crop. So trust in the power of the Most High God. It's He who'll rescue us from Caesar."

The new Simon stared in bewilderment at Joshua for a spell, and then suddenly blinked as if to refocus his attention on mundane reality.

"Yes," the new Simon said, breaking the awkward silence. "That would certainly be wonderful. I hope you're right. I really do. There *is* some debate about whether God Himself delivers the blow that rights the world, or whether God uses righteous men as His instrument to establish the renewed kingdom, but in my battered condition I'd rather put that aside for now. It's enough that we agree on the most important things—that God is the only true King of the Jews, that Caesar and Herod are our enemies, and that soon God will properly rule a new Israel in full power and glory, however it comes to be."

"Amen," Joshua said.

The new Simon stood up, stretched, and tested if he was in shape to walk. He was.

"Judas!" the new Simon said. "Are you able to walk on your own?"

Judas shook himself, stood, and walked over to his brother, whom he greeted with a quick grip on the shoulder.

"Bloodied as I am," Judas said, "I can walk."

"Come friends," the new Simon said. "We should be going. It's only a couple of hours to Tiberias. Let's find you some lodging. We'll acquaint you with Tiberias—city of too many Greeks!"

As the group shuffled back to the road, Young Jacob approached Judas.

"Friend Judas, forgive me if I pry, but I'm curious. If you don't mind telling me, did you or your brother give up any of your partners to those tax collectors when they were torturing you?"

"Absolutely not," Judas said, indignant. "We're loyal to the end. We'd die before we'd betray our friends. We learned this ethic from our father and we'll never abandon it."

"Your father?"

"Our father, Simon, was a rebel who fought under Judas the Galilean back when Coponius was procurator of Judea. He refused to pay taxes to the Romans or accept the authority of Caesar. The rebels never betrayed their principles or each other, not even under torture—even if it meant death. And that's how our father died—refusing to help the Romans rape our nation. And that's how Simon and I will go if we must."

35

Ariel and Zachariah sat on the roof of Ariel's house, leaning their backs against feather-stuffed cushions that they had brought up from the dining room. Dusk was fading into night on a warm, early summer's evening, and the almost-full moon cast its hazy glow above the shadow-shrouded foothills to the east.

"Can you imagine it, Ari?" Zachariah asked. "All those men killing their own wives and children, then slitting their own throats? I can't see myself doing the same thing in their position. It's too mad!"

"It just shows you how fanatical they were, like I've always told you. Those Sicarii, holed up in their clifftop fortress . . . they exemplify perfectly the spirit of the Zealots. In a way, it was the perfect ending—an unadulterated expression of the self-destructive lunacy that drove the rebels throughout the war. So many chances for peace—to save themselves and their families, and the whole nation too, from an utterly reckless and unnecessary leap into oblivion. But every time—defiance! In Gamala too, they killed themselves as the Romans encircled them. In Jerusalem they simply killed each other. So much thirst for blood! I suppose at some point nothing could be done. God issued his judgment, and those fools were hopelessly caught up in the storm—completely helpless in the face of divine justice."

"Yes. Perhaps you're right. Still, that Masada—such a tragedy! I heard that the Romans were planning to rape every woman and child before they enslaved them—after killing all the men, of course. Any Sicarii caught alive to be crucified, or burned to death, or both. If that's the case, then I imagine they made the right decision. Better to die with some dignity than be subjected to those horrors."

Zachariah sighed and added, "But on the other hand, it seems a little paranoid to me. The Romans had them trapped, but they hadn't even started the attack. The rebels had plenty of food, supplies, weapons—they could have put up a decent fight before doing something so desperate."

"They were doomed either way."

"Maybe so. I don't know. But apparently the Romans were expecting the Sicarii to fight them to the last man. When they approached the fortress, there was nothing but silence. They went in and saw nothing but corpses—dead fathers clutching their slain wives and children. A thousand dead. Incredible!"

Zachariah gave his cushion a violent slap with his hand.

"You know, Ari, I can't help but think that the Romans were disappointed by that grim surprise—robbed of the chance to satisfy their thirst for blood, and denied living victims for their depraved desires. But they must also have felt . . . well . . . they must have felt some admiration too. How could they not respect the way those rebels so unanimously, and so resolutely, committed themselves to die on their own terms like that? That kind of fearless contempt of death—there's an honor in that."

"Yes, maybe. But there'd be more honor to the sacrifice if there was a worthwhile purpose behind it. Ultimately, they killed themselves for a lost cause. Yes, they salvaged some pride and some dignity. But no one can deny that the war as a whole was nothing but a tragic, disastrous mistake."

Ariel and Zachariah sat in silence for a moment. Then Ariel let out a hushed, bitter laugh.

"What is it, Ari?" Zachariah asked. "Does the demise of our nation amuse you?"

"No, no," Ariel answered. "I was just remembering that shameful spectacle I saw at Machaerus. So different from

Masada! That was when I knew that the war was a sign of the end, and that Joshua will soon return. That pathetic Eleazar—the perfect embodiment of the anti-Christ spirit that brought all the catastrophes we've suffered. I still can't believe that he gave up the fight—surrendered his fortress and village—just to escape his own crucifixion. That's the evil opposite, the antithesis, of our Messiah Joshua, who handed himself over to be crucified to save his friends—to save the world!"

36

Tiberias was a new city, only a few decades old, founded by Herod Antipas and still in the throes of massive construction. A thirty-foot-high stone wall around every side of the city except the eastern lake shore was almost complete. The many docks stretching from the shore testified to the city's status as the second most important fishing and shipping port in Galilee after Magdala. This new capital of Galilee, residence of Herod Antipas himself for the last ten years, teemed with a growing population of about twenty-five thousand that was eighty percent Jewish and twenty percent Greek.

Judas and his brother Simon led Joshua's party to a weather-beaten former shipping warehouse, now being used as a barn and stable in a Jewish neighborhood in the southeast of the city. There were only three donkeys in residence, so Judas and Simon invited the disciples to each pick whichever of the many available hay bales was most to their liking and bunk in the barn for the night. They apologized for the roughness of it, but it was the best they could provide for the moment to a group of eleven.

In reality the barn and stables were a front meant to disguise the building's true purpose: storing smuggled goods, especially weapons, in feed barrels, grain baskets, and other deceptive places before being sold outside the grip of the ever-grasping tax authorities. Knives, swords, spears, archer's bows, sharpening stones, riding gear, tools, lumber, oil, fruit—if it was kosher they moved it, taking the most care with the weapons, which they sold only to other Jews. The donkeys were more than cosmetic, since they were often employed for merchandise transport, along with the occasional horse-drawn cart or boat when available.

Sometimes Judas, Simon, and their accomplices were caught by taxmen while transporting smuggled goods, especially when near city gates and other common Herodian outposts. They would compensate for the resultant losses by burglarizing tax treasuries in the city or attacking revenue-delivery crews out in the wilderness whenever they had the opportunity. Judas and Simon gained a decent livelihood from their work with the smuggling ring, and all the while they maintained their vigilance of political developments in order to discover the best ways to weaken the Herodian stranglehold on Galilee.

Judas and his brother proved to be a tremendous assistance to Joshua's ministry in Tiberias. They introduced him to the synagogues there, some of which had mikvot perfect for baptisms, and taught him the best times to use them to get an audience without interfering with the local rabbis' schedules. This helped Joshua befriend the rabbis and sometimes work with them, which in turn brought him into contact with most of the devout Jews in Tiberias. Judas and Simon also showed him several parks, amphitheaters, springs, markets, and other public spaces that he would eventually use in his mission to teach the Tiberians about the kingdom of God.

To Joshua's delight, Judas and Simon taught him the secret code words that the Tiberian Jews used to talk about Herod. This code allowed them to criticize and insult the government without arousing suspicion. In his public sermons Joshua could now fearlessly lambast Herod's crimes against the Jews, or lampoon Herod's craven sycophancy toward Caesar, by using words the local Jews perfectly understood but which Greek or Herodian ears heard as simple moral parables. Joshua might, for example, say a parable about a good and faithful dog who is rewarded by his master for bringing home dead birds from the hunt. On the surface such a tale would appear to be a lesson on pacifying

God with the proper Temple sacrifices. But his intended audience knew that the master was Caesar, the dog was Herod, and the dead birds were the economically eviscerated Jews.

In time Judas and Simon became enchanted by Joshua, and after they witnessed his public work—the authoritative but relatable teaching, the commiseration with the people's troubles, the healings, the exorcisms, and the popular adulation—they underwent baptism and became ardent followers. In short order they became disciples, proving themselves worthy by their devotion, loyalty, and enthusiastic commitment to the way of God and the ways of the group. To distinguish the new Simon from the old Simon, Joshua decided to call Judas's brother "Simon the Zealot" or "Zealous Simon," in honor of his frequent bragging about how he would rather die than acknowledge any other authority than God.

As Joshua made his way through Tiberias, developing a following little by little, supportive citizens would at times invite him to lodge with them in their homes. Joshua always politely declined but suggested that a pair of his disciples be welcomed in his stead. Every once in a while a friendly Tiberian would accept such an offer, and after a pair of months had passed Joshua had moved eight of his disciples out of the barn and into proper homes. Elder Jacob and John lodged with a family headed by a rabbi named Eliakim; brothers Simon and Andreus resided with a fisherman named Tobiah; Phillip and Bartholomeus stayed with the family of a produce merchant named Hashun; and Young Jacob and Thaddeus were the welcome guests of a carpenter named Binu.

Joshua himself remained in the barn with Matheus, Thomas, Zealous Simon, and Judas. Zealous Simon and Judas stayed there because it was their home, but Matheus and Thomas chose to live there to accustom themselves to a harder and rougher life, which they hoped would undo the softening effects of growing up with the comforts of wealth. Joshua chose the barn because he wanted to give special attention to his newest disciples. His goal was to bring the newcomers up to speed with the others in their knowledge of scripture and Joshua's own teachings.

One night, after the evening meal, Matheus approached Joshua.

"Rabbi, Thomas and I have been discussing the virtue of fasting. We want to fast—to grow closer to God by this means, but we're afraid. What if we, who have been well fed all our lives, can't endure it? Can our hunger make us weak to the influence of evil spirits?"

"I would recommend that you don't fast. Not while you're with me sowing the seeds of the kingdom all over the land. We need to eat to maintain our strength and endure the rigors of all our travelling and preaching. But if you ever find yourself unable to do this work, perhaps because you're imprisoned like John the Baptist, or perhaps because you're in some other way isolated from the people, then you may fast. But you must start small. Don't try right away to be the prophet Daniel and fast for weeks. Begin with a small fast, maybe a day long. Gradually increase the length of time. After a two-day fast, return to your normal habits, and then when you next fast try to last three days. Slowly build your tolerance this way. When you've sufficiently purified yourself through fasting, God will speak to you, probably by sending you visions. Don't be afraid of this. Have faith in God and He'll protect you. When I was in the wilderness with John the Baptist, I fasted and had visions, and unclean spirits came to tempt me. Those were the days I learned how to cast away the evil spirits. Demons are no match for the power of God."

Thomas, Zealous Simon, and Judas had been paying partial attention to this conversation from their various locations in the barn, but out of curiosity they assembled together with Matheus to listen to Joshua.

Joshua continued: "I spent days praying and fasting in the desert. I was like the Israelites when they were led by Moses through the wilderness after the Exodus. Like them I suffered hunger, fear, and the temptation to defy God's will. But I was determined to avoid making the mistakes of Moses's unfaithful followers. Remember how they grumbled at every turn, demanding water and food from God? And even after God sent them manna and well springs, they wanted more and complained, so God sent them the quails so they could have meat. And after all these miraculous gifts of providence, the moment any trouble or difficulty befell them they turned against God and demanded that Moses return them to Egypt! Faithless dogs! They were lucky to have Moses, who in his mercy begged God to spare them His wrath."

Joshua waved his hand as if to dismiss a bad memory.

"But I digress," Joshua said. "Let me return to my own experiences. Now . . . when I was out in the desert, exposed to the wild beasts and spirits, I drank from my cup of agony. Soon enough Satan came to me.

"'Eat, prophet!' the evil one said, 'God is powerful and merciful. Ask him to turn these stones into loaves!'

"'I don't want loaves,' I told him. 'I'm fasting. Right now my foods are the word of God and to do His will.'

"Satan showed me a high cliff. 'Prove yourself, prophet!' he said to me. 'Jump off the cliff. Surely God will send his angels to rescue you.'

"I said, 'That would be pointless. I'm already safe where I stand. And without the sin of putting the Lord to the test!'

"Satan showed me visions of the kingdoms of the world and all their splendor. 'All these I will give to you, with the power to rule them,' he told me, 'if you bow down before me and worship me.'

"I said to him: 'I have no use for these kingdoms. These are the same kingdoms that God will soon overturn when He establishes His righteous kingdom on earth, and when he throws you, Satan, as well as all your followers, into the pit! I worship God, and Him alone! It's His kingdom, and no other, that I seek! Be gone Satan!'"

Matheus, Thomas, Zealous Simon, and Judas stared wide-eyed at their master.

"Did that really happen, Rabbi?" Judas asked. "Did Satan himself confront you?"

"In all seriousness, brothers," Joshua answered. "If I told you every detail of my desert adventures, it would be such a long tale that judgment would probably be upon us before I finished. I've given you a parable, a brief sort of . . . summary . . . that encapsulates my overall experience of the temptations I faced while fasting. Let this parable be a lesson to you for when you fast. If you're steadfast and faithful to the Lord, you'll triumph over any evil spirit, even the king of evil spirits himself!"

* * *

The next morning Joshua and his twelve disciples met at the barn to have breakfast. They finished a basket of dried fish and a pot of lentil soup prepared by Simon and Andreus. After the meal John took Joshua aside to speak with him in private.

"Rabbi, aren't you worried about the Zealous brothers and their smuggling . . . uh . . . activities? We're all accomplices now. Surely you don't think it's right, or safe, do you?"

"Don't be so quick to judge, John. Simon and Judas pay their tithes, and they give to the needy. They rob only the Herodian extortionists, and you know those taxes aren't fair. To return what was unjustly confiscated from the people—that's not wrong. And as for safety, of course what they're doing isn't safe, but neither is what we're doing. The stooges of Rome don't like being told to repent and obey God any more than they enjoy having their ill-gotten spoils returned to their victims. We'll always be in danger from our enemies, but we can't worry about that. Our enemies are men, but our mission is from God. Don't fear men—they can only destroy the body. Fear Almighty God, who can destroy body and soul forever in the judgment of fire!"

Right when Joshua finished speaking he caught a glimpse of Simon, who looked more forlorn than he'd ever seen him. John said something, but Simon's apparent distress so disturbed Joshua that he heard none of it, and he walked that instant over to Simon as if John had ceased to exist.

"Simon, my brother," Joshua said. "You're troubled. What evil spirit has entered you?"

"Rabbi," Simon said, choking up. "Why do you put the last first and the first last? Why do you favor your newer disciples over those of us who have been with you since the beginning?"

"What? You're speaking nonsense, Simon. Explain yourself."

"Judas just told me about your fasting with John the Baptist—about how you were tempted by Satan in the wilderness. You never told me or Andreus about that. Why are you giving special knowledge to the new brothers, but not to us? Are we unworthy? Have we disappointed you somehow? Haven't we earned your trust? Why do you exclude us?"

Joshua smiled and laid his hand on Simon's shoulder.

"Simon, what am I going to do with you? How can you have so little faith in me?"

Joshua called all the disciples over to him and invited them to sit around him on a grassy patch inside the barn. When all were sitting and attentive, he taught them.

"Brothers, let me tell you a new parable about the kingdom. The kingdom of God is like a vineyard owner who went looking for workers to hire. Early in the morning he found some workers in the marketplace and agreed to pay each a denarius to work for the day in his vineyard.

"About nine in the morning he went out and saw others standing in the marketplace doing nothing. He told them, 'You also go and work in my vineyard, and I'll pay you a just wage.' So they went.

"He went out again at about noon, and again at about three in the afternoon, and did the same thing. At about five in the afternoon he want out and found still others standing around. He asked them, 'Why have you been standing here all day long doing nothing?'

"They answered, 'Because no one's hired us.'

"He said to them, 'You also go and work in my vineyard.'

"When evening came, the owner of the vineyard said to his foreman, 'Call the workers and pay them their wages, beginning with the last ones hired and going on to the first.'

"The workers who were hired at five in the afternoon came and each received a denarius. So when the earlier hires came, they expected to receive more. But each one of them, even the first hired, also received a denarius. When they saw that all would be paid the same, they grumbled against the landowner.

"'Those who were hired last worked only one hour,' they said, 'and you've made them equal to us who have borne most of the burden of the work and the heat of the day.'

"But he answered them, 'I'm not being unfair to you, friends. Didn't you agree to work for a denarius? Take your pay and go. I want to give the ones who were hired last the same as I gave you. Don't I have the right to do what I want with my own money? Or are you envious because I'm generous?'

"In this way the last will be first, and the first will be last."

The disciples, puzzled, looked around at each other and wondered what to make of the parable.

After a moment, Simon, his voice cracking with anger, said, "I hate this parable, Rabbi."

"Explain to us why you hate it, Simon," Joshua said.

Simon looked around, nervousness apparent in his eyes, took a deep breath, and began to make his case.

"I can't accept this madness that the last be first and the first be last. After all this time preaching justice, suddenly you tell us that the man who works one hour should be paid the same as the man who works twelve. This is obviously unjust, so you contradict everything else you preach. And now you seem to favor your newest disciples over your oldest. These Zealot brothers, they must have bewitched you somehow. What have you done to the rabbi, Simon and Judas?"

Zealous Simon and Judas, offended, began to rise up in protest but Joshua motioned them to stay seated and quiet.

Joshua sighed with exasperation and said, "Disciples, why do you grieve me? Can you really be so hard hearted? Don't you see the difference between man's justice and God's justice? I look around and see nothing but befuddlement in your faces, so I'll explain myself, if you have ears to hear.

"First, let me clear up this nonsense about me favoring some disciples over others. I value each of you equally. I've always insisted that the more experienced brothers help the newer arrivals learn our ways so they can be made equal to all. That's why I'm spending extra time with Matheus, Thomas, and the Zealot brothers. I'm catching them up to the rest of you. If I inadvertently teach something to one while neglecting to teach it to another, then I welcome you to come to me and get whatever instruction it is you think you've missed. For example, as far as I remember I've told all of you about my time with John the Baptist and my struggles in the wilderness. But if you have questions, come to me. I won't refuse you. What I teach to one I teach to all. So let no one claim any special status, and never try to put yourself above anyone else. Let the pagans rank each other and lord their power over one another! We don't play those games. If you're my disciple, then the humbler you are and the more you serve, the greater you'll be. And the more you try to put yourself above the others, the less you'll be. It's in this sense that the last will be first and the first will be last.

"Now I'll explain this parable which troubles you so much. It may help you to think of the vineyard workers as not all that different from you in your discipleship. If you've been with me a long time and think yourself better than the newcomers, then you're like the first-hired workers who grumble about their pay. Do you truly have a right to resent one of your brothers just because I found you before I found them? It's not like they could help meeting me when they did. The important thing is that when the spirit called, they obeyed and committed themselves completely. Was being with me such an ordeal that you envy the latecomers? Have they had it so easy? Do you wish it was you instead of Judas who was caught by the neck in that tree and getting whipped? Would you have preferred to be in Mary's position, possessed by demons as she was before I found her? Perhaps I've been stupid, assuming that you were grateful that I taught you the word and put you on the path to the kingdom! Is the kingdom not enough for you?"

Joshua paused and looked over his disciples as if he were probing their thoughts. Some disciples wore faint smiles. Others averted their eyes. Some nodded their heads. Others returned blank stares. Joshua spoke again.

"Consider, if you can, the laborers waiting in the marketplace. They couldn't help being chosen when they were. A man goes to the marketplace hoping to be hired, but stands around luckless and disappointed, pitied by passers-by, tortured by boredom and worried that he might not eat that day. Does he prefer that to decent work and pay? If he's called to work later, out of no fault of his own, is he unworthy to receive his daily bread? What's important is that he did what he could, when he could. Perhaps you think he should be paid a small fraction of what the early hires are paid, to go hungry for the crime of being hired late to the job he'd been hoping for all day long. Or maybe he should be paid his denarius, but the early hires should be paid ten or twelve denarii. A denarius per hour worked! But then the ones hired earlier, by virtue of nothing but lucky circumstance, can now enjoy several days in the security of guaranteed bread whether they work or not, while the later hires must face the next day in the same predicament as before, unsure of their next meal. And don't forget the poor vineyard owner. If he pays wages like that, he'll empty his treasury, and then what will he do when Herod's tax thugs come? He'll have to lose his vineyard to pay the taxes! We all know how that works. That's man's justice!"

Some of the disciples laughed. Joshua continued when they fell silent.

"So be grateful for the good luck that God grants you, and do all the good you can. If you're fortunate enough to be rewarded more than you need, share with the one who goes without in spite of doing all he can do. Not everyone can do as much as some others do, but everyone who does what he can deserves to eat. That's God's justice. Because God knows what you need and He knows your heart."

The disciples sat in silent and deep thought about what Joshua said. The lone exception was Simon, who grimaced as tears sild down his cheeks and into his beard.

"I'm a fool," Simon said, weeping. "I'm the worst of all of us! Now I understand your parable, Master, and I feel sorry for the world. We're so evil! Why can't we live as you describe, Rabbi? Why can't we live according to God's justice, like in the kingdom?"

"We can Simon. That's what we're here to do—to live according to God's justice and show others to do the same. It's difficult, of course, because it's not the way of the world. But *we* know this world is in its last days. It's giving way to the new one, the righteous one, God be praised."

"Amen!" the disciples cried. "God be praised!"

37

In the sixth year of his reign as emperor of Rome, Caesar Vespasian began to distribute the just-published and official Roman account of their victory over the Jews to all his important friends and associates. The book, organized into a set of seven codices, was titled *The Judaic War*, and was written by Josephus bar Matthias, a captured general from the Jewish military who switched to the Roman side and helped Vespasian and Titus defeat the Jewish rebels. Vespasian sent copies to the Roman archives, the consuls, the senate, the chief generals, the procurators of the provinces, the mayors of the important cities, and other deserving luminaries throughout the empire. When Theophilus, mayor of Antioch, finished reading his copy, he lent it to Chief Elder Evodius, the leader of the Antioch Christian community. When Evodius was done with it, he returned it to Theophilus, who then lent it to Ariel. Ariel devoured the book, which astonished and fascinated him, and upon finishing it he went to his friend Dionysius to share his excitement about what he had learned.

"Holy mother of whoredom, Dion!" Ariel said. "You have to read this book. I'll ask Theophilus to let you keep it for a while. It really is amazing. You think you know what happened during the war? You don't know the half of it!"

Dionysius pointed to a wooden box that Ariel was carrying. "Is that it? In there?"

"Yes," Ariel answered. "There are seven volumes, although the first volume is all about the Maccabees and Herod the Great, so you can skip that one and still get the whole story of the war."

"Who wrote it? Vespasian?"

"No. Josephus."

"Josephus? The traitor?"

"Yes! And he even describes how he betrayed the Zealots and became an assistant to Vespasian. It's a ridiculous tale."

"Tell it to me! Give me a short summary, right here."

"All right. Listen."

Ariel set the box down on a bench and sat down next to it. Dionysius sat opposite him in a wooden chair.

"So . . . Josephus," Ariel said, speaking in the excited tone of someone sharing a wicked piece of gossip. "He was in command of the rebel forces in Jotapata, trying to fend off Vespasian's invading legions. The defense failed, as you know of course, and when the Roman troops broke into the city and started the slaughter, Josephus and forty of his top officers hid themselves in a secret underground cavern. They brought several days-worth of food and waited for a chance to escape the city during the night. But the Romans had the city well-guarded, and Vespasian was smart enough to send out soldiers to search every possible underground hideaway. In two days Vespasian found him, and he wanted to take Josephus alive. Vespasian thought he'd be a valuable hostage with high-level knowledge of the Jewish forces.

"Now Josephus, self-preserving traitor that he was, decided to deliver himself up as Vespasian wanted. And you should read how he justifies his cowardly surrender! He claims to have had dreams in the past that were revelations from God—dreams that prophesized the future defeat of the Jews and Vespasian's rise to the emperorship. At that moment, the moment of decision to surrender or fight, the dreams came back to him in a visionary flash, and he supposedly realized that he was destined to reveal the future and help fulfill it according to God's will. Here. I have to read you this prayer that Josephus claims to have offered at that moment. Hold on."

Ariel opened the box and rifled through the volumes until he settled on one and brought it out.

"It's here in volume three," Ariel said, opening the codex and flipping through the pages. "Here it is: 'Josephus put up a secret prayer to God.' Listen to this prayer, Dion: 'Since it pleases you Lord God, who has created the Jewish nation, to defeat the same, and since all their good fortune is gone over to the Romans; and since you have made choice of this soul of mine to foretell what is to come to pass hereafter, I willingly give them my hands, and am content to live. And I protest openly, that I do not go over to the Romans as a deserter of the Jews, but as a minister from you, my Lord.' (*Judaic War,* Book 3, Chapter 8, passage 354) My God, Dion. Can you believe he had the nerve to write that?"

"Incredible," Dion answered. "Yes, it does seem to be an obscenely self-serving rationalization for his decision. But on the other hand, those prophecies of his did turn out to be true, just like those of Lord Joshua. Perhaps Josephus told the truth in that book."

"Sure. Maybe. But after all the events have occurred it's easy for him to write that he saw it all beforehand. Whatever the truth is, isn't it suspicious that Josephus justifies his surrender this way? It seems to me that Josephus concocted a pious lie to defend his treachery. I think you'll agree with me when I finish the story."

"Well, then by all means proceed," Dionysius said, eager to hear more.

"So when his officers became aware of Josephus's intent, they were furious at him, and they threatened to kill him for desertion if he didn't agree to fight the Romans with them and at least die with honor. But Josephus tried to persuade them to surrender too, arguing the immorality of making a hopeless last stand that was sure to be suicidal. Predictably, the officers rejected Josephus's proposal and remained as incensed as ever. So Josephus made his final desperate move. Since his officers were determined to die, he proposed that they all draw lots, and follow the rule that the man drawing the first lot be killed by the man drawing the second, and so on until all were slain. Amazingly, the officers agreed to this plan, and unsurprisingly, Josephus was the last left standing. Josephus claims in his book that his luck was due either to chance or God's providence. Can you believe that? Do you honestly think that there was no trickery involved in that sordid episode?"

Dionysius didn't answer. He didn't have to. The look of understanding in his eyes as he shook his head was evidence enough of his agreement.

"So," Ariel said. "Having escaped that danger, Josephus surrendered himself to Vespasian. Vespasian put him in chains and held him as an imprisoned hostage. But Josephus, when meeting Vespasian, told the general he'd had a vision from God Himself that foretold Vespasian's inevitable destiny to become emperor of Rome in the near future. According to Josephus's book, when Vespasian finally did become emperor, he remembered this prophecy of Josephus and, awed by the confirmation of it, released him from bondage and appointed him to be a high-level advisor in his retinue. Thus elevated, Josephus began his illustrious career as a Roman official, first helping Vespasian and Titus bury our nation, and next writing this history that portrays himself and his Roman masters in the most favorable possible light.

"Now, whether God really called Josephus to join the Romans, or whether Josephus is merely a self-serving opportunist, I leave that for you to decide for yourself. All I know for sure is that he's reserved for the devil, because as a Zealot or as a Roman, Josephus was in both cases a traitor to our people, and certainly no servant of the true God."

"But the way you tell it, Ari, it sounds like you sympathize with the rebels, in spite of all the things you've said against them. Is it so bad for Josephus to have been a traitor, considering that he betrayed the Zealots? Didn't they deserve it?"

"That's not the point! Of course the Zealots were villains in the war, as much as the Romans—no, more than the Romans were. Josephus himself says as much. My point is that Josephus was an opportunist. He knew how wicked the Zealots were, but he fought on their side anyway to elevate his own position in the government. And when it was convenient for him to switch to the Roman side, he did so to preserve and advance himself. If he really hated the Zealots and admired the Romans as much as he claims in his book, then why did he fight for the rebels in the first place? He didn't have to. Plenty of high-level priests and officials who opposed the war stayed out of it entirely. So I stand by my opinion. Josephus knowingly sided with one group of villains, and then another, according to the advantages he could secure from each."

Ariel held up the codex, slapped it with his fingers, and said, "Nevertheless his book about the war, as biased and embellished as it probably is, tells the story of our nation's undoing with thrilling candor. It will astound and horrify you, Dion. And despite the author's moral shortcomings, the actual facts of the war he describes only verify what I've been saying all along. You'll see, when you read it, that Joshua knew what was coming and revealed with his signs the sad events that were to unfold in our stupid, catastrophic war. I'll leave these volumes with you. I'm sure Theophilus will permit it. I'm going to buy a copy of my own for my library anyway. Just read them, Dion. Read them!"

38

Herod Antipas fretted in his grand, Greek-style palace on the east slope of the hill overlooking Tiberias from the west. Some of his spies had just informed him that John the Baptist was still causing trouble in spite of his imprisonment at Machaerus. They reported that John had been separated from the other prisoners because of his habit of preaching to them, and even in his isolation he argued to all the guards a compelling case for abandoning Herod's service and turning to piety—to avoid the fiery judgment God had planned for Herod and all the other unrepentant sinners of the world. Herod worried that John would soon have some of the guards under his spell and willing to help him escape somehow, after which John would be well placed to rouse his supporters to a possible anti-Herodian revolt. Herod wrote an order down on parchment, stamped his seal on it, and called for a courier.

"Get a sturdy group of body guards to ride with you and deliver this letter to Julius Petronius at Machaerus as soon as possible," Antipas ordered. "Stay there until Petronius gives you a package to deliver back to me."

The letter contained the order to have John the Baptist executed immediately. Julius Petronius was to send back John's head as confirmation.

When Herod received the evidence of John the Baptist's death, he ordered the news to be propagated throughout Tiberias and the rest of Galiliee, from whence it would surely pass on to all of Roman Syria. Herod's official version of the events, however, was a considerable departure from the truth. The story given to the public claimed that John had gone mad in prison, and when a pair of guards came to his cell to deliver the bread ration, he attacked them without reason, and in the fracas the guards accidentally killed him in their desperate attempt to defend themselves.

* * *

Joshua and his disciples were devastated by the news, and they refused to accept the mendacious particulars of the official report. Joshua, who had been careful to conceal his anti-Herod diatribes in allegorical parables but nevertheless was open about his association with John the Baptist, was convinced that he would be Herod's next target. At once he suspended the mission and proposed that they all get out of town for a while.

Through their smuggling activities, Zealous Simon and Judas knew of a remote wilderness beyond the hills south of Tiberias. It possessed caves hidden among rocky crags and thick coverings of brush, and the thirteen companions agreed to hide there to mourn the death of their beloved forerunner. That night they grabbed some supplies and fled under the cover of darkness. The Zealot brothers led the way.

They stayed hidden in the caves for seven days, mourning John. Joshua encouraged his disciples to fast as part of their mourning, and they all did so to different degrees. Matheus, Thomas, Phillip, and Bartholomeus fasted for one day; Zealous Simon, Judas, Young Jacob, and Thaddeus fasted for two; Simon, Andreus, Elder Jacob, John, and Joshua fasted for three. After their three-day fast, Joshua, Elder Jacob, and John went by themselves to the top of a hill to consume some of the food they'd brought: a loaf of bread, some salted tilapia, and a skin full of water. They shared their memories of John, praised his wisdom and courage, and prayed for the strength to continue the mission that he began. To close their meeting, each one of them recited a few scripture verses that each had selected as personal, pertinent expressions of their grief.

John went first, reciting from Isaiah: "So justice is far from us, and righteousness does not reach us. We look for light, but all is darkness; for brightness, but we walk in deep shadows. Like the blind we grope along the wall, feeling our way like people without eyes. At midday we stumble as if it were twilight; among the strong, we're like the dead. We all growl like bears; we moan mournfully like doves. We look for justice, but find none; for deliverance, but it's far away. So justice is driven back, and righteousness stares at a distance; truth has stumbled in the streets, honesty cannot enter. Truth is nowhere to be found, and whoever shuns evil becomes prey." (Isaiah 59:9–11, 14–15)

Elder Jacob followed with a recitation from Psalm ninety-four: "Take notice, you senseless ones among the people; you fools, when will you become wise? Does He who fashioned the ear not hear? Does He who formed the eye not see? Does He who disciplines nations not punish? Does He who teaches mankind lack knowledge? The Lord knows all human plans; He knows they're futile. Can a corrupt throne be allied with you, Lord—a throne that brings on misery by its decrees? The wicked band together against the righteous and condemn the innocent to death. But the Lord has become my fortress, and my God the rock in whom I take refuge. He will repay them for their sins and destroy them for their wickedness. The Lord our God will destroy them." (Psalm 94:8–11, 20–23)

Last, Joshua recited from Isaiah: "The righteous perish, and no one takes it to heart; the devout are taken away, and no one understands that the righteous are taken away to be spared from evil. Those who walk uprightly enter into peace; they find rest as they lie in death." (Isaiah 57:1–2)

On the seventh day of mourning, Joshua assembled his disciples and proposed a new plan for the immediate future.

"Disciples! Each one of you has become a master of the word. You know the law and the prophets as if those holy books were engraved on your hearts. You all know how to baptize the penitent and preach the way of righteousness. You can cast out evil spirits and pray for God to heal the faithful. You're now rabbis in your own right. I can say in all seriousness that each of you is an extension of myself.

"The time has come for us to separate for a short while, so that we can be in several different places at once and keep Herod off our trail. I'll send you out in pairs to different towns, towns that you already know, where you can check up on our friends and bring the word to anyone we missed. Find friends and sympathizers to stay with and eat what they give you. Spend forty days in the place I send you, and then go to Capernaum, where we'll reunite.

"Zealot brothers, sons of Simon, I want you to return to Tiberias. Stay for forty days and preach as before but never mention Herod or John the Baptist. Stay vigilant and always be one step ahead of the Herodians. Can you accept this?"

"We can," Zealous Simon and Judas answered.

"Also, can you buy a boat that will carry the rest of us out of Tiberias?"

"Easily," Judas said.

"Good. When can you get it?"

"In three days or less," Zealous Simon answered.

"Excellent. The eleven of us will meet you two at your barn during the fourth night after tonight. Take us to the boat so we can escape in the dark. Agreed?"

"Agreed," the Zealot brothers answered.

"Matheus and Thomas, we'll sail to Magdala and I'll leave the two of you there. Check up on Mary and continue the mission there for forty days. Then go to Capernaum. Will you do this?"

"We will."

"Phillip and Bartholomeus, we'll leave you in Gennesaret. Sow the word there for forty days and then go to Capernaum. Will you do this?"

"We will."

"Simon and Andreus, we'll let you off in Seven Springs, where you'll preach the word for forty days. Will you do this?"

"We will."

"Elder Jacob and John, you'll get off the boat in Capernaum. The two of you will be on your own there. Do you accept this?"

"We do."

"Young Jacob and Thaddeus, you'll go with me to Bethsaida to help me sow the word there for forty days. Do you accept this?

"We do."

"Then we're all in agreement. Good. Soon you may feel as if I've sent you out like sheep to the wolves. Don't be afraid. You're ready. Be as shrewd as snakes to avoid the snares of the wicked, but be as innocent as doves so no one can bring anything against you. Again, say nothing about Herod or John the Baptist. Rejoice over everyone you win for the kingdom, and whenever you face hostility and rejection from the scoffers, shake the dust off your feet as testimony against them and leave them for the Lord to judge. Again, don't be afraid. If you have faith, the Lord will bless and protect you. Peace be upon all of you."

Joshua and the others said their goodbyes to the Zealot brothers, blessed them, and prayed for their safe return to Tiberias. Four nights later Joshua and the remaining ten disciples sailed out of Tiberias on a twelve-man fishing boat.

39

In little time Josephus's history of the war became a sensation in Antioch. Literate Greek officials and learned rabbis passed the few available copies among themselves and engaged in passionate discussions about it with their friends. Those few who could read the Greek text were enlisted to hold readings for groups of the illiterate so all citizens could hear it. Scribes worked to make more copies in Greek and translations in Aramaic. Readers and listeners from the Jewish and Christian communities divided themselves into two camps: those who believed that the war was the beginning of the judgment that would soon expand its reach to the ends of the earth, destroy the pagan nations, and elevate the righteous elect to the heavenly kingdom; and those who believed the defeat of the Jews was a sign that God had abandoned the Jews—but only for a limited time, as He had in the days of the Babylonian Exile—and that some worthy remnant of Israel would begin the process of rebuilding the nation at some point in the indefinite future. Jews of the first camp joined Christian churches; Christians of the second camp deserted them.

One Sabbath morning, not too long before the Jewish month of Sivan, Ariel finished a synagogue service that drew a measly crowd of about twenty percent capacity. Dejected, he returned to the vestments room, changed out of his rabbi's cloak and into a sackcloth tunic, smeared ashes into his hair, and shambled out into the city. He wandered north out of the Jewish Quarter and toward the amphitheater until he reached a marketplace where the Greek neighborhoods clustered.

He drifted along the edge of the square and passed cloth-shaded stands and kiosks offering all sorts of miscellaneous merchandise that sickened him to see: gaping baskets of slimy fish and sticky fruit; textiles in an obscene variety of brash colors; rich collections of ceramic ware painted with shameless scenes of sex, swordplay, and slaughter; gleaming-metal cooking utensils on brazen, aggressive display; and the cage-incarcerated fowl, condemned and clucking. The merchants competed and conned, the crowding customers haggled and hectored, and the hot midday air slathered its dewy humidity onto every available surface of sweltering skin. Ariel wanted the earth to open up and swallow all of it.

He saw a crowd in front of a raised platform, where a man brought up almost-naked men and women to be exhibited one at a time—a slave auction. Ariel strode up to the crowd and began to accost it.

"Woe to you, Antioch!" Ariel shouted. "You'll burn like Jerusalem! Alexandria, Rome, you won't be spared either! The age of the pagans is over!"

Some in the crowd turned around and looked askance at Ariel. Unimpressed by what they saw, they turned back around and made no effort to hide their dismissive disinterest.

"Yes, turn your backs on me pagans!" Ariel yelled. "Just like the Jews turned their backs on their Messiah! And look what came of that! God's judgment is at hand! Woe to you, pagans!"

Some of the bystanders pointed at Ariel and laughed. Others looked around for city guards who might come to eject the annoying mendicant and end the disturbance.

"You have no idea what's coming, Antioch!" Ariel shouted with as much pious indignation as he could muster. "Woe and desolation! Woe upon woe! Haven't you seen what the Romans did to Jerusalem? They did it at God's command! But God isn't finished. No! Now it's the pagans' turn to drink the cup of His wrath! Isn't God mightier than—"

"Ariel!" a familiar and approaching voice shouted. "I thought I recognized you. You look . . . uh . . . not well."

Ariel turned and saw his friend Zachariah hurrying toward him.

"Zachariah?" Ariel asked as if coming out of a dream.

"Yes! It's me! Mother of Joshua, you're raving! Are you drunk?"

"No. Not at all. In fact, I've been fasting."

"Fasting. Of course. Look at you in your sackcloth and ashes. What are you mourning?"

"The whole God-damned world, Zachary. The whole God-damned world!"

Zachariah grabbed Ariel by the shoulders and started to lead him out of the marketplace.

"Come, Ariel," Zachariah said. "Let's get you back home. You're not well."

Ariel yielded to Zachariah and followed him back to the Jewish Quarter.

"By the cross, Ariel!" Zachariah said, astonished. "You were ranting like Yesus son of Ananus back there."

"Who?"

"Yesus son of Ananus. From Josephus's book. Remember when Josephus described the signs that foretold the destruction of the Temple? The doors opening by themselves, the cow giving birth to a goat, the warriors in the sky, the voice in the Temple that said, 'Let us be removed?' Yesus son of Ananus was the last of those signs. Don't you remember?"

"Yesus," Ariel said, sounding puzzled. "That's the Greek for Joshua, isn't it?"

"Yes. Of course. You still aren't fully lucid right now, are you? Don't worry, we're almost at your house. I'll explain it when you've had some rest."

When they reached Ariel's house, Zachariah eased Ariel into his bed and let him sleep. Zachariah looked around the kitchen for something to break Ariel's fast, something small for when he woke up, and settled on a jar of almonds and a small dish filled with honey. He set them on the table and went into Ariel's study to sit and rest. He looked for something to read and noticed that Ariel had a set of the seven volumes of Josephus's *Judaic War*.

After Ariel had slept and eaten, Zachariah opened the sixth volume of *The Judaic War* and showed Ariel the passage he'd referred to on the way home.

"See? It's right here in chapter five. Read it."

"Right, right," Ariel muttered as he read. "The signs at the Temple, the cow, the gate, the sky, the voice, I remember this."

Ariel started to read the Greek text aloud: "But, what's still more terrible, there was one Yesus, the son of Ananus, a plebeian and a husbandman, who, four years before the war began, and at a time when the city was in very great peace and prosperity, came to that feast whereon it's our custom for everyone to make tabernacles to God in the Temple, began on a sudden cry aloud, 'A voice from the east, a voice from the west, a voice from the four winds, a voice against Jerusalem and the holy house, a voice against the bridegrooms and the brides, and a voice against this whole people!' This was his cry, as he went about by day and by night, in all the lanes of the city. However, certain of the most eminent among the populace had great indignation at this dire cry of his, and took up the man, and gave him a great number of severe stripes; yet did he not either say anything for himself, or anything peculiar to those that chastised him, but still he went on with the same words which he cried before.

"Hereupon our rulers supposing, as the case proved to be, that this was a sort of divine fury in the man, brought him to the Roman procurator; where he was whipped till his bones were laid bare; yet did he not make any supplication for himself, nor shed any tears, but turning his voice to the most lamentable tone possible, at every stroke of the whip his answer was, 'Woe, woe to Jerusalem!' And when Albinus (for he was then our procurator) asked him who he was, and whence he came, and why he uttered such words; he made no manner of reply to what he said, but still did not leave off his melancholy ditty, till Albinus took him to be a madman, and dismissed him.

"Now, during all the time that passed before the war began, this man did not go near any of the citizens, nor was seen by them while he said so; but he everyday uttered these lamentable words, as if it were his premeditated vow, 'Woe, woe to Jerusalem!' Nor did he give ill words to any of those that beat him every day, nor good words to those that gave him food; but this was his reply to all men, and indeed no other than a melancholy presage of what was to come. This cry of his was loudest at the festivals; and he continued this ditty for seven years and five months, without growing hoarse, or being tired therewith, until the very time that he saw his presage in earnest fulfilled in our siege, when it ceased; for as he was going round upon the wall, he cried out with his utmost force, 'Woe, woe to this city again, and to the people, and to the holy house!' And just as he added at the last—'Woe, woe, to myself also!' there came a stone out of one of the engines, and smote him, and killed him immediately; and as he was uttering the very same presages, he gave up the ghost." (*Judaic War*, Book 6, Chapter 5, passages 300–309)

Ariel stopped reading and stared wide-eyed into space.

"Do you see, Ari?" Zachariah asked. "That's how you were acting, out there in the market. You were raving just like this Yesus in Jerusalem. Honestly, I was frightened for you. Just how long had you been fasting, my friend?"

Ariel seemed to not have heard Zachariah. He continued to stare, pensive.

"Ariel? Did you hear me? Are you all right?"

"He's making fun of us." Ariel said, his tone of voice grim and serious.

"What? What are you talking about?"

"Josephus. He's making fun of us. This passage, it's some kind of satire. Yesus son of Ananus isn't a real person. He's some kind of allegory for Christians in general. Josephus is ridiculing us."

"Really? How do you figure that? Josephus probably doesn't even know about us. You're not going mad, I hope. You're scaring me again, Ari. Please tell me you're not going mad!"

"Relax, Zachary. I'm completely sane. Listen. Of course Josephus knows about our sect. Aren't we Christians famous in Rome, thanks to Nero, and throughout the empire, thanks to Paul? Paul, who showed me the way in my youth, and encouraged me to learn this written Greek language when he was here in Antioch? Everyone knows about us. Most of them hate us, but they know about us. There's no way Josephus hasn't heard of us. He's probably only heard lies and slander, but that's beside the point."

"All right. So he knows about us. Explain to me how this passage is mocking us."

"First of all, look at the name of this character. Yesus is Greek for Joshua. Ananus is Greek for Hananiah, which means 'favored by God' in our language. Joshua is the offspring of the 'favored,' meaning God's favored people, the Jews. Yesus represents the sect of the Jews that acknowledges Joshua to be the Messiah."

"Or Yesus and Ananus are simply Greek versions of extremely common Jewish names."

"That would be a good point if it weren't for the highly suggestive behavior of this Yesus. He pronounces woe onto the Temple and judgment for Jerusalem. The 'most eminent among the populace' take him and give him 'a great number of severe stripes.' He has a 'divine fury' in him, and he's stoic as he gets 'whipped till his bones are laid bare' by the Roman procurator. Does this sound like anyone you know?"

Zachariah shrugged. "Maybe Josephus heard the Joshua story, but an inaccurate version of it."

"An inaccurate version, yes. But to place it at the time of the war? Even Josephus would know that Joshua died during the reign of Caesar Tiberius. Everyone who knows the Joshua story knows that."

"Then maybe it really is a true story about someone named Joshua who did things that were similar to what Christ Joshua did—an imitator who got killed in the war."

"I think that's too coincidental. Why would Josephus notice this one particular man, this Joshua imitator who preaches doom to Jerusalem? Such men always turned up at the festivals. Many Christian pilgrims acted just like this Yesus. That's why I think this Yesus character represents Christians as a group. Josephus must be familiar with Christians, and the things the louder members of our faith used to do at the festivals, so he created this composite character and named him Yesus son of Ananus because . . . well . . . what name would be more perfect than that? Just look at this part of the passage: 'this man did not go near any of the citizens, nor was he seen by them.' The more fanatical Christians behaved exactly this way on their pilgrimages to Jerusalem; they didn't go out of their way to confront people because they knew the hostility that they could get from some of the Jews. Such Christians were happy to be ignored and unnoticed by the general population. And when pilgrims of this type were targeted for abuse by unbelievers, they behaved as Josephus describes here: 'Nor did he give ill words to any of those that beat him every day, nor good words to those that gave him food.'

"Josephus is taking the most fanatical element of our sect as representative of all of us. He probably knows no better than to see us this way; it's probably his only experience of Christian behavior. And look at how Josephus ends his tale. Yesus says, 'woe to myself also' and then gets killed in a comical catapult mishap. It's a joke. The message is that those who believe in Christ Joshua are a joke, and that Joshua was no messiah—just a common prophet of doom who was as powerless as any other to rescue Israel."

Zachariah sighed.

"Well, all I can say is . . . uh . . . that you're a very clever man, Ari . . . a man of visions and special interpretations. If you're right, then Josephus mocks us. That's not surprising, given what we already know of his character. But so what? What does it change? I doubt that many others will see the same things that you do in this passage. People are going to believe what they want to believe."

40

When the disciples finished their forty-day missions, they reunited with Joshua in Capernaum and reported on all they had done. Joshua called each pair to him in turns and listened to their accounts of how things went for them. Joshua was pleased to learn that they all had found lodging with sympathizers and had evaded serious trouble from the Herodian authorities. The disciples assured Joshua that they exhausted themselves trying to reach everyone they could and persuaded many to repent in anticipation of the coming kingdom.

But without Joshua there to assist them, they also found themselves confronting unexpected challenges. For as well as they had learned Joshua's way of doing things, they couldn't project his level of charisma and authority, so they struggled to generate the same degree of enthusiasm in the populace, especially with those who were not already familiar with Joshua and his work. Likewise they were not as successful as Joshua had been in their attempts to heal the sick and cast away demons. And in spite of their remarkable command of scripture, they were often unable to provide satisfactory answers to people's questions. The disciples came to the disappointing conclusion that Joshua's baffling talents—his ability to inflame people's hearts with rekindled hope, his power to transform how his listeners saw the world, and his gift for spinning provocative parables out of the raw materials of folk wisdom, scripture, and ordinary life experience—were beyond them.

The disciples shared with Joshua the questions from the public that they struggled or failed to answer.

Simon asked Joshua, "What do I say to someone who asks me how to pray correctly or who asks me why God doesn't answer their prayers?"

Elder Jacob asked, "How can I advise someone who wants revenge on an enemy?"

Bartholomeus asked, "Rabbi, what can I say to a man who asks me how to correctly divorce his wife?"

Matheus asked, "How do I answer the man who asks for the proper way to rebuke sinners?"

Thaddeus said, "A man stumped me when he asked at what point a man's sinfulness makes him unworthy of forgiveness."

Judas asked, "What do I say to the man who asks how to tell a true prophet from a false one?"

Joshua had Matheus write all these questions down and said to the disciples, "These questions are many and deserve careful thought. Let me consider them tonight and tomorrow I'll teach you what you need to know."

That night Joshua and his disciples divided themselves into two groups, each going to a particular house for lodging. Simon, Andreus, Phillip, and Bartholomeus stayed in Simon's house, with Matheus and Thomas sleeping on the roof. Joshua, Elder Jacob, John, Thaddeus, and Young Jacob bunked with Zebedee in his house, with Zealous Simon and Judas taking the roof.

The next morning the disciples all gathered in a shady grove of olive trees near Simon's house and shared a breakfast of bread, oil, and figs. After everyone had finished eating, Joshua called them to attention.

"Disciples! With great seriousness I considered the questions you brought to me last night, and after much contemplation and prayer, our heavenly Father blessed me with the answers you seek. So listen with ears to hear.

"You told me the people want to know how to pray. I will tell you. When you pray, find a quiet place where you can be alone, and pray to your heavenly Father. As your Holy Father is unseen, be unseen by others. That way you won't be like those hypocrites who stand out in front of everyone and pray with great fanfare in order to show the world how pious they are. They only pray to win the admiration of others, and that will be the extent of their reward because God isn't impressed. But if you pray alone and with sincerity, God will hear you. There's no need to recite arcane formulas or invoke the ancients as the pagans do, as if the more strange words they speak the more they'll be heard. God knows what you need, even before you ask him, so speak plainly when you pray.

"I've composed a prayer that anyone can say—a prayer for everyone, because there are things that everyone needs: bread, forgiveness, protection from evil, and to do the will of the Father. Share this prayer with everyone who listens to you: Our Father, Lord of heaven, hallowed is your name. May your kingdom come, and your will be done, on earth as it is in heaven. Give us today our daily bread, and forgive our transgressions, as we forgive those who transgress against us. Give us time to repent before the end, and protect us from the evil one.

"I'll recite this prayer with each of you later, until you have it completely engraved on your heart. That will be easy enough. But you must do more than know it and say it; you must fulfill it. You must forgive those who have wronged you if you're to be forgiven for all the ways you've offended your heavenly Father. How many times must you forgive the one who sins against you? Seven times? Seven times seventy times! How can you expect the Lord to forgive you if you don't forgive your neighbor? I have a parable for this.

"The kingdom of heaven is like a king who wanted to settle accounts with his servants. One of these servants, a man who owed the king ten thousand denarii, was brought to him. The servant was unable to pay, so the king ordered all the man's property to be sold, and furthermore that the man himself, his wife, and his children be sold into slavery to repay the debt. The servant prostrated himself before the king and begged, 'Please give me time and I'll pay back everything!' The king took pity on the man and let him go with the debt cancelled.

"But later the servant encountered a fellow servant; this servant owed the first a hundred denarii. The first servant grabbed the other by the neck and, choking him, demanded the money owed. The debtor prostrated himself and begged, 'Please give me time and I'll pay you back!'

"The first servant showed no mercy. He had the other servant thrown into prison, to be released only when the hundred denarii were repaid. The other servants saw this and were indignant. They went to the king and told him everything that happened.

"So the king had that first servant brought to him. 'You wicked swine!' the king said, 'I cancelled your huge debt because you begged for mercy. Shouldn't you have done the same for your fellow?' The outraged king handed the servant over to the jailers and torturers, to be released only at the repayment of ten thousand denarii!

"This is how your heavenly Father will treat you unless you forgive your neighbor's transgressions against you."

Joshua paused a moment to let the lesson sink in. The disciples sat in silence.

"Now," Joshua said, tearing the disciples away from their thoughts. "People are coming to you complaining that God isn't answering their prayers. Listen carefully as I explain to you how God answers prayers.

"Ask, and it will be given you; seek and you'll find; knock and the door will be opened to you. Everyone who asks receives; the one who seeks finds; and to the one who knocks, the door will be opened.

"What father, if his son asks for bread, gives him a stone? Or if he asks for a fish, will give him a snake? If man, who is evil, knows how to give good things to his children, how much more will your Father in heaven give good things to those who ask him! Remember that David said, 'Praise the Lord, my soul, and forget not all His gifts—He who forgives all your sins and heals all your diseases, who redeems your life from the pit and crowns you with love and compassion, who satisfies your desires with good things so that your youth is renewed like the eagle's. As a father has compassion on his children, so the Lord has compassion on those who fear Him, those who keep His covenant and remember to obey His precepts. The Lord has established His throne in heaven, and His kingdom rules over all.' (Psalm 103:2–5, 13–19)

"So God will give you the good things that you ask for, *if* you fear Him, keep His covenant, and obey His precepts. But if you're arrogant towards God, violate His covenant, or disobey His law, you can't expect God to reward you. Can a disrespectful child who disobeys his father expect his father to reward him? So consider that when you think God refuses to hear your prayers. God is generous and merciful, but atone for your offenses before you ask favors of your heavenly Father.

"And consider well what you ask of Him. If your son asked you for a sword so he could go and murder your neighbors, would you give it to him? If your daughter asked for a statue of Astarte so she could worship it, would you grant her that? If man has sense enough to refuse his children such evils, how much more will God refuse to give things that offend Him to those who ask for them. Before you ask your Holy Father for something, ask yourself if that thing is good for you—if it's something pleasing to Him and consistent with His will. If it isn't, then leave it out of your prayers, lest you offend your heavenly Father and bring misfortune on your head.

"Now, some of you have been asked the proper way to rebuke sinners. This is what you're to do: rebuke yourself for your own sins. If you can face your own sins and correct your own behavior, then you can go to your brother and point out his sins. How can you complain about the speck of dust in your brother's eye when you yourself have a plank in your eye. First take that plank out of *your* eye. Then you'll see clearly enough to remove the speck from your brother's eye. Always consider well your own sins before you pass judgement on another. For however you judge others—so you will be judged.

"Some of you have faced the suspicion of the people. They look at you and wonder if you're telling them the truth or merely attempting some deceitful trick. Can you blame them for their caution? Are there not false prophets everywhere—ravenous wolves dressed in sheep's clothing? If the people doubt, you can set their hearts at ease with the fruits of your work. Do people pick grapes from thorn bushes, or figs from thistles? Every good tree bears good fruit, but a bad tree bears bad fruit. If you speak truthfully, give good counsel, heal the sick, and drive away evil, then those are the good fruits that prove you are truly a servant of God. Likewise, a false prophet will tell lies, lead people astray, and put them on an evil path. Destruction, misery, and impiety will be the bad fruits that follow a false prophet. A good tree can't bear bad fruit and a bad tree can't bear good fruit. Every tree that doesn't bear good fruit is cut down and thrown into the fire. So tell the people to recognize the true and false prophets by their fruits.

"Now, the fact that people are coming to you and asking how to get revenge on their enemies or how to divorce their wife shows me that many people lack a proper understanding of the law. So let me clarify a few things for you so you can make them clear to the people.

"First of all, the fact of the imminent judgment makes it necessary for us to embrace righteousness with greater seriousness than we're normally accustomed. If we're to be worthy of the kingdom, our goodness must exceed traditional expectations. So consider the revenge question. Tradition has taught us to love our friends and hate our enemies. But I say we must love our enemies and pray for our persecutors to find the way. Our mission is to bring people to the kingdom, and there's no time for hate and anger over past wrongs. It's hard enough already to win the kingdom; people hardly have time to put themselves on the right course, to heal their rifts, to atone for their sins, and put away all grievances before the judgment settles their accounts for them.

So tell people to set their hearts on their heavenly Father and forget about everything that might keep them out of the kingdom. Do you burn for revenge on your enemy? It's too late for you to worry about that now. Something much more serious is at hand. Doesn't God cause His sun to rise on the evil as well as the good? Doesn't He send rain on the righteous as well as the unrighteous? If you love only those who love you, how are you any better than the pagans and the tax collectors? Don't they do the same? So let goodness be the only thing you bring to the world from now on. Then you'll be doing the will of your Father in heaven.

"Likewise, consider the part of the law that says, 'eye for eye and tooth for tooth.' That was all well and good when judgment was far away and orderly society needed to endure. But now we must be better. Don't resist evil with evil. You can't afford to do any more evil. If someone slaps you on your right cheek, offer them the left as well. If you show them that you're willing to go so far as to die to stay true to righteousness, then you'll shame them to recognize their own actions. If someone sues you for your shirt, give them your coat as well. You don't need it anymore. Nothing matters anymore but the kingdom. The only thing you can't afford to lose now is your righteousness.

"Now let me tell you everything you need to know about divorce. In Genesis it's written: 'At the beginning of creation God made them male and female' (Genesis 1:27) and 'For this reason a man will leave his father and mother and be united to his wife, and the two will become one flesh.' (Genesis 2:24) They are no longer two, but one flesh. Therefore what God has joined together, let no one separate. I realize that Moses allowed men to divorce their wives, but that was a concession made for the hard hearted. If your wife is alive, then clearly she hasn't been convicted of adultery, so why are you talking about divorce? Do you suspect her of adultery? Then only proof can settle the issue, and if she's guilty she'll die. Otherwise how can you talk about divorce? You're just setting up yourself and your wife to commit adultery, because if either of you marry someone new, that's adultery. You can't afford to be committing adultery with judgment looming as it is. Accept that marriage is a sacred oath.

"And speaking of oaths, consider the tradition that says, 'Don't break your oath, but fulfill to the Lord the vows you've made.' Men are going around saying things like, 'I swear by the Temple that I'll shave my head if my field grows more crops this year than it did last year.' It's time to stop profaning the Temple with petty oaths like this. How can you test God like this while judgment hangs over your head? Don't swear by heaven, because heaven is God's throne; nor by the earth, because it's His footstool; nor by Jerusalem, because it's the Holy City. Don't even swear by your head, because you can't make even one hair white or black. Simply say 'yes' when you mean 'yes' and 'no' when you mean 'no.' Anything beyond that is from the evil one."

Joshua took a swig from his water skin. Mid-gulp, Simon asked, "So . . . are you rewriting the law?"

Joshua spit out a mouthful of water and choked.

"What?" Joshua croaked, coughing out the vaporous last drops of the ejected water. "Holy shit, no! Are you listening to me? Am I talking to the wind?"

Joshua raised his hands, looked up to the sky, and quoted from Psalm twenty-two: "My God, my God, why have you forsaken me?" (Psalm 22:2)

Joshua sighed with exasperation, brought down his hands, and looked down on his disciples.

"Listen," Joshua said, speaking with slow and solemn deliberation, "and let it sink into your hardened hearts. I'm not saying anything that contradicts the law. I'm saying that it's not enough just to follow the law. You need to obey the law, every bit of it, but don't limit your righteousness to obedience to the law. The law is filled with proper ways to settle disputes with your neighbor and atone for sins, but now you must avoid getting into disputes in the first place, and you must shun the sin before you even find yourself in need of atonement. It's too late! Again, most people barely have enough time to settle the disputes and atone for the sins that they've already amassed. With God's hand of judgment ready to strike at any moment, our repentance must be total and final. We must turn ourselves completely over to God's kingdom and never look back. That's how we fulfill the whole purpose of the law and the prophets. And until God accomplishes everything He's set out to accomplish, until this world has passed away and there remains only the new world of God's kingdom, truly not one letter, not one stroke of a letter in the law will pass away. I tell you in all seriousness that anyone who sets aside one of the least of the commands of the law and teaches others to do the same will be called least in the kingdom, but whoever teaches and practices those commands will be called great in the kingdom. And the kingdom is at hand! So now we must do more than keep within the line of the law. The Pharisees and others like them may be satisfied with simply following the law and their manufactured tradition, but your righteousness must surpass that of the Pharisees if your heart is set on the kingdom.

"Look inside your hearts. Are you satisfied? Do you feel that God has rewarded you? Are you blessed with the fruits of righteousness? What will you do with your blessings? Hide them in a cave? Bury them in the ground? Perhaps you think that's how you protect your goodness from the evils of the world. Wrong! All goodness withers and decays unless you share it with the world. If you're blessed, if you've brought forth good things in your life, then share those things and they'll multiply, adding to the good in the world and increasing your reward as well. Remember how I brought you to the Lord; now you bring others to the Lord; they in turn bring still others to the Lord; and so on and so forth—and look at how the kingdom grows! I taught you how to heal the sick, how to scare away the evil spirits, how to persuade sinners to repent and embrace the way of righteousness. Now you must give away freely the benefits of your powers, as I do. Everything good that you're given, share it—give it away. Then you'll be rewarded as much and more, for it's in giving that you receive.

"There's a parable for this, a parable that shows what the kingdom is like. It's like a man going on a journey, who called his servants and entrusted his wealth to them. To one he gave five bags of gold coins, to another two bags, and to another one bag, each according to his trustworthiness. Then the man went away on his journey.

"The man who was given five bags went at once and put his money to work and gained five bags more. Likewise, the one with two bags gained two more. But the man who was given one bag went off, dug a hole in the ground, and hid his master's money.

"After a long time the master returned and settled accounts with his servants. The man entrusted with five bags brought the other five. 'Master,' he said, 'with the five bags of gold I've gained five more.'

"His master replied, 'Well done, good and faithful servant! You've been trustworthy with a few things; now I'll put you in charge of many things. Come and share your master's happiness!'

"The man with two bags also came. 'Master,' he said, 'with the two bags I gained two more.' His master replied, 'Well done, good and faithful servant! You've been trustworthy with a few things; I'll put you in charge of many things. Come and share your master's happiness!'

"Then the man who was entrusted with one bag came. 'Master,' he said, 'I knew that you're a hard man, harvesting where you've not sown and gathering where you've not scattered seed. So I was afraid and went out and hid your gold in the ground. See, here's what belongs to you.'

"His master replied, 'You wicked, lazy servant! So you knew that I harvest where I haven't sown and gather where I haven't scattered seed? Well then, you should have put my money on deposit with the bankers, so that when I returned I would have gotten it back with interest. Guards! Take the bag of gold from him and give it to the one who has ten bags. For whoever has will be given more, and they'll have an abundance. But whoever doesn't have, even what little they do have will be taken from them. And throw this worthless servant outside, into the darkness, to be torn apart by the wolves.'"

Joshua paused to refresh himself with a few mouthfuls from his water skin. The disciples fidgeted as they sat waiting for Joshua to say more.

"Brothers," Joshua said. "That's all I have to say for now. Those of us who are familiar with Capernaum will show those of you who aren't the ways of the village. I'm curious to see if the seeds we sowed here have landed in fertile soil. It's time to let the people of Capernaum know that we've returned."

Elder Jacob, John, Simon, and Andreus got together to discuss taking the other disciples out to fish on the lake. As Joshua made his way to join them, Matheus intercepted him and took him aside for a brief word.

"Rabbi, you've unleashed a torrent of teaching on us today. I wish I was a better scribe; I'd write it all down for you."

"Matheus, don't you know me by now? You'll hear me teach those things many times, just like you've heard me share my other teachings over and over again. You yourself will teach all these things, and more besides, as we wind our way through Galilee. You'll hear it all so much, even say it yourself so much, that it will be written on your heart. You won't be able to forget it even if you wanted to."

41

Ariel sat in his study, gazing at the literature he'd arranged on the desk in front of him. The collection included scrolls, in Hebrew or Greek, of his favorite books of the Hebrew scriptures. Sitting among the scrolls were the seven codices of *The Judaic War*, Ariel's written account of his own dreams and visions about Joshua, several of Ariel's sermons, a book of commentary on the teachings of Apostle Paul, and a codex of the sayings of Christ Joshua in Aramaic. The codex of Joshua's sayings was the prize of the library—a collection of the original disciples' memories of the things Joshua taught them, passed on orally for decades, and later dictated to scribes when disciples started to die off and the survivors wanted to preserve Joshua's words for posterity. Ariel had some parchment and ink ready for writing his book, which was to be a narration of episodes from Joshua's ministry in Galilee and Judea, but first he planned to write early drafts of the scenes on wax tablets. That way he could correct any mistakes before he composed an episode's final draft.

Ariel reread the stories he'd written based on his dreams and visions about Joshua, like the Gadarene pig exorcism and the loaves and fishes miracles. He intended to include these episodes in his book, but he also planned to add several new, similar scenes that would describe Joshua's miraculous power in a way that revealed prophetic signs to readers astute enough to recognize them. There were already many stories of Joshua's wondrous deeds circulating among believers, accounts of healings and exorcisms and the like, which Ariel could mine for ideas, but those tales were generally vague and short on detail. Ariel would have to use his imagination to give such stories the desired extra meaning—the special message that would help believers who were wavering in their faith understand that Joshua's messianic identity still made sense, even in the aftermath of the unexpected and devastating results of the war.

Unsure how to start, Ariel picked up and unrolled his scroll of Isaiah.

Isaiah! No other prophet foresaw the Messiah as you did. Show me the way, Isaiah!

Ariel started reading from the beginning, and even though he'd read Isaiah many times before, he was astonished at how applicable its words were to the humiliated Israel of his own time. He wished he could assemble all the Jewish survivors of the war at the site of the demolished Temple and shout Isaiah's words to them. He imagined himself in a frenzied harangue, reciting.

You have spurned the Holy One of Israel and turned your backs on him. (Isiah 1:4)

Your country is desolate, your cities burned with fire; your fields are stripped by foreigners. (Isaiah 1:7)

Had not the Lord Almighty left us some survivors, we would have become like Sodom and Gomorrah. (Isaiah 1:9)

The Lord says: 'The multitude of your sacrifices—what are they to me? I have more than enough of burnt offerings, of rams and the fat of fattened animals; I have no pleasure in the blood of bulls and lambs and goats.' (Isaiah 1:11)

The Lord says: 'Stop bringing meaningless offerings! Your incense is detestable to me. Your New Moon feasts, and your appointed festivals I hate with all my being. When you spread out your hands in prayer, I hide my eyes from you; even when you offer many prayers, I'm not listening. Your hands are full of blood! Wash and make yourselves clean. Take your evil deeds out of my sight; stop doing wrong. Learn to do right; seek justice. Defend the oppressed. Take up the cause of the fatherless; plead the case of the widow.' (Isaiah 1:13–17)

The Lord says: 'If you're willing and obedient, you'll eat the good things of the land; but if you resist and rebel, you'll be devoured by the sword. See how the faithful city has become a prostitute! She once was full of justice; righteousness used to dwell in her—but now murderers! Your silver has become dross, your choice wine is diluted with water.' (Isaiah 1:19–22)

As Ariel read further he noticed Isaiah's fondness for symbolism and wordplay. In chapter seven Isaiah claimed to have named one of his sons Shear-Jashub, Hebrew for "a remnant will return," to proclaim the righteous Jews who would return triumphant after God's wrath subsided; and in chapter eight he named another son Maher-Shalul-Hash-Baz, Hebrew for "quick to the plunder, swift to the spoils," to satirize Assyria's pillage of sinful Israel. In chapter fifteen Isaiah altered the spelling of the Moabite city of Dibon to "Dimon" to make it sound like the Hebrew word for blood, and thereby mock how bloody Dibon would be after suffering God's vengeance. When predicting the land of Edom's undoing in chapter twenty-one, Isaiah inverted the syllables of Edom to rename it "Dumah," the Hebrew word for silence, to make a wry allusion to the condition to which Edom would be reduced after its destruction.

Ariel was inspired.

Wordplay! I should use that in my book.

42

Joshua and his disciples stayed for a while in Capernaum. They reconnected with early supporters, conducted mass baptisms, delivered sermons at the synagogue, and fished from the lake. They did the same in Seven Springs and Bethsaida, always returning at night to Simon's and Zebedee's homes in Capernaum. They drew a decent-enough following in those towns, and they persuaded some villagers to turn their lives around for the sake of the kingdom, but for most of the people Joshua's mission was old news, and with the novelty worn away they responded to Joshua with a mix of unenthusiastic tolerance and polite indifference. So Joshua led his twelve disciples out of Capernaum and into the countryside west and north of Lake Gennesaret.

They spread their news of the coming kingdom to Chorazin, Bethmaus, Arbela, Jotapata, Cana, and Sepphoris. In Sepphoris Joshua sent the disciples out in pairs to cover different districts of the city, and later he sent them in pairs on more forty-day missions to the nearby villages. Simon and Andreus went to Garis, Phillip and Bartholomeus to Gath-Hepher, Matheus and Thomas to Beth She'arim, Thaddeus and Young Jacob to Exaloth, and the Zealot brothers to Nain. Joshua stayed with the Zebedee brothers in Sepphoris, where they ministered to the city while they waited for the others to return.

After their forty-day journeys, the returning disciples reported back to Joshua, who then sent them out to new villages. Joshua next took the Zebedee brothers with him to visit the villages already served by the others, spending no more than a week in each before returning to Sepphoris. When the other disciples returned, Joshua repeated the whole process of reuniting, hearing the reports, and sending them out again to new villages. He continued this modus operandi for several months, until he believed he had evangelized the entire Galilean countryside. Then he took his disciples back to Magdala to check up on Mary.

* * *

Joshua was delighted to discover that Mary continued to spread the word to a growing flock of female followers. She even converted the courtyard of her house into a home synagogue, where she met with women to pray or discuss the nature of the kingdom. Mary inspired rich and poor women alike to embrace the way and share their blessings with each other and the less fortunate. And Mary's stepfather, Lamech, had fled to parts unknown several months back, convinced that Salome and Mary's new, Joshua-inspired religious enthusiasm was some kind of idolatrous sorcery—a conspiracy of women to entertain and promote unholy ideas like female literacy and marital celibacy. Mary was thrilled to be reunited with Joshua and the disciples, to meet Zealous Simon and Judas, and to listen to the reports of all they had done while they were away.

On the fourteenth day of the month of Adar, a month before Passover, Joshua assembled his disciples at Mary's courtyard synagogue and spoke to them.

"Brothers and sisters, it's truly a blessing from God to be here in Magdala again with our friends Salome and Mary who, with Matheus, were so supportive to us the first time we came to this city. And look at how Mary has done in our absence! She's turned a multitude of Magdala's women to the way of God and the kingdom. My heart rejoices at all the Galilean souls destined for the kingdom thanks to your efforts, my disciples. We've spread the message of the prophets about the kingdom, and taught the way of redemption, to all who have ears to hear in Galilee. The good news we've planted grows even in our absence. It spreads throughout the people as the faithful share it with their own families and communities.

"But the time is short and there's still much planting to do. I believe we're ready to sow the word in new fields. It's time to go to Judea and return her to the Lord. I propose we start by celebrating the Passover this year in Jerusalem, as is proper. Mary and Salome have already promised us lodging with Mary's cousins Martha and Lazarus in Bethany for the entire festival week—if we want. In Jerusalem we can spread the good news of God's kingdom to people from every part of Israel, and from there we can figure out how to conquer the rest of Judea for the Lord. This is the time! But I want to know if any of you have any objections or concerns, so share those now while we're here and can discuss them together. Anyone?"

There were hushed murmurings among the disciples, but only Elder Jacob spoke up.

"Master," he said, bringing an end to the whispering. "For all the success we've had in Galilee, I'm still not confident that we've reached the people of Chorazin or Bethsaida. I never felt they were persuaded, and they seem to cling to their old ways. Perhaps we should make another attempt to win them over."

"Chorazin! Bethsaida!" Joshua said, scoffing with contempt. "If they haven't turned to God by now, after all the time we spent with them, after all we taught them, and after proving ourselves with so many healings and exorcisms, then their blood is upon them! Woe to them! Our efforts there would have made Sodom and Gomorrah repent! If they haven't repented by now, it's too late for those hard-hearted ingrates. Leave them for God to judge. Let's not go picking around in weedy wastelands and trash heaps when fruitful fields beckon. How many times have I said it? The harvest is great but the workers are few. And the time is short!"

Joshua paused and calmed himself.

"Do any of you have any other concerns?"

The disciples were silent.

"God be praised," Joshua said. "Let's prepare ourselves for the journey to Jerusalem."

* * *

On the twenty-fifth day of Adar, Joshua, his twelve male disciples, Mary, and Salome set off on their pilgrimage to Jerusalem. They joined a festival caravan of about sixty other Magdalenes to ensure their safety on the road, and there were plenty of men in the caravan to put up tents when they camped and to keep watch in rotating shifts at night. Mary had tried to persuade some of her own followers to join them, but all those who had male guardians were forbidden to travel with such overwhelmingly male company, and those without guardians were old widows in no condition to make the arduous trip. All fifteen pilgrims in Joshua's group had a share in carrying the provisions, which included several days-worth of fruit and fish, several weeks-worth of beans and cheese, and oil, wine, and unleavened bread for the festival meals. Their water skins would be easy to replenish from the Jordan River, along which they would travel for most of the way.

When Joshua's travelling party reached the intersection of the Jordan and Jabbok rivers, roughly the halfway point of their journey, Joshua recognized that they were approaching the site of John the Baptist's former camp. Memories from what seemed another life welled up within him: the bitter sting of deprivation, the exhaustion of constant prayer, the exhilaration and terror of receiving God's fateful call, and the beloved friend and master whom he longed to have with him again. He sighed as he remembered how frightened he was when he first left the camp to go to Capernaum. Those worries of not so long ago seemed laughable and childish now.

Behind Joshua, Thaddeus wondered what might be happening in the lands of Perea, east of where they now walked, and Samaria to their west. He turned to his friend Young Jacob.

"Jacob?" Thaddeus asked. "The Samaritans observe the Torah, don't they? Shouldn't we share our news with them? If they're Jews, then surely some of them will accept the truth and repent, right?"

"Whether or not the Samaritans are Jews is unclear to me," Young Jacob said. "They have the Torah but reject the prophets. They think Solomon was wicked and the Jerusalem Temple a blasphemy. Didn't they try to stop the rebuilding of the Temple when the exiles returned to Jerusalem? If they reject the prophecies of Isaiah and Jeremiah and the rest, how will they accept our message, which comes from those same prophets? I think they'd be harder to teach than the Greeks."

"Rabbi Joshua, what do you say?" Thaddeus asked. "Is there room in God's kingdom for the Samaritans?"

"I hate to say it again," Joshua said, "but right now the time is short, the harvest is great, and the workers are few. We have to collect the ripe fruit first, before it rots. Once we've collected all the ripe fruit, then perhaps the late-blooming crops will be ready. We don't want to waste our time searching for good grapes in a barren vineyard—not while an abundance of fertile fields still waits to be harvested. Should we go fishing in the Dead Sea? Or shall we pick clean the olive trees and expect pearls instead of pits? Because that's how likely it would be to find a good man in all Samaria."

Joshua faced west toward Samaria, lifted his hands, and shouted to the wind: "Samaria, you whore! How many husbands have you had? I count five! Your first was a Jew and your second a Babylonian. Then the Persian . . . then the Alexandrian from Egypt . . . and then the Seleucid from Syria! Wait! I forgot one—the current one—the Roman! Six husbands! And still you claim to drink from the well of Jacob! You're utterly shameless Samaria! Where does the harlotry stop? Whore!"

The disciples had a hearty laugh at the facetious Jeremiad, and Joshua returned to the group, which he again proceeded to lead south by the river.

* * *

281

As the travelling party continued south along the west side of the Jordan, Joshua and Judas strode alongside each other about thirty yards ahead of the others. They were caught up in a lively resumption of their ongoing debate about which force dominates in the shaping of history—man inspired by God, or God provoked by man.

"Remember, Rabbi," Judas said. "Your namesake Joshua had to take up arms and fight boldly against a savage host of enemies to conquer Canaan and deliver her to Israel."

"Yes," Joshua answered. "But he couldn't succeed without the help that God promised and provided."

"Promised and provided on the condition that Joshua act bravely and not waver in his determination, and always remain faithful to the law. It was the same for David when he went to war against his enemies. God called him, but David had to rise up and face the deadly struggle to fulfill his destiny. God may guide man one way or another, but in the end man must grab the sword and take it upon himself to make changes in the world."

"Joshua and David were obedient when God called, and they did what was appropriate for their time, but man can only obey and be carried along by the much greater power of God. Consider Noah. He couldn't fight the flood by rallying his friends together into an army. He had to obey God and trust Him to carry him through to salvation. And how did Moses succeed? Did Moses send the plagues onto Egypt or open up the sea and then close it again on Pharaoh's army? God did those things! He did them on behalf of His faithful servant, yes, but it was God's power that delivered the decisive blow. Truly, all the men on earth could get together and unite in purpose, but without God's consent they'd surely fail at whatever they attempted. Man is forever at the mercy of the always-greater power of God."

"But as long as God permits us to live on His earth, it's up to man to make the right decision and win God's approval, so that the outcome's in the righteous man's favor. As men, our duty is to obey God, and God demands that we take action! Tell me, Rabbi. Have you ever been to Jerusalem?"

"Are you changing the subject already, Judas?"

"I'm attempting to illustrate a point for this discussion we're having."

"All right, I'll play along. No, Judas. I've never actually been to Jerusalem, I regret to say."

"Well I've been there, and I have friends there. I've known men who swear that they've heard the very voice of God speak to them from inside the Temple. What if you, when you're there, hear the voice of God and that voice tells you to pick up a sword and fight against the Roman occupation? Would you obey?"

"If God ordered it, I'd even jump off the top of the tallest tower in Jerusalem. I might fall to my death; I might be caught in the arms of rescuing angels and brought to a safe landing. Either way is glory. Dead, I'd wait with Abraham and the prophets for the resurrection of the righteous at the appointed time; alive I'd continue to serve God as a shepherd, gathering the lost sheep and leading them to the kingdom.

"But God won't demand such things from me, as if He were some crass magician who's amused by frivolities. And he won't command us to take up the sword either. The judgment that's coming is even more serious than the Great Flood or the Exodus, and if those events were examples of man being helpless in the face of God's power, then the judgment will be even more so. The wrath of God will extinguish all, even the Romans. Only the righteous will be rescued."

"So God alone can save us from the Romans? We have no part to play?"

Joshua looked askance at Judas.

"Do you and your friends in the Resistance really think you can take on the Romans?" Joshua asked.

"We don't have to take on the Romans. We only need to make it painfully inconvenient for them to be here raping us. To let them know that it won't be worth the tax revenue to keep us under their thumb. To bite their greedy, grasping hand hard enough that they leave us alone and stick to squeezing softer peoples for their unjust gains. Yes, there are many Resistance fighters in Jerusalem, waiting for God to reveal some fatal weakness in Procurator Pilate's tyranny—some ripe time to strike and drive the Romans to gentler pastures. If the Maccabees could drive out the Greeks, we can do the same to the Romans."

Joshua held up Judas and stopped walking.

"Maccabees? What's coming is far beyond what happened with the Maccabees! You're talking about wars and politics, but the judgment will be a greater cataclysm than any that's ever been seen. It will completely remake the world. Such things are in the hands of God, not men."

"Even if that's true, until that final Day of the Lord we still have to contend with the treachery of men. That procurator of Judea, Pilate, he's not ashamed to trample on us or our law. He raised images of Caesar in the city and stole money from the Temple treasury. He ordered his soldiers to attack those who protested. If the Romans don't like what we say or do in Jerusalem, we'll be in danger. Those friends of mine in the Resistance? We may need their protection."

"God's our protection, Judas. Only God can help us now."

43

Dionysius stood at Ariel's door holding a codex.

"I finished volume seven, Ari." Dionysius said. "It's as amazing as you said it would be."

Dionysius handed the codex to Ariel.

"Thank you for lending it to me, and give my thanks to Theophilus too," Dionysius said.

"Come in, Dion. Have a drink with me. Do you have time?"

"I suppose I can spare a moment. Is everything all right?"

"Yes, of course. I'm just working on my book. But I'm getting nowhere right now. Your visit is a good excuse to take a break and refresh myself. Please come in."

Ariel took Dionysius to the dining table and invited him to sit while he went to fetch a stone jug of water and two ceramic cups. When he returned they both drank and Ariel refilled their cups.

"By Joshua, Ari. When I read the chapter on Eleazar at Machaerus I trembled. I can't believe we were there when it happened."

"I can't believe we made it out of there alive."

"Hallelu Yah. The Lord has been merciful. Those Roman sons of harlots came too close to killing us."

"Yes . . . well . . . we're lucky we survived. Praise the Lord."

"Was your brother really in Caesarea Philippi when Titus celebrated his triumph there?"

"He was there briefly. Titus had taken him prisoner in Jerusalem. But he managed to escape, thank God."

"Thank God indeed. Aaron would surely have died in those perverse games, where the prisoners were thrown to the beasts—or forced to fight each other. What kind of horse-humping degenerates are those Romans? That's how they celebrate their victory? Hadn't they had enough bloodshed? What kind of depravity isn't sated by a complete rout of the enemy, and needs to see the subdued survivors butchered as well—as an amusement no less? That Titus is pure damnation."

Ariel held his arm up to mock the Roman Hail Caesar salute.

"Hail Titus Caesar," Ariel said, feigning the proud solemnity of an obedient Roman soldier. "Conqueror of the Jews, Supreme Sodomizer, and Royal Rapist from Rome—the pagan Lord of hell."

Dionysius laughed for a moment before fixing a sudden, serious gaze on Ariel.

"It's evil that triumphs in this world," Dionysius said. "Josephus's book confirms it. It was right there in Caesarea Philippi, when Titus was slaughtering men as if performing some kind of unholy sacrifice to himself, and reveling in his new fame as Destroyer of the Jews, when he learned that Simon of Gerasa had surrendered to Rufus in Jerusalem. Titus's primary Zealot scourge, who had so stubbornly defied him at every turn, had finally admitted defeat. Titus's conquest was now complete. The world was Titus's footstool on that day."

Ariel stared into space and pondered Dionysius's words.

"Yes," Ariel said. "On that day in Caesarea Philippi, Titus learned that he'd be immortalized in history as the great champion who delivered rebellious Judea to Rome—delivered her like a prize pig to his father as a birthday gift. And on that day the Jews learned that Simon wasn't their Messiah after all—that he was nothing but a self-aggrandizing criminal and failure."

Ariel looked straight at Dionysius.

"And what else did we Jews learn from those events, Dion?"

Dionysius returned a blank stare.

"What?" Dionysus asked. "Are you giving me another of your puzzles?"

"Think, Dion. What did we, the Jews, learn?"

Dionysius thought for a moment and shrugged.

"Well, Dion. If the Zealots aren't the salvation of the Jews, who is?"

Dionysius smiled and nodded his head.

"Oh, right," Dionysius said. "Joshua, of course."

"Exactly."

Ariel clasped his hands together and smiled.

"This talk has inspired me, Dion. Excuse me for a moment. I'll be right back."

Ariel rushed to his study and picked up a wax tablet. He wrote with his stylus:

Joshua and his disciples travelled to the villages around Caesarea Philippi. On the way he asked them, "who do people say I am?"

They answered, "They say you're a prophet, or a healer, or a holy man."

"But what about you?" he asked. "Who do you say I am?"

Simon Peter answered, "You're the Messiah."

Joshua told them to keep his identity a secret, because the time to reveal it had not yet come.

Ariel returned from his study carrying a scroll of the fifth book of Psalms and another of the book of Isaiah.

"I apologize for making you wait," Ariel said. "I had to write something down."

Dionysius waved his hand to indicate forgiveness for Ariel's brief absence.

"Why the scrolls, Ari?"

"I want you to hear some of the sermon I'm preparing for the coming Sabbath. If you'll forgive the imposition, that is."

"No, no. Go right ahead. It will be my pleasure."

Ariel assumed a stately pose and looked across the room as if he were addressing his congregation.

"How do I know that Joshua is the Messiah predicted by the prophets?" Ariel asked. "Well, let me read to you from the hundred and thirty-second Psalm of David.

"We heard it in Ephrathah, we came upon it in the fields of Jearim: Let's go to his dwelling place, let's worship at his footstool, (saying 'Arise, Lord, and come to your resting place, you and the ark of your might. May your priests be clothed with your righteousness; may your faithful people sing for joy.') For the sake of your servant David, don't reject your anointed one. The Lord swore an oath to David, a sure oath he won't revoke: 'One of your own descendants I'll place on your throne. If your sons keep my covenant and the statutes I teach them, then their sons will sit on your throne forever and ever.' (Psalm 132:6–12)

"We know that Joshua is a descendant of the line of Judah, specifically the clan of Ephrathah from Bethlehem—David's clan. This is the house from which the Messiah is to come, according to the prophecy.

"Isaiah, when he foresaw God's wrath and judgment at the end of our age, and the subsequent exaltation of the righteous remnant that would reach the new kingdom, said this: 'They'll see the glory of the Lord, the splendor of our God. So strengthen the feeble hands, steady the knees that give way; tell those with fearful hearts to be strong and not fear; our God will come, He'll come with vengeance; with divine retribution He'll come to save you. Then will the eyes of the blind be opened, and the ears of the deaf unstopped. Then will the lame leap like a deer, and the mute tongue shout for joy.' (Isaiah 35:3–6)

"So we should expect the Messiah to make the blind see, the deaf hear, and the mute speak.

"Now, when the people would bring the deaf and mute to Joshua, and ask him to lay his healing hands on them, he would wet his fingers with his saliva and put them into their ears and onto their tongues. Then he would look up to heaven and say, in our Aramaic, 'Be opened!'—'Ephphatha!' At this their ears opened and their tongues loosened, and henceforth they heard clearly and spoke plainly.

"Who could this man be, this Joshua?

"Once, a blind man came to Joshua and begged him to restore his sight. Joshua wet his fingers with his saliva and put them on the man's eyes. Then he looked up to heaven and said, 'Be opened!'—'Ephphatha!'

"Joshua asked the man, 'Do you see anything?'

"The man looked around and said, 'I see people; they look like trees walking around.'

"Once more Joshua put his fingers on the man's eyes. Then his eyes were opened, his sight was restored, and he saw everything clearly.

"This man, Joshua. Who could he be? Who could he be other than the Messiah?"

Ariel stopped speaking. The sermon was over.

Dionysius stood up and grabbed Ariel by the shoulders.

"I like your sermon," Dionysius said. "But something confuses me. In all the stories I've heard about Joshua healing people, he always succeeds right away on the first attempt. Why did Joshua have to lay his hands on the blind man twice to completely heal him?"

"Well," Ariel said. "Do you always understand my dreams and visions the first time you hear them?"

44

Joshua's party arrived in Bethany on the sixth day of Nisan, eight days before the beginning of the Passover week. Mary introduced everyone to her cousin Martha, who lived in a four-room house with her husband Hymenaeus, and to Martha's brother Lazarus, who lived by himself in a nearby three-room house. Mary, Salome, Joshua, Elder Jacob, John, Simon, Andreus, and Matheus lodged in Martha's home, while the rest stayed with Lazarus. Every morning Martha, Lazarus, and their guests got together to break their fast, and they did the same for the evening meal. Every day they spent the time between those meals in Jerusalem, preaching in the outer courts of the Temple.

They did no preaching, however, on the first two days of their stay. They spent the day of their arrival settling in and getting acquainted with Mary's relatives. The day after, the seventh of Nisan, was the Sabbath. The men took advantage of the relative calm of the labor-free day to explore Jerusalem, entering from the east through the Mount of Olives and the Kedron Valley.

Jerusalem was new to Joshua and the twelve disciples, except for the Zealot brothers, and they gazed, astonished, at the colossal stone walls, towers, and buildings that they saw as they wound their way through the labyrinth of streets to the Temple Mount. They bathed themselves in the mikvot nearby the southwest stairs to the Temple courts, ascended those stairs, passed through the tunnels leading to the Temple Mount Plaza, and ambled among the crowds in the vast Court of the Gentiles. Then they entered the gate to the Women's Court, where Gentiles were forbidden to go, and where a massive bronze gate to the west led to the Court of Israel, where only male Jews were permitted. The Court of Israel surrounded the Temple proper, which only priests were allowed to enter.

The disciples didn't bother to enter the Court of Israel right away, since it was so close to the Temple, and so crowded, that they would have missed the good view of the entire Temple that they had in the Women's Court. They simply stood in the center of that court, surrounded by cloisters supported by thirty-foot-high columns, and stared at the fifty-foot-high bronze gate to the west, behind which towered the hundred-and-fifty-foot-high Temple of marble and gold. The sunlight reflecting off the Temple's gold and marble façade was magnificent but too bright and painful to look at for more than an instant. Otherworldly singing and harp strumming by hosts of choir musicians rang out from behind the bronze gate. The smell of burning animal sacrifices overwhelmed the disciples as they watched the awe-inspiring smoke plumes rise heavenward from the unseen altar.

Joshua prostrated himself and offered up a private prayer to the Lord, which inspired the others to do the same. When the prayers were finished, Joshua stood in front of his disciples and addressed them.

"Come, my friends. Let's do our duty to the Lord and walk the circuit around the Temple seven times in the Court of Israel."

The disciples followed Joshua through the bronze gate, completed the ritual with him, and then returned to the Women's court to relax, observe the crowds of worshippers, and listen for traces of the voice of God in all they heard.

* * *

On a typical day preaching in the Temple courts, Joshua would find a well-trafficked spot in the Court of Gentiles among the rabbis, prophets, money changers, merchants, healers, exorcists, beggars, and worshippers—a spot that was spacious enough to carry his voice and allow for a crowd to gather. Usually Elder Jacob and John would assist him while the other disciples found other places in the court to either do their own preaching or encourage the public to go to hear Joshua teach. The disciples tended to work in pairs, one preaching and the other contributing supporting testimony or stoking the interest and enthusiasm of the crowd. The Zealot brothers differed from the others, however, by their tendency to forgo their preaching to disappear to parts unknown for surreptitious meetings with friends in the Resistance.

When Joshua taught in the Temple courts, he repeated the same parables, prophecies, and provocations that he'd shared with his disciples and the public in Galilee. Nevertheless there were times when Joshua would deviate from his vast repertoire and compose something new on the spot. On one such occasion Joshua was preaching while brothers Jacob and John stood with the crowd and waited to perform whatever function Joshua might demand of them during the sermon. As Joshua paused between topics, a sharply dressed and well-groomed young man approached Joshua.

"Rabbi," the young man asked. "What exactly must I do to gain acceptance into God's kingdom?"

"First, you must know the commandments of God written in the law," Joshua answered, as much to the crowd as to the young man. "But don't just study them or agree with them. Fulfill them. Obey them. The law can be summed up in two commandments: love the Lord your God completely, and love your neighbor as you love yourself. But actually accomplishing this is difficult. At every turn we're tempted by evil, so be careful. If anything and everything you do can rightly be called love of God and love of neighbor, then the kingdom will be open to you."

"Rabbi," the young man said. "I always live within the law of God, and God has blessed me for it. Is that all I must do?"

"If you're determined to be perfect in the eyes of God, sell your possessions and give the money to the poor. Then dedicate yourself to saving others from the coming wrath. If you're as righteous as you claim to be, join us. We could use you."

The young man gasped, offended. He wheeled around and strode away through the crowd.

"Ah ha," Joshua said. "Simple but difficult! How hard it is for some to enter the kingdom of God! Not everyone has the stomach to humble himself to the extent demanded by the kingdom. You must be small in this world to be great in the kingdom. What parable can we use to describe the kingdom of God? It's like a garden. Think of the mustard seed. It's the smallest of all seeds, but when planted it grows into the largest plant in the garden, with such big branches that birds can perch in its shade. In this way the last and the least of our current evil time will be the first and the greatest in the kingdom.

"Likewise the first and greatest of these evil times will be the last and least in the kingdom, if they can manage to enter the kingdom at all. What if you're grand indeed, possessing many houses and owning extravagant wealth while so many suffer in destitution and hunger? Then you're like a great tree towering above all others. What can the gardener do with you? Will he tear out every other plant and seed to make room for you? You're too big for the garden!"

Joshua looked across the court and pointed to draw his audience's attention to the crowds squeezing through the gate into the Women's Court.

"The gate into the kingdom is a narrow one!" Joshua shouted. "Every time you share what you have with your brothers and sisters, every time you humble yourself and serve the good of all—you unburden yourself a little bit more of the excess baggage that makes you too big to fit through that gate. And every time you hoard your goods for yourself alone, every time you make yourself greater at the expense of others—you encumber yourself more and more with the dead weight of injustice. Then you're like a giant trying to squeeze through a tiny door—or like a camel trying to pass through the eye of a needle. The man of great wealth trying to get into the kingdom of God—he's like that camel trying to go through the eye of a needle!"

The crowd was silent, struck by the imagery of Joshua's parable.

"The kingdom," Joshua said, "is like a king who prepared a wedding banquet for his son. He sent his servants out to those who were invited, to tell them the banquet was about to begin. The servants enticed the invitees with promises of butchered lambs and fattened cattle and every other culinary delight, but each and every one of them made some excuse or another for being unable to attend the banquet.

"'I must meet a man I found who will buy my field,' said one.

"'I must go and buy some oxen for my plow,' said another.

"When the servants reported to the king that all those who were invited made excuses like this and declined to attend, the king was enraged.

"The king said to his servants: 'The banquet's ready but those I invited didn't deserve to attend. So go out to the streets and invite whomever you can find, including the poor, the lame, the deaf, and the blind. My house will be full of guests at my son's wedding banquet!'

"The servants did as the king ordered, and the banquet was a great success. None of those who were first invited got a taste of that banquet.

"God calls you to his kingdom. But are you even interested? With what are you busying yourself so much that it's keeping you from the kingdom?"

Joshua motioned to Jacob and John to take over while he took a break to drink some water. As the two brothers took his place in front of the crowd, Joshua said one word to them, "Psalms," before sitting nearby and opening his water skin. Jacob and John understood that Joshua wanted them to recite a passage of their choosing from the Psalms that would be an appropriate complement to the sermon he'd just given. They gave it a moment's thought, and John, with Jacob soon joining him, began to recite from the middle of Psalm fifty-two.

"Surely God will bring you down to everlasting ruin. He'll snatch you up and pluck you from your tent; He'll uproot you from the land of the living. The righteous will see and fear; they'll laugh at you, saying, 'Here now is the man who didn't make God his stronghold, but trusted in his great wealth and grew strong by destroying others!' But I'm like an olive tree flourishing in the house of God; I trust in God's unfailing love for ever and ever." (Psalm 52:5–8)

* * *

On another day, Joshua was preaching in the Court of Gentiles and he noticed all the money changers and merchants doing business there. The money changers traded Tyrian silver shekels for the public's Greco-Roman coins. This exchange enabled worshippers to carry their coins into the Temple because the Tyrian shekels were devoid of the images of Caesar that made drachmas and denarii forbidden. The merchants sold animals for Temple sacrifice: birds for the poor, goats and lambs for the fortunate, and cows and oxen for the rich. Joshua yelled across the court at the merchants, but he knew that the merchants wouldn't hear him. His words were for the people gathered around him.

"Forgiveness for sale!" Joshua shouted. "Buy forgiveness for your sins! The merchants grow rich from all the sinning! It's time to put the sacrifice sellers out of business! Repent for good!"

Joshua returned his attention to his audience.

"There's nothing wrong with proper worship in the Temple as established by Moses and the law," Joshua said. "But things have changed here in the Promised Land, and not for the better. People allow themselves as much sin as they can afford—as much as they can atone for with their sacrifices. The rich think they can get away with so much sin! But you can't buy your way into the kingdom! You're better off giving your money to the poor. The more you give, the greater your treasure will be in heaven. But the merchants here will take your money, buy more animals, and then sell you those animals so you can keep atoning for your sins, and on and on—the cycle of sin spins around and around until judgment comes. Break the cycle! Repent and find your way to the kingdom!

"That Temple . . . look at it! It's the Temple of God! But the priests who serve inside it, who are they? Are they the sons of Aaron, Moses's brother? No, they're not. Are they the sons of Zadok, David's high priest? No. If they're not the sons of Aaron or Zadok, then where do they come from? Where?"

Joshua paused to allow his listeners to think. After the brief moment of reflection passed, Joshua resumed his sermon.

"I regret to tell you that those priests aren't the servants of God, they're the servants of Herod! They won their positions not by tradition, or study, or worthiness. Their fathers were appointed by the Herods for how well they fulfilled the plans and purposes of those Herods—those dogs of Caesar—and it was from those corrupt fathers that they inherited their priestly titles.

"And now we don't even have a Herod to act the part of a Jewish king here in Judea. Rome has dropped the pretense. We have a Roman procurator reaching into the Temple treasury whenever he wants. The Temple treasury, God's Temple treasury, established for the good of the people of Israel, is now Caesar's personal cash box! Those priests who claim to act on your behalf take your donations and use them for their own purposes, the most important of which, to them, is to gain favor with the Romans. Such are the shepherds of Israel in these dark days. Your self-appointed shepherds are selling God's Temple, God's city, and God's nation to the Romans!

"Ezekiel saw that this would happen. When the Lord showed him what it would be like before the judgment, the judgment that we'll see in this generation, He said this to Ezekiel: 'Prophesy against the shepherds of Israel! Say to them: "Woe to you shepherds of Israel who only take care of yourselves! Shouldn't shepherds take care of the flock? You eat the curds, clothe yourselves with the wool, and slaughter the choice animals, but you don't take care of the flock. You haven't strengthened the weak or healed the sick or bound up the injured. You haven't brought back the strays or searched for the lost. You've ruled them harshly and brutally.'"
(Ezekiel 34:2–4)

"The Lord said: 'I'm against the shepherds and will hold them accountable for my flock. I will remove them from tending the flock so that the shepherds can no longer feed themselves. I'll rescue my flock from their mouths, my flock will no longer be food for them.' (Ezekiel 34:10)

"The Lord said: 'I'll search for the lost and bring back the strays. I'll bind up the injured and strengthen the weak, but the sleek and strong I'll destroy. I'll shepherd the flock with justice. I'll judge between one sheep and another, and between rams and goats. Is it not enough for you to feed on the good pasture? Must you also trample the rest of your pasture with your feet? Is it not enough for you to drink clear water? Must you also muddy the rest with your feet? Must my flock feed on what you've trampled and drink what you've muddied with your feet? I myself will judge between the fat sheep and the lean sheep. Because you shove with flank and shoulder, butting all the weak sheep with your horns until you've driven them away, I'll save my flock, and they'll no longer be plundered.'" (Ezekiel 34:16–22)

Many of Joshua's listeners had walked away by the time the sermon reached this point. The rest were nervous and looking around to see if any Romans or priests were near. Joshua himself did a quick check to see if he was in any trouble. Satisfied that he was safe, Joshua continued to speak to the remaining crowd.

"After God comes with all His angels to judge the world—after all that must be toppled is toppled and after all that must be saved is saved—there will be a great resurrection of the dead. God will gather the living with all those who have ever lived and He'll sit before them on his glorious throne. He'll separate all the people one from another as a shepherd separates the sheep from the goats. He'll put the sheep on his right and the goats on his left.

"Then the Lord will say to those on his right, 'Come, you who are blessed, and take your inheritance, the kingdom prepared for you. For I was hungry and you gave me something to eat, I was thirsty and you gave me something to drink, I was a stranger and you invited me in, I was naked and you clothed me, I was sick and you looked after me, I was in prison and you came to visit me.'

"Then the righteous will answer Him, 'Lord, when did we see you hungry and feed you, or thirsty and give you something to drink? When did we see you a stranger and invite you in, or naked and clothe you? When did we see you sick or in prison and go to visit you?'

"The Lord will reply, 'Truly I tell you, whatever you did for one of the least of these brothers and sisters of yours, you did for me.'

"Then He will say to those on His left, 'Depart from me, you who are cursed, into the eternal fire prepared for the devil and his angels. For I was hungry and you gave me nothing to eat, I was thirsty and you gave me nothing to drink, I was a stranger and you didn't invite me in, I was naked and you didn't clothe me, I was sick and in prison and you didn't look after me.'

"They will also answer, 'Lord, when did we see you hungry or thirsty or a stranger or naked or sick or in prison, and didn't help you?'

"He will reply, 'Truly I tell you, whatever you didn't do for one of the least of these, you didn't do for me.'

"Then they'll go away to eternal punishment, but the righteous to eternal life."

Joshua paused to drink some water. The crowd stood silent, waiting to see if Joshua would say anything more.

"The judgment is coming soon," Joshua said after finishing his drink. "Will you be ready on that day?"

45

One evening Ariel was having trouble finding the right words for an episode in his book. He wanted to write a series of exhortations that Joshua would deliver to his disciples—exhortations that would be consistent with Joshua's known teachings but would also be pertinent to the concerns of readers who might be wavering in their faith. So far Ariel had written only two sentences, both of them warnings to stay faithful and avoid hindering the faith of others:

"If anyone is ashamed of me and my words in this adulterous and sinful generation, the Son of Man will be ashamed of them when he comes in his Father's glory with the holy angels."

"If anyone causes one of these little ones—those who believe in me—to stumble, it would be better for them if a large millstone were hung around their neck and they were thrown into the sea."

Ariel lifted his heavy eyes to look at the piles of open scrolls and codices littering his desk. He felt like he was drowning in a sea of scripture. He pushed back his chair and stood up, dizzy with frustration. He grabbed his cloak and exited his house.

Maybe a walk will clear my head.

Ariel walked in the general direction of the synagogue and pondered that he might go there to pray to God for some inspiration. On the way he saw a man in the distance beating a donkey colt with a stick. As he approached he could hear the man rebuke the animal.

"Lazy son of an ass's cunt!" the man shouted. "Move it!"

The man struck the colt's hindquarters with the stick again, but the colt sat motionless on all fours near a hitching post at the entrance to a courtyard. The man grunted in frustration and struck the animal again. He raised the stick to deliver yet another blow when Ariel rushed up and grabbed it in a flash. Ariel wrested the stick from the man, who staggered back surprised and shaken.

Ariel brandished the stick at the man and shouted, "Stop beating this ass! You're just going to kill it!"

The man backed away with his hands up and terror in his eyes. Ariel held the stick with both hands and raised it over his head.

"This is Zechariah's staff of Favor," Ariel said before cracking it in two over his own knee. "There! The covenant with the nations is broken." (Zechariah 11:10)

"What the hell is wrong with you?" the man asked.

"Haven't you read Zechariah?" Ariel asked. "He foresaw the Day of the Lord, which is at hand."

Ariel took the half of the stick that was in his right hand and poked the man in the chest with it four times, each time enunciating a syllable: "Ze-cha-ri-ah."

The man tried to grab the stick, but Ariel threw both pieces out into the street before he could.

Ariel waved his hands as if he were pushing tall reeds out of his way and said, "Let the dying die, and the perishing perish. Let those who are left eat one another's flesh. Zechariah said that, too." (Zechariah 11:9)

"You're insane. You have a demon!" the man cried.

Ariel fell to where the colt lay and embraced it around the neck as if it were a beloved pet.

"Show some compassion for the colt!" Ariel shouted. "The colt is dear to the Lord. Haven't you read Zechariah?"

Ariel recited Zechariah 9:9: "Rejoice greatly Daughter Zion! Shout, Daughter Jerusalem! See, your king comes to you, righteous and victorious, lowly and riding on a donkey, on a colt, the foal of a donkey."

"The ass is yours," the man said. "Take it. Just leave me alone."

The man ran away down the street.

Ariel kissed the colt and looked up to the sky.

Of course! The Messiah entered Jerusalem riding on a colt! This is another sign from the Lord!

Ariel released the colt, went down on his knees, and bowed down in the direction of Jerusalem.

Thank you, Lord, for this inspiration. I will share it with the faithful.

Ariel ran home, energized and ready to continue his work.

46

It only took a few days for Joshua to become the most popular speaker in the Temple courts. At times hundreds crowded around him to hear his impassioned and provocative sermons. On one particular day in the middle of Passover week, a crowd of about three hundred assembled around the southwest corner of the Court of Gentiles to see and hear the notorious Nazarene broadcast his grim good news about the soon-to-be-realized fate of Israel. Joshua's twelve disciples were standing nearby with the audience in front, watching Joshua with both admiration and apprehension. Joshua paced and gesticulated. He gave extensive justification from the prophets for his claims about the judgment and the kingdom. He pronounced his usual blessings and woes, and railed against lust, hate, dishonesty, and hypocrisy. He told his parables of the sower, the unmerciful servant, the workers in the vineyard, the wedding banquet, and the bags of gold. He explained how people are defiled by what comes out of them rather than what goes into them.

As he finished his lesson on the roots of true defilement, Joshua noticed a group of well-dressed Pharisee legal scholars striding through the crowds along the south wall. There were four of them, sporting long, ostentatious fringes on their cloaks and wearing thick, semi-conical headdresses which were shrouded under expensive linen mantles. They seemed to delight in having the public clear the way for them like the waves before Moses, and they strutted by the alms beggars with visible contempt, not bothering to give them so much as a glance.

Joshua drew the crowd's attention to the Pharisees and said, "The Pharisees and teachers of the law—they know the scriptures well. Heed what they say but don't be like them, for they don't practice what they preach. They're happy to burden people with cumbersome loads but refuse to do their own share of the labor. Everything they do is done for people to see: they wind wide phylacteries around themselves and hang long tassels from their garments; they love the place of honor at banquets and the most important seats in the synagogues; they love to be greeted with respect in the marketplaces and to be called learned by others.

"Woe to you, Pharisees! Woe to you, scholars of the law! Hypocrites! You give a tenth of your produce but neglect the more important matters of the law—justice, mercy, and faithfulness. You should practice the latter without neglecting the former. You blind guides! You strain out a gnat but swallow a camel!

"Woe to you, hypocrites! You clean the outside of the cup, but inside it's full of greed and self-indulgence. Blind guides! First clean the inside of the cup, and then the outside will also be clean.

"Woe to you, vain scholars! You're like whitewashed tombs, which look beautiful on the outside but on the inside are full of the bones of the dead and everything unclean. On the outside you appear to people as righteous, but on the inside you're full of hypocrisy and wickedness!"

One of the four Pharisees had heard the end of Joshua's rant and hurried over to the front of the crowd. With his head upturned and a smug smile, the Pharisee said, "Aren't you the Nazarene? Joshua is it? This year's popular Passover prophet?"

"I'm Joshua of Nazareth," Joshua answered. "That much is true."

"It's my honor to meet you, Joshua," the Pharisee said with obvious disdain. "Rabbi, you're surely a man of integrity, unimpressed by the wealth or position of others. I hear you teach the way of God in accordance with the truth. So tell me, wise teacher, is it right to pay the imperial tax to Caesar, or is it wrong? Should we pay or not? What do you say?"

The Pharisee waited while Joshua ran his hand through his hair and pondered a response.

Joshua sighed and said, "You're trying to trap me. But I'll play along."

Joshua looked around and addressed the crowd. "Who here has a coin, a drachma or a denarius, that I can look at. I promise I'll return it."

Several people scrambled to open sacks and find a coin for Joshua. After Phillip, Andreus, and the Pharisee each placed a coin in Joshua's palm, Joshua put up his hands to signal that he was satisfied. He looked at the three coins one at a time and then settled on one, giving the other two back to Phillip and Andreus.

"Tell me, Rabbi," Joshua said as he handed the coin back to the Pharisee. "Whose image is this on the coin? Whose inscription? What does it say?"

"Caesar's," the Pharisee answered.

"Then give back to Caesar what belongs to Caesar, and give back to God what belongs to God."

The crowd was silent as it pondered Joshua's statement. Soon everyone was in suspense, waiting for Joshua, or the Pharisee, or anyone to say something and bring a resolution to the tension.

The silence broke when a man in the crowd, it wasn't exactly clear which man it was, spoke out: "He's saying we should pay the tax! Give to Caesar what's Caesar's—that means pay the tax to Caesar!"

Murmurings ran through the crowd. The Pharisee laughed.

"He says pay the tax!" the Pharisee shouted, triumphant. "He sounds like a collaborator to me!"

The murmurings grew to grumblings, scattered shouts broke out, and the disciples fidgeted in fresh sweat.

"No!" Joshua shouted, quieting the crowd. "That's not what I'm saying! I said give back to Caesar what belongs to Caesar, and give back to God what belongs to God. Think about it! Do you know the difference? Why are all these coins with Caesar's image on them here in our land? Are we Romans? Why does everything we do require the approval of Caesar? Again, are we Romans? Why are all your shekels getting carted off to Rome, along with your produce? Is Caesar a Jew? Why do the priests fear Caesar more than they fear God? Is Caesar greater than God?

"All of you who consider yourselves so pious for refusing to pay the Roman taxes, what difference does your defiance make now? You're like the shepherd who chases away the wolf after all his sheep are dead and devoured! What are your coins compared to what you've already delivered up to Caesar—your land, your city, your government, the Temple, and all the other holy things that once belonged to God? The prefects, the priests, the Herodian kings—they take the treasures of your fathers and sell them to lavish gifts onto the pagans. They even help them build temples to Caesar! So now Caesar is worshipped and God is reduced to a tax collector, who for the right price will even exempt you from his holy law!

"But this is exactly what the prophets said would happen in the time right before the judgment—that you would abandon God and give Israel over to the pagans. Judgment's at hand! Do you hoard up money thinking you can bribe God to forgive you your sins? I tell you in all seriousness that not even all Caesar's wealth will buy admittance to the kingdom. It's too late to be worried about money. Worry about God and the kingdom. Let all of Caesar's money go back to Caesar, let the Romans go back to Rome, and give back to God everything that belongs to God. You know what belongs to God: this land, this city, that Temple right there, and all the holy things due Him according to the law—the very things you've given to Caesar!

"So I repeat to you, all of you with ears to hear, give what belongs to Caesar back to Caesar, and give back to God what belongs to God!"

Joshua paced, agitated. Sweat glistened on his face. The crowd was silent. Some listeners gazed at the ground as if ashamed. Others nodded their heads in apparent agreement with Joshua's words and looked around to read the reactions of the other spectators. The din of the activities going on in the rest of the court—the people moving, singing, laughing, shouting, and praying; the commerce, the animals, the sounds echoing off the walls—it was all a distant roar, superfluous.

Elder Jacob started to chant: "Caesar's back to Caesar, God's back to God!" The chanting was slow at first, rhythmic. John joined in, then Zealous Simon and Judas.

"Caesar's back to Caesar, God's back to God!"

The rest of the disciples joined the chant, followed by some in the crowd.

"Caesar's back to Caesar, God's back to God!"

More people in the crowd added their voices to the chant. Soon most of the crowd was chanting—a moment later almost all of it.

"Caesar's back to Caesar, God's back to God!"

Everyone in the court looked in the chanting crowd's direction. Some people ran over to join it.

"Caesar's back to Caesar, God's back to God!"

The crowd erupted into sporadic fits of clapping, foot stomping, hooting, and fist raising.

"Caesar's back to Caesar, God's back to God!"

Some Temple guards ran down from the balconies of the Women's Court to investigate the commotion in the Court of Gentiles. Roman soldiers came up out of the tunnels to do the same. They crept up to the crowd with their weapons at the ready. The chanting was lively but the crowd was contained for the moment. Some bystanders hustled themselves into the tunnels and down the stairs to get away from the Temple Mount as soon as they could. Others joined the chanters.

"Caesar's back to Caesar, God's back to God!"

Merchants and money changers started to pack up their supplies. Someone threw a rock at the Temple guards at the north end of the court, and the guards, after dodging the rock, rushed the back of the crowd. The crowd broke away from the guards and fled in all directions. People knocked over money changers' tables, released animals from their bonds, and unleashed pandemonium. Amid all the random collisions between man and beast, the chanting continued.

"Caesar's back to Caesar, God's back to God!"

Young men took advantage of the chaos to steal what they could from the spilled money and merchandise. Women covered their children, huddled with them along the walls, and hurried to the exit tunnels. It took but a moment for the merchants' area to become a vortex of violence as men fought over the loose loot or assaulted anyone in possession of coveted property.

The Temple guards ran to the fracas and bludgeoned the unruly, hoping to pummel peace into them, while the Roman soldiers stabbed, kicked, and clubbed anyone not already immobilized or dead. The mob swarmed the soldiers in retaliation and smothered them with their sheer numbers, which enabled some rioters to steal weapons from soldiers and kill a few of them, but that did little to slow the soldiers' prolific butchery of the mob.

Meanwhile Joshua and some of his disciples saw the Pharisee wander off to a guard, say a few words to him, and point in their direction.

Zealous Simon grabbed Joshua and waved over the disciples.

"Right now!" Simon shouted as he waved his friends toward the nearest tunnels. "We need to get the fuck out of here before more soldiers arrive!"

"Follow us!" Judas shouted as he and his brother led the way.

Simon and Judas dodged, shoved, and darted to carve a path through the panicking hoard of fleeing civilians. Once through the tunnels and down the stairs, they jumped to the side as a squad of Roman troops ran past them and up the stairs. They all gasped for breath and flattened themselves against the wall on the side of the stairway.

Zealous Simon tried to calm his frantic nerves while he assessed the situation. If they ran through the streets they would look suspicious, but with the security forces focused on the Temple, and the populace in a panic, it probably wouldn't matter. Furthermore, if they took their time walking at a normal pace, other Temple fleers might spot them and alert the authorities.

Running seemed to be the best option. So the Zealot brothers cut short their moment of rest and rushed their companions south at a run along a ravine that separated the upper and lower parts of the city.

After about ten minutes they headed east into the lower city. They zigzagged through the streets, causing everyone who crossed their path to jump out of their way like startled cats, until they reached a grain storage barn. They went inside, where Judas pulled open a trap door hidden under a pile of grain sacks and guided the group down stairs to a long tunnel. Now safely hidden, they slowed to a walk.

"This tunnel goes out to the Valley of Kedron," Judas said. "From there we can climb up to the Mount of Olives."

"Will we be safe enough there to rest?" Joshua asked. "I don't think I have the strength to go straight on through to Bethany."

"There's a place there where we can hide for the night," Judas answered. "It's totally safe. We should stay away from Bethany. Lots of people know who you are and I'm sure your name is already circulating in witnesses' reports and among the soldiers. The authorities will be looking for us, and soon they'll be able to trace us back to Bethany. But where we're going we'll be well hidden."

After exiting the tunnel, Simon and Judas led their party northeast, up and out of the Kedron Valley, and onto the base of the Mount of Olives. It was midday and throngs of pilgrims were camped there, gathered with family in tents and around cooking fires. Joshua's group wandered northward alongside the crowded hills and olive groves, waving away smoke and tiny flies, until they reached the base of a hill with the entrance to a cave on one side. Zealous Simon whistled a short, high-pitched note and two young men dressed in the rough flax tunics of farm workers emerged and saluted Simon.

"Shalom, Eli, Hani," Simon said. "We'll take over now, brothers."

Eli and Hani clasped hands with Simon and Judas and ran off. Four more young men of similar appearance exited the cave, clasped hands with Simon and Judas, and followed Eli and Hani into the hills.

"Resistance fighters?" Joshua whispered to Judas.

Judas made the gesture of silence, wiping his fist across his lips to signal that yes, they were Resistance fighters, and yes, it would be wise to say nothing about it.

The Zealous brothers led the other eleven into the cave. It was approximately thirty feet long, sixty feet wide, and twelve feet high. Four natural rock columns stood evenly distributed throughout the cave and spanned from floor to ceiling. There was an olive press at the left end of the cave and a cistern at the right end. It wasn't the season for harvesting olives, so the press had no baskets of olive pulp in it, just a stone slab on top of a stone pedestal cut to hold oil in reservoirs around the circumference. A wooden beam connected to the top slab extended out of a hole in the wall, and stone weights, meant to hang from the beam to apply pressure, lay stacked on the ground nearby. The cistern sat beneath a spout that brought rain water in from the outside via a channel drilled through the rock. Several wooden crates and clay jars sat against the back of the cave.

"Welcome, brothers," Zealous Simon said, "to Gethsemane, 'the olive press.' I love this cave. Spread yourselves around and feel the air. Dry and mildly cool. It's always like that. Perfect for storing food and wine."

Zealous Simon opened his arms to show off the jars in the back.

"We have olive oil pressed from the last harvest, and some honey too."

"What's in the crates?" John asked.

"Mats and blankets for sleeping. You can see that there's plenty of space here for all of us to sleep comfortably. But this cave is still beautifully small, at least compared with the others around Jerusalem. Too insignificant and unnoticed to attract trouble."

Joshua looked over the cave and said, "You're not storing any leaven in here, are you?"

"No, of course not," Zealous Simon said. "Not during Passover week. Don't worry about a thing, Rabbi. Right now we're just foxes in our hole. Curl up and get comfortable."

Joshua breathed a deep sigh and slumped down on a bench along the back wall. Then he sat up, leaned back, and motioned for his disciples to sit on the ground in front of him.

"It's time we talked about what happened back there," Joshua said. "We went too far. Even if there'd been no violence, we made a mistake agitating the crowd like that. That's exactly the kind of thing that attracts the wrong kind of attention. We all should have been more careful, like we were with Herod in Galilee. No more political provocations, not even disguised in secret code words. We blundered. Today was a victory for the evil one."

"Rabbi," Judas said. "Forgive me, but I respectfully disagree. We, and you especially, aren't to blame for any of the violence. You just told the people the truth, and that awakened something in them. If the people want to act on it, let them. If the people, not just resistance fighters and rebels, but the people too—if they rise up against the occupiers, then we'll have the advantage. The Romans don't want to kill civilians. Remember what happened when Pilate ordered his soldiers to attack the crowds protesting his images of Caesar. The people offered their necks, showing that they'd rather die than offend the Lord. Pilate had to back off and cancel the whole thing. The Romans won't massacre civilians; it's dishonorable for them and they know it would only turn our entire nation against them."

"So," Joshua said. "You think the people are ready to resist, but non-violently, to shame the Romans? Because that's what you're describing, but what happened at the Temple was violent resistance."

"Either way, if the Romans see how many are willing to die to return our nation to God, they'll leave us alone. It's too much trouble for them otherwise."

"So you want to sacrifice the people to regain the land? What's the point of the land if most of the people are dead?"

"No! I'm saying we show them that we're *willing* to die, so that they're forced to *not* kill us."

"Even if I understood your argument, Judas, I would still consider it irrelevant. I'm not interested in riots, or shows of force, or uprisings, or resistance that's violent or non-violent. I was called to bring the people back to God. That's all."

"But what if God brought you here specifically to inspire the people to reclaim their birthright? This could be the moment. The people might finally be ready to strike back at Pilate."

Joshua ran his hand through his hair and looked up as if beseeching the heavens outside.

"What can I do now?" Joshua asked, almost groaning. "If I'm a wanted man, then where can I go? Back to Galilee? Is this how it ends?"

Zealous Simon chimed in: "Rabbi, let's not blow things out of proportion. Even if the Romans are after you, which may or may not be the case, they only have so much patience for manhunts. Eventually they'll forget about you. For now, you can change your appearance, change your name, and hide out until it all blows over. This kind of thing happens all the time."

"Pray the Lord has mercy on us, Simon," Joshua said, turning his gaze toward Zealous Simon, "and that you're right."

Joshua leaned back and held the top of his head in his hands.

"Shittiest of shits!" Joshua said, almost spitting. "What a setback!"

A short, high-pitched whistle sounded from outside the cave, startling the ten disciples who had been transfixed by the debate between Joshua and the Zealot brothers. Judas and his brother looked at each other.

"I'll check it out," Judas said, motioning to his brother to remain seated.

Judas jumped up and hurried out of the cave. Eli and Hani were waiting at the entrance. The three of them moved to a giant olive tree and leaned against its thick trunk under a shady canopy of twisting branches.

"So," Eli whispered. "Is it a good time to make a move?"

"What about him?" Hani asked, pointing to the entrance of the cave. "Will the Nazarene help us? Will he get the public to support us?"

"Probably not," Judas said. "That's my answer to both of you. But the people could already be persuaded, so it might not matter. What have you heard?"

"The whole city's on edge—pissed off and fuming," Eli said. "There was a lot of bloodshed at the Temple. Everyone's talking about it. People are getting together and cursing the Romans."

"I'm going to have to check with some of our friends in the city today," Judas said. "I'll get a sense of the mood and find out if there's a good plan in the works. Meet me here tomorrow and I'll tell you all I know."

Eli and Hani clasped hands with Judas and walked west toward Jerusalem. Judas returned to the cave.

"What was that about?" Joshua asked as Judas sat down with the other disciples.

"It was Eli and Hani," Judas said. "They wanted to know if the Resistance is going to launch an uprising."

Everyone looked at Judas with the tell-tale wide eyes of visible trepidation.

"What did you tell them?" Joshua asked, nerves straining his voice.

"I told them I didn't know, and I don't. What do you think?"

"I have nothing more to say about uprisings," Joshua answered, indignant. "I'm just a fox in a hole."

Zealous Simon tried to change the subject: "It's still Passover week. One or two of us should buy or trade for some matzah and wine from some of the pilgrims outside. Do any of you have money? Or do we have to trade some of our foodstuffs?"

"I have a few coins," Andreus said.

"Me too," Phillip said.

"Good," Zealous Simon said. "One of you can get the matzah and the other can get the wine. Do you approve, Rabbi?"

"Do what you have to do," Joshua told Andreus and Phillip. "Just don't get into any trouble. We've had plenty of that for one day."

47

One day Ariel again grew tired of sitting at his desk and trying to conjure up the right words to describe Joshua's portentous signs to the world. So he left his house to take a walk, hoping the break would invigorate him. He was also hungry, so he walked to the marketplace in the center of the Jewish Quarter to find something good to eat.

In the marketplace Ariel encountered a man selling produce at a cloth-shaded kiosk. Baskets, boxes, and bowls displayed a bounty of various fruits, but two particular large baskets of figs attracted Ariel's attention. One basket held plump, ripe figs of a rich purple color. Ariel picked one up and felt its heaviness and its flesh, which was a perfect balance of firm and supple, and his mouth watered at the promise of lush, sweet reward. The other basket contained wrinkled, misshapen figs well past their prime, with skin discolored by the grime of leaking juice drying in the heat. Ariel touched one and its flesh gave way as if it were made of warm, flabby custard—the fruit's skin tore open and pulp dripped onto his finger.

"Is your name Jeremiah?" Ariel asked the merchant.

"No, lord," the merchant answered. "My name's Amos. You must have me confused with someone else."

Ariel laughed.

"Well, Amos, whoever you are, you have Jeremiah's baskets of figs."

"I assure you they're mine, lord."

Ariel laughed again.

"No, no, friend. I'm not accusing you of stealing your figs. I'm talking about the book of Jeremiah. Don't you remember? When Nebuchadnezzar exiled the skilled workers of Judah to Babylon, God showed Jeremiah two baskets of figs, one with good figs and one with bad figs. And that's what you have here. This basket has beautiful, perfectly ripe figs, and this other has ruined, inedible figs."

"They aren't inedible. Those figs may be over-ripe, and I've lowered their price accordingly, but they're perfect in that condition for making dips and sauces, or for embellishing cakes. They're good figs for the right purpose."

"If you say so. But again, I'm really talking about Jeremiah's two baskets of figs. God said the good figs were like the exiles in Babylon, good and faithful Jews who would return and rebuild Jerusalem. But the bad figs were like the survivors left behind in Jerusalem, the sinful Jews whom God would destroy with sword, famine, and plague. Don't you remember?"

"Yes. I think I remember that story from Jeremiah. Chapter . . . which was it?"

"Chapter twenty-four."

"Right. Twenty-four."

"And Jeremiah was right, was he not?"

"I suppose so."

"Jeremiah was a true prophet of God. God spoke to him and showed him the fate of the wicked in Jerusalem."

Ariel raised his arms and scowled as if preparing to deliver a prophecy of doom to a crowd. With his voice low and grim to feign that of a prophet, Ariel recited from the eighth chapter of Jeremiah: "The Lord declares: 'I'll take away their harvest; there will be no grapes on the vine. There will be no figs on the tree, and their leaves will wither. What I've given them I will take from them.'" (Jeremiah 8:13)

Ariel dropped the prophet act and laughed.

"Do you remember what else Jeremiah said?" Ariel asked. "He faced the sinful and idolatrous people at the Temple and asked them, 'Has this house, which bears my Name, become a den of robbers to you?' (Jeremiah 7:11) Doesn't that remind you of what happened to the Temple in this latest war? Doesn't that describe the Temple with those brigands Simon, Eleazar, and John fighting each other within? A den of robbers! It's perfect."

Amos just stared at Ariel.

"And Joshua, the Messiah, foresaw this latest destruction of Jerusalem," Ariel said. "He told us it would happen when judgment was at hand. He showed us the signs. Joshua's words and signs are now confirmed. He saw the war, the famines, the abominations . . . and he warned us. We're the generation that will see the judgment!"

Ariel stopped speaking. He and Amos were both silent for a moment.

Then Amos spoke: "I don't believe in the Nazarene."

Ariel frowned and narrowed his eyes.

"Then you," Ariel said, "belong to this basket of figs, the rotten ones. Repent! Repent before you get swept away with the pagans. Take up the cross and walk the way of Christ Joshua. The time is short!"

"I don't believe in Joshua the Nazarene and I don't believe in any Messiah. When we sin against God, He punishes us, and when we obey He rewards us. It's as simple as that. If most of the people grow sinful, enough to infuriate the Lord, He destroys and disperses us. Then, when we're obedient again, He restores us. That's how it's been for many centuries and that's how it will be for many more. No ultimate salvation is coming—not soon anyway."

Ariel sighed, indignant.

"Let these figs be a warning to you!" Ariel shouted. "The fig tree's twigs are tender and its leaves are out; the time for the harvest is here! Join the remnant that follows the way and be one of the good figs, from the good tree, or you'll be cursed. Christ

Joshua will curse your fig tree, and it will wither, never to bear fruit again. Look at what happened to Jerusalem and tremble!"

Ariel knocked the basket of bad figs down to the ground, where the contents spilled at his feet. Amos tried to grab Ariel, but Ariel was too quick and ran away the instant he'd toppled the basket. Ariel ran without stopping until he reached his home, where he hid himself away and tried to relax. When he was calm again, he sat down to resume his writing.

48

During the Passover festivals Pontius Pilate always removed himself from his usual residence in Caesarea and occupied Herod the Great's old palace in west Jerusalem. He did this because he had to stay on top of things during those dangerous days when the influx of pilgrims increased the city's population fourfold. As soon as Pilate learned of the disturbance at the Temple, he rushed with his entourage to Fortress Antonia to meet with the high priest, Joseph Caiaphas. When Pilate arrived, soldiers and Temple workers were still cleaning up the mess left by the riot. Dozens of arrested rioters were locked up in the fortress stockades, and the dead bodies were laid on sheets outside the city walls east of the Temple, waiting to be claimed by relatives or dumped in mass graves in the wilderness.

Pilate and Caiaphas met in a reception hall on the lower floor of the palatial fortress. Before entering, Pilate told his bodyguards and slaves to wait outside, and he walked in accompanied only by his translator. Caiaphas was waiting for him and glaring under his wide, flat-brimmed turban while standing dignified in his immaculate blue robe draped with a purple and scarlet sash. Pilate was annoyed and sweaty, and his moist, hairy arms poked out of his purple-bordered, wool toga. After the requisite formal salutations and expressions of mutual respect, the two leaders began their discussion in Greek, the translator at their side waiting to be called upon when necessary.

"Explain what the hell just happened in the Temple!" Pilate demanded.

Caiaphas flinched. "The crowd got carried away with excitement at the words of a particular preacher, a man known as Joshua the Nazarene. He's the man of the moment it seems. Very popular with the pilgrims."

"What's a Nazarene?"

"The title means he's from Nazareth."

"I've never heard of such a place."

"Nor I, until now. It's in Galilee, apparently. Or perhaps it's completely made up. It sounds like 'Nazirite,' which is our word for a monk devoted to the holy life. Maybe this Joshua is from a community of Nazirites, or wants people to think he is."

"Joshua the Nazarene, Joshua the Nazarene, Joshua the Nazarene," Pilate repeated the name to engrave it in his memory. "How does he inflame the crowds? What does he tell them?"

"I hear he cites the prophets—says the final judgment is coming. He tells parables about the nature of the Most High and urges people to repent of their sins. In this he's similar to other so-called prophets that I've seen come and go. But the people have taken to a particular saying of his: 'Return to Caesar what belongs to Caesar and return to God what belongs to God.' It's become a popular rallying cry of protest throughout the city."

"Hmm. I heard some people shouting a short, repeated phrase like that on the way here. It was in Aramaic I think. I didn't understand it, but whole groups of people were shouting it from the rooftops. Maybe that was it."

"It probably was, lord. My men tell me that's exactly what people are shouting at their protest assemblies."

"So what exactly belongs to Caesar, and to God, according to this Joshua?"

"I'm not completely certain, but I think the gist of it is that Rome and the Romans belong to Caesar and Judea and the Jews belong to God."

"Of course. 'Romans go home.' You know the danger of these types of agitators. Why didn't your men detain him?"

"In the chaos he got away, apparently. He probably slipped out while the guards and soldiers were busy putting down the violence."

"It sounds like your security at the Temple is lax!" Pilate shouted. Pilate pounded his own head with his fist. "Caesar's piss! I can't let that obscene Nazarene get away with this insult. I need to make an example of him before this stupidity spreads, or else I'll have to treat your people to a severe chastisement. Does anyone in your Sanhedrin know him, or where he might be found?"

"I doubt it. And the Sanhedrin doesn't meet during the festival anyway. All members are with their families celebrating like everyone else."

"Well, I'm sending my men after this Joshua, and all who help or imitate him, and I expect you to do the same. Arrest anyone who professes to support the Nazarene or his message. Some of them must know where he's hiding. Send the agitators to me, here at Fortress Antonia; this is where I'll be for the foreseeable future. But before you do, bribe or torture them to give up whatever they know about him."

"With respect, lord, bribery and torture will be useless with these people, whether you or I conduct it. There's a code among our people, a matter of solemn honor, that forbids us to betray or inform on our own compatriots when they're pursued by foreign authorities. This code is especially strong among the kind of rebels we're dealing with. They'll die before giving anyone away."

Pilate groaned from exasperation and disbelief. He lowered his head and held the top of it with the palm of his hand, as if in troubled concentration. Then he lifted his head, looked at Caiaphas, and spoke.

"If you can't bribe or torture them, then figure out some clever way to trick them into giving him up to you, like that king of yours, Solomon. How does the story go? There was a boy . . . yes. I remember. Two women claim to be the mother of the same boy, so Solomon proposes that the boy be split in two and one half given to each woman. The true mother surrenders her claim to the boy to save his life. Yes. Use that kind of trickery to get the truth out of the rebels indirectly. I'll try to devise some kind of ruse too—something for my own men to use in case bribery and torture fail them."

49

Ariel lay in deep sleep on his bed. He dreamed that he was a servant waiting on Joshua and his disciples at the Last Supper. As he poured water into their cups, he saw Joshua—handsome, dignified, and radiant with righteous authority. Joshua reclined on a large cushion and scanned the room with eyes expressing deep suspicion.

"You can't hide yourself," Joshua said. "I know you're here among us, traitor."

One of the dining disciples stood up and said, "Surely I'm not the traitor, am I? Please Lord, don't let me be the one!"

The others did the same, one by one, until a last disciple faced Joshua and said, "I know I'm not the traitor. I would die before I'd betray you. Could a dead man possibly harm you, Lord?"

The disciple then flashed a dagger with a curved blade, the kind used by the Sicarii, and sliced open his own throat with it. Pulsating gushes of blood sprayed from his neck and splashed onto the table and floor. Another disciple caught some of the spraying blood with his cup, drank, and fell to the floor writhing.

Some disciples drew swords and decapitated others who exposed their necks to them like proud martyrs. The remaining disciples unsheathed swords of their own and confronted the decapitators. Each man thrust his sword into his opponent's chest in an act of mutual impalement. The impaled pairs fell in paroxysms to the floor.

Ariel looked for Joshua and saw him still reclined on the cushion, but now Joshua was transformed into a shimmering body of white flame. Ariel wanted to escape the room, but the floor disappeared and left him to sink into a deep pit of slimy, blood-soaked flesh and viscera. He sank until he was submerged and drowning in the gore.

In a sudden flash Ariel woke and found himself in his bed again, soaked in sweat.

Was this a dream from the Lord?

Ariel rolled himself off his bed and onto his knees on the floor.

He prayed: "Lord Joshua, son of the Most High, have you sent me a sign? If so, what are you trying to tell me?"

50

Andreus and Phillip returned to the cave in the late afternoon, Andreus with a basket of unleavened bread and Phillip with a stone jar containing about fifty ounces of wine. They set their purchases down near the jars of oil and honey and joined the other disciples, who were on their knees and deep in prayer. The disciples faced west, toward the Temple, and prayed for safe deliverance from their pursuers. Joshua asked God to protect not only himself and his fugitive disciples, but also Mary, Salome, and their relatives in Bethany, whom he prayed would be spared any visits from the authorities looking for him. Judas beseeched God to reveal to him what to say to his Resistance comrades. Judas wanted to know if they should coordinate a massive attack on Herod's Palace or Fortress Antonia, or if they should hold out and wait for a better opportunity in the future.

After a couple of hours of prayer, the disciples found themselves shrouded in thickening darkness as sunset approached and the day's waning light fled from the already dim cave. Zealous Simon and Judas lit some oil lamps and spread them around the cave, bathing it in a flickering, orange glow.

"Brothers," Joshua said, calling his disciples to attention. "You need to be prepared to carry on in case I'm taken from you."

The disciples erupted in anguished protest.

Simon, revealing the sentiments of all the disciples, said, "Wherever you go, Rabbi, we'll go, even if it means death. May we never separate."

"Listen," Joshua said, gesturing for calm. "I'm not saying that it will happen, but we have to accept that it might. And I don't want you to give yourselves up for my sake. I'm the one the authorities want. You can still get away. You still have anonymity. If I must be taken, then I want you to escape and continue the mission. Do whatever you have to do—deny that you have anything to do with me, avoid mentioning my name—but continue to proclaim the truth to the people. You know in your hearts that you must do this if, God forbid, our enemies take me."

"It would be better if the twelve of us were handed over and you were saved!" Phillip cried.

The others chimed in with distressed supplications to heaven to preserve their master. They touched and embraced Joshua like children afraid to part with a beloved parent. They huddled around him as if their clinging bodies could shield him from all the evils of the world.

"Enough!" Joshua shouted. "What demons have entered you to make you all act like hysterical women? Let go of me before I drown in your tears!"

The disciples backed off and sat down, embarrassed.

"Listen, my brothers," Joshua said, his voice gentle again. "I need you to have faith. Remember that our final destination is the kingdom. But before then we each must drink the cup the Lord gives us. Who here has a cup for holding wine?"

Andreus withdrew to a nearby carrying sack, searched inside, and pulled out a plain, smooth, and polished limestone goblet.

"I have one, Rabbi," Andreus said, handing it to Joshua.

Joshua set the cup down next to the wine jar. He grabbed the basket of matzah and stood up straight as if called to attention by some unknown authority.

"Stand up, brothers," Joshua said. "I'm going to give you each some of this bread. This bread is my body. By taking it and eating it, you're giving me your solemn oath to faithfully continue our mission in the event that I'm no longer with you, as if your body were my body—as if I were acting vicariously through you."

Joshua recited the Kiddush prayer of thanksgiving over the basket and handed a piece of matzah to each disciple. They all ate, some with eyes moist from welling tears, others composed and firm in stoic resignation. He set the basket down and poured wine from the jar into the cup, filling it. He raised the cup and recited the thanksgiving blessing.

After the blessing, Joshua said, "This cup of wine is the cup of tribulation. It's the hardship and sorrow you must endure on your mission. It's my blood. By drinking it, you're giving me your solemn oath to accept whatever trials you may face in the event of losing me, and to remain faithful to your mission even if it costs you your life, as if your blood were my blood and your life my life."

Joshua took a sip from the cup and handed it to Elder Jacob, who drank from it and passed it to his brother John, who drank and passed the cup to the others so all could drink in their turn. After the last disciple drank from the cup and handed it back to Joshua, Joshua raised the cup again and repeated the thanksgiving prayer before setting the cup down by the wine jar. Then he led the disciples in singing the Hallel hymns (Psalms 113–118).

While he sang along with the group, Judas decided that Joshua's exhortation to stay strong and carry on meant that Joshua was giving up on his own public role in their ministry. It seemed that Joshua, now a marked man, would be henceforth confined to the shadows, exerting influence from behind the scenes or perhaps even abandoning the disciples to spare them the danger of his association. Judas doubted that without Joshua the disciples would have the charisma or wisdom to inspire the people to free themselves from Roman oppression. Judas thought about how incensed the city was at the Romans at that moment, and about how few days there were before most of those outraged Jews would be leaving Jerusalem. He could sense the window of opportunity closing. When the singing ended Judas took his brother outside, said a few words to him, and slipped away into the darkening valley that led to the city.

Several minutes later Joshua approached Zealous Simon.

"Simon! Where did Judas go?"

"He said he was taking a brief trip to the city to speak with Hilkiah."

"Hilkiah?"

"He's the chief Resistance leader in Jerusalem. An old friend."

"Why? Why would he do that now, with this shit storm brewing?"

"I wish I knew," Zealous Simon said. "He just said that he was inspired to preach, now that he has your body and blood coursing through him."

* * *

Judas knew that on a night like tonight, with the population in tumult and Pilate's soldiers on high alert, Hilkiah would be in his subterranean hideaway in southeast Jerusalem with his band of twenty or so fellow Resistance officers. The hideaway, a complex of four linked caverns that was accessible from the city only by underground tunnels with secret entrances, contained valuable weapons and supplies that were always under guard, but Hilkiah would want to be there in person to distribute them to his men at a time when the Romans were agitated and prowling.

After navigating the city streets for about half an hour, Judas met a man sitting on a boarded up well and pronounced the secret password, "dumah," the Hebrew word for silence. The man lifted the wooden planks capping the well and Judas climbed inside. A ladder led twelve feet down to the bottom, where a seven-foot-high passageway began. Judas wandered the tunnel until he reached the entrance to the first cavern, where a guard admitted him after hearing the password. Judas found Hilkiah, hulking and hirsute, sitting on a mat in the armory and plotting with several comrades amid racks of swords, slings, and clubs.

"Judas!" Hilkiah cried when he saw Judas enter.

Judas and Hilkiah embraced and exchanged greetings.

Hilkiah addressed his men: "Friends! This is Judas, a comrade from long ago. We used to sabotage Roman supply caravans together, back when Gratus was procurator. A great help to the movement and a pain in the ass to the Romans!"

The men offered Judas welcomes and pleasantries for a moment until Hilkiah took him aside to speak in private.

"How long has it been, friend?" Hilkiah asked. "What mischief have you been up to all this time?"

"I've been in Galilee. Smuggling mostly. But for the last year I've been assisting a rabbi—a rabbi who saved me and Simon from some of Herod's thugs in Tiberias."

"Saved? That sounds like a good story. What happened?"

"I'll tell you later, if there's time."

Judas moved closer to Hilkiah and lowered his voice as if he had a secret to spill.

"Don't you think the time is ripe for a strike? Everyone's cursing the Romans, and think of the numbers. Their soldiers can't take us on, not with the people on our side."

"Of course. We've been going over plans—figuring out the best way. Right now we're thinking about placing ourselves around Fortress Antonia, weapons hidden until—"

Hilkiah snapped his fingers and made an upward stabbing motion with his hand.

"How many men can you get?" Judas asked.

"Each man here can cover a district and round up about a hundred men. All together we'll be some two thousand. With the public occupying the guards with disturbances and such, we can probably take the fortress."

"Yes. With the weapons from the fortress we can arm even more men."

Judas grabbed Hilkiah by the shoulders.

"Let me speak to your men. I feel inspired."

Hilkiah released himself from Judas's grip and called over his officers.

"Comrades! Judas wants to make a speech! Shut up for a minute and listen!"

Judas raised his hand to signal quiet until the chamber hushed.

"Friends," Judas said. "God has sent opportunity our way. If we're brave and seize it, we can throw off the pagan yoke. Everything is lining up in our favor! Just look at what's happening. The people are inflamed—driven to rage, justified rage—by the words of Joshua the Nazarene. I know this Joshua—I'm his student and his friend."

Gasps and murmurs erupted at the mention of Joshua. Judas paused and waited for the chatter to die out.

"Joshua knows the prophecies better than anyone, and he knows that the days of our liberation are at hand. It's time to return to God what belongs to God. Listen to Hilkiah. He has a good plan. God grant us victory!"

The men shot questions at Judas. They asked him where Joshua was, what Joshua knew, and if Joshua would help them persuade the people to attack the Romans.

Judas held up his hands for quiet.

"Listen. All I can say about my master is that it's not safe yet for him to come out of hiding. I have nothing more to say than that."

The men started to raise an excited clamor, and Hilkiah motioned for silence. The men quieted.

"Thank you for your encouragement, my friend," Hilkiah said, slapping Judas's back and taking the floor. "Men! I'm going to give each of you your assignment. Listen for your name!"

Hilkiah paused and looked at Judas.

"Will you be coming with us?" Hilkiah asked.

"No, brother. I can't. I wish I could. But I'll pray for you. I have to get going—right now. I've been away too long as it is. Success to you, friend."

* * *

When Judas emerged from the false well above the caverns of southeast Jerusalem, the well's guardian was gone. The streets of the city were lit here and there by hanging oil lamps, wall-installed torches, and the rooftop fires of Passover celebrants.

Many people, indoors and out, were still assembling themselves into parties to indulge in group condemnation of the Romans. They chanted curses, sang insults, and recited litanies of Roman crimes against the Jews. Every once in a while some version of "Caesar's back to Caesar, God's back to God" rang out.

When Judas reached the alley that led to the storage barn—the one containing the secret entrance to the tunnel to the Kedron Valley—he found a group of five men in hooded cloaks loitering against a wall. Judas tried to sneak by unnoticed, but one of the men saw him and walked over to stop him. The man raised a hand and made a secret Resistance sign of peace, and then said one word: "dumah."

"Dumah," Judas answered, eyeing the man in a futile attempt to identify him.

"I recognize you, friend," the man said. "I saw you at the Temple with the Nazarene, Joshua. You know him!"

Judas's instincts warned him to be wary. He didn't recognize any of these men.

"Excuse me," Judas said. "I'm in a hurry."

"Hold on! Let me walk with you. We can help each other."

"Please, you've mistaken me for someone else, I don't know any Joshua the Nazarene."

The four other hooded men approached and stood nearby. The man spoke again.

"Relax, brother. We're on the same side. My friends and I are admirers of Joshua—he's waking the people up to the truth. I've heard him myself. I want to know more about the kingdom and how to reach it. I want to be baptized."

"I'm sorry. I can't help you."

The men surrounded Judas. They took turns entreating him.

"Baptize us."

"Show us the way to forgiveness."

"Take us to him."

Judas looked around for the easiest way to escape. He racked his brain to come up with some way to distract the men and flee to safety but his wits failed him. He clutched a dagger under his cloak.

"Please," the first man said, coming closer. "We seek the kingdom. We know judgment is near."

The man tried to grab Judas by the arm, and Judas sprang back and brandished his dagger.

"Stay the fuck away from me, pigs!" Judas yelled, waving the blade at them.

One of the men grabbed Judas's arm from behind and tried to dislodge the knife with a violent shake, while another man kicked Judas in the groin. Judas doubled over and dropped his dagger. The other men pounced. They pummeled him until he was weakened enough to subdue, and then tied his wrists together behind his back.

The first man lifted his hood and whistled a long, high note. In less than ten seconds a troop of twenty-six Temple guards, armed with swords and clubs, ran up and took Judas into their custody.

"Who is this?" one of the guards asked, looking at the first man.

"I don't know," the man said. "He's uncooperative. But I know he belongs to the Nazarene. I've seen him with him."

The guard grabbed Judas by the back of the head.

"What's your name?" the guard asked.

Judas tried to wriggle himself free from the guard, but the guard tightened his grip and forced Judas's face to within an inch of his own.

"I said, what—is—your—name?"

"I am," Judas said, "he who fucks your mother."

The guard slapped Judas on the side of his head.

"Nathan!" the guard shouted, looking at the first of the hooded men. "What did you get out of this prick?"

"Just his dagger and his insults," Nathan said.

The guard punched Judas in the face.

"Where's your Joshua? Tell us and we'll let you go."

"Let me go? How dumb do you think I am? You stupid steed strokers!" Judas shouted. "Do you really think I'm some kind of coward? That I'd just march you dumb donkey dicks right up to Get—"

Judas stopped himself and shuddered.

"Ah ha!" the guard cried, raising his fist in the air. "'Get'—'press.' Your Joshua's at the press! Wine press or—"

The guard looked up to the Mount of Olives.

"Olive press!" the guard shouted. "Joshua's at one of the olive presses—or a wine press."

"He's probably not talking about any wine press, Reuben," Nathan said to the guard. "There are places called 'olive press' in the hills, but I don't know of any place near here called 'wine press.'"

"Right," Reuben said. "Gethsemane. Gethsemane Mount . . . Gethsemane Garden . . . Gethsemane Grove . . . Gethsemane this, Gethsemane that."

Reuben kicked Judas in the groin.

"Which is it, you shit?"

"Fuck you! I'm not saying anything more!" Judas was curled up in pain.

"Name your price," Reuben said. "How much silver will it take to make you sensible?"

"Just kill me right here. I'm not giving you anything more, not for anything."

Reuben sighed and looked up again at the Mount of Olives.

"You know what?" Reuben said. "Don't say anything. Be a hero and protect your Joshua. We'll just go to every place called 'olive press' in the hills and kill everyone we find. Their blood will be on your head."

Reuben turned to Nathan.

"What is it, five places?" Reuben asked. "We can finish the job tonight!"

Reuben pulled Judas up by the neck.

"There's really no point resisting, you mule," Reuben said. "We know all about your plans to attack the fortress. Pilate has spies even in the underground tunnels. Your plan will be shut down before it can even start. You're giving up your life for nothing."

Reuben shoved Judas to get him moving.

"Come on, hero," Reuben said. "You're coming with us. You'll get to see a lot of innocents die—all because of *your* stubbornness."

51

One evening, an hour or so after the Sabbath ended, Zachariah and Ariel sat together on a stone bench in the courtyard of Zachariah's home. They had just finished a supper of mutton stew and had gone out to enjoy the mild outdoor breeze and get some relief from the stifling heat of the house.

"The people are impatient," Zachariah said. "More and more I'm accosted by members of my church. 'When's Joshua coming?' they ask me. 'How much time is left?' and 'Why does he delay?'"

"I get the same from my flock," Ariel said. "What do you tell them?"

"I tell them I can't answer those questions. How could I? Only God knows the day and the hour of the final judgment. How do *you* answer them?"

"I say the same. And I tell them to watch for the signs. We need to be alert and ready when the master returns. Too many people are letting themselves forget about Joshua as the time of his return approaches. 'Stay faithful and stay awake,' I tell them. 'Don't lapse into sin or unbelief. He could return at any moment.' I'm actually thinking of putting something about this in my book."

"Really?"

"Yes. I want to have a scene in which the disciples ask Joshua these kinds of questions about when God's wrath will come. After he tells them about the wars and famines and destruction of

Jerusalem—the signs of the beginning of the end—he urges them to keep watch and stay awake, because only God knows the exact time. He tells them they're like servants tasked with watching over their master's home while he's off on a journey. The master will send them away if he finds them sleeping when he returns. Joshua says it to the Twelve but he's also saying it—"

"To us? This is really a message for *our* time, isn't it?"

"Exactly."

Zachariah smiled. "I know your methods well, friend."

Ariel laughed. "That's fortunate for both of us; the better you understand me, the less difficult it is for me to explain myself."

Zachariah nodded. "So . . . Joshua tells his disciples to keep watch and stay awake. What happens next?"

"Next there's the whole sordid episode with Judas, which you know all about already. But then, as Joshua is about to be arrested, he returns to my theme. Imagine Joshua at that moment. Imagine him telling his disciples to stay awake and keep watch while he goes off to pray—to pray for his Father to give him the strength to face his impending, sacrificial death. When Joshua returns, he finds his disciples sleeping. They fail to keep watch."

Zachariah's brow furrowed. "But there's nothing in the traditional account of Joshua's arrest that says the disciples fell asleep."

"No, of course not. I know. But it's a symbol, a sign. It's a warning to people *today* to not fall into temptation and abandon the Messiah right as he's about to return. It's a message to the sleepers among us right now."

"But don't you think you're taking liberties with our Lord and his disciples? How can you say they failed Joshua like this? Isn't this slander?"

"No. Not at all. I'm just telling the truth in a new way. Surely you understand me as well as you claim to, don't you? Hear me out, Zachary. Doesn't Joshua want us to remain faithful until he returns?"

"Yes. Of course."

"And didn't the disciples abandon Joshua when he was arrested, only to be ashamed of their cowardice when Joshua came back to them after rising to glory?"

"Yes. That's the official story."

"Then I invent nothing and slander no one. I simply take actual events and use them as a lesson for today. Shouldn't I do what I can to encourage people to keep the faith? Isn't that my duty as a rabbi and servant of the Christ? Yes. I think I'll put this episode in my book. The people should hear it."

"If you say so. I won't dare argue with you. You win every time."

Ariel smiled.

"Oh, and another thing," Ariel said. "I had a hideous dream a few nights ago."

"Yes?"

"It was horrifying. I was at the Last Supper, but it was all wrong. The disciples all killed each other or killed themselves."

"Joshua too?"

"No. He turned into some kind of angelic being. But the rest went mad. Stabbings, decapitations—at the end of it I was drowning in blood."

"Mother of mercy, Ari. Had you been drinking?"

"No. When I woke, I was afraid the dream was a sign from the Lord—some terrible omen. I prayed for understanding but I still wonder about its meaning, if it even has any. It did remind me of something though."

"What?"

"Masada."

Zachariah paused to think for a moment.

"Yes, of course," Zachariah said. "All that murder and suicide."

"Right. So I opened up the last volume of *The Judaic War* and reread chapter eight, the one about Masada. I tried to find any similarities with the Last Supper. At the time I thought the Lord might have wanted me to connect the two somehow, to use the Last Supper to allude to Masada in some way perhaps . . . something like that."

"Did you find anything?"

"Maybe. They're both final events of sorts. Masada was the last stand of the Sicarii and the end of their movement. Likewise, the Last Supper was the last meal Joshua had with his disciples before his death. But *that* movement was really just about to begin, because after Joshua appeared to them risen from the dead, the disciples went out and spread the news of the resurrected Messiah and established the churches. So consider this: Masada was an assembly of a thousand rebels, hoping to hold out indefinitely against the Romans, and it ended in complete failure and mass suicide. The Last Supper was a small gathering of Joshua and the Twelve that soon turned tragic, but ultimately it led to a great victory. So in that sense the Last Supper is something of an antithesis of the Masada tragedy. It might be worthwhile to tell the story of the Last Supper in a way that alludes to Masada, to contrast the rebels' false salvation of Israel with Joshua's true way to the kingdom of God. I've recently been working on this idea actually."

"How's that going?"

"Not well. But I'll share my silly idea with you. You see, back when I reread that chapter on Masada, I was struck by how much Josephus wrote about the peculiarities of that fortress—its elevation on top of that almost insurmountable tower of rock, its abundant and expensive furnishings, and its perilous isolation in the desert. For all the strategic advantages it had to protect it from attack, Masada had the disadvantage of having no nearby source of water—not even a single spring. It was completely dependent on the rains to fill its cisterns—in a desert with unreliable rainfall! When the Romans went to Masada, they had to bring all their water with them from far away.

"From these details I got an idea for how to introduce the Last Supper scene. Imagine this: the disciples ask Joshua where they'll celebrate the Passover meal. Joshua tells them to go into Jerusalem and look for a man carrying a jar of water. 'Follow him to the house he goes to,' Joshua tells them. 'The owner of the house will take you to a large, upstairs guest room, well-furnished and ready. We'll have our meal there.' It's a subtle allusion to Masada that readers of *The Judaic War* should catch—a reminder of how the Zealots' movement, and its fate, was the evil opposite of ours."

Zachariah frowned and stared at Ariel.

"I hope you won't actually put that in your book. It completely changes the location of the inauguration of the Eucharist. And for what? A sly swipe at the Zealots? I know you want to answer those who use *The Judaic War* to discredit our faith, but isn't this a bit much? You're obsessed with Josephus and that book of his. I don't think many people will grasp the allusion anyway. So why bother? It will just confuse people."

Ariel laughed.

"Yes, you're probably right, Zachary. I told you it was a silly idea. I think I'll take your advice and leave it out. What was I thinking?"

52

Joshua sat with his back against a rock column in the cave, fretting. He tried to imagine what Judas might be up to. Perhaps he was getting some of his Resistance fighters together to commit some act of sabotage against the priests or the city guards. Such a stunt, whether Judas got away with it or not, would surely only increase the heat on Joshua. Maybe Judas had abandoned Joshua and the mission because he didn't believe in it anymore. Or maybe Judas was attempting to recruit his friends to help Joshua and the disciples escape Jerusalem. Whatever the case was, Joshua feared Judas's return. Even if Judas was careful to steer clear of danger, he nevertheless might come back with Pilate's agents following him in secret pursuit.

Joshua hopped up and headed toward the cave's exit. John intercepted him.

"Hold on, Rabbi," John said. "It's not safe for you to be seen outside. Is there something I can do for you out there?"

Joshua sighed, exasperated.

"I need to see who's out there. I need to know if Judas is coming back. I'm beside myself with worry."

"I'll climb up the hill and be a lookout," John said. "I'll check if anyone's heading our way."

"Take your brother with you, and Judas's brother, too. He knows Judas better than anyone. Come tell me if you see Judas or anyone suspicious approaching."

John rounded up Elder Jacob and Zealous Simon and the three of them ascended the hillside above the cave to keep watch over the area. The valley between Jerusalem and the campfires of the pilgrims on the Mount of Olives was pure darkness. The three watchers peered into the night, determined to spot any and all shadowy or torch-lit movement that drew near.

Meanwhile Joshua faced the west wall of the cave, prostrated himself, and prayed out loud: "Lord of heaven, Father of Israel, Creator of the world—protect us, your faithful servants, in our hour of need. Let all evil and danger pass over us on this night. Protect Judas; whatever he's doing, let him do it quickly and return safe and without trouble. Give him, and us, the strength to resist the evil one . . ."

When Joshua finished praying, Simon came to him.

"Rabbi, I ate the bread and drank the cup, but I don't think I can fulfill my promise, not if we're to lose you."

Simon started to choke up.

"I couldn't bear it, Master. I'd die of grief."

Joshua laid a hand on Simon's shoulder and looked at him with an expression that exuded warmth and sympathy.

"Simon, you're my rock—my cephas."

"Rock?"

"When I took you into my fold you were like a rock: hard and unformed. You were the first true man of the people to join me—simple, uneducated, troubled, and lost."

"You insult me, Rabbi? Even now?"

"No. Just listen. You began humbly, but look at what you've become. You were a rough block of stone, and now you're chiseled, carved, and polished—a solid vessel of truth. You, more than any of the others, proved to me that the people of Israel were ready to hear the news of the kingdom. If any of my disciples can carry on the mission, you can, because you've come farther than all of them. You're my solid rock. I ought to call you Rock—Cephas— from now on. Whatever happens, don't be afraid—stay firm, be unstoppable—because that's what you are now."

Simon blushed and took Joshua's hand.

"If I'm your rock, then you're my earth. How can I stand if my earth falls away? I'll fall with it."

"No. I'm just another rock. Without me you'll fall gently to the ground, only to find yourself supported by the Lord. He's your earth. It's God who's been holding us up the whole time—trust Him."

At that moment John, Elder Jacob, and Zealous Simon rushed into the cave.

"Rabbi!" Zealous Simon shouted. "I saw Judas. He's with a band of Temple guards—about thirty. It looks like they've taken him prisoner. They're coming this way."

Joshua gasped and started to pace.

"Oh God, what has he done?" Joshua asked, speaking to no one in particular. "How close are they?"

"It's only a matter of minutes before they find us," Zealous Simon answered.

"Brothers, come gather around me!" Joshua shouted.

At once the disciples assembled before Joshua.

"You all must flee now," Joshua said. "Go back to Bethany. Stay with Mary and Salome and wait for me there. If I don't return to you in three days, go back to Galilee—to Magdala. I'll meet you at Mary's house as soon as I can."

"What will you do, Rabbi?" John asked.

"Don't worry about me. With God's help I'll figure out what happened to Judas and maybe rescue us both. Judas may have some kind of ruse going. There may be a way out of this trap, but I won't risk getting all of us captured or killed. So flee. Now!"

Joshua chased the disciples out of the cave. They all saw and heard the armed band approach from the west—torches blazing, boots scuffing, and weapons rattling. Terrified, the disciples dashed eastwards up the slopes and into the darkness, scattering themselves among tents and trees.

Simon Cephas found a thick-trunked olive tree, hid behind it, and took an instant to look back in Joshua's direction. He glimpsed Judas on his knees in front of Joshua, with the soldiers closing in on them. A sickening wave of dread coursed through him, and the paralysis of fear began to grip him. Somehow he shook it off enough to take a deep breath, summon all his strength, and rejoin the others in their frantic ascent to safety.

* * *

Judas ran ahead of his captors and fell on his knees before Joshua.

"You, the ever-loyal Zealot, betray me?" Joshua asked.

"They tricked me!" Judas shouted. "Spies have infiltrated the Resistance. They were going to find you no matter what I did. They were going to kill everyone up here and burn it to the ground. It was a choice between giving you up or letting you and everyone else get slaughtered."

"It was a choice between trusting God and trusting men. You picked the worst time to go plot with your friends, or whatever it was you were doing. This is how the world repays you for trying to impose your will upon it."

"Forgive me, Rabbi." Judas glanced back at the pursuing soldiers. "You can talk sense into these men, Master. Persuade them! Work a miracle!"

The soldiers grabbed Joshua, who didn't resist when they bound his hands, and recaptured Judas.

"Are you Joshua the Nazarene?" Reuben asked.

"I am. Let this one go. He's useless to you."

"Where are the rest of your followers, Joshua?" Reuben asked.

Reuben turned to his men and shouted, "Search the area for suspects!"

"My friends abandoned me long ago," Joshua said. "You'd be wasting your time trying to catch up to them. Leave the innocent alone. I'm the one you want."

In a moment the searching soldiers returned.

"It looks like they were camped in that cave," a soldier said, pointing. "There's food and bed matting, but everyone's gone."

Reuben selected ten men.

"You ten go looking for any suspicious people hiding around here. Bring any captives to Fortress Antonia."

Reuben turned to the remaining men and said, "Let's go. Pilate's waiting at the fortress. These two will fetch a handsome reward."

Joshua spoke to the guards: "Aren't you Jews? Don't you know the prophets? God's wrath is at hand. Repent and save yourselves. Stop working for the pagans."

"Listen to him," Judas said. "He's a man of God. He has powers. You're sealing your own doom if you don't."

Reuben dismissed Judas's and Joshua's comments with a wave of his hand. The soldiers laughed and marched their captives down into the valley.

* * *

Upon entering Fortress Antonia, Reuben and his troops brought Joshua and Judas straight to the praetorium, where Pilate waited to interrogate each of them himself, one at a time. Pilate chose to meet with Joshua first, so Reuben took Joshua into the designated courtroom and left him in the custody of two Roman soldiers. Pilate stood in front of a marble dais with his translator at his left. Two Roman bodyguards, dressed and equipped like centurions, flanked the dais, upon which a scribe sat on a wooden chair. Joshua, hands tied behind his back and flanked by the soldiers, stood facing Pilate.

"Do you speak Greek?" Pilate asked in clumsy Aramaic.

"No." Joshua answered.

Pilate signaled to his translator and began to speak in Latin, which the translator converted to Aramaic.

"You're the one called Joshua the Nazarene, correct?"

"I am."

"You stand accused of inciting insurrection and rioting in the Temple. Do you have anything to say in your defense?"

Joshua was silent.

"Nothing? This is a serious accusation. I can have you crucified. You have nothing to say for yourself?"

Joshua remained mute. Pilate moved closer to him.

"I want to hear it from you—your words. What do you preach?"

"My message is for the people of Israel. It's of no use to pagans."

"Be that as it may, I want to know what you teach the Jews. Well?"

"I simply tell the truth."

"And what's the truth?"

Joshua looked straight at Pilate.

"You, the Romans, the first and the greatest on this day—savor your moment. Soon God will topple you. He'll wipe the earth clean of you."

"Really? How can you know such a thing?"

"God sent his prophets to warn us of the judgment that's at hand. So far everything they've written has happened—as written. All will be fulfilled."

"So your prophets told you to incite the people to rebel against us?"

"No. I teach repentance and righteousness. I teach the way of God's kingdom."

"God's kingdom? You mean Judea?"

"I mean the kingdom that's coming to welcome God's faithful and save them from His wrath."

Pilate paused and scratched his head. "This kingdom's coming here? To Judea?"

"Yes."

"From where?"

"Heaven."

"Of course. I should have known that. There's no room for pagans in your kingdom, is there? You'll have to get rid of all the Romans and Greeks to make room for your kingdom, I imagine. That's why you preach 'Romans back to Rome and Judea back to the Jews.'"

Joshua paused to gather his thoughts.

This Pilate is going to kill me no matter how I answer his questions. What does he want? Resistance secrets? A list of rebel accomplices? Whatever he does to me, he won't get anyone else. He'll get nothing from me.

Joshua said, "I merely told the people to let Caesar have what belongs to Caesar, and let God have what belongs to God. It's simple justice."

"Which the mob naturally took to mean: 'Let Caesar's people stay in Rome and let the Jews pacify their jealous god by driving the Romans out of Judea.' You've just admitted it. You're an agitator."

"Whatever anyone took it to mean, I was only saying that the priests had exchanged God for Caesar by handing over the holy things to Caesar—and by turning God's Temple into a Roman tax-collection agency. All that's true, isn't it? You can't deny that the priests work for you now."

"You're still talking like an agitator. Your testimony only further demonstrates your guilt. I judge you to be—"

"I'm not afraid of your judgment!" Joshua shouted, cutting Pilate off. "The only judgment that matters is the judgment of the Most High. I face my Judge without fear—conscience clean. But woe to you and Caesar and Rome! The Lord is far mightier than Rome. You'll perish in the fire. Burning coals and sulfur will rain on you. The scorching winds will erase you from memory. The earth will open up and swallow you into hell!"

Pilate signaled to the soldiers to restrain Joshua.

"Joshua the Nazarene, I sentence you to crucifixion," Pilate said. Pilate addressed the soldiers: "Don't bother sending the other one in. There's no reasoning with fanatics. Take all the insurrectionists you're holding and crucify the whole lot of them."

53

Ariel stood at the podium in the synagogue before a good attendance of about eighty percent capacity. Larger crowds were to be expected at that time—the beginning of the Hebrew month of Tisri—when the Day of Atonement was less than two weeks away and people were mindful of their sins.

"I know, brothers and sisters," Ariel said, "that some of you are struggling with your faith. You look at all that's happened to us— the destruction of our Holy City and Temple, the forced exodus of our people to foreign lands, the unprecedented slaughter of our compatriots, the Roman yoke around our necks as tight as it ever was—and despair of any salvation to come. Perhaps you hoped the Zealots, with the help of the Lord, would achieve a miraculous victory over the Romans and resurrect the glorious kingdom of Israel. Maybe you've had enough of would-be Messiahs and their promises. I know some people have resigned themselves to defeat, convinced that God has abandoned us to the Romans for our collective sins—sins that could take centuries of reform and rehabilitation to atone for.

"If you're one of those who've let this kind of pessimism weigh heavily on your heart, let me assure you that you're mistaken. Those of you who know me are already well acquainted with what I've said so often about this—about how Joshua predicted that wars and famines would be signs warning that judgment was near—and how still further destruction, even of the pagans, will precede the glorious return of Christ Joshua, who will bring the angels of heaven with him to overturn the current reign of evil and finally found the long-prophesized kingdom of God. But as a mercy to those who have borne with me for so long, I'll defer repeating those things to a later time.

"Instead I want to remind those of you who have lost or are wavering in your faith, or worse still, are discouraging the faith of others, what Christ Joshua said to the people of Galilee: 'If anyone causes one of these little ones—those who believe in me— to stumble, it would be better for them if a large millstone were hung around their neck and they were thrown into the sea. If your hand causes you to stumble, cut it off. It's better for you to enter life maimed than with two hands to go into hell, where the fire never goes out. And if your foot causes you to stumble, cut it off. It's better for you to enter life crippled than to have two feet and be thrown into hell. And if your eye causes you to stumble, pluck it out. It's better for you to enter the kingdom of God with one eye than to have two eyes and be thrown into hell, where, as Isaiah said, "the worms that eat them will not die, and the fire that burns them will not be quenched."' (Isaiah 66:24)

"Joshua also said, 'Salt is good, but if it loses its saltiness, how can you make it salty again? Have salt among yourselves, and be at peace with each other.'

"When Joshua said this, he evoked Leviticus chapter two, verse thirteen: 'Season all your grain offerings with salt. Don't leave the salt of the covenant of your God out of your grain offerings; add salt to all your offerings.' In other words, stay faithful to the covenant. We who acknowledge the Messiah Joshua have a covenant with him. Stay faithful to that covenant.

"And remember what Joshua said to the Pharisees who asked him if it was lawful for a man to nullify his marriage contract and divorce his wife. Joshua told them that Moses—not God, but Moses—gave them the option of writing a certificate of divorce, but only to appease their restless and hardened hearts. Joshua invoked *God's* law and told them: 'What God has joined together, let no one separate, and anyone who divorces his wife and marries another woman commits adultery against her. And if she divorces her husband and marries another man, she commits adultery.'

"If this is true about the marriage covenant, then even more should you shun breaking your covenant with the Messiah. If you entered into the covenant with Christ Joshua, then God has joined you to His son and to the salvation that comes through His son. Don't separate what God has joined together!

"Now, if you *have* separated yourself from the Messiah, not all is lost. You can return to him. It's not too late. You may be surprised to hear this, but Simon Peter himself, the prince of the apostles, lost his faith once. It's true. Even he once denied his allegiance to Joshua."

The congregation stirred. People looked at each other with questioning eyes, and doubtful murmurs rose and fell before fading into a resurgent silence.

"Yes. It's true, brothers and sisters," Ariel said. "When Joshua was arrested, Peter tried to follow at a distance to see what they would do to Joshua. Some people saw him and questioned him, saying, 'You're a friend of the Nazarene aren't you? I've seen you with him.'

"But Peter denied it. He said, 'I don't know who you're talking about.'

"'You must be,' they said. 'I can tell from your accent that you're Galilean.'

"Peter wouldn't relent. 'You're mistaking me for someone else,' he told them. 'I may be Galilean but I know no Nazarene. Leave me alone!'

"Peter got away, but when he realized what he'd done, he broke down and wept with shame. Yet we all know that he eventually reconciled himself with Joshua. Now he's the most honored of all the apostles. So you *can* return to the fold and recommit yourself to the Messiah. If you need to renew your faith, do it now. The judgment is near.

"If you were seduced by the Zealots—duped by their lies and false promises—don't let your disappointment with *them* discourage your faith in the real Messiah. I know that the Zealots deceived many, even some of our most eminent compatriots. Many of the high priests, and some of the best scholars, supported them. They put their hopes in the wrong saviors. If they'd been at Joshua's trial, and if Pilate had offered them a choice: to send Joshua to crucifixion and free a murderous bandit, or to crucify the bandit and free Joshua, they would have chosen to free the murderer and crucify the Messiah. Weren't the same priests who supported the Zealots the same who killed Jacob, Joshua's brother? They put their trust in robbers and murderers, but disdained the prophets and the very Messiah proclaimed by those prophets. That's why God, using the Romans as His instrument, destroyed them. Let the results of the war be a lesson to you, a proof that God's wrath is real. Embrace the way, if you haven't already done so, and be prepared for the great judgment that will come when Joshua returns."

* * *

After the service, Chief Elder Evodius, who had been among the crowd that heard Ariel's sermon, took Ariel aside and confronted him.

"What's gotten into you?" Evodius asked. "Who gave you the authority to say those things about Peter? Peter denied that he knew Lord Joshua? By what authority do you say such things?"

"Let me ask your honor one question," Ariel said, "and I will tell you who gives me the authority to say these things."

"Ask your question."

"When Josephus met Vespasian for the first time and predicted that he would soon become emperor of Rome, did that prophecy come from God or not?"

Evodius pondered the question. He realized that if he said the prophecy didn't come from God, he would have to explain why it came true, because in Deuteronomy 18:21–22, Moses wrote that the test for whether a prophecy is from God or not is whether it comes true or not. But he also understood that if he said the prophecy was from God, then he would have to acknowledge that Josephus, a man whom Evodius had often lambasted for being a cowardly opportunist, liar, and traitor, had spoken with divine authority.

"I don't know how to answer your question," Evodius said.

"Then neither will I tell you by what authority I say the things I say."

54

Joshua felt like he'd been baptized in flames and his own blood. The scourging had ripped little nuggets of flesh from all over his back, chest, and legs. His bloody and beaten body was a seething cauldron of searing, incomprehensible pain. He wanted to find Judas, wherever he was, and berate him for his stupidity. But he knew Judas had suffered a savage flogging of his own, which was sure to be aggravated by staggering feelings of guilt and regret, and Joshua, in spite of his fury, could not help wanting to reach out to Judas and console him somehow, perhaps by reassuring him that his brutal degradation at the hands of sinners would earn him God's forgiveness in the kingdom.

But Judas was lost in the crowd of seventy-one rioters and rebels selected by Pilate to be crucified that morning. While on the death march, Joshua would on occasion try to spot Judas among the condemned crew shuffling its way to the killing ground, but before he could get a glimpse of his hapless friend a quick blow from a Roman-wielded rod would always goad him to redirect his gaze to the ground in front of him.

Joshua wanted to cry out insults to the Romans and praises to God. He imagined leading all his crucifixion-bound companions in chants: *Woe to Caesar! The last shall be first and the first last! Prepare to be judged, judges! God will make you pay!* But his broken state and pain-induced delirium had sapped his spirit, and he knew that merely attempting speech would bring an instant rebuke from the rod.

Since leaving the fortress, the Roman crucifixion squad had led its charges down dirt roads outside the walls of Jerusalem. Joshua, like the others, wore a thin wooden plaque that hung from his neck and identified his crime. Two words, one Greek and the other Aramaic, were branded onto the plaque. They both read "Insurrection." A small crowd of onlookers, some of them friends or relatives of the condemned, others just strangers motivated by morbid curiosity, followed the march from a short distance along the sides of the path. At times spectators would try to approach one of the captives, either to embrace a loved one or to spit at one of the disgraced, but the soldiers beat back all such attempts, assuming that anyone coming so close was a potential rescuer or saboteur.

Early on in the march the soldiers brought the condemned to a clearing where each captive received his crossbeam. A pair of soldiers placed a heavy wooden beam on Joshua's shoulders, and Joshua held it in place by wrapping his arms over it from behind. The friction of the beam against the raw nerves of his brutalized back awakened new waves of torment. He swayed back and forth as he attempted to keep his balance with the added weight. When his stance was stable enough to start walking, he took small, cautious steps, straining torn muscles with every lift of a foot, and almost buckling under crushing spasms of pain with each footfall. Several times along the way he stumbled and dropped the beam, raising the ire of impatient soldiers who kicked and pummeled him until he got up to submit to a refitting.

After a few hundred yards of anguished and arduous slogging, they reached a quarry where two hundred vertical stakes were anchored into the ground, most waiting to have a crossbeam fit onto the top, some complete and still bearing the festering, bird-pecked remains of earlier victims. There were fifty Roman soldiers already at the quarry, mostly just standing guard, and the fifty that arrived with the fresh batch of victims enlisted their aid to carry out the crucifixions. A group of soldiers chased away a few scavenging dogs, and then they forced the spectators to stand about two hundred yards away from the killing ground to prevent anyone from attempting to pull anyone off a cross or otherwise disturb the proceedings.

There were sixty-seven men to crucify, four of the original seventy-one having died on the way to the quarry, and the soldiers stripped them all of any remaining clothing. Since it took at least two soldiers to crucify one man, the soldiers divided the condemned into two cohorts to be dispatched in succession, with Joshua selected to be in the first.

Two soldiers fit Joshua's crossbeam onto the top of a stake and tied Joshua's arms to the crossbeam with rope around his wrists. Joshua's arms draped over the beam from behind as they had when he carried it. The soldiers further secured his arms by driving iron nails into the top face of the crossbeam through his forearms, which caused Joshua to scream in agony at each pound of the hammer. Next they secured his feet to the bottom of the vertical beam. With the inner heel of his left foot against the left face of the beam, they drove a nail (which was already embedded in a small slab of wood) into the beam through the heel, so that the slab of wood held the heel in place between itself and the beam. Joshua again cried out with each excruciating drive of the nail. The soldiers repeated the process with the right heel against the right face of the beam, and then left Joshua to hang.

* * *

At noon Joshua's hell was at its zenith. The sun scorched his ripped skin, baking his open sores where flies fed and deposited their eggs. He itched without remedy, and his dried out orifices cracked and stung. His strained muscles cramped, his pierced tissues tore, and his torn flesh seared. His warping bones ached with all-consuming ardor, his vital organs felt crushed beneath his rib cage, and his oppressed heart squeezed his ever-diminishing blood supply through dilapidated and collapsing vessels.

The immobilization was maddening, confining him to helpless impotence while the cruel outrages of the elements assaulted his exposed and harrowed body. More than anything it was the slow suffocation that was killing him, and gasping for breath required him to pull himself up by his pinned arms and legs—a maneuver that agitated his puncture wounds and set off a fresh cascade of throbbing misery.

Joshua tried to distract himself from the torture by reciting prayers in his mind. Psalms of lament and woe, like Psalm thirty-eight, came to him first.

I'm bowed down and brought low; all day long I go about mourning. My back is filled with searing pain; there's no health in my body. I'm feeble and utterly crushed; I groan in anguish of heart. (Psalm 38:6–8)

Such verses hit too close to home to provide any consolation, however, so he struggled to remember more upbeat compositions like the last Hallel psalm, which was fresh in his memory from Passover.

When hard pressed, I cried to the Lord; He brought me into a spacious place. The Lord is with me; I won't be afraid. What can mere mortals do to me? The Lord is with me; He's my helper. I look in triumph on my enemies. I won't die but live, and proclaim what the Lord has done. The Lord has chastened me severely, but He has not given me over to death. Open for me the gates of the righteous; I'll enter and give thanks to the Lord. (Psalm 118:5–7, 17–19)

Joshua also tried to block out the pain with pleasant memories of his friends, disciples, and family. He thought about the eleven surviving male disciples carrying on without him. He remembered Mary Magdalene, Mary his mother, Joseph his father, his brothers, and John the Baptist. Deep and distant feelings of love washed over him, tempered by rage at being ripped from life too soon. He thought about Judas hanging on his own cross somewhere in that gruesome garden of gasping groaners. Then he shook his head in horror at the enormity and absurdity of his own stunning reversal of fortune. A wave of anguish shot through him as he contemplated the hopeless reality of his imminent demise. He hung his head in a futile attempt to hide his face from the sun, which he imagined to be gazing down in disgust at the vile spectacle below it.

* * *

At three hours past noon, after he'd lost all feeling in his arms and legs, Joshua began to drift in and out of consciousness. When unconscious, Joshua's lungs were squeezed under the pressure of his slumping body, incapable of any but the shallowest of breaths. Whenever the involuntary struggle for oxygen jolted him gasping back to consciousness, his throbbing torment returned. His conscious moments became disorienting as well as painful, with a growing sensation that he was anchored to a spinning earth that was causing him to career forward as if he would face-plant onto the ground. It was like falling into indeterminate space toward an inevitable collision that somehow never came. Whenever that experience sickened him to the point of feeling that he might vomit up the dust that seemed to fill his bowels, he slipped back into unconsciousness.

* * *

By sundown Joshua had escaped consciousness for the last time. In his mind's eye he saw the sun descend beneath the horizon to usher in a darkness which consumed everything but the tiny light beams that fled from heaven through the pinholes that pocked the firmament. A gentle, low-droning hum reverberated through his bones, followed by the sense that he was no longer inside his body. He floated in the void, shedding his pain like old skin. Far in the distance a flame flickered among the stars. It moved toward him, enlarging as it approached. Soon Joshua could see four gleaming-white, winged horses flying abreast and pulling a resplendent golden chariot. The chariot's pilot was a blinding, fluid figure of fire. Joshua soaked in a nebulous euphoria, elated that his Lord had at last come to rescue him.

* * *

The soldiers walked through the foul-smelling killing ground of the quarry and performed a cursory inspection of the crucified corpses. After their subjection to the ravages of birds and beasts, the bodies were unrecognizable—men reduced to grimy, skeletal cadavers in various states of decay. Fly larvae squirmed in any decomposing flesh left clinging to the bones.

The centurion in charge gave an order to his underlings: "Take the bodies to the pit."

The soldiers pulled out the nails, untied or hacked loose the ropes, collected the crossbeams, and tossed the bodily remains onto some donkey-drawn carts. As soon as everything was properly retrieved, they walked the corpse-carting donkeys to a depression dug out of some soft ground about a hundred yards away. There they dumped the remains of Joshua, Judas, and the rest. Then they covered them with the dug-up earth piled nearby.

55

Ariel paced and fidgeted while Dionysius sat at Ariel's desk and read the latest section of Ariel's book. When Dionysius finished, he set the parchment sheets down on the desk and rubbed his eyes.

"Well?" Ariel asked as he took a seat next to Dionysius. "What do you think?"

Dionysius took a deep breath and cleared his throat.

"You've done it again, Ari. As usual you've delivered treasures both old and new. It won't surprise you that I have questions."

Ariel laughed.

"Of course," Ariel said. "Ask me."

Dionysius pointed to the end of the first page.

"The first thing that puzzled me was this," Dionysius said. "You have Judas son of Simon written as 'Judas Iscariot,' as if he called himself 'Judas, the man from Kerioth.' Are you trying to say something about the Moabites? The traitor Judas wasn't from Kerioth, or anywhere else in Moab. He was from Galilee like all the other disciples. What does it mean?"

"You really don't see?" Ariel asked. "Let me help you. It's wordplay, just like you find in Isaiah or Jeremiah. Simply invert the first two letters of 'Iscariot.' What do you get?"

"Sicariot. Oh, of course. The Sicarii. You're taking a swipe at the Sicarri."

"I couldn't resist. You can't deny that the Sicarii were traitors to Israel just like Judas was a traitor to Joshua."

"Are you going to go back into the earlier parts of your book now and write 'Judas Iscariot' everywhere you had 'Judas' or 'Judas son of Simon.'?"

"Maybe. I might do that when I put all the pieces together in the final version."

Dionysius flipped over two pages of Ariel's manuscript.

"And here," Dionysius said, "at the part where Joshua is arrested. 'One of those standing near drew his sword and struck the servant of the high priest, cutting off his ear.' That's not part of the traditional version. What does it mean?"

"I was inspired to put that in after rediscovering an interesting passage in Amos."

Ariel rifled through the scrolls on his desk, picked up a thin one, and unrolled it.

"Look here, Dion, at chapter three: 'As a shepherd rescues from the lion's mouth only two leg bones or a piece of an ear, so will the Israelites living in Samaria be rescued, with only the head of a bed and a piece of fabric from a couch.' (Amos 3:12) Amos was writing about the few righteous Jews in Samaria, back when Samaria was the seat of the kingdom of Israel during the schism with Judea. Remember how rampant sin was in Samaria then? From that nation of wicked idolators, God would rescue a tiny remnant of loyal believers from destruction at the hands of the Assyrians.

"But the metaphor applies equally well to our time—to the minute fraction of Jews from the priestly class who'll be among the elect to enter the kingdom when judgment comes. Out of that whole corrupt body, no more than an ear will be undefiled enough to escape God's wrath."

Dionysius laughed. "Ha! An ear! If that!" When he stopped laughing, he pointed back to the manuscript. "So what about this next part, after the disciples flee. You wrote something completely new: 'A young man, wearing nothing but a linen garment, was following Joshua. When they seized him, he fled naked, leaving his garment behind.' What's that supposed to mean?"

Ariel frowned.

"You more than anyone should understand it, Dion. It comes from another inspiration from Amos. Here, look."

Ariel moved his finger two columns to the right, to an earlier section of Amos. He read the last verse of the second chapter: "Even the bravest warriors will flee naked on that day." (Amos 2:16)

"That verse reminded me of Eleazar at Machaerus." Ariel said. "Naked Eleazar, cowering before the cross, begging his compatriots to surrender their village to save him—the antithesis of Joshua, especially at that moment when Joshua courageously faced *his* cross."

"Of course," Dionysius said, slapping himself on the forehead. "How could I be so blind?"

Ariel laughed.

"We were there, Dion."

"But you were the one who actually saw it."

Ariel paused a moment to think, and then said, "You know, maybe the joke about the naked man is a bad idea. Perhaps no one will appreciate it, or maybe people will read something ugly into it. Should I get rid of it?"

"No. Keep it in. Even if no one understands it, at least it doesn't hurt the story. But it makes a good point to those who might catch the meaning. I like it."

Dionysius flipped three pages ahead in the manuscript.

"I see you've left the crucifixion scene mostly unchanged from what the original apostles handed down to us, and what David predicted about it in his twenty-second psalm. Except for this one sentence: 'A certain man from Cyrene, Simon, the father of Alexander and Rufus, was passing by on his way from the country, and they forced him to carry the cross.' Alexander? Rufus? You're making some kind of statement about Tiberius Alexander and Terentius Rufus, aren't you? And Simon? Do you mean Simon bar Gioras? You know he was from Gerasa, right?"

"You're catching on, Dion. Yes, I know Simon was from Gerasa. But hear me out. Simon bar Gioras's murderous banditry brought a double Roman scourge onto our nation: Tiberius Alexander, the epitome of Jewish treachery in service to the Romans, and

Terentius Rufus, the paragon of Roman hatred for our people. Traitors like Alexander and bigots like Rufus would never have come to destroy us had it not been for the Zealots, epitomized by Simon. That's why I wrote that Simon is the father of Alexander and Rufus—he brought them onto us. And he carries the cross because he did his part to help kill righteousness and turn people from the way."

"But why Cyrene?"

"Because . . . look, let me explain. In *The Judaic War,* Josephus says that the Sicarii movement started way back when Augustus was Caesar and Coponius was procurator of Judea. A Roman senator named Cyrenius came to impose taxes on Judea, now that Herod Archelaus was gone and Rome had taken direct control. Judas the Galilean started the Sicarii movement specifically to revolt against this Cyrenius and his taxes. Josephus even mentions it in his chapter on Masada, because the Sicarii leader Eleazar at Masada was a descendant of that same Judas the Galilean.

"Now, at the very end of *The Judaic War,* Josephus says that the Sicarii suffered their final defeat in Cyrene, Libya, where the last-remaining dregs of those rebels were crushed by the Cyrenean pagans. Isn't it ironic that the Sicarii movement began as a rebellion against Cyrenius and ended with their defeat in Cyrene? That's why my Simon is from Cyrene. He's a symbol, not just of Simon bar Gioras's Zealot group, but all the Zealot groups, including the Sicarii."

Dionysius sighed.

"I can't accuse you of failing to stretch your imagination in this work of yours," Dionysius said.

Dionysius flipped two more pages ahead.

"I see here in the burial scene that you've written about this man, Joseph of Arimathea. Is this more wordplay? I've never heard of a place called Arimathea."

"Say the name out loud in Greek."

"Yo-seph-o-a-po-Ar-i-ma-the-as."

"Say it faster."

"Yo-seph-wa-po-Ar-i-ma-the-as."

"Faster."

"Yo-seph-wa-puar-i-ma-the-as. Oh, of course. Yoseph bar Matthias. It sounds like the Aramaic for Joseph son of Matthias—Josephus. I figured you would work Josephus himself into this at some point."

"How could I not?"

Dionysius returned his attention to the manuscript.

"Let me see if I can figure out your meaning. 'Joseph of Arimathea, a prominent member of the council.' All right, that sounds like Josephus, since he was a high-ranking priest and official. 'He was himself waiting for the kingdom of God.' Well, Josephus was a Pharisee, so he hoped for the resurrection at the final judgment, so that fits. 'He went boldly to Pilate and asked for Joshua's body.' Hmm. This I don't understand. Why would Josephus want Joshua's body? And then he wraps Joshua's body up in linen and puts him in a tomb cut from rock, sealed with a stone. What does it mean?"

"Remember, Dion, what Josephus did. He went to Vespasian and asked to become his assistant—his assistant in burying the Jews. When I say, 'boldly asked for Joshua's body,' I use the term 'boldly' with sarcasm to make fun of Josephus's cowardice. He helped Rome put Israel in the tomb, but he nevertheless made sure to tell his readers how much he still respected his ancestral people and the Jewish religion. So he buried us, but with respect, or so he would like the world to believe. But he's full of shit. I know he mocked Joshua, and our sect, with that story of his, the one about Yesus son of Ananus. Under the spell of pure, shameless opportunism he tried to bury all of us—all Jews and Christians—and pretended to do it with respect. He put his own people into the tomb that should have been his! He's nothing but a gutless, groveling traitor. Josephus—what a God-forsaken, bastard son of a whore from a long line of whores—generation after generation of whores!"

Ariel took a few deep breaths and calmed himself.

"So, Dion. Are you out of questions?"

"About this manuscript? Yes. But you still have to write the ending. You have to write about Joshua's resurrection. Will you be adding new things to that as well?"

Ariel's face turned serious.

"There will be no resurrection in my book," Ariel said, as if proclaiming some sacred resolution.

"What? How can you leave out the resurrection?"

"I'm going to end it right when the disciples feel just like our own brothers and sisters feel right now. Lost. Afraid. Worried that Joshua is gone and never coming back. Imagine it—Mary of Magdala and Salome go to the tomb. They find the stone rolled away somehow. When they enter the tomb, the body's gone. But an angel appears, and tells them that Joshua has risen. He tells them to inform the disciples that Joshua has conquered death and will visit them again in Galilee. Mary and Salome flee from the tomb, terrified. That's where the story ends.

"Let everyone who reads or hears my book fill in the ending themselves. We all know the resurrection story. Let the people figure out that they're now in the same position that Mary and the disciples were in back then. And let them realize that they'll get their answer, just as the disciples got theirs. If they believe in the resurrection, they'll understand why they have to stay faithful in these times of terror."

"But if the people are to believe, then you at least have to acknowledge the resurrection in your book."

"I do. The angel, remember? He tells Mary and Salome all about it. And again, everybody already knows the story."

Dionysius shook his head.

"The angel?" Dionysius asked. "A second-hand report? With all the particulars missing? And I assure you, not everyone knows the story. What about all the pagans and Jews we haven't reached? Don't we want our churches to grow?"

Ariel thought for a moment.

"You make a good point, Dion. Maybe I'll foreshadow the resurrection, in all its glory, at an earlier place in the book somehow. That way I can acknowledge the resurrection but still keep my ending."

56

The disciples reached Martha's house in Bethany in the middle of the night. They woke Mary and told her everything that had happened.

"You cowards!" Mary said. "How could you just run away like that? You need to go back to Jerusalem and rescue Joshua. And I'm coming with you."

"No. It's too dangerous," Simon said. "Joshua ordered us to flee, even though we wanted to stay with him. He saved us. If you go to Jerusalem asking around for Joshua you'll get arrested for sure. Joshua wants us to wait here for him."

"We can't just leave him there at the mercy of the priests' goons," Mary said. "They might kill him. We need to help him."

"And get captured or killed ourselves?" John asked. "What good will that do? Joshua doesn't want any more of us to get taken. He wants us to be safe while he escapes. He'll return. He knows what he's doing."

"And," Elder Jacob said. "If Joshua goes the way of John the Baptist, God forbid, we need to continue the mission. We promised him that we would."

"Yes," Simon said. "If we disobey the master it will only make things worse."

Mary glared at the rest of the disciples and asked, "Do you all feel this way?"

The disciples nodded in agreement and hung their heads.

Mary threw up her arms and clenched her fists as if she were crushing walnuts in her hands.

"I can't believe this!" she cried. "How can this be happening?"

Mary's eyes welled up. She closed them and clasped her hands to pray: "Be merciful, Lord. Bring Joshua back to us. Protect and deliver him from all evil . . ."

Matheus embraced his sister and held her tight while tears flowed, hers and his.

* * *

At Lazarus's house the next morning, Younger Jacob went to speak to Zealous Simon.

"This must be especially difficult for you, Simon, with your own brother in trouble as well."

"Judas is not my brother—not anymore. I denounce and disown him. He betrayed Joshua and the rest of us too. If Joshua returns and brings that traitor with him, I'll kill him myself."

"Just like that you judge him? What if Judas isn't as guilty as you think he is? Maybe someone betrayed *him*. Maybe there's something we don't know that would help us understand what happened, why it turned out as it did. Whatever Judas did, maybe it's forgivable. Remember what Joshua said about forgiveness—"

At that moment Matheus arrived and interrupted them.

"Jacob, Simon," Matheus said. "Round up the others and come to Martha's house. The women want to make an announcement to the men."

Younger Jacob and Zealous Simon looked at each other and shrugged.

"What are they up to?" Younger Jacob asked.

"I don't know," Matheus said. "Everyone's going crazy. Just come so we can be done with it, whatever it is."

Lazarus and all his boarders went to Martha's house and met the others in the courtyard. Mary stood in front of everyone and spoke.

"Friends and brothers, please listen. Martha, my mother, and I are going up to Jerusalem to find out what's happening to Joshua—"

"It's too dangerous!" Matheus cried, interrupting.

"Joshua himself forbids it!" John added.

"Quiet! Let me finish!" Mary shouted. She glared at the men until they fell silent and gave her their full attention.

"There's no reason to worry," Mary said. "Think about it— we're women. No one will suspect us of anything. We won't let anyone know about our connection to Joshua. We won't need to. We can find out what we need just by mingling innocently with the public. We're just three harmless ladies. When we learn anything we'll tell you."

The men began to stir but Mary gestured for quiet.

"Don't bother raising objections," Mary said. "This is decided and it's right. You know it is. We can't just sit here waiting. If we can save Joshua then we must, especially if it's no more dangerous than doing nothing. If there's anything you can do to help we'll let you know. Meanwhile keep careful watch here. May God preserve and protect you."

The men said nothing.

* * *

It didn't take long for Mary, Martha, and Salome to learn what had happened. Pilate had sent out an official report throughout the city that scores of insurrectionists were to be crucified that day. The report mentioned only one particular insurrectionist's name—Joshua the Nazarene.

Fearful of inspiring assemblies of people to new rioting, Pilate didn't make the location of the executions public, but through casual conversations with various members of the populace the three women discovered it. By about noon they found their way to the quarry northwest of the city.

Mary, Martha, and Salome stood with the crowd of onlookers. The soldiers prevented the crowd from getting close to the killing ground, so the women could only see a multitude of indistinguishable men hanging from crosses. Any one of them could have been Joshua. They asked other onlookers if they knew which of the crucified was the Nazarene, but none could help them. The three women embraced, wept, and shook with grief at the bloody scene. When evening approached the soldiers ordered the crowd away, but they promised that the Jewish crucified would be taken down as soon as they were confirmed to be deceased, and therefore their dead bodies would not hang on their crosses overnight in violation of the Torah's desecration laws.

Mary and Salome spent the night in Jerusalem but sent Martha back to Bethany to deliver the bad news. The disciples were devastated and went into immediate mourning. They changed into sackcloth tunics, covered their heads with ashes, and fasted. In their grief they lambasted themselves for abandoning their master and began a fervent session of anguished prayer for forgiveness.

The next day Mary and Salome returned to the quarry and noticed that every one of the condemned seemed to still be hanging from a cross. Mary asked a soldier why none was taken down. Weren't all or most of the crucified Jews? Mary accused the soldiers of violating Jewish law. But the soldier assured her that they didn't take anyone down because all the victims were still alive, as was to be expected after only one day. Mary and Salome were incredulous but said no more. They just stared at the obscene orchard of crosses in the distance and stewed in their helpless rage.

On the third day Mary and Salome returned to their quarry vigil. When they saw birds pecking at some of the bodies and dogs tearing at the legs of others, they protested to the soldiers.

"Those men are dead!" Mary shouted. "Give us the Nazarene. We won't let you desecrate his body. Give him to us, you lying jackals!"

A soldier drew his short sword and pointed it at the women.

"You rebel bitches," he said, sneering. "Fuck off and don't come back. Be thankful you're women and run on home. If we see you here again we'll kill you, you rebels' whores!"

Mary and Salome ran back to the city, terrified.

The next day Mary and Salome tried to approach the quarry by stealth, taking a new route. They exited the city through the Garden Gate in the western wall near Herod the Great's palace, and then took the road heading northwest toward Joppa. About five hundred yards from the city wall they turned northeast to climb to the top of the hill of Gareb. From there they had a good view of the quarry below. They saw that the bodies had all been removed, even the upper crossbeams. All that remained were rows of bloody stakes sticking out of the ground and a few Roman soldiers patrolling.

Mary and Salome hurried back to the city to find out what happened to the bodies. Near Herod's Palace they encountered a Pharisee scribe offering his services at a booth. Before saying anything, Mary laid a silver shekel on the counter.

"Shalom, Rabbi," Salome said.

The rabbi nodded. "Shalom, sister."

"Please," Mary said. "You know the city well, don't you?"

"Of course. How may I help you?"

"When the Romans execute Jews, what do they do with the bodies?" Mary asked.

The man grimaced and said, "Oh. I hope you haven't lost anyone to the Romans, but if so, I offer my condolences. But to answer your question . . . by law, they're required to take them to the Jewish cemeteries, and leave them with officials there who bury them according to the regulations of the Torah."

"Do you know where they took the bodies of the crucified, the ones just outside the walls in the quarry under the hill of Gareb?"

"I'm sorry, I don't. But they surely took them to one of the nearby cemeteries or crypt yards. If you ask the workers there, they should be able to tell you if they have whomever it is you're looking for."

"Can you tell us where to find those cemeteries and crypt yards?"

"I know all of them, I believe. The Jewish ones in Jerusalem anyway."

The Pharisee wrote a list of the locations, including nearby landmarks, onto a leaf of parchment and handed it to Mary.

Mary and Salome visited every burial ground on the Pharisee's list. A few had recently interred someone named Joshua, but none could say with certainty that he was Joshua the Nazarene. One site had received a load of corpses from Roman troops, but the original source of the bodies was unknown. Discarding their customary fear of the unclean presence of dead bodies, the women made pests of themselves searching burial grounds and peeking into empty tombs to recover any clues they could about the whereabouts of Joshua's remains. In the end they surrendered to frustration and returned to Bethany, with nothing more than the hope that Joshua's body had been treated with some modicum of propriety and decency.

The news of Mary and Salome's fruitless search, with its grim suggestion that Joshua might have been denied even a proper burial, compounded the disciples' grief and guilt. Simon Cephas even started to feel his faith slipping away. If Joshua was right in all that he taught and proclaimed, why did God allow him to be cut down in such a horrifying and unjust way? Was Joshua wrong? Was it a mistake to follow him? Had all that time spent with Joshua been a waste—a foolish pursuit of a crazy dream?

In his anguish Simon resolved to walk alone back to Capernaum, the whole way starving himself and letting the bandits and beasts do as they pleased with him. If somehow he survived the trip, he would drown himself in the Sea of Galilee.

57

After Ariel finished his book, he often read from it at the synagogue. He had copies made and distributed them to the other Antioch church officials, who read from it to their own congregations. Soon it became so popular that it came to be seen as a complement to the famous book of Joshua's sayings. Believers referred to the so-called Book of Sayings and Book of Signs as if they were a natural pair, and considered the two books to be worthy additions to the new, emerging canon of Christian scripture. Neither book had an official title or author, although everyone assumed the Book of Sayings came from an original apostle, probably Matheus, and Ariel's acquaintances all knew that Ariel was behind the Book of Signs. Christians propagated the Book of Signs throughout the lands around the Mediterranean Sea, in both Aramaic and Greek, and in time its official title became *Evangelion*—Greek for "The Good News"—from the book's first sentence: "The beginning of the good news about Joshua the Christ, the son of God."

* * *

When Dionysius went to deliver a copy of the Book of Signs to Chief Elder Evodius, Evodius met him at his front door but did not invite him inside.

"This book of Ariel's—I'm loath to take it," Evodius said, holding up his hand to refuse the codex that Dionysius offered him. "I'm afraid the book might be cursed."

"Seriously, lord?"

"Yes. Ariel is guided by forces that I don't trust. I think he has a demon. He changes the tradition handed down to us from the apostles. He corrupts the teachings with his own fancies. That man and his book are dangerous."

"With all respect, lord, I believe you're mistaken. Ariel hasn't taken anything out of the tradition. Nor has he changed any of it. He's simply added his visions and dreams, which evidently come from the Lord. Ariel would have you approach his additions as you would a puzzle designed to make you think, or a lesson on how to interpret Joshua's teachings in light of the times. It's nothing to be afraid of."

Evodius, silent, arms crossed, and motionless, stared at Dionysius.

"Lord," Dionysius said. "Everyone's reading it. It's good. There's nothing in it that contradicts Joshua or the tradition or anything. The things that are new or unfamiliar to you—you don't have to take them literally. They're symbolic, like so much of Joshua's own teaching, and like so much of scripture too. Give it a chance. If it offends you, you can give it back and forget you ever saw it. Condemn and criticize it if you must. But at least read it first."

Dionysius held out the codex again for Evodius to take.

"How am I to understand it," Evodius asked, "if Ariel is trying to perplex me with puzzles? What's the secret?"

"He doesn't want to perplex anyone. He wants to challenge, teach, provoke—enlighten. Here. Let me read you a bit of it, something that should help you."

Dionysius opened the codex to a page.

"Here, lord," Dionysius said. "It's right here after Joshua's parable of the sower. I know you know that parable from the Book of Sayings. A very symbolic parable, that one. Let me read you this short passage: 'Joshua said to them, "Do you bring in a lamp to put it under a bowl or a bed? Instead, don't you put it on its stand? For whatever's hidden is meant to be disclosed, and whatever's concealed is meant to be brought out into the open. If anyone has ears to hear, let them hear.'"'

Dionysius closed the codex and again held it up to offer it to Evodius.

"May the Lord shine His light to expose whatever evil you're hiding in that book!" Evodius shouted before shutting the door and leaving Dionysius alone outside.

Dionysius shrugged, returned the codex to his knapsack, and headed back home.

58

Simon sneaked out of Martha's house while everyone was asleep and slipped into the night, taking the paved highway to Galilee through Samaria. The road was busy enough to keep the cheetahs and other predatory beasts away most of the time, and even at the loneliest stretches, Simon's weak, shambling figure failed to tempt the prowling animals away from the more promising wild targets available. Bandits were even less impressed, taking his wretched walk and vile smell as an indication that he had a disease or a demon that was best left alone. Simon even failed to starve himself, because he gave in to the occasional temptation to visit a spring, fig tree, or date palm for a sip or a nibble. He further thwarted his suicidal intentions by sleeping in craggy ditches and brushy basins that kept his body well hidden from passers-by.

After about ten days Simon reached a place on the road where he could hear the Jordan River to his east and see Mount Tabor to his west. He knew that just beyond the mountain lay Nazareth, Joshua's hometown. He felt compelled to climb Mount Tabor and perhaps get a look at Nazareth from the summit. Why not? Somehow he'd survived thus far. Maybe God had protected him and still had something to teach him.

When Simon reached the foot of Mount Tabor, he walked west along the southern face of the mountain, ascending along the way but in no great hurry to reach the top. He meandered past the carob and mastic trees of the lower altitudes until he reached higher ground where oak and terebinth trees dominated. By the time he knew he was on the western face of the mountain, he was four-fifths of the way to the summit.

He leaned against the thick trunk of an old oak and rested in its shade. He decided to climb no higher. He was exhausted, and he knew there was an old Hasmonean military fort on the plateau on the mountaintop. The fort was in an official state of disuse, but Herodian troops were known to occupy it on occasion to watch over the surrounding terrain. Simon could avoid trouble and still have a good view of the villages to the west by staying right where he was.

He saw several villages in the distance below, but he wasn't sure which of them was Nazareth. At that height the villages all looked the same, and he wondered what he'd expected to see now that he was in a position to see it. He thought of Joshua and looked up to the heavens to offer up a prayer that had been running through his mind all day. It was from the Psalms, but he didn't remember anymore which one it was. In his weakened state he could only speak with a soft voice and hope the winds would carry his prayer to where it needed to go.

"Lord, you're the God who saves me; day and night I cry out to you. May my prayer come before you; turn your ear to my cry. I'm overwhelmed with troubles and my life draws near to death. I'm counted among those who go down to the pit; I'm like one without strength. I'm set apart with the dead, like the slain who lie in the grave, whom you remember no more, who are cut off from your care. You've put me in the lowest pit, in the darkest depths. Your wrath lies heavily on me; you've overwhelmed me with all your waves. You've taken me from my closest friends and have made me repulsive to them. I'm confined and can't escape; my eyes are dim with grief. I call to you, Lord, every day; I spread out my hands to you. Do you show your wonders to the dead? Do their spirits rise up and praise you? Is your love declared in the grave, your faithfulness in Destruction? Are your wonders known in the place of darkness, or your righteous deeds in the land of oblivion? But I cry to you for help, Lord; in the morning my prayer comes before you. Why, Lord, do you reject me and hide your face from me? From my youth I've suffered and been close to death; I've borne your terrors and am in despair. Your wrath has swept over me; your terrors have destroyed me. All day long they surround me like a flood; they've completely engulfed me. You've taken me from friend and neighbor—darkness is my closest friend." (Psalm 88)

Simon turned around and looked up at the summit. What did he care if Herodian soldiers saw him or even killed him? Wasn't this supposed to be the end? He wanted to climb to the top but he couldn't get himself to move. He craved water and longed for food, but all he could do was sit with his back against an oak and stare up at the mountain's crown. He wondered if it had been two or three days since he'd last eaten anything. He couldn't remember and he didn't care. He was as immobile as the tree. He fell asleep.

* * *

Simon woke to the irritation of a leaf scraping against his cheek. Cold wind gusts buffeted him and rattled the limbs of the trees. It was night and no moon was visible. He heard a voice call him.

"Simon."

Simon tried to move but couldn't. He felt completely paralyzed. He heard the voice again. It was familiar.

"Simon. Simon Cephas."

"Joshua?" Simon asked, terrified.

"Simon, listen to me."

The voice indeed sounded like Joshua's.

"Rabbi?" Simon asked the darkness.

A blinding-white light flashed and Simon saw Joshua standing in front of him, clad in glowing, golden robes.

"Simon, my Cephas, don't be afraid." Joshua said. "I bring good news."

Simon tried to reach out to touch Joshua but he remained paralyzed.

"Cephas," Joshua said. "I've joined Moses and Elijah."

An ancient-looking man with long, white hair and matching beard appeared on Joshua's right, and a younger, but still old, bald man with a long, black beard appeared on Joshua's left. The two new apparitions were dressed in glowing garments identical to Joshua's.

"Moses," Joshua said, spreading his right arm and opening his hand to present the ancient lawgiver. He did the same with his left arm and said, "Elijah" to introduce the prophet.

The two great luminaries nodded. They looked just as Simon had imagined them when he'd heard the scriptures as a child. Simon recalled the legends he'd heard in his boyhood about the great heroes of Hebrew history visiting the tents of families celebrating the Feast of Tabernacles.

"I'm so sorry, my lords," Simon said, his voice cracking from fear, "but I have no sukkot to build for you. Please forgive me."

Joshua laughed and clasped Simon's left shoulder. It felt like it always had before when Joshua touched him.

"Cephas," Joshua said. "Why are you talking about tabernacles? Forget about that and listen. The Lord has assumed me into His heavenly kingdom, like Moses and Elijah before me. Tell Mary and the disciples to stop looking for my body. My body's right here, before you. Look!"

Joshua grabbed Simon by the shoulders and shook him. Simon felt Joshua's hands on him and the shaking. He tried to embrace Joshua but he still couldn't overcome his paralysis. Joshua let go of Simon and spoke again.

"They never found Moses's or Elijah's body either. Don't you remember? God took them to Himself. He's done the same to me. I was crucified and I died, but I've risen! The Lord resurrected me and now I sit at His right hand. Tell the others. God has appointed me to return as the Son of Man, the Messiah, to judge the world and begin the new holy age. Continue my mission, as you promised. I'm coming soon. Tell everyone I'm coming back soon."

A shining cloud that radiated flashing beams of light in all directions descended and enveloped the divine trio.

"Lord?" Simon asked.

In an instant the cloud disappeared and Simon was alone again.

"Lord!" Simon called.

Simon heard nothing but the wind in the trees. He tugged at his oily and filthy hair.

I can move again! I'm awake. It wasn't a dream!

He ran down the hill the way he came and kept going all the way to the Jordan, where he drank and bathed. He resolved to go to Sennabris to join a safe caravan and return to Bethany. He felt reborn. He was beside himself with joyous excitement and eager to share the glorious news with his friends.

Simon's visitation experience on Mount Tabor, however, was a hallucination—brought on by exhaustion, fasting, and grief. But Simon was convinced to his core that it had been real—that his beloved friend and rabbi had risen from the dead and taken an exalted place at the right hand of God.

* * *

Mary and Salome sat staring at the entrance to an open, empty tomb in a crypt yard in southeast Jerusalem. They were led there by some strangers who claimed to be admirers of Joshua, and who insisted that they witnessed the Romans bring his body, and the bodies of those crucified with him, to the site. Nevertheless Mary and Salome got nowhere with the graveyard workers and made no progress on their own either. They decided that they'd been tricked. But they still had reason to haunt the cemeteries of Jerusalem, because they were convinced that Simon had gone looking for Joshua's body on his own when he disappeared from Bethany three weeks earlier. They were afraid he'd gone mad with grief and was now wandering into certain doom, but they clung to hope that they would somehow find him in the end. The other disciples went looking for him on the way to Galilee, supposing that he'd followed the Jordan to return to his home in Capernaum.

"Mary!"

Mary and Salome turned and saw Simon standing above them. He looked clean, lucid, and happier than they'd ever seen him. He was radiant.

"Simon!" Mary and Salome cried. They smothered him with hugs and kisses until he was wet with their joyful tears.

"Where have you been?" Mary asked. "We were afraid we'd lost you forever."

Simon laughed and released himself from their embraces.

"I was called to Galilee, and now I'm back. I ran into the brothers on the way down, by the Jordan. They came back with me to Bethany. We're all back together now, God be praised."

"Who called you to Galilee? You didn't tell us. We thought you'd gone mad." Mary said.

"I thought so too. But it was the Lord. The Lord called me!"

Mary and Salome looked at each other and worried that they had been right about Simon going mad after all.

Simon laughed.

"Martha told me you'd be here, looking for Joshua. Well, stop looking! You won't find him among the graves and tombs. I found him."

Mary and Salome gasped.

"Yes. I found him. Or he found me. He came to me in Galilee. Alive!"

"What?" Mary and Salome shouted, almost collapsing from shock.

"So they never killed him?" Mary asked.

Simon frowned.

"They killed him, yes. But God raised him from death! Joshua came to me on Mount Tabor, and he was with Moses and Elijah too! He said he was resurrected back to life and taken up to heaven. He sits at the right hand of the Lord."

Mary and Salome were afraid and speechless. They didn't know whether to rejoice at a great miracle or mourn the loss of their friend's sanity.

"I know it's hard to believe, but it's true. Joshua touched me. I felt it! It was him, in the flesh. He's the Messiah! God has exalted him and he'll come back. He's coming back to judge the world and establish the kingdom."

Mary and Salome stared at Simon, their welling eyes dripping like fresh wounds.

"Come on Mary, Salome. Let's go back and rejoin the others. Forget these tombs. Joshua's with the Lord. You'll never find his body. Never. Stop looking. He's not here!"

Endnote

This book's depiction of events in the war between the Jews and the Romans (66 C.E. – 73 C.E.) is based on *The History of the Jewish War Against the Romans* by Flavius Josephus (37 C.E. – circa 100 C.E.). Ariel's stories of Joshua's miracles and signs in *Nazarene Dream* are based on *The Gospel According to Mark*. Joshua's teachings, outside of quotations from *The Old Testament* and *The Book of Enoch*, are based on *The Gospel According to Matthew, The Gospel According to Luke*, and the author's imagination.

Printed in the United States
By Bookmasters